D0375130

# TIME WILL TELL

## BARRY LYGA

LITTLE, BROWN AND COMPANY
New York   Boston

Little, Brown and Company
Hachette Book Group
1290 Avenue of the Americas, New York, NY 10104
Visit us at LBYR.com

First Edition: September 2021

Little, Brown and Company is a division of Hachette Book Group, Inc. The Little, Brown name and logo are trademarks of Hachette Book Group, Inc.

The publisher is not responsible for websites (or their content) that are not owned by the publisher.

Library of Congress Cataloging-in-Publication Data
Names: Lyga, Barry, author.
Title: Time will tell / by Barry Lyga.
Description: First edition. | New York : Little, Brown and Company, 2021. | Audience: Ages 14 & up. | Summary: Relates the efforts of teens Elayah, Liam, Jorja, and Marcie to solve a 1986 murder, and the actions of their then-teenaged parents leading up to the crime.
Identifiers: LCCN 2020048675 | ISBN 9780316537780 (hardcover) | ISBN 9780316537803 (ebook) | ISBN 9780316537841 (ebook other)
Subjects: CYAC: Criminal investigation—Fiction. | Murder—Fiction. | Bigotry—Fiction. | Mystery and detective stories.
Classification: LCC PZ7.L97967 Tim 2021 | DDC [Fic]—dc23
LC record available at https://lccn.loc.gov/2020048675

ISBNs: 978-0-316-53778-0 (hardcover), 978-0-316-53780-3 (ebook), 978-0-316-39411-6 (international)

Printed in the United States of America

LSC-C

Printing 1, 2021

For J, J, S, R & D

We did the things and we can't take them back.

*I'd sit on his lap in that big old Buick and steer*
    *as we drove through town*
*He'd tousle my hair and say, "Son, take a good*
    *look around*
*"This is your hometown"*

                        **—Bruce Springsteen,**
                        **"My Hometown" (1984)**


*I awoke from a quiet night, I never heard a*
    *sound*
*The marauders raided in the dark*
*And brought death to my hometown*

                        **—Bruce Springsteen,**
                **"Death to My Hometown" (2012)**

*I'm sorry*

# THE PRESENT: ELAYAH

**B**earing shovels and a pickax, they made their way up the hill that morning. Liam started whining about the climb halfway up, pleading exhaustion already, to the annoyance of the others. Elayah rolled her eyes.

Marcie did more than roll her eyes—she turned to Liam and held out her shovel, stopping him in his tracks.

"Are you in or are you out?"

"I only had a grande this morning," Liam said with a wretched pout.

"Grow up," Marcie told him, tossing her hair back. "Stop being a pussy."

"Microaggression!" Liam cried. "Hashtag me too!"

The last of their foursome, Jorja, snorted. She had the pickax, which somehow imbued her with additional gravitas. Everyone turned to look at her.

"Girls are *allowed* to say *pussy*," she informed Liam. "We're reclaiming it from the patriarchy."

"Sucks to be you," Marcie added with a healthy dose of snark.

"Wait, wait!" Liam made an almost mechanical sound deep in his chest. "I think...I think I know what the problem is." He gagged up a wad of something thick and yellowish, then spat it into the grass at his feet.

Elayah was the only one to react. "Gross!" she exclaimed.

Liam chuckled under his breath. Tall and dirty blond and crinkly-grinned, he was pretty much every aftershave and men's deodorant commercial come to life. He had a face made for YouTube and a body made for making girls swoon. Straight girls, at least. Elayah had done her fair share of swooning, and even knowing that he was playing her for the reaction to his phlegmy, male raunch, she was still frozen by those blue eyes and that saucy quirk of his lips.

"You're disgusting," she said just a moment too late. Liam laughed. He took a bizarre pleasure in tricking her, then pulling back the curtain. Always had.

"It's up there." Jorja pointed to a spot just atop the hill.

"The lady hath spoken!" Liam shouldered his shovel and—grande or not—dashed up the hill at a pace that made Elayah feel like a slug. "First one up is ruler of the world!"

Jorja reacted instantly, her long legs carrying her up the hill only a foot or two behind Liam. "No fair!" she screamed, racing.

Just then, Liam crested the hill. He spun around and lofted his shovel like a medieval knight's sword, striking a legs-akimbo pose. "I have conquered the mountain!" he bellowed.

"Not a mountain!" Jorja yelled back, just a few feet from him.

Marcie sighed and shook her head, adjusting her glasses. She raised an eyebrow at Elayah. "Are we going to race like those idiots?"

"Please, no."

Marcie laughed. "I'm glad."

Together they made a steady but unhurried trek up the hill. The incline rolled over into a broad, wide expanse of grass and trees. It would have been a mesa if it had been higher and drier. And in the Southwest. From here, they could see the dinky "sprawl" of town to the north, the Wantzler factory—still chugging along, barely—to the west, and the high school to the south, down the slope. Elayah allowed herself a moment to enjoy the view, then hustled over to where the others had gathered.

"I think it's this tree," Liam said, now all serious. "It is, right?"

Everyone glanced over at Elayah, who had already dug into her pocket for her phone. She consulted a document, pinching it wider. It was a scan of the yellowing sheet of paper she'd found in one of the old yearbooks in the school library. There was a map of sorts there, with a scraggle of lines to indicate the copse of trees they faced right now, then a hasty circle to indicate the sun. Some ruled lines formed a right triangle between the sun, one tree in particular, and a spot on the ground.

The tree on the map had a callout to it, showing a capital *B*. The tree Liam had indicated had a rough, scraggly *B* carved into its bark, nearly overgrown but still distinct enough to identify.

"Looks right," Elayah said. It had been more than thirty years since the makeshift map was drawn. They were damn lucky the tree was still there. Hell, they were lucky the *hill* was still there.

When she'd told her dad about the "treasure hunt," he'd laughed and said, "Honey, are you sure there's even a place to look anymore?"

Fortunately, there was. The hill and the trees were older, slightly eroded, more than a little weary-looking, but still in the same places they'd occupied in 1986.

"Time to measure," she told them.

The lines forming the right angle had foot demarcations on them, meaning that figuring out the location of the spot on the ground should have been as simple as facing the right direction, watching the shadow of the tree, and judiciously applying old man Pythagoras's theorem about $a^2$ and $b^2$ equaling $c^2$. But the tree had grown over the past few decades, so they had to fake it, using the measurement on the old paper to calculate where the shadow would have fallen back in 1986 and then going from there.

Elayah had aced trig, so she got to do the math while Liam and Marcie used their shovels to measure off the appropriate distances.

"Why didn't they just write down the longitude and latitude?" Liam grumbled.

"Because no one had GPS back then," Jorja told him gently. Physically, Liam was almost always a step ahead of the three women; mentally, he was almost always a step behind.

It was simple enough to find the spot. Now they just had to hope that, for example, the tree hadn't shifted because of erosion or ground movement in the preceding thirty-plus years. Or that the slope of the ground hadn't changed too much. Or any of a million other little things that could throw them off.

She kept those fears to herself. No point stressing anyone out. This was supposed to be fun. *A lark*, Jorja had called it when Elayah first suggested they dig the damn thing up.

"How far down do you think they buried it?" Marcie asked as the four of them clustered around the spot.

Elayah shrugged. "I don't know. They didn't write that down."

"Six feet?" Liam said with a mix of confidence and inquisitiveness.

"That's dead bodies," Jorja informed him.

"Just how many dead bodies *have* you dug up?" Liam asked.

"Only the three," Jorja deadpanned, then shoved Liam lightly. He nudged her back with his shoulder.

They could have been brother and sister. Both of them tall, both of them blondish—though it was tough to tell with Jorja, ever since she'd started buzzing her hair. Their easy repartee infuriated Elayah, which she never let show; she didn't want Liam to know she cared.

But...damn, sometimes she wished she were Jorja instead of herself. To be so relaxed and at ease around Liam...

"So, six feet, right?" Liam said, jostling Elayah from a world in which she, not Jorja, lived next door to Liam and got to joke around with him and even touch him on occasion.

"Not technically," she said, going on autopilot. "That used to be the law for graves, but that was hundreds of years ago, in Europe, when they had to bury victims of the plague deep enough that the bodies couldn't contaminate the living. In the US, the only relevant law is that there has to be eighteen inches of dirt between the body and the open air."

There was a moment of silence during which they all regarded her. Jorja seemed to be absorbing this information, filing it away in her personal data vault. Marcie just grinned.

"Geek Girl rides again!" Liam sang out. Elayah pursed her lips in mock anger. It was the easiest way to keep herself from blushing. Why did she crave his attention, even when it was negative?

Oh, right, because she was madly—

"For definitions of *geek* meaning anyone smarter than you," Marcie snapped at him.

"So...everyone, then," Jorja chimed in brightly, ignoring Liam's look of feigned outrage. "Let's get started."

Liam was a bit taller and stronger, but Jorja had an almost poetic sense of movement. She briefly struck a Rosie the Riveter "We can do it!" pose before applying the pickax to the ground, breaking up the turf so that the shovels could find easier purchase.

She leaned back, slid the pickax's handle through her threaded fingers almost to its end, and then skip-stepped forward, bringing the ax up and around and then down in a perfect arc, biting the earth with its steel tooth.

*Ch-chm!*

A devotee of a brutally exhausting form of yoga and a regular in the school's weight lifting room, Jorja had the lithe shape of a dancer, wedded to a swimmer's muscles. She seemed to enjoy attacking the innocent turf.

She and Liam swapped pickax duty until there was a wide, ragged oval of broken earth. Then the foursome took turns with the shovels, one of them digging the hole, one keeping its edges from collapsing, while the other two rested. It was deeper than eighteen inches, but fortunately nothing like six feet—an hour later Liam's shovel sang a sour, metallic note and shivered so strongly in his hands that he nearly dropped it.

"Rock?" he said, arming sweat off his forehead.

"Didn't sound like it," Jorja replied, and crouched to peer into the hole. She'd stripped off her overshirt, and sweat soaked through her ribbed white sleeveless tee. "Looks shiny. Step back."

For once, Liam obeyed, scrambling out of the hole. Sunlight glimmered off something that was most definitely not made of stone.

"Hells yeah," Liam whispered. "Time capsule, baby."

"Time capsule..." Mr. Hindon, the high school's long-serving media specialist, had drawn out the words as though remembering the lyrics to a song, then executed a very brief series of eye spasms. He had Tourette syndrome (*not Tourette's*, he'd been explaining to generations of students; there was no possessive), and when he focused hard, sometimes his eye muscles did a little involuntary dance.

"Time capsule," he'd said again, musing over the yellowing sheet of paper they'd handed him. "Yeah, I remember that now that you mention it. Some kids from the class of eighty-seven buried a time capsule."

"But I found this in the yearbook from 1984," Elayah told him.

He shrugged almost extravagantly. "Who knows? It's a mystery!"

Turned out it wasn't the only one.

Liam and Jorja were slick with sweat, their bare arms streaked with dirt, their faces smeared. They'd been in the hole for only ten minutes, trying to wrestle the thing out, but it was proving difficult.

"This thing feels like a greased pig."

"Really, Farmer Brown?" Jorja asked, chuckling. "Have a lot of experience with greased pigs, do you?"

"You don't know everything about me," Liam told her.

"Oh yeah, you're large. You contain multitudes."

Liam stared blankly. Walt Whitman was not his forte. In fact, anything before, say, the year 2000 might as well be dinosaurs.

"We'll explain it later," Marcie promised him.

Elayah couldn't help it—her brain flashed pieces of the poem, whether she wanted it to or not.

*The past and present wilt—I have fill'd them, emptied them.*
*And proceed to fill my next fold of the future.*

After some more bickering, Liam and Jorja finally set themselves up in new positions, but to no avail. The thing didn't budge. "What were they thinking?" Liam demanded.

"It lasted all this time," Marcie said. "So I guess they were thinking right."

"Let me try this myself," Liam said.

"Ooh," Jorja said, deepening her voice and slackening her jaw. "Me big man. Me lift heavy thing for dainty ladies."

"I'm just thinking, y'know, too many cooks—"

"Can you guys work *together* for once?" Elayah's exasperation finally overcame her attraction.

Jorja and Liam pulled wounded expressions and looked at each other. "Wow, that hurt."

"No need to go all Mom on us," Jorja added. "We're working through it."

"Just . . . do something!" Elayah erupted. The damn thing was *right there*! "Sheesh."

"Who died and made her boss?" Jorja asked.

Liam shrugged. "I don't know, but I guess we better get serious before she, like, gives us demerits or something."

Jorja crouched and worked her hands under the time capsule. "I'll try to tilt it toward you," she said to Liam. "See if you can get it into your arms."

"And then what? Use my superpowers to fly out of here?"

Elayah nudged Marcie with her elbow and gestured. They took up a position just behind Liam at the edge of the hole. "Try to shift it toward us and we'll roll it out."

Liam considered, shrugged, nodded. He whipped off his shirt and dabbed his forehead before tossing the garment a few feet away. Elayah took in his crisp shoulder blades and the hard ridges of muscle in his back. She exchanged a look with Marcie, who mouthed, *Keep it in your pants.*

Elayah shot back a death glare. Her lust for Liam was a secret between just the two of them.

Marcie shrugged as though to say, *He's not even looking this way.*

True. But Jorja was facing them. And Jorja and Liam were tight. *Tell-you-everything-I-see* tight.

"Let's do this shizz," Liam said. "My dad said we'd never find this thing, and I really want to prove him wrong."

He hunched down. Sweat gleamed on his skin. For the moment, Elayah had nothing to do, so she watched the beads meander.

Jorja groaned with effort. The time capsule was much bigger than they'd expected. The sheet of paper they'd found in the old yearbook was titled *Contents of Time Capsule* and had listed maybe two dozen things, most of which were small. Elayah had figured that the entire thing would be the size of two or three shoeboxes.

What they'd unearthed was more like the size of a small filing cabinet. Cylindrical and made of stainless steel, it had the words PRESERVATION INC. stamped in an arc on one end, with STORAGE VAULT rounding out the other arc. It lay diagonal in the dirt, so they'd had to dig a deeper, wider hole than they'd anticipated to reveal the entirety of its length.

"I hate our parents!" Jorja cried in anguish as she strained with all her might. Miraculously, the thing moved, shifting enough that it collided with Liam, who was ready for it. He backed up against the side of the hole for stability and flexed, managing to lift the capsule by rolling it up his body. Elayah and Marcie leaned over the rim of the hole and stabilized the cylinder until Jorja could come over and help push it out onto the higher ground. Somewhere during all this, Elayah's hands ended up on Liam's back and shoulders, but she was too focused to realize it and wasn't even embarrassed until they had the capsule out of the hole and Liam mock-shouted, "El's copping a feel!"

"You should be so lucky." Marcie always had Elayah's back.

Liam climbed out of the hole. "How does it open?" he asked, nudging the time capsule with his toe.

The cylinder was about three feet long and a foot in diameter. Elayah crouched and wiped dirt away from both ends, figuring one of them would unscrew like a jar lid. Sure enough, there was a seam at one end, with an inset groove where her hand fit perfectly. She twisted and turned, eventually grunting with effort, but the thing wouldn't budge.

Liam slid up behind her, put his arms around, and captured her hand with his own. "Let me help," he said, and winked when she glanced over her shoulder at him.

Liam knew how she felt. He had to know. And here he was, practically *hugging* her—

"On three," he said, almost softly, into her ear.

They twisted at the same time. For a too-long moment, nothing happened. Her fingers tightened and strained, and then she felt Liam's hand press with a near-crushing force on her own and the lid slowly ground to the right.

There was a slight popping sound, like a Coke bottle that's been opened too suddenly. Air pressure stabilizing, Elayah knew. Gases finding equilibrium between the hermetically sealed cylinder and the outside world. There were formulas and equations that explained it, but she was too lost in the twin thrills of the opening time capsule and the nearness of Liam, the tang of his sweat in the air, the husk of his breath at her ear.

"Nice," he murmured.

She cleared her throat, suddenly highly aware of his closeness, of Jorja's and Marcie's attention. With a shimmy of her shoulders, she shook him off and applied herself to the lid, twisting it farther until it came off entirely in her hand.

With Marcie, she spread out a blanket they'd brought along, and then—before she could react—Liam upended the canister.

"Welcome to prehistory," he joked.

Elayah suppressed a yelp of horror and outrage. She'd hoped for a little pause, a moment to reflect. It had been more than thirty years since the air in the canister had mingled with the air of the world. Decades since these things had been touched or even seen. She'd wanted to pull each one out, compare it with the list, maybe record the moment....

"We were supposed to take it slow!" Jorja admonished him.

"It's not an unboxing video," Liam told her, then began pawing through the spilled contents. "I mean, look at this crap."

"It's the ultimate unboxing video," Jorja fumed. "Or would have been."

There was nothing for it, though. Liam had already dumped everything out, so Elayah settled for shooting some video for Insta as Jorja and Marcie got down on their knees with him and raked through the stuff.

"Look at this." Jorja held up a rectangular plastic box. It was transparent, with a paper insert tucked into the front, on which some words were scribbled in black ink. She opened it and clucked her tongue. "My dad has a box of these in the garage."

"It's a mixtape," Elayah said. "It's like a playlist." In preparation for the dig, she'd done a ton of research on the 1980s. She spied a Walkman in the sprawl of artifacts and picked it up. "We can play it later."

Jorja shrugged and moved on. Elayah surrendered her fantasy of doing this in an orderly fashion and instead started looking for one specific item. The one her dad had mentioned when she'd first told him about the time capsule.

At first, he'd had no reaction at all...and then his eyes lit up, as though remembering a long-forgotten dream. "The time capsule! Oh my God, I forgot all about that!"

Elayah had been surprised that her father remembered it at all. What were the odds that she and her friends would stumble upon this thing *and* that her own father would remember it?

"We came up with it in a social studies class," he recalled, closing his eyes, straining to revisit the past. "Mr. Ormond? Mr. Almond? I can't remember his name. There was a project we did where he gave us a bunch of old junk and we were supposed to try to figure out what kind of society had made it.

"So then one of us had the idea of burying our own time capsule and then digging it up...." He trailed off, eyes now open, staring up at nothing. "Oh, right..."

His voice had gone soft.

"What?" Elayah asked.

"We buried it in the fall of eighty-six, before the ground got too hard. We figured we'd dig it up fifteen years later," he told her. "We agreed to meet again on September twelfth."

He spoke as through the date had significance. She did the math. "Oh."

"Yeah, we had other things on our minds. We all forgot about it, I guess." He grinned at her. "If you guys are really going to dig it up, make sure you grab something for me, okay?"

She spied it quickly. Her father's description had been spot-on. Long time ago or not, he remembered.

She snatched it up. It was a small rectangle lined with a faded burgundy felt, hinged on one side. When she opened it, it revealed a set of glassed-in photographs, still as bright and crisp as though printed yesterday.

On the left side were two teen boys, not much older than her. Wisps of mustache. One in Jheri curl, the other a high-top fade. Otherwise identical in their blue-and-green Canterstown High varsity jackets.

It was the last photo taken of her father and his twin brother. Before Uncle Antoine, whom she'd never met, ran off to Mexico and other points south. He'd sent a few postcards early on, then nothing. Her father's eyes, usually so wide and joyous, always narrowed when he spoke or thought of his brother. In this photo, they looked both boisterous and radiant, in that way teen boys apparently always had. The smiles killed her. Her father was generally a happy man, but she knew his joy had a corroded center.

The other photo was the Jheri-curled boy (the twin whom she now knew to be her dad...and he would definitely get some ribbing about that hair) and a beautiful girl about Elayah's age. She wore a floor-length lavender gown with matching lipstick and heels, her shoulders bare, her hair a slick cap of finger waves. He was decked out in a shiny monstrosity of a tuxedo that looked to have been made out of stamped tin, his tie and cummerbund matching the dress.

Her parents. At homecoming. Wow.

She was lost in the moment. Why had her father chosen this item for the time capsule? It was significant to no one but her and her family. It had nothing to do with the state of the world in 1986.

"Hey, El, is this on the list we found?" Marcie was holding up a raggedy old doll, its fabric a tattered mess. The vinyl head lolled atop the body, which was partly rotted away. "And shouldn't it have been better preserved?"

Elayah contemplated. "Maybe it was already in bad shape when it went in," she said.

Marcie nodded, looking at the thing quizzically. Elayah called up the contents document again and skimmed it. "Nope. Nothing about a doll."

"Huh," said Marcie.

Elayah scanned over the cluster of items again. There seemed to be too many.

She took charge. Liam was goofing around with a couple of action figures he'd found (*M.A.S.K. toys,* according to the inventory list). She stopped him and had him join her, Jorja, and Marcie in dividing the items into categories—paper, plastic, cloth, metal, other.

At her direction (and with only minimal "Buzzkill" grumbling from Liam), they started out by identifying the thirty-one items on the inventory. A *Time* magazine cover sporting a portrait of a reader delving into Stephen King's *It*. A vinyl record sleeve that looked like a smear of colors abutting a severe black-and-white portrait. *True Colors*, it said. *Cyndi Lauper*.

More. Another cassette, this one with an insert as blank as the day it'd been bought. Three plastic squares that looked vaguely familiar. She read their labels: *400k floppy diskette*. Oh, right—they looked like the Save icon in Word. Floppy disks. They were like old-fashioned USB keys.

There were more pictures. Newspaper clippings. All of which were on the list.

But after they separated out the stuff on the list, there was still more. A *lot* more.

There were several pins. One read, *We'll get along fine as soon as you realize I'm God.* The rest were along the same allegedly humorous lines. There was a US Mint proof set of coins from 1985, the dime, nickel, penny, quarter, half-dollar, and dollar still gleaming. A stack of comic books bound together in a plastic sleeve, titled *Camelot 3000*. A stapler . . .

A *stapler*! What on earth?

"This makes no sense," Jorja said, running a hand over her fuzzy head. "It's like they used it as a trash can."

"What's the point of the inventory if you're just gonna throw in a bunch of old junk?" Marcie asked, fanning herself with one of the floppy disks.

"There might be interesting data on that disk," Elayah said. Why did she feel so defensive about the contents of the time capsule? Why was she so invested in it? It had been her idea to dig it up, yeah, but only because Liam had . . .

Oh.

Yeah. Because basically Liam had brought it up to his dad and his dad had laughed and said, "That old thing? You'll never find it." And then Liam had wanted to prove his dad wrong, so of course Elayah just *had* to make it happen for him.

They combed through the remaining items, taking pictures and tapping notes along the way. There was a total of thirty-four additional items, most of them junk (she admitted in the privacy of her own head), some of them quite large. No wonder the capsule had been so much heavier than they'd expected.

"Is that everything?" she asked.

"Let's check!" Liam exclaimed, and then made a show of sticking his face right up against the opening of the cylinder. "Hey, there's something in here!"

"Quit goofing around," Jorja said.

"I'm serious!" Liam pulled away from the cylinder, his face sweaty and red and impressed with an arc of the circumference of the tube. "It's not a joke."

As if to prove his seriousness, he tilted the time capsule and shook it. "It must be stuck," he said, and shook harder, banging it against the ground a bit.

Something clattered down the length of the tube and spilled out onto the ground. It was a length of white cloth, wrapped around something roughly six inches long, fastened with what looked like masking tape.

"I thought you were kidding," Marcie said.

Liam feigned horror. "I've never been so offended in my life! Hashtag puh-lease."

Elayah picked up the object and hefted it. It wasn't terribly heavy. The tape came loose easily.

She unwrapped it and nearly dropped it. They all stared.

It was a knife.

Not a butter knife or a steak knife. This was a pretty wicked-looking *knife* knife. Like the kind you used to go hunting. Or to…to…

She didn't know what else. The kind of knife you see in action movies, strapped to the belts of tough ex-soldiers with serious PTSD. There were streaks of dark red along the base of it, where the blade met the handle, stuck in the little crevices there.

"Whoa," Liam said without a trace of humor or goofiness.

"What the hell?" Marcie asked.

That was when Elayah dragged her eyes from the blade in one hand to the fabric in the other. There was a slip of paper tangled up in the cloth. She unwound it.

There was a murrey blemish in one corner of the paper. And some printed words. It took her a moment to decipher them.

*I'm sorry*, it read.

And then: *I didn't mean to kill anyone.*

# 2

# THE PRESENT: LIAM

Liam couldn't conjure a joke or even a morsel of snark to puncture the uncomfortable silence that followed after El read the note aloud. Like the others, he just stared silently at the knife for a long time. Then Marcie cleared her throat.

"Looks like we need to call your dad," she said to Liam.

Liam blinked a few times. Finally, something he could blow up into a joke.

"My *dad*? What's *he* gonna do—cook this thing in a béarnaise sauce?"

Jorja sighed. "Your *other* dad, you moron."

Liam slapped his forehead, pretending to remember who his bio-dad was and what he did. "Duh. Right."

His japery had punctured the uncomfortable quiet, but not for long. Now they all stood around in silence again, staring at the knife El held in her hand.

"We messed up a crime scene," she said after a moment, and her anguish was so real and so potent that he immediately sought another needle with which to puncture it.

"I don't think anyone actually got killed *in* the time capsule," he said.

Jorja shrugged into her plaid overshirt. "Yeah, but still...we should take pictures of everything, just the way it is. To preserve as much of the initial scene as possible."

And then they all looked at Liam, as though being the son of the sheriff made him an expert in crime-scene forensics. Liam nodded gravely, thinking, and then whipped out his phone, crouched, and started snapping away, keeping up a running commentary as he did so:

"That's right, old *Time* magazine—give me sexy! Pouty! Oh yeah, Walkman—you're fierce! You go, girl!" And on and on, until they all surrendered and started taking their own pictures. Whew. Awkwardness avoided.

When they were done: "We need to get this to the cops," El said very seriously, brandishing the knife.

"Come on," Liam said. "Guys. Are we *really* saying that one of our parents killed someone and hid the murder weapon in a time capsule?"

They all went silent for an excruciatingly long time. He'd meant it as a joke, a way of knocking back El's too-serious concern. But by the time the words left his mouth, he realized what he was actually saying, and the joke fell facedown, dead on arrival.

"Well, damn," Jorja said, and produced her fidget spinner from a pocket. Light sparkled and arced from it, racing spots along the shadows cast by the trees. "Good point. This thing belonged to our parents. This is *their* stuff."

They all exchanged a worried look.

"For real?" Marcie said in a low, almost feeble tone. "Like...our *parents*?"

None of them wanted to contemplate it, but here they were. Liam racked his brain for something incredibly stupid and inappropriate to say.

"Maybe..." El held her hands up helplessly, rescuing him. "Maybe someone else sneaked it in?"

*Sneaked.* She was the only person he knew who said *sneaked* instead of *snuck.*

"Well, I know my dad didn't do it," Liam said. "He's one of the *good* cops. And my other dad didn't grow up here. The rest of y'all...who knows?"

They all stared silently at the knife. He could feel each of them wondering if their parents had it in them to kill someone.

"We really, really need to go to the police," El said quietly.

"But we can't just leave this stuff here," Marcie pointed out. "Two of us will go to the cops. Two of us will stay behind to watch this stuff. Liam, you drove. And, El, you unwrapped the knife. So..."

Liam pretended to be annoyed, but his heart hammered. He wanted to be alone with El—he pretty much *always* wanted to be alone with El—and this time he swore to himself he wouldn't blow it. He would actually say something real, not something stupid or snarky or just plain dumbass.

"Fine," he said in his best grumble. "We'll go bug my dad. C'mon."

He grabbed his shirt from the ground, turned, and walked back down the hill without even a glance at El. Hardest thing he'd ever done.

The Canterstown Sheriff's Department and Department of Public Safety occupied a building just off Founders Street, the main boulevard that cut through town, leading from the WELCOME TO CANTERSTOWN! sign to the east to the Wantzler factory in the west. The office lay at the end of a curl of road that wound through a series of dusty, undergrassed, unused lots. It was a plain brick building with beige-and-gray clapboard shingles, rising an imposing two! whole! stories! As a kid, Liam had spent so much time here that he thought of it as a second home. He knew which of the prisoner cells were the best to play in, and in which ones lingered a permanent *parfum* of mingled vomit and piss.

He parked in the space marked FOR DAY-WATCH COMMANDER. There was no day-watch commander.

"You okay?" he asked, glancing over at El. She'd been quiet the whole way here—the whole fifteen minutes—and he'd managed to keep his joking to a minimum, which hadn't been easy. Now the sound of concern in his own voice caused a wellspring of hipster irony and bad taste to gush up from his gut. Against everything he held dear, he swallowed it down.

"Yeah," she said, not looking up. "This is just...super weird, you know?"

"I don't know about *super* weird," he said, hearing his own thoughts for the first time as they came out of his mouth. "Maybe, like, *ultra* weird, which is one step down."

She sighed something that was almost a laugh, papery and ephemeral.

Inside the office, half-height panels divided the room into six evenly sized areas. At the front was a high counter, behind which sat Loretta Blevins. Her official title was "sheriff's office assistant," but she knew for certain that this position was one step above the Lord God Himself on the org chart. She'd been sneaking Liam candies and cocoa since before he could remember, and while she jealously guarded the sheriff and her other charges, she had a weak spot the size of Kansas for her boss's only child.

"Hi, Loretta!" he said brightly. "We have, like, a murder weapon for Dad. Is he in?"

She shook her head and chuckled. "Murder weapon, eh? Go on in. He's back there."

He pushed open the swinging half door at the counter and led El through the open floor plan, through the little hallway back by the watercooler. The place stank of stale coffee and cigarettes, even though smoking had been banned in municipal buildings a million years ago. Liam knew the odor was repellent, but he couldn't help it—it smelled like home to him.

At its end, the hallway T'd. One branch led to the holding cells and records room. The other led to the sheriff's office. Liam didn't bother knocking.

"Hey, Dad!"

And there sat the sheriff of Canterstown, a.k.a. Dad Number One, a.k.a. Bio-Dad. He was what old people called "a tall drink of water," topping out at around six two, which portended well for Liam, who was just a tad over six feet right now but still growing. Other than that, they had little in common physically—Dad was wiry and thin where Liam was solid and muscled. Dad's hair was black-going-gray, while Liam's was sun-kissed blond. Liam had always thought he looked more like Chef Wally, a.k.a. Dad Number Two, a.k.a. Adoptive Dad, a.k.a. Pop, which just proved that maybe genetics was a science, but it wasn't an exact one.

"Shouldn't you be in school?" Dad asked mildly, not even looking up from his computer screen. The office was dimly lit, save for a desk lamp and the light from the computer. This room had originally been for some kind of evidence processing, but Dad hated sitting in the big glassed-in office out front that the previous sheriff had used. So he'd knocked it down to make more space for the deputies and tucked himself away in his little dungeon.

"We were digging up the—"

"The time capsule, oh yeah, right." Dad pushed back from his desk and swiveled to face them, hands clasped behind his head as he leaned back. "Hi, Elayah. How'd it go?"

"A little murder-y." Liam stepped aside and gestured to El, who stepped forward nervously, holding out the knife—rewrapped in its fabric—reverently, the way he kinda-sorta remembered priests holding out the host.

Dad arched an eyebrow. "I don't have time for nonsense, Liam. Elayah, I expected better from you."

"Sir, it's not nonsense." She placed the knife on his desk and stepped away, as though afraid of an eruption of some kind. "My fingerprints are on it. I'm really, really sorry."

"I told her to burn them off with acid *weeks* ago," Liam chimed in. "But did she listen? Nooooo…"

Dad frowned and leaned forward, scooting back to the desk. He hesitated a moment, hand outstretched toward the slender bundle, then thought better of it and plucked up his letter opener. He used the thin blade to pry the fabric apart, revealing the blade.

"Okay," he said calmly. "Guys, this is a pretty standard-issue hunting knife. Or at least, it was back in the day. Everyone around here had one. Hell, *I* had one. Probably up in the attic right now. Someone tossed it into the time capsule. That's not a crime."

El was frozen, just standing there. Liam nudged her with his elbow because that seemed safe—if he touched her with his hand, he was afraid he'd never stop.

"Dude," he forced himself to say, "the note."

El nodded as though to herself. "Under the knife," she said. "Paper."

Dad gently pushed the knife to one side to reveal the piece of paper. It was turned perpendicular to the desk, so he stood up and craned his neck to read it without touching it. Then he sat gingerly in his chair.

"Kids, I doubt this means what you think it means."

"What *does* it mean, then?" El said with some steel in her voice. Liam wanted to pat her on the back and congratulate her. As long as he'd known her, she'd been cowed by anyone over the age of twenty-five.

"I'm saying…" Dad shook his head. "Look, let me…"

He wheeled up to the desk again and started tapping at his keyboard. "It can't be a murder confession," he said, "because…"

"Because there were no murders back in 1986?" El asked.

Liam hadn't considered that. It was a different town then, a different era.

"On the contrary," Dad said, and turned his monitor so they could see it.

"There were four killings in the eighteen months leading up to the day your dad and I and the others buried that time capsule. See here?"

Liam came around the other side of the desk so that he could see without interfering with El, who was practically diving into the computer screen. Four windows were open, each showing a scanned document that he recognized as a standard municipal D&R summary. *Disposition and recapitulation.* It was the form that summed up the contents of a police incident file. He'd seen them scattered around the kitchen table growing up and could recite portions of the municipal legal code by heart.

All these cases were solved.

"Four unnatural deaths," Dad said. "And there was a kid who drove his car into a ditch when he was driving drunk and died, so five if you count that one. We solved each one of them. Well, the guys in this office back then did. Three were by confession. Eyewitnesses to the other one. More importantly," he went on, holding up a hand to forestall El's interruption, "none of them involved a knife, so even if the cops messed up back in the dinosaur days, it still wouldn't prove anything. Four bodies, no knifings."

"Maybe they never found the body." El straightened up, defiant. Liam licked his lips. Oh, Lord, determined El was even more awesome than shy, nerdy El. He ransacked his memory to conjure the name of the patron saint of hopelessly horny teen boys and came up empty.

Dad considered what she'd said. "Look, there *are* several still unclosed missing persons cases from that time. Including…" He hesitated a moment. "Including your own uncle."

"He's not missing," El said. "He's in Mexico. Or was."

"Well, be that as it may, the case is still officially open." Dad heaved out a prodigious and world-weary sigh. "Things were a lot different in those days, guys. Especially in small towns like this one. Nothing was connected. Nothing was computerized. People up and left all the time, never to be heard from again. Is it possible that one of them was actually murdered with this"—he tilted his head at the knife—"and we just never found the body? Sure. Anything's possible."

It was either a charming sign of brotherhood or an early indicator of dementia that Dad kept saying *we* when referring to the Canterstown cops of 1986.

"But," he went on, "the overwhelming odds are that someone back in eighty-six thought it would be funny to put 'evidence' of a crime in the time capsule, figuring it would trigger some huge manhunt in the future when the thing was dug up."

"'Someone'?" El raised her voice about as high as she was capable in the presence of an adult. "There were only five of you, right?"

Dad clucked his tongue nonchalantly. "That's right."

"So one of you put it in there. Shouldn't we find out who?" Liam was surprised that the voice was his own. El must have been surprised, too—she turned to look at him, her brows knitted together, her mouth half-open, no doubt about to say the same thing.

Liam shrugged and gave her a lopsided grin, then worried that he looked like he was having a stroke.

Dad was usually easygoing, but he had his limits, and Liam could tell from the set of his father's jaw that those limits were within view. "Of course we will, Liam. But this is what I do—let me handle it. The right way."

"Of course!" El said, the words almost exploding from her.

"Sure." Liam shrugged again.

"And I don't want you mouthing off around town about murders and such," he warned them both, but gazing more sternly at Liam. "Like I said, this is probably a prank. One that's going to waste time and resources. I don't want whoever did it getting their jollies off us running around to figure this thing out."

"Did you actually say 'getting their jollies'?" Liam asked. "How old *are* you?"

Dad shut his eyes for a moment and rubbed the bridge of his nose. "Liam..."

El saved him from a minilecture, probably a repeat of the one Liam had titled *Not Everything Is a Joke, Son.*

"Everyone knows we were digging the thing up," she interjected at just the right moment. "The *Loco* was even going to do a little story."

*The Lowe County Times*—both affectionately and not-so referred to as the *Loco*—was the local newspaper. *Paper* might have been a misnomer, as printing costs had driven it online years ago and it existed now in digital form only, as something between a blog and a fledgling social media network.

Given that its design was at least ten years out of date and its reportage tended toward local "news" everyone already knew—recapped with a surfeit of exclamation points—it was surprisingly popular and boasted a thriving message forum.

"That's fine," Dad told her. "They can do their story. Just don't say anything about the knife or the note, okay?"

"And what about the rest of the stuff in the time capsule? Isn't that technically evidence?"

Dad smiled a little too tightly. Liam recognized the look; it was the same look he had when he watched any cop show on TV.

"I'll send someone over to photograph it and take statements from you guys, but there's no sense impounding it. The relevant evidence is right here on my desk."

Liam could tell that El had more to say, but he could also tell that Dad had reached his limit of what he no doubt considered absolute nonsense and a waste of time. He touched El lightly on the back of her hand; she jerked away as though prodded with a soldering iron, and his heart sank into his shoes, along with all his hopes and dreams.

*Oh, hey, sorry to startle you, El, but remember how when we were in fifth grade Jorja came out and you and me and Marse formed the Queer/Straight Alliance to help her out and then we kept it going through middle school and high school, but the thing is for me it was really just an excuse to stick around you because you guys were headed off to the Ungodly Genius classes and I was destined for the Well, He Can Tie His Shoes classes and I was like, holy crap, Elayah is the most amazing human being on the planet and I've had a thing for you since, like, ever, but you were off being a genius and somehow the QSA kept us being friends and now it's like a legacy thing, even though we never really get to hang out because you'd never actually be with an idiot like me, right, so why am I even saying any of this, oh, wait, I'm not saying it I'm just thinking it because I'm a gigantic coward.*

"Overreact much?" he said instead, then immediately wished he could take it back. "C'mon."

As they headed to the door, Dad called out to them. "Hey, kids?"

They turned back at the door. "Thanks for bringing this to my attention," Dad told them with a lot more earnestness than Liam would have expected.

# 1986: DEAN

He knew he looked good; he didn't even need to look in the full-length mirror mounted on the back of his bedroom door, but he went ahead and did it anyway, checking himself out. The new jeans were snug, but they were supposed to be. His pink T-shirt was set off perfectly by the new white sport coat, which was rumpled just right, the sleeves rolled up like Crockett's on TV.

The door swung open. Jenny, his sister, never knocked when she wanted to use his mirror.

"What do you think?" he asked, stepping back and opening the jacket so that she could get the full effect.

"Not *totally* grody," she said, sniffing as though it pained her to pay him a compliment. She fluffed her hair in the mirror. She'd gotten a blowout the day before, and her hair was permed around her head in a massive blond ball of frizz. She wore a short, flaring skirt with a purple halter top and matching headband, one bra strap exposed along her shoulder. She also wore an expression of bored contempt, her default since falling into the world of the Valley girls. Adjusting her bra strap a little farther along on her shoulder, she nodded in satisfaction to her reflection and left him alone with his own.

And yeah, man, he liked what he saw. His hair was too dark to be Don Johnson, so he'd just gone ahead and slicked it back with some Dep. You were supposed to use a little dab, but his hair was too thick for that, so he used a palmful. By third period, his hair would be frozen solid, but at least he could be sure it wouldn't move out of place.

And he had to look good. As of today, he was vice president of the student government. He had to look the part, right?

Out in the kitchen, Mom and Dad were already eating breakfast when he and Jenny arrived.

"Bye, family," Jenny said. Dean immediately turned around to watch the fireworks.

"You're not leaving this house looking like that!" their father thundered from the table. "Jesus Christ! Look at you! I can see your, your, your *brassiere!*"

"What*ever*, Daddy," Jenny said. "I'm, like, nineteen. You can't, like, tell me what to do."

"You live in *my* house!" he told her. "I didn't catch a bullet in my leg in Vietnam so that my daughter could dress like some kind of whore."

*No, you got a bullet in your leg because you were too slow to turn around when your lieutenant shouted to retreat,* Dean thought, but did not say, would never ever, *ever* say.

Mom put a calming hand on Dad's shoulder. "Bob. She gets to make her own decisions." She shivered a little. "I just wish you would *decide* to dress a little nicer, Jenny."

Jenny shrugged indifferently and grabbed a piece of toast on her way out the door.

"What about your son?" Mom asked, nudging Dad, who grudgingly looked up from his paper again.

"Forget to wash your hair this morning?" Dad asked.

"It's slicked back."

Dad frowned, but then relented. "You want to look like a greaser, that's your lookout. What's with the pink shirt? Are you a girl now or something?"

"Guys can wear pink now, Dad."

"Did we forget something this morning?" Mom interrupted, stroking her own chin meaningfully.

"Mo-om!" He dragged the word out to more syllables than it needed, hating the whining note in his voice. He rubbed a hand over his carefully cultivated stubble. "It's the style."

"*Style*'s not the word for it," Dad grumbled from the table. He had gone back to reading the *Morning Gazette,* which he prided himself on plowing through before leaving for work. Then, when he got home, he would go through the *Evening Gazette.* They were a *Canterstown Gazette* family—none of that *Lowe County Times* nonsense for them. "I don't trust a paper that only publishes one edition," Dad would say to anyone who dared ask. More like he didn't trust a paper that had endorsed Mondale.

"Anyway..." Dean had nothing else to say, but he knew he had to say *something.* He let the word trail off into infinity, then smiled thanks at his mom and rushed out the door with his toast.

At school, he immediately sought out Brian, Jay, and the twins. He was excited, not just about his first day as SGA VP, but also for the first Monday morning *Miami Vice* death pool check-in with the guys. He had guessed three in the pool last Friday afternoon, and there had been four killings on the show that night. As long as no one else had guessed four, he would win.

Marcus had agreed to hold the guesses and the money. He and his twin, Antoine, showed up a couple of minutes late. Brian, Jay, and Dean were clustered in the cafeteria, waiting for the homeroom bell to ring when the twins hustled in, out of breath.

"Sorry," Marcus said. "We missed the bus. Had to run from the house."

The Laird twins were known as the two fastest runners at the school, maybe even the county, depending on the outcome of the spring's track season. Dean had nicknamed them Black Lightning, like the guy in the comic books, and the twins had really taken to it. Rarely did you see or think of one without seeing or thinking of the other. They routinely finished each other's sentences and seemed to communicate telepathically.

Antoine was the quieter of the two. Yes, the Laird boys finished each other's sentences, but usually Antoine had the shorter end of the communal utterance. What he lacked in verbosity he made up for with a wicked grin that spoke volumes.

"Open it!" Brian demanded. "We don't have long! It's almost first bell."

Marcus fumbled for a moment with the envelope. It was a large manila affair, its flap gummed shut, five signatures overlapping the line of closure.

They'd come up with the idea while watching reruns over the summer:

Every Friday afternoon of the new season, the five of them wrote down their names and guesses on slips of paper, then deposited those slips and two bucks apiece into an envelope.

Antoine, silent, leaned over to right the envelope in his brother's hands. Marcus tilted his head in thanks—Dean imagined radiating concentric circles like Aquaman's telepathy on Saturday mornings, transferring a *Thanks* from twin to twin—and tore open the envelope.

Just then, a hand slapped out from nowhere and knocked the envelope out of Marcus's hands. Brad Gimble—football prodigy and overall tool—snickered. "Oops!"

"Knock it off, Gimbo!" Dean snapped.

"Bite me, loser!"

Before Dean could retort, Brad disappeared down the hall, flipping the group off as he went.

"How is he calling *me* a loser?" Dean marveled as the twins recovered the envelope.

"He's never going to get over you beating him," Brian said.

"Forget him." Jay gestured to Marcus. "Hurry up."

"Dean, three…," Marcus read quickly, shuffling the papers. "Jay, eight…Brian, fifteen…Come on, man!" An eye roll.

"It could happen!" Brian protested. "A big drug bust with lots of…" He mimed spraying lead all around the room with a machine gun.

"Uh-huh," Marcus said, ignoring him. "Antoine, five. And me…five…"

Dean grinned broadly. He'd won!

"Of course you two guessed the same number," Jay complained as Dean scooped up his winnings.

"It's a coincidence," Marcus said defensively.

"You share one brain," Jay told them. "Lame death count anyway."

Antoine shrugged as the bell rang and the boys dispersed to homeroom.


Third period was Dean's free period, which usually meant loitering in the cafeteria or goofing around in the library, but now meant he could hang out in the SGA office. There were two desks in there, and he looked forward to the empty space and the free time.

As long as Dean could remember, he'd wanted to be a writer. He spent his free time conjuring science fiction novels, fantasy epics, extended runs on the comic books he still loved. When not doing homework or chores at home, he spent his time at his desk, outlining and plotting. Now he had a free period every day and a space of his own to work in. He just knew something great would come of it.

The office was on the second floor, a tiny room crushed between the math and science departments. He experienced a minute thrill on opening the door with his key and was slightly disappointed to see Mr. Grimm there, sitting at one of the desks, grading papers.

"Oh, hi," Dean said, hoping that his displeasure didn't come through.

Despite his name, Mr. Grimm generally had a broad, friendly attitude and was well liked by the student body. Which, Dean realized, was probably why he had wound up as the faculty adviser to the student government.

"Good morning, Mr. Vice President," Mr. Grimm boomed. He couldn't help it—he *always* boomed. "I'm just wrapping up. I'll get out of your way."

It was weird to have an adult—and a teacher—defer to him, but Dean wasn't sure what to do about it. Besides, he liked the idea of having the office to himself.

"You know, I'm not supposed to say things like this, but I'm glad you won and not Brad Gimble," Mr. Grimm said. "I get the feeling he was just looking to pad his college applications."

Dean shrugged. He still wasn't 100 percent sure how he'd managed to eke out a victory over the more popular football player, but he wasn't going to question it.

Mr. Grimm gathered up his things, then paused at the door. "Did you guys hand out the teacher survey?"

One of Dean's first jobs as SGA vice president was to write up and distribute a survey to the school's teachers to see how they could work better with SGA. He had spent the weekend trying to type it up at home, then given up after a dozen typos. Mom had sat down with his handwritten version and produced a clean copy in five minutes.

"I have it," he told Mr. Grimm, "but just one."

"You can make copies now, during your free period, and put them in the teachers' mailboxes."

Dean's nose wrinkled. He didn't mind cranking the mimeograph machine, but he hated the smell of the toner.

"Do I have to?" He gestured to his pristine white jacket. "I don't want to get purple all over my new—"

"No mimeos for this," Mr. Grimm interrupted. "You can use the Xerox machine in the principal's office. Remember to let it warm up for a few minutes before you push any buttons."

Dean had used the photocopier once before—it was as big as a doghouse and coughed and chuckled like his dad's old Chevelle. Still, it was a million times better than hand-cranking the mimeograph and breathing in the Purple Death.

Mr. Grimm waved and headed out the door, then stopped once more. "Forgot—you're going to need to get some paper from the supply closet." He fished around in his pockets and produced a key ring with over a dozen keys. "It's one of these. I think the one labeled 2QR."

Mr. Grimm handed the keys over and disappeared down the hall. Dean hefted the key ring and then tucked it into his pocket. Time to get to work.

As the school day ended, Dean made his final locker stop. Jay caught up to him as they headed for the door and the buses. They were laughing about something on *The Cosby Show* when Mr. Grimm ran up to them.

"Dean, you forgot to give me my keys back."

Dean froze. He *had* forgotten. How? He sheepishly handed them over.

When Mr. Grimm was gone, Dean kept walking, then stopped when he realized Jay had fallen behind. Peering around, he saw his friend standing in the same spot as before, staring off into the middle distance.

Dean knew that look. A good time usually followed. Or trouble. Sometimes both.

"I'm gonna miss the bus," he said, returning to Jay's side. "Come on."

"I'll drive you," Jay said with an almost vacant expression on his face; he was building something in his head. "He just . . . gave you his keys?" Jay asked slowly.

"I needed paper. For the copier. So I had to unlock the supply room."

A savage and utterly unrestrained grin split Jay's face. "I have an idea. . . ."

# THE PRESENT: ELAYAH

In her garage, Elayah stared at the relics laid out before her on an old garden tarp.

*Relics* was probably kind. Most of it was, she had to admit, junk.

There were postcards from such mundane places as Philadelphia and the Jersey Shore. A few sheets of paper containing what appeared to be emo poetry of the very worst, most high-schoolish sorts. A blue envelope containing a love letter from "*L*" to "*M*" that was alternately so overwrought and so dirty that she blushed in embarrassment for the writer and the recipient, then for herself for reading it. The word *girth* actually appeared more than once.

There were vinyl 45s and those cassette tapes. Ancient video game cartridges. A magazine called *Byte*. A collection of *Garfield* comic strips. (Wow, that cat was *old*!) A couple of old VHS tapes that she could identify only because her dad still had one of him and his brother crushing the hundred-meter relay their junior year, long before Uncle Antoine ran off to Mexico. Dad kept saying he was going to digitize it but never got around to it.

There was a VCR in the attic. Maybe she could watch the old tapes.

Maybe she could listen to the old cassettes and 45s. And find a way to access the data on the old disks.

And...

And she sighed, gazing at her empire of crap. After a deputy had photographed everything, a reporter from the *Loco* had—as promised—stopped by and photographed everything again, then interviewed the four excavators. Afterward, Jorja had pointed out that they needed to do *something* with the capsule contents...and the three others had looked pointedly at her.

"This *was* your idea...." Marcie had said, then trailed off.

*Gee, thanks, bestie.*

So she had packed everything up and brought it home. Twenty-four hours ago, she would have been *thrilled* at the opportunity to paw through the remnants of her dad's teen years, to sift through the late twentieth century and learn things that you couldn't find on Wikipedia and in old movies.

But that was before she'd held a murder weapon in her hands.

It *was* a murder weapon. She was sure of it. Elayah didn't believe in ESP or second sight or psychic powers, but she believed in gut instinct, and every part of her—including her gut, *especially* her gut—cried out that the knife was exactly what it seemed to be: the ender of a life. A cutter of the cords of Fate.

Yeah, okay, she was getting a little poetic in her excitement. Still. The point stood.

She left the tarp and its contents for another day and went inside, flicking open her phone as she did so. The *Loco* site had been updated, and the story about the time capsule was now the top link:

### Local Teens Unearth a Piece of Our Past

With the byline Rachel Sagura. Rachel was not much older than Elayah, a comms major at the nearby community college with journalistic aspirations. Or at least a desire to end up on TV.

*For more than thirty years,* the piece began, *it has lain beneath the ground, deposited there in years past by a group of high school friends who thought they themselves would dig it up someday. Instead, that task has fallen to their children.*

*Ronald Reagan was president when the time capsule went into the earth on the hill overlooking Canterstown High School in the fall of 1986. Cyndi Lauper, Bon Jovi, and Huey Lewis and the News made the music that had everyone in town dancing. The Berlin Wall still stood, and the Challenger disaster was still fresh in everyone's mind....*

Elayah groaned a bit and skimmed down, eager to skip the part where Rachel proved that she possessed core competencies in both Wikipedia and copy-and-paste.

*The capsule was unearthed by a quartet of current Canterstown seniors, led by Elayah Laird, who describes herself as "something of a polymath, I guess."*

Elayah winced. She'd said it wryly, with a healthy dose of self-deprecation, but that color didn't come across in black-and-white text.

Rachel introduced the others and then went on:

*Rising early, the foursome gathered at the school, having been given permission by the town to dig on municipal property. With the map they'd discovered already digitized for safekeeping, they puzzled out the location of the capsule and dug it up, uncovering a treasure trove of 1980s memorabilia sure to spark to life the nostalgia center of any self-respecting Gen Xer.*

"We were kinda hoping for gold doubloons," Liam said. "But I guess you can't always get what you're hoping for."

Liam's deadpan delivery fared about as well in text as had her own.

Rachel evenhandedly included some comments from Jorja and Marcie, then wrapped up with the information that "the four plan to examine their booty and perhaps present it as an exhibit at the Canterstown Public Library this winter."

*Examine their booty?* Really? That was Rachel's idea of wordsmithing? Elayah shivered in sheer repulsion and hoped for the sweet release of death. She would hear a *lot* of "Examine *this* booty!" tomorrow at school for sure. No doubt some of it from Liam.

There were photographs of the stuff currently laid out on the tarp—two wide shots of everything and then a gallery of close-ups. Below that, the usual comment section.

**I remember those shoes! Best shoes I ever owned!**

**OMG—I had that exact same Walkman! My kids would never get it if I showed it to them.**

**That ALF lunch box could have been mine!**

A bunch of oldsters reminiscing, going all nostalgic. What would they say if they knew, though? If they knew what else had been in the time capsule?

Still staring at the phone, she walked through the living room. Dad had gotten home from work and lay on the sofa, swiping through his iPad. "Eyes up!" he admonished her, and she juked her line of sight up just in time to avoid colliding with the coffee table.

"Sorry," she said sheepishly.

"Kids these days," Dad said, clucking his tongue for effect. He smiled as he said it.

"Adults these days," she retorted. It was their usual back-and-forth.

"What's got your head in the clouds, sweetheart?"

Elayah flopped down onto the sofa next to him. "The time capsule."

"I saw the story." He waved his iPad in the air a bit.

"I found your thing," she said. "It's out in the garage with the rest of the stuff. I'll go—"

"Don't worry about it," he told her. "I'll see it later. What's bothering you?"

She hadn't yet told him about the knife. Liam's dad had seemed pretty serious about keeping it under wraps. "What was the point of doing an inventory if you didn't actually keep it accurate?"

He pursed his lips and tilted his head back, time traveling. "Well, look, we were sloppy. What can I say? I guess we didn't bother to inventory it all."

Sloppy or not, though, one of them had put that knife in there. What did he know? What did he know that he wasn't telling her?

"Honey?" he asked, sitting up straighter. "You're doing that thing where you disappear into yourself. What's bothering you?"

She considered telling him about the knife, right then and there. But she couldn't do it. She had to give the sheriff time to start looking into it. And besides, there was nothing for her dad to do about it.

"Nothing, Dad. I just have to ask Liam some stuff." She sidled away, slipping into the kitchen, tapping at her phone.

Elayah: **hey**

Liam: **yo**

Elayah: **has your dad said anything about the** 🔪 **!?**

Liam: **oh yeah he always shares case information with me** 😄
Elayah: **come on**
Liam: **I'll ask him when he gets** 🏚️
Elayah: **promise?**
Liam: ✌️

After dinner, she went out into the garage and recovered the hinged photo frame from the tarp. She presented it to her parents with a little drumroll playing on her phone. Mom took it from her and stared at it for a long while, her eyes glistening.

"Look at you. Both of you." She held it out to Dad, who nodded and said nothing, his lips pressed together.

"I'm sorry," Elayah said. "Should I not have showed it to you?" She'd never known her uncle Antoine and probably never would. His last communication from Mexico had been something like fifteen years before she was even born.

"Baby," her dad said softly, and stood to put his arm around her. "You did just the right thing."

They squeezed each other for a moment. It was quiet for too long.

"I just don't remember your hair being *so* greasy!" Mom said abruptly, and she and Elayah cracked up as Dad spluttered a nearly incoherent defense of his teen self.

Later, she sat in her room, staring at the ceiling. It was long past time to go to sleep. There was still no news from Liam, nothing at all about the police investigation.

And why would there be? The sheriff, she realized, didn't really take this seriously. His first step should have been to call the other people who'd contributed to the time capsule. Well, he definitely hadn't called her dad, and a quick hop into her QSA group text told her that he hadn't called anyone else's parents, either.

He had obviously been humoring her when he'd promised to investigate. He thought the whole thing was just a joke, so he'd probably just handed off the knife and the note and the cloth to a deputy who had it filed away in the evidence room in one of those dusty, old cardboard boxes you see on cop shows all the time. And it would sit there for *another* thirty-five years, a different sort of time capsule, and no one would ever know what had actually happened.

But people needed to know. People *deserved* to know. Somewhere out there, a family was missing a piece of itself. She knew how that felt, vicariously if nothing else. Just from her dad's expressions, from the way her mom had said *Both of you.*

It had happened to another family, too. A loved one had disappeared thirty-five years ago, and they didn't know why or how. They had the right to know, didn't they?

*Just don't say anything about the knife or the note, okay?*

That was what the sheriff had said. Those were his exact words. Elayah had a very good memory for what people said—it made taking notes in class pretty much redundant—and she knew that Liam's dad had been very specific. She was allowed to talk to the paper, just as long as she didn't say anything about the knife or the note.

Her dad had a saying: *Sometimes you just gotta kick the mule if you want it to kick back.*

It was a pretty stupid saying. As far as she knew, her dad had never even *seen* a mule. And, like, why would you *want* a mule to kick? But whatevs. The point still stood.

Liam's dad wasn't going to do anything about the murder unless he was compelled to.

So.

Elayah: **hey there I wanted to add something to the story. is that cool?**

It took a while for the response to come. She whiled away the minutes playing *Bold-or-Dash!* on her phone.

Rachel: **like what?**

She chose her words carefully.

Elayah: **we found something. I can't tell you what because the police are investigating.**

This time, the response was nearly instantaneous.

Rachel: **Police? What did you find? I can update the story.**

Elayah folded her lower lip in against her teeth and worried it back and forth a bit. She had already figured out exactly what to say. Had already written it, in fact, in her Notes app. She copied and pasted her response in and hesitated not even the slightest bit before pushing Send.

Rachel did not, in fact, update the story that night. She posted a new one instead.

## Police Investigating Evidence Unearthed from Time Capsule!

The lede was as good as it could get in local news, she figured:

*Four teens who dug up a thirty-five-year-old time capsule this morning found more than just the music and amusements of their parents' generation. They also found evidence of a crime.*

Not bad.

From there, the article quickly summarized the earlier piece, along with a link back to it, then got to the nitty-gritty:

*"I can't say much," said Elayah Laird, who led the group that excavated the capsule, "but there was evidence of something pretty horrible in there. We know what you did. And now the police know, too."*

*We know what you did.* That hadn't been a part of her original text. Rachel had texted her back and asked, *What would you say to the person who put this evidence in there, if you could talk to them?*

And Elayah had thought about it and figured *We know what you did* was pretty neutral. But seeing it in black and white, it suddenly seemed threatening.

Furthermore, she hadn't expected Rachel to use her name—they hadn't discussed it—but oh well, there it was.

*When pressed for more information, Laird demurred, stating that she had been asked to say nothing of the specifics of the evidence.*

*The Canterstown Sheriff's Department did not respond to our request for comment. We will update this story if that happens.*

Elayah nodded to herself triumphantly. There. *Now* let Liam's dad ignore the knife. He would have no choice but to take it seriously.

*Now* she could sleep.

She thumbed off her phone, turned out her light, and rolled over, secure in the knowledge that things would be different in the morning.

And woke up in the dead of night, suddenly, completely.

There was the pressure of another body on her bed, the heat of someone behind her, a slender, sharp line of metal at her throat, and then a soft whisper in her ear:

"Don't scream."

# 1986: MARCUS

Try that one," Marcus said, pointing.

Jay sighed heavily and shrugged Marcus off. Marcus gritted his teeth and counted to five in his head. He didn't have the patience to count to ten, which he knew was sort of the point, but he just couldn't make himself do it.

"I have a system," Jay said. "I'll get it."

There were twenty-one keys on the ring that they'd duplicated, with no way to tell what key opened what lock. As a result, the five of them loitered quite conspicuously outside the school, huddled together in the gloaming of the parking lot lights. It was early October, and the air had yet to chill. They'd chosen the door on the east side of the school because it had the least exposure to the road, but Marcus knew that the police often used the parking lot to turn around or take a quick break during their nightly patrols. He told Jay this.

Jay shrugged. "I'm not worried about the police."

Jay was in the Civil Police Corps, a countywide organization of teens who planned on becoming cops someday. Once a week and for two weeks in the summer, he dressed in a cut-down police uniform and drilled with the local sheriff's office. When someone ran away from home or didn't come back from a Sunday hunting trip in the woods, the CPC was called in to support the police in the search and rescue.

Marcus thought it was a joke, but he knew Jay took it very, very seriously. And it was one thing for whiter-than-white Jay Dearborn to stand in the headlights of a Canterstown sheriff's cruiser, quite another for Marcus and Antoine to do the same. But there was no way to explain that to Jay.

Marcus had tried once.

"You think the police here are racists?" Jay had hooted. "You remember that one time there was a Klan rally over in the old March field?"

As though Marcus could forget.

"The sheriff had cruisers parked at the property line all night to make sure nothing got out of hand," Jay said. "Would they do that if they were racists?"

And that had been that. Jay had a way of speaking that tended to shut off further debate, whether you agreed with him or not.

Jay was okay for a white kid, Marcus thought. A little too into the cop stuff, but Marcus remembered that as a child, even he had wanted to be a policeman at one point. The idea had obsessed him, until one day—he must have been about seven—his father sat him down out on the old wooden steps of the porch that hung off the back of their house.

Pops had leaned in and pried open his mouth, showing Marcus a sore-looking gap about halfway back. At that point, Marcus himself was missing two teeth, which he understood to be a part of the aging process, plus a way of getting twenty-five cents from the tooth fairy. But he didn't know *adults* lost teeth, too.

"Marching down in Baltimore, about ten years ago," Pops said without preamble, staring into the middle distance as though it were the past. "Police came, of course. Always expect that. Sometimes it got rough; sometimes it didn't. No way to tell which it would be. It was never about us, mind. It was always them. Who's feeling it? Who's giving the orders? Who's ignoring the orders?"

Pops sighed and massaged his temples. "Took a nightstick to my face. I felt that tooth come out. It rattled around in my mouth for a second; then I spit it out when he got me in the gut with that stick. Beat the hell out of me, but I was the one who spent the night in jail."

Marcus didn't know what to say.

"You want to be police," Pops said, "you go on and do it. Bet you'd be a good one. And we need good ones. But just know who you'll be working with and what it's about."

And then he'd put a hand on Marcus's shoulder, squeezed tight, and kissed him gently on the forehead. Marcus didn't cry until later that night, when he was alone in bed while Antoine was brushing his teeth. He hid his tearstained face against his pillow until the lights went out.

Even now, he couldn't watch *T.J. Hooker* like the other guys did because he knew, deep down, that old Captain Kirk could easily be the guy who knocked Pops's tooth out of his face if someone gave him the order. *Miami Vice* was different—those guys didn't wear uniforms, and they seemed tight for a Black guy and a white guy. Plus, their boss wasn't white.

He was a little uncomfortable following Jay's lead, but Jay had been leading them all around since they were kids. It was just a natural pattern for them.

"Just hurry, okay?" he said now to Jay.

"Ah, yassa, Kingfish!" Jay said in his very best *Amos 'n' Andy* voice.

Marcus and Antoine exchanged a glance. Once, that glance would have communicated volumes to Marcus, but recently . . . recently he'd felt closed off from his twin. People always thought that twins had some kind of telepathy or ESP, but Marcus had never been willing to go that far. Still, he and Antoine had always been able to read each other's moods, their expressions not transparent, but at least at a level of legible translucency.

Now, though, Antoine had gone opaque. When Marcus looked at him, he saw only himself, reflected back, mute and stony.

"Got it." Jay's voice was a hushed whisper of excitement. This was the moment they'd been waiting for since Dean borrowed Mr. Grimm's keys a second time . . . and handed them off to Brian, who raced home during lunch and made dupes on the key grinder his dad kept in the garage.

"Wait." Dean reached over between Marcus and Antoine and grabbed Jay's wrist before he could haul open the door. "Do you think there's an alarm?"

The five of them pondered this, eyes flicking to one another. Dean, clearly concerned. Antoine, still a blank. Jay, nostrils vibrating with exhilaration. Brian, twitching his jaw muscles in anticipation. Marcus wondered if his own expression accurately reflected the counterbalancing combination of outright terror and utter electricity racing through his nervous system at the moment.

"Who would want to break *into* school?" Brian pointed out.

This was true.

Dean released Jay's wrist and let him tug at the door. Marcus half expected the door not to open—it couldn't be *this* easy to break in, right?—but the door pulled out just as though the morning bell had rung.

They all looked at one another, grinning. Even Antoine. It was nice to see.

"Let's go find that pool," Jay said with a glint in his eye.


The pool. The Canterstown High swimming pool. Spoken of in whispers, passed down through word of mouth from senior classes to juniors, spreading through the student body like pink eye.

Legend had it that when the high school was built, it counted among its gymnastic accoutrements a swimming pool, for use in phys ed. But an obscure regulation decreed that all schools in the county must have equal access to the same facilities. Since only Canterstown High had been built with a pool, this meant that other students in other schools would be at a disadvantage.

The pool was already built, so the solution had been simple: Close it off and don't let anyone in. Depending on whom you'd heard the story from, details varied. Some said, for example, that the pool was actually under the gym, which had a retractable floor.

Marcus had heard that one. He'd also heard that the pool lay behind a stout, locked door in the basement. That made a lot more sense, but he hoped the retractable-floor story was true. That would really be something to see.

He slipped into the building right after Jay, holding the door open for Antoine and Dean. Brian came in last, closing the door almost tenderly. Given that Brian was built like a John Deere, such delicacy was comical. No one laughed, though.

After a moment, Marcus's eyes adjusted to the dark and he could barely make out the trophy case mounted on a nearby wall. The Steingard Trophy—"the Cup"—stood in the center on a shelf lined with purple velvet, its place of pride undisturbed since 1972. A slight smell of disinfectant lingered in the air.

"Now what?"

Dean gestured with a flashlight he'd brought along. Silvery and ridged for a better grip, it was about average size—a foot long and as big around as a Coke can.

"Not yet," Jay said, brandishing his own extinguished CPC flashlight, this one a serious, sleek black cylinder of metal. "Wait until we're away from the doors and windows."

Using the weak spill of light from the parking lot and their own years of memory, they made their way down the hallway toward the cafeteria, where they finally lit up the flashlights. The cafeteria seemed somehow old and haunted in its emptiness, the tables rolled against the walls, the doors to the kitchen and the lunch line closed. Without the raucous noise of a hundred students and the dead-fried smell from the lunch line, the place felt funereal. Sepulchral.

"We should split up," Brian suggested, hauling his own flashlight out. It looked tiny in his enormous paw. For five years, football coaches had done everything but drop to their knees and beg for Brian to go out for the team, but he had precisely zero interest in sports.

"I'll take Antoine," Dean said. "We'll check out the basement."

"I'll go with you guys," Marcus offered. "We can go through the gym on our way." Those were the two best bets for the location of the pool.

"What does that leave us to do?" Brian asked, pointing to Jay and then back to himself.

"I have some ideas," Jay said. The wavery yellow glow of the flashlight cast harsh shadows up the contours of his face, glimmering wetly in his eyes. But Marcus recognized the expression on Jay's face, the vanguard of realization and ignition.

That look both thrilled and frightened Marcus. Or maybe the two were the same, in the end. Maybe fear and excitement existed on opposite sides of the same coin, bearing the same weight, displacing the same amount of air, and only chance determined which one landed faceup in any given situation.

"Okay," Marcus said, a little doubtfully. "You ready?" He nodded to his twin, who could only be bothered to offer a half shrug in return. *Damn, Antoine. What is with you?*

# JAY

Jay led Brian down the big, double-wide corridor that stretched from the cafeteria, past the auditorium, toward the main office.

"What are we doing?" Brian whispered. The painted cinder blocks that lined the empty halls carried that whisper and echoed it back to him. They were alone in the building. Why was he whispering?

Jay said nothing, simply raised the hand without the flashlight, hoisting aloft the ring of keys.

"I don't get it."

Jay sighed. Brian was a good guy, but he was the dumbest of the smart kids Jay had surrounded himself with. Which still made him smarter than a lot of the other kids in school and some of the teachers, but talking to Brian wasn't like talking to Dean, for example. Dean *got it*. Instantly. Every time. Jay tolerated Brian's presence in their group because Brian usually had access to pot.

So, with an air of forbearance, Jay rattled the keys. "We have every key to the building. We can do a lot more than just find a pool. We can go *anywhere*. But first we have to figure out which keys open which doors."

Brian stopped dead in the middle of the hall. "I thought we were going to just find the pool...."

"There *is* no pool, Bri. It's just a rumor someone started years ago. I asked my dad."

Jay's dad was on the board of education. He would know.

"We have the keys to the kingdom," Jay went on, trying each key in the lock to the main office door. "It's a moral imperative to do something with them."

"A moral imperative?" Brian shivered. "Man, this is illegal. Don't you want to be a cop someday?"

Jay shrugged, his attention entirely focused on the lock and the plethora of key options before him, juggling the keys in one hand while keeping the flashlight focused on the lock with the other. "This is no big deal. We're not hurting anyone. You guys are all under eighteen, right? It's nothing. Stop worrying."

The lock clicked. Jay pushed open the door and motioned for Brian to enter.

Brian shook his head.

"Fine. Stay out here. Alone."

Brian folded his arms over his chest, then relented.

Jay grinned. He was a leader. He got his way. This was why he would be a great cop. Someday, he'd probably end up being sheriff of this town. And *that* would be a great day for Canterstown. Truly.

Brian sidled up to him. "Now what?"

Jay splashed the beam of his flashlight around the room. This was the outer administrative office ("Admin," as it was called over the PA). Two secretaries sat here during school hours, pecking away at their electric typewriters, filing paperwork, and generally acting like too-stern grandmothers to all those summoned here.

A short corridor led to three other rooms, offices for the principal and two vice principals. Jay knew which one he wanted, but first...

He stepped around one of the secretary's desks. MRS. WISTERN, said the nameplate. The desk wasn't locked.

"Ever feel like skipping class?" he asked Brian, brandishing a yellow pad of hall passes.

"C'mon, man," Brian said. "They'll notice if you swipe that."

Jay chuckled. "They're not gonna notice. Anyway..." He ripped a half dozen passes off the pad and handed them to Brian, who took them, albeit reluctantly, and shoved them into his pocket. Another half dozen went into his own pocket.

"Now what?" Brian asked, arms folded over his chest. "Stealing lunch tickets?"

Jay shook his head and crooked his finger in a *Come here* gesture. Together they walked down the short corridor until they came to the door with a nameplate reading MARSHA TOOMBS, VICE PRINCIPAL. It took only a minute or two to locate the right key, and soon they were in.

"I didn't know Mrs. Toombs had one of those," Brian said, pointing.

Jay grinned and strode over to the desk, upon which lay the object of Brian's attention: an almost-new Apple IIe computer, sleek and snowy white. "The school board approved it a couple of months ago."

Jay's dad nominally ran the board of education, but like most parents, he knew absolutely nothing about computers. Jay had been obsessed with them since playing his first video game. He scrounged junk shops and yard sales for components and boards and cases. He had a copy of *Newsweek* with a guy named Steve Jobs on the cover.

So when the school had requested a computer for the administration to use, Dad had come to Jay for advice.

"Is this just them trying to squeeze more money out of us?" he'd asked. "Or is there actually a use for one of these things in a school?"

Jay had enthusiastically endorsed the idea and had even tried to persuade Dad to buy one of the amazing new computers he'd read about in *Byte*: a Macintosh. But his father had been scandalized by the thought of spending two thousand dollars for something useless like a computer. So Mrs. Toombs ended up with an Apple IIe.

The screen came to life. The board hadn't sprung for the color monitor, so it was just black and white.

"Shall-we-play-a-game?" Jay asked in his very best robotic voice.

*Now* Brian got it. He'd been leaning with casual exasperation against the doorjamb, but now he jerked upright and dashed around the desk to join Jay.

"Do they keep grades on it?" he asked. "Like in *WarGames*?"

"Yeah. That's why they got it for her in the first place." Jay flipped through the box of floppy diskettes he'd discovered in her desk drawer. One had a label that read GRADE BOOK. He fed it into the disk drive and he and Brian waited, breathing quietly into the grinding noises coming from the drive.

Eventually the program booted up. *Press any key to continue*, said the screen, so he did. After a little while, the application came up, asking him how many disk drives were attached and reminding him that unauthorized copies of the software might not work. Soon the main menu came up and he chose option three, to see the current grades.

*Loading main grade-book program,* the screen flashed at him. Jay grinned.

"Here we go! What class is giving you the most trouble these days?"

**6**

# 1986: MARCUS

The gym doors—all of them—were locked. Marcus fiddled with his own set of keys, swapping them out in the thready light that bled through the windows to the parking lot. Eventually he found the one that turned the lock.

"Got it!" he whispered excitedly, and turned to find...

Dean and Antoine were gone. They'd stolen away while he'd been focused on the keys.

And taken the flashlight with them.

Marcus swore under his breath. He could use a good dose of that fabled twin telepathy right about now. He would use it curse out his twin for disappearing on him.

Fortunately, the gymnasium had big, wide windows up near its ceiling, across from the bleachers. They let in enough light from the parking lot that he could see once he got inside. His breath and his footsteps echoed hugely in a way they never did during phys ed class, when bodies packed the room.

Wandering almost at random, he began checking the edges where the floor abutted the walls, the bleachers. He had never seen a retractable floor before, but he imagined such a thing would look different from an ordinary floor. Gaps or hinges or rollers, tucked just out of casual view.

None of these appeared during a cursory examination of the floor, nor during his more focused search, down on hands and knees, crawling along the bleachers, blowing and brushing dust out of the way as he sought evidence that the floor could roll away to reveal a pool beneath.

The gym was a bust.

He slipped out into the corridor, careful to lock the door behind him. A light stabbed out of a nearby cross corridor, the one that led toward what was officially called the Health Suite, but known to all and sundry as the Sex-Ed Room. Stashed down here near the gym, as though all bodily functions— no matter their origin or intent—must be relegated to one corner of the building.

Once his eyes adjusted again to the darkness, he strode down to the cross corridor, turned. Nothing. Even darker down here. One hand outstretched to maintain contact with the wall, he progressed slowly until his hand encountered empty space.

As he turned this new corner, a flashlight's beam threw a glow in his direction. Antoine lay on the floor, reaching up for Dean's outstretched hand.

"You all right?" Marcus asked, jogging over to them. If one-half of Black Lightning was out of commission, the school's chances in track this year would be dim, and the twins' odds of getting into the University of Houston would drop precipitously. He scooped up the flashlight, which had dropped to the floor and rolled back and forth, twisting and turning shadows on the walls like psychotic marionettes.

"Get that light out of our faces," Dean snapped, holding up a hand to shield his eyes.

Fuming, Marcus jerked the light back and forth from his twin to Dean. "What the hell, you guys? You just ditched me."

"You were taking forever with the gym keys," Dean complained, "so we went to check out the basement."

"And?"

Antoine merely shrugged.

"Nothing. You?" Dean asked.

"Nope. I'm starting to think there's no pool."

Dean snorted. "I bet there isn't. That was just Jay's way of getting us to go along with this."

Marcus frowned. "Really?" But he knew, deep down, that Dean was right. "What's the point?"

Antoine shrugged again. His favored mode of communication these days.

"Jay always has some ulterior motive. I bet he's doing something like sneaking into the girls' locker room. I could have been hanging out with Kim tonight," Dean said with some asperity, "instead of wasting my time here."

Antoine seemed just as upset as Dean. Marcus thought about it and decided that he, too, was angry on behalf of his buddy. *He* could have been making out with Dinah. He saw her little enough as it was. Wasting an entire night on a wild-goose chase made it even worse.

He opened his mouth to commiserate, but just then the PA system exploded to life with a too-loud crackle and a brief burst of feedback.

"Attention all skulkers and those who are breaking and entering," Jay's voice boomed, echoing down the empty halls, "please report to Admin." Then, in his best Valley girl voice: "Like, totally *now*, totally."

# DEAN

Dean insisted they all run. The twins easily outpaced him, even in the dark. He followed their forms with the bouncing beam of his flashlight.

It seemed ridiculous, but some part of him was afraid that the PA was loud enough to be heard outside the school, that Canterstown's still night air would carry the broadcast past the Wantzler factory store (closed and empty this late at night), over the nearby crest, through the copse of trees, and down into town itself. And then there would be a rush of police and parents. He wasn't sure which of those would be worse.

Antoine and Marcus pulled up outside Admin before Dean had even finished scampering up the nearest staircase. They waited for him at the door, arms folded over chests, chiseled, sculpted out of the darkness around them.

They weren't even breathing hard. Dean's forehead was dotted with sweat.

"Join us, won't you?" Jay leaned out into the corridor. "We have something to show you."

Soon they were all arrayed around Mrs. Toombs's desk, studying the grade book on the computer.

"Computers are gay," Marcus said. "You can tell because they always start with 'see colon enter.'"

Brian and Dean chuckled. Jay sniffed in something akin to offense. "This is an Apple, not an IBM. There's no C: prompt."

Dean rolled his eyes. "Fine."

Jay flounced into Mrs. Toombs's chair with a little more drama than the moment called for. "Guys. This is big, okay? I'm offering you the promised land. Moses never had it so good. I can switch up your grades and make your lives a whole lot better. And easier."

"They'll notice," Brian said.

"He's right," Marcus put in. "I have a C in chemistry right now. If you change it to something else, Mr. Chisholm will definitely notice."

Jay shook his head. "Jism won't notice a thing. Not if we wait until right at the end of the semester. Once Toombs has Mrs. Wistern enter the final grades in, the computer does all the work, figures out your average, and has the report cards printed. The teachers never even see them again."

"So you're saying we have to come back at the end of the semester?" Marcus sounded incredulous. "What was the point of coming here now if we have to come back in a few months?"

Jay shrugged. "To be sure we could do it. To be sure I could get into the computer."

"You're gonna start a nuclear war," Brian warned him.

"I'm not gonna start a nuclear war," Jay batted back.

Dean had been watching Antoine the whole time the others had been speaking. Antoine was the only one not even looking at the computer monitor. Instead, he leaned against the wall, arms folded, gazing steadily back at Dean, an expression of quiet exasperation on his face. Dean knew the look well. Antoine communicated mostly without words, as though he and his twin had been allotted a joint vocabulary stipend in the womb and Marcus was using up the verbiage too quickly for Antoine to use his share.

"I'm not sure they'll be happy with this when you apply to the police academy," Dean pointed out.

Jay spun around in Mrs. Toombs's chair. "What does that have to do with the price of tea in China?"

"Breaking and entering. Cheating. That doesn't sound like a great cop to me."

With a wave of his hand, Jay dismissed the idea like a bad smell. "I want to be a cop because *other* people need to follow the rules. I'm okay on my own. So are you. All of us. We're all smart enough to keep it together and keep ourselves in line." He arched an eyebrow. "Marcus's C in chem notwithstanding. But most people aren't. Most people need discipline."

"It's just that damn stoichiometry," Marcus grumbled.

"So we're the elite that gets to cheat?" Dean asked.

"Are you serious?" Jay launched himself out of the chair and planted his fists on his hips. "You act like this matters. I can get straight As without cheating at all. You all know that."

It was true. They were all—modesty aside—smart. Marcus was struggling with chem, yeah, but they had solid grades. Jay was the smartest... probably.

"I do know that. So why do we need to change our grades? They're already good enough."

"Wouldn't you rather get As without having to do so much work? Cruise along senior year with steady Bs or even Cs, then we jack them up right when college applications go out at the end of the semester. Stop wasting so much time on school stuff and work on other things."

"What other things?" Marcus asked. "What have you got going on that's so important?"

Jay laughed. "Pretty much *anything*. School is just a means to an end. The only reason you go to high school is to go to college, right? The only reason you go to college is to get a job. School doesn't actually mean anything in and of itself. Just get through it and move on to the real world."

Tempting and persuasive, Dean had to admit. Schoolwork wasn't *that* hard, but he would enjoy taking it easy and dropping some of the anxiety of getting good-enough grades to attract a topflight college. His family was comfortable, but not wealthy. If he wanted to go anywhere other than a state school or avoid joining Jenny at community college, he needed exceptional grades.

"You could spend that extra time studying for the SAT," Jay said suddenly. "Think about it."

And that, Dean acknowledged, made a lot of sense. If grades were one component of getting into, say, Princeton (his dream school), then the SAT was the other big chunk.

"We can't fake our lives like you can," Marcus said, interrupting Dean's internal calculations. "We can't just show people a piece of paper that says we can run the two hundred under twenty. We gotta actually *do* it if we want to go to college."

Jay arched an eyebrow. "Do you? Straight As in every class? Two Black kids? Affirmative action? You're a shoo-in."

Marcus's jaw tightened. Jay didn't notice—Jay was ever oblivious to such cues—but Brian and Dean exchanged a glance.

"Maybe there's more to it," Marcus said very, very evenly after a long pause.

"You guys just don't get it," Jay complained. "Fine. Screw you. I'll just fix my grades."

With that, he stomped out of the office.

The four of them stared around at one another. Antoine still hadn't spoken.

"We have to go get him," Brian said quietly.

"He'll calm down," Dean assured him.

"Not that." Brian indicated the computer. "He's the one who knows how to shut this thing down."

# 1986: MARCUS

True to Dean's prediction, Jay had calmed down and broken through his sulk by the time they made sure all the lights were out and the doors were relocked before leaving. As he slid behind the wheel of his Chevette, Jay looked over his shoulder at Marcus, who had lost the coin toss and sat in the middle of the back seat, between Brian and Antoine. He was pinned on both sides, his knees practically to his chest.

"You'll come around," Jay prophesied with that ineffable sense of confidence he always projected. "I bet by homecoming you'll be begging me to change your grades."

Not for the first time in his life and—he knew—not for the last, Marcus considered how different the rules were for white kids. Jay could break into school, break into the principal's office. He could go jogging in a white neighborhood any time of day or night. He could tell off a teacher.

He could do all these things and get a slap on the wrist, at most. Marcus would be *lucky* to get away with a slap across the face.

Jay was—as Dean had once said—"all balls and no dick." He had zero impulse control, zero sense of self-preservation, and because he seemed like a nice white kid from the right part of town, he never had to suffer the consequences. And there was no one who would ever say precisely that to his face.

There weren't many Black folks in Canterstown proper. Most lived on the outskirts of town, closer to the factory. And of those who did live in town, very few had kids in their teens. Marcus and Antoine made up an amazing 13 percent of the high school's Black population. There were even fewer kids of other colors.

And the truth, Marcus acknowledged, was that most of those white kids were pretty cool to them. Polite. He knew his athletic prowess buttressed him against some of the more overt expression of racism; school pride trumped racial animus, it seemed. He'd learned that lesson early, in elementary school. Chosen last for a game of Smear the Queer at recess, he'd wowed everyone with his stamina and evasive maneuvers. Suddenly he was chosen first any time anything athletic was involved. Which was almost as bad, really, because suddenly everyone thought all he was good for was sports.

Good or bad, it stuck. He and Antoine became the first and second picks each and every time, and the two became legendary. Then Dean dubbed them Black Lightning, and it was as though the nickname solidified the legend, made it something fated.

That was good enough for now, he supposed. But he couldn't rely on the sufferance of white people for his whole life. So he and Antoine were going to relay-race their way to University of Houston, home of Kirk Baptiste and Carl Lewis. And they would keep having each other's backs, and they would make sure that if one of them got up one more rung on the ladder, then he'd lean back and give the other one a hand up.

All of that occupied him so much that he didn't speak to Antoine at all after Jay dropped them off on the corner. They walked in silence to the middle of the block, then up the driveway to the house.

"Man, you were quieter than usual tonight," he told his twin as they unlocked the front door and slipped inside. Mom and Pops had already gone to bed, even though it was only ten. Pops had early shift this month, and Mom tried to sleep on his schedule.

Antoine just shrugged. Sometimes Marcus wanted to punch some words into his twin's mouth. At first, the silence hadn't bothered Marcus. He and 'Toine had always communicated mostly nonverbally anyway, able to read each other glances, moues, and eye rolls as easily as other people read comic books. When 'Toine pared back on his talking, Marcus just picked up the slack. It felt natural, almost instinctual.

Which meant that Antoine's silence went on much longer than Marcus realized before he really even noticed it.

And lately, his twin's moods and thoughts had become undefinable even to Marcus. He knew it was past time to broach the topic with his twin, but they'd never needed to have that sort of serious conversation before. Now Marcus felt as though he had a low-grade headache all the time, as though something were constantly nagging at his brain, worrying at the neurons and delicate cradle of blood vessels surrounding it.

He brushed his teeth. Wiped foam from his mouth. Enough was enough. It was time to tell Antoine to knock off the silent treatment. He would just do it. Rip off the Band-Aid.

He marched into their room. Antoine sat quietly on his bed, hands clasped before him, and lifted his gaze to his brother's.

Before Marcus could speak, Antoine said, "I want my own room."

# THE PRESENT: LIAM

Liam was awakened by a crash, then a thud, then a string of muffled curses. He lay blinking up at the ceiling for a moment, orienting himself in space and time. The sleep had been deep. Dreamless. Rudely interrupted by a series of noises he knew all too well.

Another slight thump. More curses. Liam couldn't help it; he smiled in the darkness at the familiar routine.

It happened at least once a month—Dad would get an emergency call in the middle of the night, something his deputies either couldn't handle or didn't feel comfortable handling. Every time, Dad would drop his gun belt while fumbling in the dark, then trip over it and collide with the nightstand. Then he would bang his head on the nightstand while bending down in the dark to pick up the belt.

"Sweetheart," Pop often said, "why don't you just turn on the damn light?"

"Because I don't want to wake you up," Dad would respond, and then look perplexed when Liam and Pop would laugh out loud at it.

Liam waited for the plod of his dad's feet down the hall past his bedroom. He glanced at his phone on its charging stand—it was a little after two in the morning. Which meant *both* dads would get up, with Pop insisting on brewing a thermos of coffee for Dad before he left. So, two sets of plodding feet. And then he could roll over and go back to sleep.

As a kid, he hadn't been able to do that. Awoken in the middle of the night, he'd leap out of bed, pull back his curtains, and stare out the window as Dad backed out of the driveway, his headlights cutting the night. Then, weeping, he'd run to his fathers' bedroom and launch himself into their bed, snuggling close to Pop, who would kiss his forehead and stroke his hair and promise him that Dad would be okay, that he would come back to them, that everything would be all right.

He still worried about his father. Canterstown was small, but it was the kind of town with a lot of guns, many of them bigger and more powerful than the service revolver Dad strapped to his hip. Anything could happen, especially in a town where employment was scarce while opiates and ammo were plentiful.

But he was old enough now to know that he could do nothing about it. As a child, he'd thought that staying awake and hoping and worrying would somehow magically protect his father. That as long as he didn't sleep, Dad would have no choice but to come home safely.

He'd discarded that sort of magical thinking a long time ago. He worried about his father but didn't obsess over it. There were jobs a lot more dangerous than being a cop. Twenty-five years in the sheriff's department and his dad had drawn his weapon in the field exactly twice... and one time was just to put a bullet between the eyes of a rabid dog snarling and foaming its way across someone's backyard.

The second time had been to talk down a guy with a knife to his girlfriend's throat at a local bar. As soon as Dad unholstered his weapon, the guy's eyes had "popped like something from an old Bugs Bunny cartoon," Dad reported, and he immediately dropped the knife and held his hands in plain sight. "I didn't know you were *serious!*" the guy had complained.

Liam listened, half-drowsy, practically back in dreamland as his dad's feet clomped toward his door. Pop's followed, lighter, unshod, creaking the old floorboards.

But the footsteps didn't march past his door. They stopped there. The next thing Liam knew, Dad threw open the door to his room and thrust out his hand, forcing an unwelcome glow into the room that made Liam groan and shield his eyes.

"What the hell, Liam?" Dad yelled. "What the actual hell?"

"Good... morning?" Liam asked, still hiding his eyes behind one hand.

It was Dad's cell phone, he realized. Who kept the brightness cranked up like that at night? Old people, he supposed.

"Sweetheart..." There was Pop, coming up behind Dad, belting his bathrobe, his hair tousled and twisted up like licorice sticks. "Calm down. Let him wake up."

"He's up," Dad snarled. "He's wide awake, aren't you, Liam? What the hell are you and Elayah up to?"

After a moment of blinking confusion, he lowered his hand, his eyes adjusted. "El? She's not here." *More's the pity.*

"Don't screw with me, Liam." Dad's voice was tight, hoarse. Behind him, Pop put a hand on his shoulder, trying to calm him down.

Liam sat up and rubbed his eyes. "Dad, seriously, I don't know what you're talking about."

Wordless and fuming, Dad handed over the phone. Liam stifled a yawn—he could just picture Dad: *Am I* boring you, *Liam?*—and scanned it quickly. The *Loco*'s home page.

## Police Investigating Evidence Unearthed from Time Capsule!

Uh-oh.

"Do you have any idea what kind of trouble this is going to—"

"Dad, I didn't know. I swear." He felt bad throwing Elayah under the bus, but it was the truth.

Before Dad could retort, the phone vibrated in Liam's hand, popping up a notification. "It's the station," he told Dad, handing the phone back.

Dad swiped to answer and held the phone to his ear. His expression of anger melted into shock, and his rage-suffused face paled. "Are you sure?" he asked, then said, "Okay, on my way."

"What's going on?" Liam asked.

Dad hesitated on his way out the door as Pop stepped aside. "It's Elayah," he said after a moment. "It's not good."


Liam figured he would fall asleep leaning against Pop in the waiting room at the hospital, but it never happened. His nerves hummed as though he'd mainlined cold brew for a week, and his stomach clenched as though he'd eaten nothing but five-alarm chili.

Eventually Dad returned from wherever he'd gone to coordinate cop stuff and told them that El was out of surgery, awake, alert.

"And believe it or not, she asked for you," Dad told Liam, and gestured for him to follow.

They wandered through a maze of hospital corridors, each one paler and more poorly lit than the last, until they arrived outside a room where Mr. Laird stood, waiting for them.

They'd been closer, once. Once upon a time, Liam had spent after-school hours at El's house, along with Marcie and Jorja. Before the separation in middle school, when their brains dictated their schedules. They were all still friends, but there'd been a disconnect. He still saw Jorja all the time because she lived next door, but even that tight relationship had its fissures—Jorja was almost as smart as El and had no reason to keep hanging out with a dummy like Liam.

El's dad nodded to him as they approached El's room, as though it being almost sunrise and his daughter having nearly died, of *course* Liam would be here. Most natural thing in the world.

"Uh, hello, sir." Liam was surprised to find his voice coming out in a whisper.

Mr. Laird offered a tight smile. His hands, Liam noticed, were shaking.

Dad noticed, too. He touched Mr. Laird's arm lightly, a gesture Liam had never witnessed before with a member of the public. Then again, they'd been friends in high school.

"It's all right, Marcus. We're on it."

"No offense, but this isn't exactly what you guys do all the time," Mr. Laird said.

Dad took it in stride. "True. But there's something or other about detective work in one of the manuals back at the station. We'll figure it out."

At that, Mr. Laird cracked a smile. Dad too. They clapped each other on the shoulder in the manner of men who've shared a past.

"Liam," Mr. Laird said. "She'll be glad to see you."

"The only reason I'm letting you in here," Dad said, his tone the same as when he used to tell Liam to finish his homework, "is because she's asking for you. You're going to keep it short, and don't imagine for a minute that you two will be alone together."

Liam had never in his life spent *less* than a minute imagining himself and El together, but he nodded anyway.

Dad opened the door and stood there for a moment, blocking Liam's view. "Dinah, you okay?" he asked.

Liam heard El's mom say something he couldn't quite make out, and then Dad stood aside to let Liam in as Mrs. Laird squeezed past. She favored Liam with a struggle of a smile on her way.

Inside, El sat up in a hospital bed. Her hands clutched each other in her lap, her head inclined down. She didn't move her head at all when Liam entered, but her eyes fluttered up in his direction. A bandage swaddled her throat, stark and white against her skin. Its existence enraged him in a way he hadn't felt since second grade, when Billy Huntsman had pushed him on the playground and taunted him for not having a mother.

"That bandage color's all wrong for you," he said, not quite sure where the words were coming from. "And cotton? Really? I'm thinking a tulle, maybe something in mauve, and my dads are both gay, so I know what I'm talking about."

From behind him, something strangled that was either a snort or a chortle from Dad.

"And if you were trying to get attention, El, there are so many better ways. Haven't you ever heard of using drugs? Suicide attempts? Getting pregnant? Come *on*. I know you're an overachiever, but this is a little extreme, even for you."

The right corner of her mouth twitched ever so slightly. Not a smile. Just the promise of one to come.

Job done.

He approached her and opened his mouth to continue, but she spoke first.

"Can I ask you a favor? For real?" Her voice was hoarse, strained, earned.

"Sure."

"Can you just sit here and hold my hand and maybe not talk? Just for a little while?"

Liam bit the inside of his cheek. Everything in his body—every organ, every blood vessel, every *atom*—cried out to quip something like, *I can—the question is, will I?*

Instead, he sat down next to her and a series of neurons lit up with *I am sitting on a bed! With her!* and he stomped all over them like a man in flammable pajamas stamping out a speckling of red embers strewn by the wind. He took her hand, which was cool and dry.

Dad crossed his arms over his chest and leaned against the doorjamb, watching them without really watching them. El seemed not to realize he was even there. Her grip tightened on Liam's hand. With every bit of strength in his body, he prevented himself from making a joke about her crushing his hand.

After a moment, her breath hitched in her chest. She wasn't crying. She was very specifically, very intentionally *not* crying.

Her request had been very clear, so clear that even a dummy like him could understand and heed: Sit. Hold hand. Keep big fat yap shut.

But that catch in her chest, her hand shaking so slightly.

He disobeyed. He dropped her hand and put his arm around her shoulders. She stiffened, then leaned into him, eyes tightly shut, extruding two fat, glistening tears.

"You're gonna be okay," he whispered, feeling the weight and heat of her against him.

She nodded into him. When Liam looked up, Dad was staring at them, his expression a mingled chaos of anxiety and pride.

# ELAYAH

Why had she asked for Liam? Because she knew his father was on the way? Because she'd heard her dad say the sheriff's name and the first thing she'd thought of—as she emerged from the sleep-haze of anesthesia—was the boy she ached for? Because the thought of him here, when she was at her most vulnerable, was a more potent balm than the numbing gel the doctors had slathered on her throat?

Maybe some of those. Maybe all of them.

No one could figure out how to make the bed change position. With a gentleness she had not known he possessed, Liam helped her sit up and propped pillows behind her back. The sheriff stood nearby while her parents sat in the room's two chairs, clutching each other's hands.

Liam held her hand, occasionally tightening his grip for no reason at all.

Liam's dad asked her if she felt like talking, and when she nodded, he told her was going to record their conversation and pressed a button on his phone's screen.

"Let's start at the beginning, okay, Elayah?" The sheriff's eyes, deep set and blue, ringed by crinkles she imagined had to be well earned, did not leave her as he spoke. And as she spoke, they never moved away.

She told them everything she could remember: She'd texted Rachel at the *Loco* with the new quote. She'd watched for the update, then read the new article. She'd been surprised, but not overly so, that her name was used.

"Of course she used—"

"Marcus." Mom cut Dad off before he could go any further. Dad settled into a grumbling quiet.

Then she'd gone to bed, awakened sometime later when she felt something—

—someone—

Someone in her bed.

Tears again. She didn't want them. Didn't know where they were coming from. Wiping at them with the heel of her hand, she sniffed back tears and then a fresh jolt of pain from her throat hit her and the tears doubled.

With his free hand, Liam snatched a tissue from the box on the nightstand and held it out to her. She wasn't sure yet what blowing her nose might do to her throat, which was, basically, held together with string and tape at this point, but she wiped her eyes and squeezed his hand in silent gratitude.

"You woke up...." Liam's dad prodded.

She told them how she'd felt the presence of a body behind her, and how—before she could move or react—the hand had come around her body, pressing the blade to her throat. *Don't scream.*

He'd kept his hand over her mouth. His breath in her ear, his voice lower than a whisper. His lips brushed her earlobe when he spoke again.

*Where is it? I know you. . . . I saw it. Where did you put it?* A hush of desperation in his tone. A man seeking water in the desert. A man frantic for succor on a dead, lonely street at midnight.

And then, just before he removed his hand, he reminded her not to scream.

"What did you do next?" the sheriff asked.

"I screamed," she said very matter-of-factly.

The sheriff grinned almost imperceptibly. Liam whispered, "Hells yeah," under his breath.

"I don't think he meant to cut me," she added. "I think he was startled when I screamed and he jerked away and the knife just…" She put a hand to her throat. Through the gauze, her numbed throat throbbed gently. The sensation of her skin parting, of the sudden spill of blood all over the front of her pajama top, all over her bed…in that instant, she'd flashed to her own death, imagining her windpipe savaged, her carotid severed. For seconds that lasted years, she'd lain on the bed, frozen in terror as the side of her neck spurted blood in syncopation to her horrified heartbeat.

"Are you sure it was an accident?" the sheriff asked.

Elayah shrugged. "He said something. . . . His voice when he said it—he sounded scared. Like he couldn't believe he'd cut me."

"What did he say?"

"It was swearing." Her eyes flicked to the phone and the voice-recording app displayed on the screen.

The sheriff nodded. "You don't have to repeat it if you don't want to. Would you recognize his voice if you heard it again?"

"I think."

"What happened next?"

Next? It had all happened simultaneously. That was how it had felt at the time, at least. Her scream. His movement. The abrupt, hot line of pain. A cry from down the hall, her dad, woken from sleep. The bed shaking, the mattress rising as the alien body clambered out…

All of it happening in the same, single compressed instant, a nugget of hypercondensed time.

"So he goes out the window," the sheriff said. "Had the window been open when you went to sleep?"

"It was a cool night," Dad said a tad defensively. "There was no reason to have the air on."

"Thanks, Marcus." Again, Liam's dad never stopped watching Elayah, even as he spoke to Dad. "I want to be sure of something: You're positive it was a man?"

She nodded. No mistaking the roughness of his hands. The timbre of his voice, even at a whisper.

"Elayah, is there anything else you can remember? Was there a smell? Cologne? Something like that? I know you only saw his hand, but maybe he had a tattoo?"

She shook her head. "It was too dark. I didn't smell anything except..." She hesitated. Liam offered a supportive squeeze, and her parents gave her that *go ahead* look.

"He was white. He, you know, white people smell a certain way."

"Elayah..." Mom groaned.

"I'm sorry! It's true!" It hurt her throat to speak at anything approaching normal volume, but she couldn't help herself.

Next to her, she imagined Liam lifting his arm to sniff his pits. Somehow, he wasn't doing that. Maybe this was all a dream.

If the sheriff was offended, he didn't show it. "Anything else make you think he was white? Could you tell from his hand?"

"I didn't see his hand that well. It was too close to focus on. But his smell. And his voice..."

She closed her eyes. The very last thing she wanted was to relive those stark moments, those clock ticks of trepidation, but there was something else, she thought. There was something she was missing. Something she was forget—

"Whiskers." It popped out, much to her own surprise. Her parents and Liam blinked at her as though she'd grown a unicorn horn.

But Liam's dad just clucked his tongue thoughtfully. "He had a beard."

"I felt it on my ear."

The sheriff took a moment, glancing around the room. She knew he could stay here for hours, interrogating her, but her parents were on edge. It had been hours since her emergency surgery, and the sun was already up.

*I can do this all day*, she thought, channeling her inner Captain America. But she knew, at the same time, that she couldn't. She was fading fast.

"This is all good stuff, Elayah," said Liam's dad, tapping off the recording app. "Thank you. If you remember anything at all, no matter how small or insignificant it seems, tell your parents or call and tell me, okay?"

She nodded gravely, but she knew there would be nothing else. It had happened so fast. It had been over almost in the same instant it had begun.

"Marcus, Dinah." He turned his attention to her parents now, telling them to leave her room as it was, not to go in there. A forensics unit would come later to fingerprint and take samples for analysis.

"Can you have someone watch the house?" Mom asked. "In case he comes back?"

Liam's dad hesitated in his answer, then pinched the bridge of his nose as he spoke. "Sure, sure. I can have a deputy keep a lookout."

As they ironed out the details, Elayah's energy dropped further, sending her into that eyelid-drooping stasis that precedes sleep. She hadn't fallen asleep while sitting up in a very long time, but it was going to happen right now, she thought. Sitting next to Liam. Holding his hand. She just wanted to curl into him, her head on his chest, and dream of absolutely nothing.

She got part of her wish, at least.

# LIAM

Pop had already gone home by the time Dad was finished interrogating El, who fell asleep midsentence much to everyone's amusement. Dad made some calls to arrange for protection for the Lairds, and Liam thought they would be headed home, but at the last minute, Mr. Laird called out Dad's name. They huddled in a corner of the hospital corridor for a moment, Mr.

Laird's expression urgent and somehow reluctant at the same time. Dad shook his head a few times, brushing him off as politely as he could. Their brief conversation ended with a handshake and then an awkward one-armed hug that—even at a distance—felt more obligatory than earned.

"What was all that about at the end?" Liam asked as they got into the car. The sun was just edging its way into the sky off to the east. Liam should have been exhausted, but his body hummed with energy.

"He made a lot of homophobic jokes back in the day. When we were kids. I guess it's been eating at him, and he just figured now was the time to apologize."

Liam considered. "He didn't know you were gay. They weren't aimed at you."

"No. But he feels bad. Which is his prerogative."

"And what did you tell him?"

"I reminded him that I used to tell the same damn jokes."

# 1986: JAY

School meant little to Jay, which he thought both fair and somewhat retaliatory, since school didn't seem to think much of him, cramming him into useless classes like phys ed and language arts, enslaving him to someone else's schedule. He supposed some would have called his dislike of school ironic, given his father's position on the board of education. But he'd known since kindergarten that he was smart—one elementary school teacher had, within earshot, called him "the smartest kid I've ever had in my classroom"—and so he'd come to understand that his boredom in and with school was not his fault. It was the fault of the system, which sought viciously and dispassionately to cram the square peg of him into the round hole of public education.

Brad Gimble sat a few desks over, which always managed to infuriate Jay. This was supposedly an advanced class—jock morons like Gimbo shouldn't have been allowed in. But the school system didn't have the money to break the advanced class off, so they were stuck with encroaching average idiots.

Gimbo, no matter his prowess on the football field, had peaked in third grade, as far as Jay was concerned. And even that had been mere luck.

Back then, they had gone on a class field trip to the Canterstown Public Library, a small brick edifice on the north side of town. From there, the Wantzler factory was just a triple jut of smokestacks rising from beyond a hill, identical triplet plumes of deep gray smoke rising and dissipating like old memories.

To the side of the library was a stale and crumbling cemetery surrounded by a precarious, half-height stone wall. Jay had been coming to the library since before he could read, and some part of him had assumed that all libraries had cemeteries attached to them. It made an eerie, juvenile sort of sense: Libraries stored old books; cemeteries stored old bodies.

In third grade, Canterstown began indoctrinating its young into the history and mythology of the town. Jay had had the story of town founders Ezekiel Canter and Jakob Wantzler already drummed into his head by that point, but one thing he hadn't anticipated was exactly how far the school system was willing to go to make an impression on the impressionable.

After some noodling about in the library, the class reconvened just outside the gate to the cemetery. There, Miss Dell explained the final part of their trip: They would be let loose in the cemetery and tasked with finding the grave of Ezekiel Canter himself.

Even at that young age, Jay was competitive. Deep down, he understood that the stakes in this particular race were nonexistent. Still, he wanted to be the one to find it. Because someone had to be first, and why shouldn't that be Jay?

He started with the big monuments, zeroing in on the biggest. To his dismay, that was what everyone else had determined, too. He was one of a crowd clustered around a large plinth topped with a weeping angel, wings spread, eyes downcast. It was a little too much, and it was also the grave of REV. JEDEDIAH MOORE. Oh, and—on a smaller side plaque—HIS WIFE.

He checked the next-biggest monument, then the next and the next. Names and dates swam at him. He started to wonder: Who made sure the dates were right? It had to be the family members left behind, didn't it? Sure, that made sense. And parents usually died first, so that meant the children would have to know the dates.

It occurred to him, in that instant, that he didn't know in what years his parents had been born.

He stood absolutely still in the middle of the graveyard, his eyes staring yet unfocused. Kids milled around him, looking for Ezekiel's grave, and Jay tried to remember exactly how old his mother was and what that worked out to...1948? 1947? He would have to know. It was his job. He would have to memorize it or write it down or—

Miss Dell shouted out, "We have a winner!"

And there stood Gimbo, smirking from a patch of browning grass. When the rest of the class rushed over, they beheld not a towering monument... or even a midsize statue... or even a regular gravestone. At the edge of the smudge of grass, nearly concealed from view by weeds, lay a small stone no bigger than a picture book. The chiseled letters—worn and barely legible—spelled out EZEKIEL CANTER and then GONE TO GOD and the dates of his birth and death.

"It's so little!" someone shouted.

Miss Dell nodded, putting a hand on Gimbo's shoulder. "You all thought it must be the biggest one here, didn't you? But the obvious answer isn't always the right one. Don't make assumptions. Just because the town is named for him doesn't mean he had the biggest or the best grave site."

It felt like a trick. Like a setup. And Miss Dell's smirky little smile, the way she rested her hand on Gimbo's shoulder, possessively, as though to say, "Brad only figured it out because *I'm* his teacher and *I* taught him," just made it worse.

In the sudden present, Dean's voice dragged him from his reverie. He liked Dean, but Dean was a little too goody-goody. A little too eager to answer. *Better him than me, though*, he thought as Dean expounded on the New Deal.

Jay didn't care. His A in this class was already guaranteed.

But he thought about the idea Dean had approached him with, the one inspired by an earlier history class. And when they stood up into the anarchy of class change at the bell, Jay sidled up to Dean and said, "You know that time capsule idea? Let's do it."

# 10

# THE PRESENT: LIAM

He'd not slept since being awoken at two, and Pop had suggested taking a mental health day, but Liam couldn't imagine lingering around the house with nothing to distract him from thinking about Elayah's night. So, fueled by an obscene quantity of Pop's best cold brew with a triple shot of simple syrup, Liam grabbed his backpack from the back seat, beeped his car locks, and headed for the school's side door, the closest one to the student lot.

Much to his surprise, a reporter buttonholed him before he made it. Liam sized him up instantly with the practiced eye of a kid whose cop dad took him to work way too often. The reporter was in his early thirties, stubbly beard, too much gut, not enough pecs. White ball cap with #1A stenciled on it in black. He wielded an iPhone like he thought it was Captain America's shield.

"Hi there!" the guy said. "Hey, do you know Elayah Laird?"

*She's carrying my baby*, Liam didn't say.

*She's actually my twin sister*, he also didn't say.

*Like, biblically?* he further didn't say.

Those were just three of the dozen retorts that blazed paths from his brain to the tip of his tongue before he managed to swallow them back down. They were twelve of the hardest things he'd ever done in his life.

"*No hablo inglés*," he said instead, shrugging. It was *October*. There were statewide elections in a couple of weeks—shouldn't *that* have been the big story?

"*¿Conoces* Elayah Laird?" the reporter replied in immediate and excellent Spanish.

Liam stared. "*No hablo español,*" he blurted in a panic, and ran for the door. The reporter gave chase, then stopped at the walkway as he realized Liam would make it inside before he could catch up.

"Curses, foiled again!" Liam shouted over his shoulder, and then disappeared into the school.

For third period, Liam had study hall, which was hilarious because he never ever studied. But it was an opportunity to head to the media center. Where it had all started.

El had been working on a project for the yearbook, a retrospective page. It was supposed to be a simple one-pager, a look back at the first year or two of the yearbook. One of those "Look how far we've come!" sort of things that got geeks so excited.

In typical El fashion, she'd gone overboard. She'd spent hours in the media center, paging through the old yearbooks, noting local dynasties, print upgrades, the procession of time. What began as a page in the yearbook morphed into an online multimedia project for the school website. Because of course it did.

And then she stumbled upon the list of the time capsule's contents. And then she'd talked to her dad. And then Liam had talked to *his* dad, who'd laughed with foggy reminiscence and said, "My God, that thing is buried and gone, Liam!"

"What if we could find it and dig it up?" he remembered her saying to all of them, clustered around a pizza in her living room. Marcie had sort of shrugged and Jorja had nodded thoughtfully, and the idea would have died right there. *Should* have died right there because Liam thought it was sort of pointless, but also it was El's idea, and *also* also, his dad thought it was useless, so of course Liam was now all for it. And he bubbled up with enthusiasm, which got Jorja nodding thoughtfully again, but this time with more energy, and Marcie clucked her tongue like she did when she had an idea....

And then someone slit El's throat in her own bed in the dead of night. So, yeah, good job there, Liam.

The media center was quiet, empty except for Mr. Hindon behind the circulation desk, tapping at his keyboard. He looked up when Liam entered, looked back down at the keyboard, then startled and did a double take.

"Liam! Have you seen Elayah? How is she?"

Mr. Hindon was ticcing like crazy, his eyes aflutter, his nose working like a bunny on crack. When he got excited or stressed—every kid in school knew this—his Tourette symptoms really kicked into high gear. "She brought me that inventory, and I told her about your dad and her dad and the others...." He grimaced. "I feel like it's my fault."

*Makes two of us.* "Pretty sure it's the guy with the knife's fault," Liam said with an airy insouciance he did not truly feel. "You got a minute?"

Mr. Hindon's eyes narrowed. "I have several. Do *you?*"

Liam flashed his hall pass. "Study hall. Do you remember anything else about the time capsule? Like, was there anyone else involved?"

Dad had said it was just the five of them, but thirty-five years was a long time. There could have been another participant.

He remembered the expression on Marcie's face when he'd made his ill-considered joke (most of them were ill-considered, honestly) about one of their parents having wielded the knife. She'd been shocked, dismayed, disbelieving all at once. He didn't want it to be true. His dad, both of Marcie's parents, Jorja's dad, El's dad...and El's missing uncle. Six of them had conceived of the time capsule, put things inside. Five buried it. As far as he knew, no one else had been involved.

But anything was possible, right?

*Please*, he thought, *let someone else be involved.*

With a sigh, Mr. Hindon came around the desk and dropped into a chair. He motioned for Liam to sit, too, so Liam perched one hip on a table.

"I wasn't directly involved, you understand? They came to me with some questions about archiving." Mr. Hindon shook his head, a small smile on his lips. "I can't remember which of them, whether it was your dad or one of the others. They wanted to bury a time capsule, and they came to me and asked about how to do it."

"And?" Liam licked his lips. Someone had to know *something*.

A shrug. "I helped them figure out where to buy one. I think…" He leaned back, staring at the ceiling for a moment. "It was a long time ago… but back then, I probably put in for an interlibrary loan. Got a catalog with time capsules in it for them. I think I tried to explain some best practices for preservation and selection…."

"But it was a long time ago," Liam supplied as Mr. Hindon drifted off.

"It was. I'm sorry I don't remember more."

Liam chewed on that for a moment.

"Is there anyone you can think of who might know more?" Liam asked.

"Most of the faculty back then were older. They're either retired or no longer with us." He tapped a pin he wore on his chest: CHISHOLM FOR STATE SENATE. The county superintendent of schools was running for the General Assembly. "*He* taught here back then, but I doubt we could get in touch with him now."

"Are you allowed to wear that to school?" Liam asked.

"Oh. I didn't even think about it." He removed the pin and tucked it into his pocket. "I was canvassing before work. Thanks for reminding me. Anyway, I could put together a list of the others who are still around, but…"

"But what?" Liam asked into the hesitation.

"But, well, Liam…you should really be talking to your parents. Yours. Marcie's. Jorja's. Elayah's. They were the ones who did it, after all."

# ELAYAH

Mom sat in what appeared to be the more comfortable of the hospital room's two chairs, tapping away at her phone. Dad was nowhere to be seen. Elayah came awake slowly and reached for the cup of water by her bed.

"Your father had to go into work. I took the day off."

Elayah nodded as though she understood. Took a sip. She knew her mom really couldn't afford a day off.

While she slept, the analgesic gel had worn off. The outside of her throat itched and burned. It felt threadbare, as though something as simple as a hard swallow would rip it right open.

"I'm okay." Her voice surprised her—it was low and husky, almost sexy. "You can go to work."

Mom laughed hollowly. "Not a chance, baby girl. Some fool comes into my home and threatens my daughter. You think I'm letting you out of my sight? Besides, the doctors say at least a day, maybe more, depending."

Elayah fumbled for her phone. Someone had brought it for her and plugged it in on the nightstand. Her notifications were blowing up, a steady stream of round rects popping up like soap bubbles on the lock screen.

Twitter.

Insta.

And email notifications from the *Loco*. She'd signed up for them the previous night, thinking there might be something interesting that would pop overnight. Not knowing that she'd conjured herself into a horror movie, not a documentary.

Fiddling with the phone, she tried to scroll Insta, but her mentions were clogged. She caught a word here and there—*knife, wow, murder, parents*—just enough to know that everyone who knew her wanted to talk about nothing more than what had been reported in the paper and what had happened afterward.

Yesterday, all she'd wanted to do was talk to people about the knife. Now she didn't even want to think about it.

Mom sat stirring a paper cup of coffee, staring out the window. She had a magnificent view of the parking lot and a big air conditioner condenser on the nearby roof.

"Did you put anything in the time capsule, Mom?" Elayah had been so focused on the knife and then on getting the picture to her dad that she'd never considered what Mom might have preserved.

With a wistful little smile, Mom shook her head. "Honey, I don't expect you to understand, but...your dad and I weren't *that* close back then."

"You were his girlfriend! You went to homecoming with him."

"I know. But we weren't in love, baby. Not yet. That happened later, after..." She drifted off into that territory of fog and mist that occluded her uncle Antoine and his life in Mexico. "We liked each other. We dated. I know people don't really date anymore. You just…" She mimed swiping right on an invisible phone, and Elayah suppressed a giggle at the thought of her mom on Tinder.

"We went out on Saturdays. We went to dances together. But your dad was always running. Always training. He was so dedicated and devoted. And he had his friends."

"Like Liam's dad," Elayah supplied.

"All those white boys." Mom shook her head, tsking. "Can't really blame him. There weren't a lot of Black kids in this town back then. You had to get along with the white kids, especially if you wanted to compete."

Elayah pondered this. She attended the same high school her mom had, but the place was easily 40 percent students of color, with more than half of those being Black. Hearing about the old days was like visiting Mars.

"And then Antoine disappeared," Mom went on. "It was the week after homecoming. Right around the time they buried that thing. At first, everyone thought he'd just…" She gestured wordlessly and helplessly, sketching in the air. "I don't know. We thought he was in a snit about something. We figured he was off sulking."

"Really?" Elayah tried to imagine herself disappearing for more than an hour and her family and friends just shrugging their shoulders and not worrying about it. Someone would fire up their GPS locator and ping her phone in minutes.

"'He, uh, probably hopped a bus to New York to see m'cousin,'" Mom grunted. Her impersonation of Dad was dead perfect—she nailed the bass tone of his voice, the almost-Southern inflections. Elayah laughed with delight. Who knew that parents could keep on surprising you?

"That's what everyone thought for the first day or two. But he never showed up in New York." Mom leaned back in the chair, tucked her legs under herself, still staring out the window. She kept stirring the coffee, never raising it to her lips. "And then a couple of days turned into a week. And everyone got scared. And it was a Black boy gone missing in a town that didn't care about Black boys. A *country*," she corrected herself. "We posted signs. We called radio stations, and we tried to get the TV people to come out. And then one day, the first postcard arrived."

"From Mexico."

"Yeah." Mom looked down into her coffee, realizing it had gone cold in her hands. With a moue of disgust, she set it aside. "Anyway, that's how your dad and I got close. Love close. Looking for Antoine."

She dabbed gently at the corner of one eye with the pad of her finger.

"I'm sorry, Mom."

Mom shook her head. "It's all in the past, baby. Nothing to be done for it. Why don't you get some more sleep?"

She didn't really want to, but the next thing she knew, she was asleep again.

# THE PRESENT: ELAYAH

Mom had—at last—gone home, lured there by the promise of a hot shower and clean clothes. She vowed to return as quickly as possible. In the meantime, a deputy was stationed outside the hospital room. Elayah was pretty sure this was overkill, but she felt better anyway. She had never really trusted the police, but the sheriff was different; he was Liam's dad.

Then she heard voices outside her door. A moment later, the door opened and Liam, Jorja, and Marcie spilled in, bearing wonderfully greasy bags from Five Guys.

"You better not have brought the little," she warned them. "I want the double or GTFO."

Liam arched an eyebrow and presented a bag to her with an air of stage magician theatricality. "Double *bacon* cheeseburger," he informed her with deadly seriousness. "*Large* fries. And, yes, we brought malt vinegar."

Elayah had thought her ardor for Liam had grown about as much as possible, but his gift of salt-and-fat-laden goodness overwhelmed what now seemed a small, petty love.

"How are you holding up?" Marcie asked. She perched on the edge of the bed, primed to take Elayah's hand or give her a shoulder to cry on at the slightest provocation.

"She's good," Liam spoke up from the foot of the bed. He'd brought a rubber ball and started bouncing it against the linoleum tiles, the sound echoing and boisterous in the enclosed space. "She looks good. I mean, fine. She looks fine. Are you fine, El?"

"I'm okay," Elayah said. She couldn't tell if it was the truth or not, but it seemed to be the thing to say in the moment. "I'm glad you're here."

And she was. It was a fluke of nature that led to their foursome, the confluence and coincidence of their parents—friends in high school—all having children at around the same time. Or maybe it wasn't a fluke at all. Maybe nature itself bent and perturbed in the face of friendship, warped with its own special gravity.

Nothing but their parents' connections would have brought these four together, certainly not for any length of time. Jorja was destined to be the next Margaret Atwood or Rebecca Traister, depending on which way the dice landed. Liam would end up on his first magazine cover soon enough… and then would never be off them for the rest of his life. Marcie's ambition was to be the second or third female president of the United States—she was convinced, perhaps correctly, all things considered, that someone else would beat her to first before she was eligible to run.

Which left Elayah…

Elayah, who had—in the words of one early report card—"almost limitless potential." Who was "the smartest kid I've ever had in my class." (Ms. Bachman, eighth-grade social studies.) Who "thinks around corners," according to a guidance counselor. Who "could be anything she wants to be," said her violin teacher. She could code. She could paint, a little. She could do obscenely complicated math in her head.

It was magnificent, and it also sucked donkey balls. (Liam's favorite expression of discontent.)

There had been studies years ago that showed that when you presented consumers with multifarious choices—like, say, fifteen different types and brands of jelly—they had a harder time deciding, took longer to make up their minds, and were less satisfied with their ultimate selection than those who'd chosen from a narrower band of options.

Elayah feared buying the wrong jelly. Only the jelly was her life.

When she had "almost limitless potential" and "could be anything she wants to be," the panoply of options whelmed her. And now it was senior year and decisions loomed in the middle distance, and Elayah feared that she would put herself on the wrong path, choosing a set of initial conditions that would result in a suboptimal outcome.

Sometimes, it really sucked to understand chaos theory.

"What have you been up to?" Marcie asked.

"Other than, y'know, getting your neck to stop gaping wide open." Liam had figured out how to "walk" the ball back and forth over the backs of his fingers.

"Liam!" Marcie snapped.

"Don't be a dick," Jorja admonished, and punched him in the shoulder.

"Wait, I can't say *pussy*, but you're allowed to say *dick*?"

"You *can't* say *pussy*, but you just did!" Jorja threw her hands up in the air. "Have I taught you *nothing* in all these years?"

She snatched the ball away from Liam as though taking a toy away from a toddler midtantrum. "And balls are for good boys who don't say stupid things about gaping neck wounds."

"Dick, balls…" Liam crossed his arms over his chest. "I'm feeling harassed."

"Congratulations," Jorja said dryly. "Today you have become a woman."

Elayah couldn't help laughing at Liam's hangdog expression.

"Do the police know anything yet?" Marcie asked. She clearly yearned to lean forward and hold Elayah's hand, so Elayah moved a bit to make it easier for her. She did it more for Marcie than for herself but had to admit it felt good.

Would have felt better if it was Liam, though.

Her eyes flicked to him now, waiting. Marcie had set him up perfectly, and she waited for the list of things he would conjure that the police knew.

But instead of rising to the challenge of Marcie's question, he simply turned both palms up to show he was empty-handed. "It's not like TV. It takes time."

Marcie nodded, still clasping Elayah's hand. "But what does your dad *think*?" she asked Liam.

Liam pursed his lips, deep in thought for a moment. "Not sure. We haven't had our usual homicide-consultation meeting."

"Well, now you're never getting this back," Jorja said, and stuck the ball into the waistband of her jeans, where it jutted out like a horror-movie tumor.

"You two." Marcie had the maternal tone down pat. It didn't work on Liam, though—he'd never had a mom to smack him down. "This isn't why we're here."

Liam flashed his supermodel grin and laughed shortly. "My dad hasn't told me anything. Can I please have my ball back now?"

Jorja shrugged indifferently. "Was that so difficult?" Then, almost as a peace offering, she handed his ball back to him.

The four of them dove into their food with a vengeance. For Elayah, it was the first real food she'd eaten since the dinner hours before her throat was cut, and with her friends making snarfing, growling eating noises around her to match her own, she could almost pretend the late-night attack had never happened.

Almost. Because every time she swallowed, she was too aware of the tug at her stitches, the pain as her throat worked its peristaltic magic to get the delicious burger and fries down.

"What's new in school?" she asked as brightly as she knew how.

Jorja, sitting in the chair Mom had vacated, made a show of exaggerated chewing. The bright overhead lights reflected off her glasses, hiding her eyes, rendering her expression inscrutable. Jorja was tough to read under the best circumstances; this didn't apply.

Marcie sat on the bed, closest to Elayah. She grinned weakly, swallowed hard. Said nothing.

Liam, having scoffed down his food first and fastest, leaned against the wall, arms crossed over his chest. He shrugged. "The usual. Stocks up; bonds down. Reporters there, believe it or not. I told them you were squirreled away in a secret government training facility, learning jujitsu and how to shoot guns in order to become a supervigilante, dedicated to eradicating crime everywhere. But never, tragically, able to get the one criminal who hurt you. Pretty good superhero origin, right?"

"It'll do," Elayah said. "Are there really reporters?"

"Circling the school like sharks after someone busted open a blood piñata," Liam recounted.

"A *blood* piñata?" Marcie exclaimed. "Liam!"

"Racist *and* stupid," Jorja reproved him.

Liam shrugged. "I didn't say *whose* blood."

No one had a rejoinder to that.

"Are we gonna talk about it?" Marcie asked eventually.

Liam sighed heavily. "I guess we have to, huh? I say Rams/Pats in the Super Bowl, but the season is still young and—"

"Not now," Elayah said. "Please."

Because it was time, she realized. Time to be serious. The moment had been stalking her for a while now, creeping along, keeping to the shadows. Until this instant, when it pounced. She was ready.

Liam swallowed audibly. "I don't want to."

"El's ready," Marcie insisted.

"What if I'm not?" Liam fired back.

Jorja shot her arm out, arcing her wadded-up burger wrapper into the air. It sank into the trash can without so much as brushing against the rim.

"It has to be done," she told Liam. "We don't have the option of not talking about it."

Liam banged the edge of his fist against the wall. "Would you change your mind if you knew your dad was going to jail?" he said, his voice smoldering and ready to ignite. "Because that's where this is all headed. One of our parents in jail."

He told them about his conversation with Mr. Hindon. "'They were the ones who did it, after all.' That's what he said. He meant buried the time capsule, but it's more than that."

"Yeah, you said before—"

"I was kinda joking," he told Marcie. "But, well, yeah. I mean, look—there's the knife, right? And I'm pretty sure that was blood. So we're saying someone was killed. And one of our parents did it, and then came after El. The only thing we know for sure is that it wasn't my dad. I heard him getting up in his room when it all went down."

"My dad was at home, too." Jorja hmmphed.

"Were you awake at two AM?" Liam replied. "You saw or heard him in the house?"

Jorja went silent. Elayah wondered how it felt for the child of a defense attorney to be so thoroughly lawyered.

Marcie shrugged. "My dad doesn't live around here. I don't know where the heck he was last night. Probably shacking up with his latest girlfriend. And who cares about my mom—it was a man, right, El?"

Elayah nodded. The peanut-oil-coated ball of fried potato in her gut felt like a baby ready to start kicking. She laced her fingers over her belly the way she'd seen pregnant women do and leaned back, parsing her words carefully before she spoke.

"The thing is," she said at last, "I don't trust any of them. Not even your dad, Liam. Not entirely."

"Come on!" Liam protested. "He *couldn't*—"

"It's not that. But he could be covering something for someone. Right?"

"Nope." Liam shook his head fiercely. "Not my dad. He takes this stuff seriously."

Elayah slumped back against her pillows. The pleasant fullness from the burger and fries had morphed into a thick, clunky lumpiness in her gut. She was suddenly enormously tired, but her mind refused to let her give in. There was a mystery to solve, and her own life could depend on it.

The door opened and Mom stepped in. Her nostrils flared for a moment, scenting the burgers and fries, and her worried expression relaxed into something that was almost normal. Almost pre-attack.

"It's great to see you guys," she said, "but Elayah needs her rest, so I'm going to ask you all to go now."

# LIAM

Jorja showed up at Liam's house before school the next day. Liam was slipping on his shirt when Pop opened the door and ushered her in.

"Whassup?"

Jorja fidgeted, stalling until Pop disappeared into the kitchen, where he began yelling at Dad about something involving eggs. A joke involving two gay men with a child but no woman occurred to Liam, and he filed it away for the next time an egg fight broke out.

"I talked to Marse last night," Jorja said. "She was on with El all night. I know she seemed okay yesterday when we were there, but according to Marcie…she's not doing well."

Liam cracked his neck to one side then the other. "Okay. Talk."

"It's one thing during the day. When people are around. But she didn't sleep well last night," Jorja said with the reluctant air of someone breaking the Girl Code. "Even in the hospital. She was texting all night. Marcie and I got to talking, and we think…we think she needs a distraction. She needs to *do* something."

Unsure of his line in this impromptu one-act play, Liam said nothing and simply crossed his arms over his chest to wait her out.

"I think we should look into the time capsule stuff. Try to figure out what happened back in 1986."

Liam froze in place and stared at her.

"Liam. Say something."

"Sure. How about…have you lost your mind?" He hissed this last, coming over to her and grabbing her by the arm. "Look, I don't try to cook Pop's steak tartare, and I don't investigate crimes."

"I'm not saying we're going to solve a crime or anything. I'm just saying we take the stuff from the time capsule and try to match it up to our parents and whoever. See what we can find out about what happened back then. Your dad will figure out the deal with the knife. We'll just…" She shrugged. "We'll just nibble around the edges. El comes home tomorrow, and being home will only make it worse for her. This'll give her something to think about. A distraction."

Liam shook his head and stepped away from her. He'd been through a lot with Jorja, but this was too much.

"Come on, Li. For El."

He was 100 percent dead set against it until she said that.


*They were the ones who did it, after all.*

Mr. Hindon's words scrabbled like desperate mice in the back of Liam's head all through school that day, colliding with Jorja's crazy idea, bouncing off poor El's savaged throat. He couldn't focus in any of his classes, which—truthfully—wasn't much different from a typical day for him. But today's distractions seemed more pernicious, more demanding. He went through English and drama and couldn't recall a single damn thing he'd allegedly learned in either of them.

At lunch, he plopped down with Marcie and Jorja.

"Guys," Liam said.

*They were the ones who did it, after all.*

*Did it.*

*It.*

Did what? What, exactly, had their parents done?

"Guys," he said again, this time clearing his throat to get their attention. Marcie looked up from her phone, her eyes a little puffy. Had she been crying? Over what—El?

"I think El's getting cabin fever," Marcie said quickly. "She just texted me that she's actually watching live TV."

"Alert The Hague." The two of them chuckled over Jorja's comment, the only clue Liam had that it was a joke. He had no idea what The Hague was. He offered an indulgent grin, an expression that said, *Not really funny, but I'll crack a smile for you out of pity.* His default response to jokes he didn't understand.

"Did Jorja tell you our idea?" Marcie asked. "About looking into the time capsule stuff? The knife?"

Liam shook his head. "Look, I'm up for whatever will help El, but do we really want to go poking around into that stuff? We might not like what we find."

Marcie sat up straight, slamming her phone down on the table. "Why, Liam? Because you think one of our parents tried to kill El?" She pointed to herself and Jorja as she said this.

"Hey…" Jorja put a hand on her shoulder, but Marcie shook it off.

"We know that's what you think, Liam," she went on. "Because it can't be *your* dad, because you saw him at your house that night. So what you're saying is that either my—"

"You're both upset because of El," Jorja interrupted. "No point fighting between ourselves. This is when we need to come together."

"Truce." Liam held up both hands. Dad always said that 90 percent of police work was convincing people they didn't really want to commit crimes in the first place. Sometimes it paid to lay back and play it cool.

"Look," Jorja said, "we don't have to accuse anyone of anything. But if we figure out what happened *then*, maybe we'll know what happened *now*."

Jorja and Liam stared at each other across the table. Liam considered a sudden belch—he'd always been able to burp on command. It would certainly puncture the seriousness of the moment. But for the first time that he could remember, he wasn't sure he wanted to skewer gravity.

Jorja blew out a breath and looked away. Liam stiffened; he knew what this meant. Jorja always looked away when she was going to say something deep and real.

"I'm not sleeping," she said, her voice toneless. Only those who'd known her for a long time knew that the less emotion she showed, the more she felt. "I feel helpless. And scared."

"Me too." It came out before Liam could stop it. He wasn't afraid for himself, but someone had cut El. And that person was anonymous and, as his dad sometimes said, at large.

As a kid, Liam had always laughed at the phrase *at large*. He thought it meant the criminal was overweight.

Wasn't funny anymore.

Liam burst through the front door that afternoon after school, his bladder about to explode. He knew he shouldn't have ordered the trenta. What had he been thinking?

"Outta my way!" he yelled. "I'm gonna pee my pants!"

Dad was alone on the sofa. He peered over the top rim of his laptop. "Why? There's a bathroom right there."

Liam's lips twisted into a grimace, and he ripped open the bathroom door. "You think you're funny," he shouted as he dashed inside, slamming the door behind him. "But you're not!"

He relieved himself with an audible sigh, washed up, and went out into the living room. Dad glared at his laptop as though it had insulted his mother. A reality show about people working on a yacht played on TV, muted. Which actually made it more entertaining, in Liam's opinion.

"Pop left some stew in the fridge. It's amazing," Dad said without looking up. "Three minutes in the microwave, but tell him we heated it up on the stove top."

Ignoring his grumbling stomach, Liam leaned against the entryway into the living room. "Dad, how's the case going?"

Dad blinked repeatedly, as though clearing something from his field of vision. "You know I won't discuss a case with you."

"Come on. It's El."

"All the more reason. Listen to me: I promise you we're doing everything we can to find the person who attacked El. We're combing through all the evidence we pulled from her room. Fingerprints, fibers. Stuff I can't tell you about. Everything."

"The ladies think it has to be connected to that knife."

Dad sighed. "I'm sure. But, Liam, that knife...like I told you, it's probably a dead end."

"Pun intended?"

"Nope." Dad cracked a grin. "I'm not telling you what you're about to hear, okay? Lab report came in on the knife. Results were inconclusive. Probably deer blood—those knives were used a lot for dressing deer."

"What about the note? Have you talked to everyone who put stuff in the time capsule?"

Dad shook his head. "Some of them. Not as easy to get in touch as it used to be. You kids are tight, but we've all got our own lives."

Liam pondered that. It had been a long, long time since the four families had convened for a barbecue or a cookout. He hadn't really noticed how the adults had drifted over the years.

"Look, Liam, no one remembers anything. We buried that thing close to Halloween. Someone probably thought it was a funny prank. Take a deer knife with some blood on it, make it look like a confession. A couple of the guys had that kind of sense of humor. But it wasn't a big thing. People forget."

Liam didn't even ask if Dad was one of those guys. His dad hardly even laughed.

"One thing you learn as a cop," Dad went on, "is that the percentages are usually right. A woman goes missing? You check the boyfriend or the husband. Money disappears from a cash register? You look at the cashier. But the percentages aren't *always* right. And for something like this...well, it's entirely possible that someone *disturbed* saw that story online. And they constructed a whole narrative in their head about what it meant."

"Someone crazy, you mean."

With a wince, Dad shook his head. "Most people with mental health issues are victims, not perpetrators. But it's possible someone with some sort of delusion or hallucinatory disorder thought the story was about them. And took action."

"I don't know," Liam said doubtfully. "Seems a lot simpler if someone was trying to get rid of evidence." He left unsaid the *One of your friends* part.

Dad stood up and stretched. "Trust me, that would be *less* simple. Could you imagine all the coincidences that would have to line up? No, Liam. Odds are that the knife is just a prank or a goof, like I said, and the person who attacked El isn't related to it at all." He clapped his hands together. "Can I warm up some stew for you?"

Liam's gut warred with his brain. His gut, as usual, won. "Sure, Dad."

# 1986: DEAN

Since the age of ten, Dean had had trouble sleeping. His parents saw this as a struggle to be won, not a problem to be solved. They had tried commanding him to bed earlier and earlier, then had tried letting him stay up later and later; the former on the theory that he needed more time in bed to relax and unwind from the day, the latter on the theory that he needed to be exhausted before his head touched his pillow.

Neither had worked. Eight o'clock or eleven o'clock, Dean would lie awake, staring at the ceiling, turning to glare at his clock, the red glowing bars of the digits steadfastly refusing to change under his gaze. It would be midnight forever, and then it was one in the morning and he was still awake.

Sometimes, he tried music. Other times, he tried talk radio. He'd recently discovered Dr. Ruth's show and had been surprised that something so explicit and so sexual could be heard for free over the public airwaves. Perhaps as a sop to propriety and decency, Dr. Ruth's show did not air until midnight.

It was called *Sexually Speaking*, but Dr. Ruth's heavy German accent rendered it *Zexually Zpeaking* whenever she introduced it. "Hello, zis is *Zexually Zpeaking* vit Dr. Ruth Vestheimer."

The accent and the subject matter combined into a jarring, utterly *un*soothing experience, an almost unsettling juxtaposition of the harsh Germanic syllables—the intonations of the Nazi villains in everything from

*Hogan's Heroes* to *Raiders of the Lost Ark*—with Dr. Ruth's puckish, playful ribaldry. She spoke like a horny Teutonic elf, but seriousness and sincerity crackled like static in every exchange with every caller. Dr. Ruth never put him to sleep, but she made it possible for him to pass the minutes between midnight and twelve fifteen AM without obsessively checking the time. When she signed off, he always groaned into his pillow and settled in for the long, dark caesura between sign-off and sleep.

Tonight was not a Sunday. He had no Dr. Ruth to look forward to in— he checked the clock—forty-seven minutes.

With a defeated sigh, he flipped his pillow, looking for a cool spot. It was a beastly hot Indian summer. A thin breeze wafted in through his open window, but only enough to tease him with the promise of cool air.

He went to the window and pressed his hand against the screen, willing more air to find him. Imagining that he could control air currents with his mind. Closing his eyes, he tried to conjure wind, not mere breeze.

Nothing.

Except a sound.

He opened his eyes and looked out into the dark. Dean's bedroom window opened into the backyard, a quarter acre of flat grass rolling out to a barbed wire fence that separated his family's plot from a huge field attached to the Winslow farm. During the days, the Winslows' cows wandered in that field, eating grass and leaving enormous piles of flat cow dung that Dean's mom had him steal for fertilizer for her garden. At night, there should be nothing out there. Nothing except for bats in the old cherry tree that rose against the moonlit sky.

By the tree, something moved. Something much bigger than a bat.

# 13

# THE PRESENT: LIAM

Back in Elayah's hospital room that afternoon after school, Liam thought her mom seemed almost grateful to see them this time, slipping out moments after they arrived.

"I think she's going stir-crazy in here," El said.

*She's not the only one*, Liam thought. As El's health improved, she seemed more manic. Her eyes were brighter than the day before, and there was a sort of nervous energy shedding from her; excitement flung like sweat with every movement.

"How'd everyone sleep last night?" she asked with an almost wicked gleam in her eye. "I slept like a baby—up every couple of hours to cry and complain."

Liam had slept perfectly well but wasn't about to admit it. Not when he knew El had been up and had been keeping Marcie up.

"How about you, Jorja?" El asked.

Jorja said nothing, then shrugged, eyes downcast. "You know."

Liam knew Jorja had spent her life learning how to be tough. Even around friends, it was difficult to be weak.

"Tell us," Marcie said gently.

"Yeah, I couldn't sleep, either," she said eventually. "My father. I see him and it comes into my head, without warning: *Did he kill someone? Did he help cover it up?* He's a public defender; he spends his life making sure people aren't abused by the system, and I always thought that was noble, but what if it's self-serving? What if—"

"Calm down." Marcie put a hand on her wrist. Jorja, once started, was a boulder rolling downhill. "We're not there yet."

"This doesn't bother you? At all?" Jorja pulled her arm away. Not aggressively or angrily. More in a self-protective way.

Marcie pondered for a moment. "I don't know. You've always thought your dad was perfect. He's always been there for you, no matter what. My mom...my mom had a drinking problem for a while, you know? And my dad cheated on her when I was little, I guess. I mean, if I'm reading between the lines right. They've been divorced so long I don't even remember them ever being together. I never had any illusions about them being perfect. But I know they didn't kill anyone."

"I'm not deluded," Jorja sniffed.

"No one said you were," Elayah told her. "And for all we know, they just covered it up."

"I don't want to think that." Marcie's voice, usually so confident, was small.

"I like all your parents," Liam said, unbidden. "And I don't want to think any of them had anything to do with this. Not my dad, not any of our dads or your mom, Marse. But...there's this thing called *linkage blindness*. It's where cops don't see the evidence right because they don't *want* to. And I think my dad's getting that. Because all the suspects that make sense were his friends."

"This sucks," Marcie pronounced.

"Dad always says that cops need to be aware of what they *don't* know as much as what they *do* know."

"So let's do this the right way, then." Marcie dug into her shoulder bag, a wondrously large cornucopia of every sundries and necessities you could imagine. She emerged with her iPad and Apple Pencil. "Let's walk through this, okay?" She held up the tablet and wrote *THE MURDER* across the top of the screen.

"We don't know it's a murder," Jorja said immediately.

"Someone stabbed someone," Elayah argued. "The note mentions killing someone."

"We don't know it's blood on the knife." Jorja had a way of being infuriatingly reasonable about very important things that demanded a sense of drama.

"Well, it might be animal blood," Liam told them. "But the results were inconclusive, so who knows?"

"We know someone put the knife in the time capsule," Marcie put in. "And it had to be one of our parents, right?"

Marcie looked around the room after this pronouncement. No one spoke. El shifted uncomfortably and prodded gently at the stitches on her throat. They knew it had to be true.

Except it didn't have to be true.

"All we know for certain is that they came up with the idea and they buried it," El pointed out. "Maybe someone else put the knife in there. Did anyone else know about the time capsule back then?"

"Mr. Hindon did," Liam supplied.

"Anyone else know?" Marcie enunciated as she wrote the same words under *THE MURDER*. No one spoke. "Okay, so our parents buried the thing. They put stuff in there. We start with them."

Jorja cleared her throat meaningfully. "Have we considered...I mean, *I've* considered, but have the rest of you considered that whoever put the knife in the time capsule..."

"Is the same person who held a knife to my throat," Elayah finished for her.

Marcie jumped in. "We don't know that for a fact."

Jorja shrugged. "Occam's razor."

Liam didn't know what that meant, but Jorja, Elayah, and Marcie all nodded grimly at one another as though they'd just solved an impossible equation, so he figured it was significant. As hard as he tried to keep a puzzled expression from his face—he hated showing off his stupidity—Jorja knew him too damn well. And took pity on him.

"Occam's razor is a—"

"Doesn't matter," he told her. Jorja's heart was in the right place, but he couldn't bear to listen to another dumbed-down version of some obscure fact. "Say it *was* one of our parents. That still means we're looking in our own houses."

Jorja nodded soberly, and then she said...

# ELAYAH

**M**ost likely candidate is El's dad."

Jorja had the grace to say it with a note of apology in her voice.

Before El could speak, Liam jumped up from his chair and told her, in very Anglo-Saxon terms, to attempt sexual reproduction with herself.

"We have to consider everything," Jorja replied. If Liam's outburst shocked her, she didn't show it. "El, you know I think your dad is great. But he was already in the house. It makes him the prime suspect."

Liam snorted in disgust and kicked his chair. Elayah couldn't decide if she was touched by his anger on behalf of her father or annoyed that he was sucking up all the oxygen that would allow her own outrage to flame.

"The guy was white, though," Marcie said, then arched an eyebrow at Elayah. "Right?"

"And you really think Mr. Laird would put a knife to his own daughter's throat?" Liam insisted before Elayah could jump in.

"He would if he didn't want to be a suspect," Jorja said with infuriating calm. "I'm sorry, El. But you said he sounded white. That's not much of a trick. Voices are easy to change. And he could have worn some kind of cologne or something that reminded you of the way white people smell."

"Right," Liam said, his voice edged with a nasty, dark sarcasm. Elayah couldn't remember a time she'd ever seen him so angry. "He just stopped off at the drugstore and bought a bottle of *Eau de Cracker.*"

Again, Jorja's tone was annoyingly calm, as though she knew it was the only way to keep Liam in check. "I'm not saying he was *trying* to smell like a white person. Just that whatever he wore happened to *seem* that way to El."

Of course it was all nonsense, all conjured from Jorja's fecund imagination. This was, after all, the same Jorja who'd gone as Harvey Weinstein in Hell for Halloween. Twice.

But as rapidly as she dismissed it, Elayah had to force herself to reconsider. It had been late. She'd been awoken from a deep sleep, rattled into wakefulness by a blade at her throat. She'd been positive of what she'd told the sheriff, but now, she couldn't be. Jorja was wrong, she knew. She also knew that there was a chance—small, but not zero—that Jorja was right.

"We have to consider my dad," she said quietly, not daring to look at Liam. He seemed more upset than she was at the idea.

"It wasn't your dad." Liam's tone was concrete, definite, embedded in confidence.

"We can't make assumptions," Marcie admonished.

"Don't talk to me about assumptions," Liam shot back. "We know what we know."

"We're like Jon Snow; we know *nothing*," said Jorja with infuriating confidence. "Nothing at all. We're just stumbling around, figuring it out. We won't know anything until we know it."

Her words hung alone and heavy and true in the air.

"Well, that makes *perfect* sense," Liam grumbled.

"We still don't even know it's a murder," Elayah reminded them all. "Someone could have been stabbed and still lived."

"Any of our parents have weird scars?" Marcie asked, half joking.

"We're going about this all wrong," Liam said, and the serious tone of his voice caught them all off guard. "I know I'm the dumbass of the group, but I grew up around this stuff. You have to think like cops: motive, means, opportunity."

"Who wants to kill someone, who was able to kill somebody, who had the chance to kill somebody...?" Elayah hated herself for ending it in a question. She knew she was right. But this was a whole new arena for her, and Liam's sudden take-charge attitude threw her.

"Yeah," Liam said. "But also: Who had the motive, the means, and the opportunity to use the time capsule to throw away the knife?"

"Just our parents," Elayah said, miserable as she said it. "And I guess Mr. Hindon."

Silence. For too long.

"Guys," Marcie said, her voice almost a whisper, "I'm really not cool with thinking any of our parents could have done this."

"Other people could have gotten to the time capsule...." Elayah said. "It was a long time ago. We don't know who might have—"

"Means?" Marcie interrupted. "Sure. But motive? Why would someone uninvolved in the time capsule think to put a murder weapon in there?"

"We still don't know it's a murder!" Jorja nearly shouted, her face twisted in aggravation. "Stop calling it a murder weapon when we don't have proof there was a murder!"

"Be cool!" Liam hissed, glancing toward the door. "We don't need parents in here."

"Why not?" Jorja fired back. "Let's invite them in so that we can interrogate them right now and get to the bottom of this."

Liam chuckled without mirth. Elayah had never witnessed such an expression of solemnity on Liam before. It was as disturbing as though an alien face-hugger from that old movie had glommed onto his face.

"Guys, you aren't thinking this through," Liam said. "We're talking about our parents. We're saying—"

"All we're saying is one of them might have been involved somehow," Jorja assured him. "Maybe covering it up. Maybe hiding the knife for a friend, right? I don't think any of us believe one of them actually *killed* someone."

"What if *all* of them did?" Liam asked quietly.

Elayah hadn't even considered it. And now that Liam said it out loud, it was the only thing that made any sort of sense. From the moment she'd seen the knife, she'd operated under the assumption that one of the group of parents had hurt or killed someone and used the time capsule to get rid of the knife, probably assuming—correctly, as it turned out—that they would never actually dig it up. Not accounting for Elayah stumbling upon its existence.

But that "lone gunman" theory now seemed naive and oversimplified.

"They all had access to the time capsule. They all knew each other and were around each other all the time. And they conveniently didn't bother to dig it up." Liam was still talking, as though he had to convince anyone of anything. Marcie wore a gut-punched expression. Jorja was studying the ceiling tiles, avoiding everyone's eyes.

"We could *all* be living with criminals," Elayah whispered.

Elayah couldn't sleep after they all left. Her parents once again filed in as soon as her friends left, first Mom, then Dad when his shift ended at the factory. He leaned in to kiss her, and she smelled the unique combination of his aftershave and the chemicals they used to process the tapes at the factory. It was a smell she'd known her whole life—Dad found an aftershave he liked and stuck with it—but on this night, she didn't find it comforting. Dad's sad eyes and concerned expression seemed more a mask than reality to her.

*Did you do it?* popped into her head unbidden. *Was it you?*

Pleading exhaustion, she turned over in bed without so much as a "Hi" to her father, closing her eyes, pretending to sleep. She hated herself for thinking this way, but suddenly her father was a different person to her.

He was a suspect.

Which was an absolutely *insane* thing to think. It *couldn't* be her father.

Then who?

It had to be one of the friends, the group that had buried the time capsule. One of her friends' parents.

Jorja's dad worked for the county as a public defender. Probably could have made a lot more money somewhere else, but he was—in his own words—"a true believer." Elayah couldn't imagine him killing someone. He was gregarious and funny and brewed his own root beer. That didn't strike her as the homicidal type.

Marcie's parents had split when Marcie was four—her dad lived down in Finn's Landing, near the river. Elayah didn't know him terribly well. He tended not to show up for events or parties, and when he did, he usually lurked near the door and disappeared halfway through. Unlike Kim—Marcie's mom—he always insisted on being called "Mr. Ford." He was a writer, she knew—he wrote technical manuals and stuff like that. She'd spent some weekends with Marcie at his apartment when they were younger; the place had been clean, but cluttered, and smelled of something stale and sweet that years later she identified as marijuana.

If she was being honest, Elayah didn't like Marcie's dad. But that didn't mean he was capable of murder.

And Kim was...well, Kim was Kim. As a child, Elayah had spent many a day and sleepover at Kim's apartment, which seemed cozy and cluttered in the best possible way. Marcie had had bunk beds back then, and they'd kept track of who slept on the top and who slept on the bottom, alternating, occasionally trading, sometimes turning the top bunk into the prize for a bet.

Kim kept them plied with a steady stream of junk food that was forbidden in Elayah's house, often leaving them unattended for hours at a time while she worked one of her jobs. It had seemed magical to Elayah, and only now did she notice the creases in Kim's forehead, the wrinkles around her eyes, the hard sighs.

Impossible to imagine this woman with a knife in her hands.

That left Liam's dad, and yeah, he'd definitely been home in bed when she'd been attacked.

*Good job, Detective Elayah—you've eliminated every suspect! That's not how this is supposed to work.*

# Ep. 001

INDIRA BHATTI-WATSON, HOST:

This is *No Time Like the Present*, an NPR podcast. I am Indira Bhatti-Watson, reporting from Canterstown, Maryland.

(SOUND BITE OF MUSIC)

BHATTI-WATSON:

The town itself seems not so much developed or planned as emerged from the surrounding fields of corn, soybeans, and tobacco.

If you are of a certain age, you probably remember Wantzler cassette tapes, with their distinctive blue-and-green packaging, and perhaps the company's late foray into videotapes and floppy disks. In a digital world, such media have fewer and fewer uses, and the factory's attempts to adapt to the times have failed more often than not. In recent years, a risky factory reconfiguration to begin producing components for computer flash memory seemed like a gamble that would pay off ... until the coronavirus temporarily shut down the factory and wiped out many local businesses. Unemployment and opiate addiction rose hand in hand here in Canterstown, but back in 1986, this was an example of President Ronald Reagan's paean to "morning in America," a thriving slice of small-town America where the collars were blue, the moms were stay-at-home, and the cars were built in Detroit.

We came here for many reasons: an attack on a young woman in her own bed. A time capsule unearthed, bearing mysteries. And we found not just the story of a group of friends trying to understand the past, but also a town on the precipice of its own unknowable future.

On this podcast, we're going to take you through Canterstown. Its history. Its present. Its likely future. We're also going to try to answer the question on everyone's mind: Who attacked seventeen-year-old Elayah Laird in her own bed . . . and why?

MARTIN CHISHOLM, LOWE COUNTY (MD) SUPERINTENDENT OF SCHOOLS:

This town was once a thriving example of middle-American values and initiative. It can be again. Send me to Annapolis to represent you, and I will do whatever it takes, fight whatever battles there may be, to revitalize and reenergize our community after the destruction wreaked on us by the economy, by the coronavirus, by decades of politicians who just didn't care!

(CROWD NOISE)

CHISHOLM:

If you need any further evidence for why there needs to be a change in Annapolis, just look at what happened the other night!

BHATTI-WATSON:

That's the voice of Martin Chisholm, running for Maryland state senate. In the 1980s, he was a teacher at the school

Elayah Laird now attends. We spoke to him between campaign appearances.

CHISHOLM:

You know, it was different back then. I hate it when old people like me say that! But it's true. You didn't have to watch your kids every single second. They could go outside and play unsupervised or run over to a neighbor's house. It wasn't all sunshine and dandelions, don't get me wrong. But is there maybe a way to incorporate the good parts of the past into our future?

BHATTI-WATSON:

Forgive me for saying so, but that sounds pretty regressive for someone running as a Democrat.

CHISHOLM:

I'm trying to be realistic. I don't want every part of the past back. God, no. But I can tell you this: Back then, nothing like what happened to poor Ms. Laird would have happened in this town.

**14**

# THE PRESENT: ELAYAH

While Mom was at the nurses' station haggling over some insurance thing on the day of her release, Elayah got dressed, packed her pajamas and some toiletries into a canvas tote Mom had brought, and then sat on the bed to wait.

Eventually, she had to start sorting through her phone. Now was as good a time as any.

holy snap @elayahlairdrox got stabbed!!!

not stabbed you idiot SLASHED. There's a diff.

whatevs

guys I heard @elayahlairdrox got killed last night!

FAKE NEWS! She wasn't killed. Just got her throat cut.

Just?

Whew! That's good news. She's my lab partner.

She couldn't bear much of it. The people she truly cared about—her family, her teachers, her friends—knew the truth, and that was what mattered. For the first time in a long time, she tapped out of Twitter and Insta without looking at every tweet and comment. Social media was too much noise, not enough signal.

Opening her browser revealed the last page she'd visited before going to bed that fateful night—Rachel's second story, the one that had gotten serious. The comment section on that particular article had lit up with gossipy speculation. Elayah was accustomed to such behavior from her peers and the occasional putative "real housewife" on TV, but to see actual adults in her actual town—people with jobs and mortgages and kids—descend into a murk of guesswork, supposition, and baseless surmise was disheartening.

Worse yet was the story about her own attack, linked in an update squib at the bottom of the story. LOCAL TEEN ATTACKED IN HOME AFTER HINTING AT DARK SECRET screamed the bold, red, overwritten headline. Rachel had the byline again, no doubt fist-pumping at the memory of the day she'd met Elayah and the others.

The story was lean, thankfully, devoid of most facts. The phrase "The Canterstown Sheriff's Department refused to comment" was deployed.

But the basics came through: Elayah had spilled the tea and then had her blood spilled. Light on actual content, Rachel's four breathless paragraphs compensated with attitude, verve, and lurid implication. Was her attack connected to the mystery from decades ago? How could it not be? All the story lacked was an autoplaying audio of a dramatic drumbeat to drive home the point.

She had to scroll past two screens of trackbacks before the first comment appeared.

Lots of speculation, lots of rumor. Half-true tidbits, links to personal Facebook accounts with "pix from right across the street!" Elayah realized, to her dismay, that photos of her being wheeled out of her house on a stretcher would now live forever in the depthless, borderless tracts of the internet. Image searches for *Elayah Laird* would, years from now, regurgitate grainy, half-dark cell footage of her unconscious body, covered in blood.

*Splat!* went her phone. It was the alert sound she'd chosen for Twitter

DMs. At some point, the idea of a direct message landing on her phone with a wet thud, like bird poop, had seemed amusing. Now it just seemed juvenile and idiotic.

She tapped to get into Settings and change the sound but missed the icon, her thumb sliding along the notification panel instead. The next thing she knew, Twitter opened and spat out the DM:

"Hi, Elayah!

"My name is Indira Bhatti-Watson, and I'm a producer at NPR in the podcast division. I'm wondering if anyone has approached you about the rights to your story? I'm already in town, and I'd love to bring a crew to interview you about your discovery. Maybe you'd be willing to walk us around town and give us a local's perspective?"

There was another paragraph—this one all business—including an email address, two cell phone numbers, and a link to an NPR bio page.

Okay, so first of all: She had to close up her DMs because what on earth had she been thinking? But second of all...

NPR. National Public Radio.

*National* Public Radio.

*National.*

What the hell?

Elayah pondered for a moment, then went back to the article about her, sliding her finger up the screen until she hit the trackbacks. This time she didn't skip them.

cnn.com

msnbc.com

foxbaltimore.com

wjla.com

The list went on. A local TV affiliate picked it up on a slow news day from the local news. And then a network decided to throw it into the nightly report. Weird angle, time capsule. Sins of the past and all that. And then, as best she could tell, Black Twitter picked it up and ran with it precisely because the story of a young Black girl having her throat slashed in her own bed wasn't getting the sort of traction it would have gotten if it had happened to a white girl.

Which led to cable news and the news cycle that eats itself alive.

Yeah, that was the Hansel and Gretel of it all. Whatever the specifics, she'd gone viral, and there was no sign of the bug abating anytime soon.

Well, Instagram would be safe, right? Just pictures of pretty people. She switched over only to find a DM there as well. This Bhatti-Watson person was persistent.

She tapped into DMs to erase it, but it wasn't from the NPR lady at all. And it was short and to the point.

**You weren't supposed to get hurt**, it said.

Wait, *what*?

She had no idea who *notarealaccount237483423* was, but she had a sneaking suspicion it might—*might*—be a burner account.

**You weren't supposed to get hurt**, the DM began. **No one else needs to get hurt. Leave it behind the statue of Susan Ann Marchetti in the park tonight at midnight and this all ends.**

Elayah skimmed it another time. There wasn't much there, and there were no lines to read between. Pretty obvious. Pretty *blatant*.

When she tried to respond, she got an alert telling her the account was deactivated. Yeah, a burner.

"What the hell?" she murmured.

A phalanx of photographers greeted Elayah and her parents when they left the hospital late that morning, along with a slew of locals wielding smartphone cameras as though they'd taken an online course in photography and general asshattery.

Dad shielded Elayah's face with his hand, while Mom shucked off her jacket and put it over Elayah's head, a measure that was at once absurd and comforting.

At home, her room had been cleaned and straightened, but she experienced a tiptoe tingle of fear and memory up her spine as she stood in the doorway. A mélange of half memories eddied around her, a clutter of stumbles, hitched breaths, slick warmth pooling in her palm. Her Solange poster was gone, four tiny pinholes at its missing corners the only evidence of its past presence. She imagined it blood-swiped, a smeared handprint emblazoned along its surface. Imagined her parents glancing at each other in silence before taking it down, throwing it away.

Or had the police taken it as evidence? There were smudges of black powder here and there, and some dim memory from years ago struggled to the surface: Liam, regaling the class with a report on police procedure. *And the thing most people don't know,* he'd blurted out, his words always racing to catch each other, as though desperate to unite into a single unit of sound, *is that fingerprint powder is* really *messy and it's not white like on TV; it's black and it gets* everywhere *and my dad says you probably don't even want to bother having them fingerprint your house because it's a hassle and they probably won't get anything usable anyway.*

How was she ever going to sleep in here again? There was a new lock on the window, a stout one. The problem hadn't been the original lock, though—she'd had the window open, after all. What was her dad going to do, put bars over the window?

Actually, yeah, she could see him doing exactly that.

"When you're ready." Mom's hand on her shoulder. Mind reading Elayah's own thoughts. "You don't have to sleep in here until you feel like you can."

Elayah shook her head, though what she was trying to communicate in that moment, she couldn't say.

Her phone buzzed for her attention. She'd turned off most notifications, allowing only people she actually knew to get through.

Marcie: **u doing ok? want me 2 come over?**

She really, really didn't, and she really, really did. She didn't know what she wanted anymore, other than to not be afraid of her own bedroom.

**u home yet? feeling ok?**

Liam, this time. Her heart skipped a beat and the pulse in her throat strained against the stitches.

**Not bad**, she thumbed to him. Then added:

He dapped back: 

**u need anything**  he sent after a moment.

She considered. An idea was forming. **actually could use a favor. talk later?**

It was the middle of the day; Dad was at the factory. Mom would usually be at the real estate office, making copies, making coffee, doing whatever. When Elayah found her in the kitchen, she seemed out of sorts, being at home during the day.

"Mom, you can go to work."

Mom sat on the floor by an open empty cabinet, rearranging the plastic containers, matching bottoms to lids. "No, no," she said without looking up. "I'm fine."

The people at Morris Realty were pretty understanding, but Mom was hourly, not salaried. Every hour she stayed home with Elayah was money out of her pocket.

"Mom, really. I'm okay." Her own voice surprised her. It sounded stout and confident, utterly at odds with the turmoil that roiled her gut in the same instant. She knew her mom *should* go, but she truly, almost desperately didn't want her to.

Mom snapped a lid into place, realized it didn't quite fit, and stood up, arching her back, then looking around at the Tupperware she'd scattered all over the floor. "How is there one lid that doesn't match anything?" she asked the universe. "How does this always happen?"

Elayah sank into a kitchen chair. "You used a container to bring water outside for the plants, remember?"

Mom heel-palmed her forehead. "Right. Right. It's in the garage." She smiled wanly at Elayah. "Thank you, baby."

*Baby.* She was an only child, and she knew she would always be her parents' baby, but normally that word rankled, chafed. She was a woman. Hell, she'd survived a knife attack.

"I'm okay, Mom," she said, and this time she almost believed it.

Mom nodded, absorbing the lie. "But, baby," she said, a small, sad smile tugging at her lips, "I'm not."

# THE PRESENT: LIAM

They had a dishwasher but almost never used it. From a young age, Liam had been washing the dishes to help out in the kitchen while Pop put away the leftovers and the left-out ingredients from dinner. It had been a way for Liam to be closer to Pop at first, an unconscious and unfathomed attraction to his nonbiological parent. Liam understood Dad too well, on a visceral level. But as a kid, he'd been drawn to Pop, who was blond where Dad was dark, heavy where Dad was light, boisterous where Dad was reserved. The kitchen became their nightly ritual. By mutual understanding and no words whatsoever, Dad was barred from the kitchen after dinner. Pop and Liam time. Sacrosanct.

"Hear from El?" Pop asked, shutting the fridge door on leftover risotto and mushrooms.

His back to Pop, his hands working in the soapy water, Liam shrugged.

"Not so loud," Pop admonished, and Liam chuckled.

"Just a text," he said. "I'm trying not to crowd her, you know?"

Pop came up behind him and kissed the top of Liam's head. He had to go up on tiptoe to do it—Liam had taken an inch over Pop a year ago. "You ever going to tell that girl you love her?" Pop asked.

"I'll get around to it one of these days."

Pop patted Liam on the shoulder. "Don't wait too long, kiddo. Life's short."

"So're you."

"No one likes a smart-ass kid, Liam. Don't forget the pan in the oven."

Pop kissed him once more, on the cheek, and left Liam to finish the dishes.

Liam set the pan to soak, then pulled out his phone. **now a good time?**

El sent back a screen grab of her Insta DMs. It took Liam a moment to register what he was seeing.

**I'll show it to dad right now**

**NO!**

Liam flicked his gaze through the archway that led to the dining room. Dad and Pop sat at the table, scrolling their phones in that silent communion married people have.

**why not?**

**we don't know who we can trust**

Fuming, Liam almost shut off his phone. El was being paranoid. They *knew* his father hadn't attacked her.

**chill out**, she texted, as though she could read his mind. **i have a plan.**


Liam tried not to move, but he was cold and his body wanted to dance back and forth to generate heat.

El's plan was simple and to the point: Stake out the statue and see who showed up. Liam wouldn't have done this for any other human being on the planet.

And yet here he was at close to midnight, twenty minutes from home and practically begging to be grounded for life if he got caught.

**Leave it behind the statue of Susan Ann Marchetti in the park tonight at midnight and this all ends.**

*Yeah, we'll see about that,* Liam thought.

*The park* could mean only one place, in context: Susan Ann Marchetti Memorial Park, a popular municipal park in Brookdale, not far from Canterstown. And there was only one statue in the park, that of the eponymous lady herself. So Liam got to the park around eleven thirty and secreted himself in some bushes with a line of sight to the statue. He hadn't left *it* there, partly because screw this guy, but mostly because the knife was locked up in Evidence Control.

He shivered. It was a cold fall night, and he suddenly had to pee. Shouldn't have downed a Coke on his way, but he'd needed the caffeine and sugar boost.

Fumbling at his fly, he relieved himself into the bushes, suppressing a sigh of relief as he did so. No sooner had he tucked himself back in than he spied movement by the statue.

A thrill ran through him, supercharging his body beyond the chemical capabilities of caffeine or sugar. *Holy crap. It's happening.*

It suddenly occurred to him that the odds were very good that he was about to see one of his friends' parents skulking about, and his excitement crashed.

Shifting slowly into a better viewing position, careful not to make noise or rustle the bushes, he peered out to the statue. The lighting was poor here, as throughout most of the park. He wished he had night-vision goggles. Not just for this, but in general. It would be cool to have night-vision goggles.

A figure broke loose from a cluster of shadows. Dressed in black pants, black boots, and a long black jacket, as well as a black wool cap. Nice. The figure glanced around, then casually meandered over toward the statue.

Liam leaned forward a bit. Looked like a guy, but in that coat, who could tell for sure? He didn't *think* it was Marcie's mom, but...

The figure stepped around the statue, and Liam realized the flaw in his part of the plan—the best concealed spot near the statue had a *very* obstructed view of the back of the statue. Which is where *it* was supposed to be left. Once the mysterious person in black went around to the back of the statue and saw that the knife wasn't there, he or she or they would just disappear into the park and vanish for good.

*I should have planted something there. Like a decoy. Duh. Next time I sneak out in the middle of the night to catch a bad guy, I'm totally going to think it through.*

El had told him not to improvise, but he figured now was the time to improvise.

As quietly as he could, he emerged from the brambles and leaves surrounding him. His legs, cramped from squatting in the bushes for so long, seized up on him; he sacrificed a few seconds to do some deep knee bends to get the blood flowing again. Then he crept closer to the statue, sidled around it—

And was busted immediately. He damn near crashed into the figure in black, who was crouched at the base of the statue, running his—yeah, it was a dude after all, big shock—fingers along the concrete. The man yelped and sprung up from his squat. Liam, off-balance from the near collision, flailed, snagging the hem of the guy's coat with one hand.

His grasp was tenuous at best. Liam fell to the ground, still clutching the coat. The man grunted in surprise, threw a look over his shoulder. Liam caught a glimpse of high cheekbones, shaved smooth. A smallish nose. A flip of honey-dark hair protruding from under the cap.

"Let go!" The man lurched forward.

Liam flung his other hand out, grasping the coat up higher this time, tightening his grip. The man stumbled and dropped to one knee. Progress!

With a heave of breath and a groan of effort, Liam pulled himself into a wrestler's crouch, now landing both hands higher on the coat. It occurred to him that if the guy just slipped his arms out, he'd be home free, leaving Liam with nothing but a jacket as a trophy.

Instead, the guy stumbled as he tried to rise, collapsing on all fours. Liam pounced, tackling him around the midsection, bearing both of them to the ground. The statue stood in a circle of cobblestones; Liam's left hip and elbow sang their pain; he tuned them out. He was *not* letting go of this dude.

"Get off!" the guy cried. His voice was low-pitched, slightly nasal. Liam twisted, hugging the guy from behind and above, trying to tip them over so that he could get him in a headlock. Wrestling lessons from gym class were a million years ago, but muscle memory saved the day.

The man thrashed under him, hands scrabbling against the cobblestones for purchase, for stability. Liam rocked them back and forth. Anything to keep the guy from gaining any sort of leverage.

*Smash his face against the ground.* The savagery of the notion startled him, as did his immediate acceptance of it. Yeah, smash the guy's face. That would stop him.

He released his grip, counting on his weight to hold the guy down while he reached for his head. *Grab the ears. Lift. Smash. Repeat? Maybe. Let's see how it goes.*

But in probing for the man's head, he shifted his weight, and in that moment, the man rolled to one side, knocking Liam off-kilter. Shimmying like a snake, the guy wriggled out from under Liam.

Liam cursed under his breath and stretched to clasp the man's ankle. But the guy kicked out, knocking Liam's hand aside, then lashed out with his other foot, catching Liam fully on the left side of his face with the bottom of his shoe.

The world exploded red, then white, then black. Sparks danced before Liam's eyes. Through a fuzzy haze of static, he witnessed the man scramble a couple of feet away, then rise to his feet and dash off through the bushes.

Back in the car, Liam gulped air until his breathing returned to normal and his heart rate subsided. Then, in a move that he knew would make his dad proud (after his dad finished berating him for being here in the first place, of course), he whipped out his phone and tapped out a quick list of everything he could remember about the man and their scuffle.

His ribs hurt and the side of his face throbbed, but his vision had cleared and showed no signs of impairment. Skimming his list, he determined that it met with his satisfaction. He began composing a text to El, but a look at the time told him she was probably asleep. And it was too much for a text anyway.

*And besides, do I really want to leave evidence that I did this?*

He lifted his gaze to the vanity mirror and stared at himself. Was this how it was going to be now? Thinking like a cop and a criminal? Covering his tracks while searching for someone else's?

Jorja's voice in his head: *Come on, Li. For El.*

*Well, yeah.*

He texted El that he would fill her in in the morning and then drove home.

**16**

# THE PRESENT: ELAYAH

Elayah had told herself she could sleep in her room. She was very persuasive—top scorer in debate club *and* mock-trial team, three years running, thankyouverymuch—and she convinced not only her parents, but also herself.

Pajamas on. Shea butter on. Stitches lubricated to prevent scarring.

New sheets. The guest duvet cover because hers was covered in blood and, hey, let's not think about that, okay, let's just think about that nice, stout lock on the window. Gee, it sure is hefty-looking and, according to the locksmith site she'd checked, was rated number two in the world. Which would probably suffice since they weren't trying to keep the CIA out.

With a deep breath, she had stepped into the room, threw back the duvet and top sheet, climbed into bed, and turned off the lights. Then she'd rolled right out of bed, marched out of the room, and walked down the hall to her parents' room, where she stood in the doorway and announced, "Yeah, that's not gonna happen after all."

Mom and Dad exchanged a knowing glance. She figured one of them had just won ten bucks from the other.

That night, for the first time since seventh grade, Elayah slept in her parents' bed, curled up next to Mom. Dad slept in her room. She put her phone under her pillow, set on vibrate.

It woke her from a thin sleep sometime after midnight. Next to her, Mom breathed regularly and steadily. Dad's snores echoed down the hall.

The text from Liam was mysterious, frustrating. Sort of like Liam himself.

**success? kinda-sorta? 💀 ❓ talk tomorrow**

She sighed and slipped the phone onto the nightstand. Unable to fall asleep again, she rolled out of bed silently and stretched. What had happened? Should she text Liam back? He was probably on the road, so bad idea.

Above and behind the nightstand was a window looking out into the backyard. Elayah quietly peeled back the shade to peek outside. The moon was high and bright, almost full.

And someone stood in her backyard.

Her heart jumped once. Her brain immediately rejected the evidence of her eyes. A high fence separated her yard from the adjoining houses. It's not like someone could just wander back there accidentally or unintentionally. It was after midnight. Therefore, her brain insisted, you're not seeing what you think you're seeing.

But someone was there. Standing underneath the cherry tree that grew in the northwest corner of the property.

Elayah's mouth went dry. Her eyes darted to Mom's slumbering form. Wake her? Go get Dad? Call 911?

Picture. Take a picture of the guy first. Right?

She bobbled her phone plucking it from the nightstand, finally righted it, and peeled back the shade again.

There was no one there.

*Told you so,* her brain said smugly.

# LIAM

Liam woke to his own hiss of pain. In his sleep, he'd rolled to his left, pressing the tender side of his face against the pillow. He crawled out of bed less than six hours after crawling in.

A brief look in the mirror over his dresser told the tale: A massive black-and-blue continent had arisen from the ocean of his face, folding around his left eye and inflating down to his cheek. He appeared as though he'd taken a boxing glove to the face.

It could have been worse, he supposed. It could have been a footprint.

*Well, you snuck—sneaked, sorry, El—out of the house, down to the park, back home, and back inside without being caught. You couldn't expect the night to go perfectly, right?*

Dad and Pop milled about the kitchen. Pop had hash browns on the griddle, and Dad's head had disappeared into the fridge. "Where *is* the cheddar?"

"Behind the mushrooms," Pop said without so much as a glance up from the potatoes.

"But where are the mushrooms?"

"In front of the cheddar," Liam said helpfully.

Dad chuckled dryly and closed the fridge door. He startled at the sight of Liam's face. "What the hell happened to you?"

"Well," Liam said slowly, as Pop turned and added his gasp to the conversation, "first I was born. And then at some point I hit puberty. And then—"

"Not funny!" Dad snapped. Pop abandoned his griddle to come to Liam's side, taking his chin in his hand and turning his face this way and that against the light.

"I'm fine," Liam protested, gently disengaging from Pop. "It only hurts when I stare at something really hard."

"What happened?" Dad demanded again. "Were you in a fight?"

Liam shrugged. "Masturbation accident. We've all been there, right?"

He knew it wasn't working when Dad and Pop both—without so much as a glance at each other—folded their arms over their respective chests and glared at him.

"Okay, okay," he said with a sigh. "I fell out of bed. Got tangled up in the sheets, fell, hit my stupid face on the stupid nightstand. Can I score some of those hash browns now?"

Pop clucked his tongue and relented, stroking Liam's face for a moment before returning to the stove. Dad nodded thoughtfully. Liam figured he'd pulled it off.

Maybe.

# 1986: KIM

Kimberly Tate—one of many Kims in school and therefore known mostly as Kim T. or even K. T.—had no illusions about her artistic abilities, thanks mostly to her artistic sensibilities. She could identify good art, pick it apart, analyze it. And that same ability made her painfully aware of her own shortcomings when it came to creating art.

*You need to learn how to take enjoyment in something you're not good at*, her dad told her once. *It's okay not to be the best at something.*

Tough lesson to learn, she thought, sitting in art class, but one she'd taken to heart. As proved by the fact that she—stubbornly? obstinately? idiotically?—took an art class every single year of her high school career, even knowing that she would never be great at it.

Art class had a lot to recommend it, actually. With grades totally subjective, the pressure to *succeed* dissipated, replaced with a gentler sense of accomplishment. No questions; no answers. Just the work.

Plus—and this was more important than she'd initially thought when signing up—art class was mostly girls. It was a welcome break from all those booming, assertive, insistent masculine voices and attitudes in the rest of her classes.

Fortunately, she had found Dean.

Dean, who was unlike the rest of the boys. Oh, he could be as gross—as *grody*, her Val-speaking friends would say—as any other boy. As loud. As unyielding. But his core was kind and empathetic. He possessed an inner gentleness that she'd never witnessed before.

It all went back to sixth-grade social studies, Ms. Grimaldi's class.

With no particular reason for doing so—the lesson that day was on the Trail of Tears—Ms. Grimaldi suddenly segued into a discussion on the very nature of America itself. In America, she claimed, anyone could be or do anything. Anyone could grow up to be president. Even a girl.

There'd been a ripple of slightly astonished, slightly bemused laughter at that, as the boys in the room chuckled at the idea. Ms. Grimaldi slapped her hand against the blackboard. The dull thwack of her hand and the resultant cloud of chalk dust had halted the class's reaction, and she'd repeated herself firmly, in an almost-defiant, *I dare you to laugh* tone.

But Kim had—through sheer coincidence—not been watching Ms. Grimaldi during the literal and figurative dustup. She'd turned to check out her friend Becky's hair, which had been a *disaster* in homeroom, sending Becky in a panic to the lavatory. Kim wanted to see if some hair spray and time with a brush had managed to rescue Becky's coif, but she'd been distracted by Dean, who sat just in front of Becky.

When Ms. Grimaldi made her comment about a girl someday being president, when the boys reacted, Dean hadn't said anything at all. Made not a sound. Instead, he simply nodded, his expression thoughtful, as though absorbing the information.

And then . . .

Just the tiniest smile.

A smile, she thought, of approval.

She was too young, she knew, to be in love. But she also knew that when the day came, she would be in love with Dean.

And that had happened, almost as though foreordained. Their friendship grew throughout middle school, deepened and burgeoned during freshman and sophomore years, then turned into something much more before Thanksgiving junior year.

Most days, she sat with the boys at lunch. In truth, she missed sitting with Jenny A. and Jenny M. and Becky and Sarah and Missy, but Dean was her boyfriend and she knew it was right to sit with him. Besides, the guys were funny, and she heard things at their table that she never would have heard at her own.

And by sitting there, she had more time with Dean. More time to figure out how to take things to the next level.

Early in their relationship, Kim had told Dean that she thought sex should be for after marriage, and he'd surprised her by agreeing. Was he just trying to accommodate her, or did he really mean it? Dean's family didn't go to church, so she couldn't be sure.

But now…she'd changed her mind. Big-time. She felt an empty, yawning ache at her core when they were together, and whenever they kissed, she caught fire in the most incredible, loveliest way. Her thighs went hot, and on Saturday nights, when he left her house after they'd spent the night down in the den, kissing and sucking at each other's necks, she immediately plunged her hands down, hunting for relief.

She didn't want him to think she was a slut, but she was tired of her own fingers. She wanted more. She wanted to feel him inside her, a thought that made her blush every time she had it, which was too often.

But she couldn't just *tell* him that. She *wasn't* a slut. She needed *him* to make the first move, and then she would acquiesce. Let him chase her to where they both wanted to go. She'd started wearing clothes that were a little more revealing, a little tighter. Today, for example, she wore a bulky sweater, but skintight yellow-and-green-patterned pants she'd found at the mall over the weekend.

"Hey, check it out!"

So swaddled in her own thoughts was she that it took a physical shake of her head to bring her back to the present, to art class. Brad Gimble, sitting next to her, was one of the very few boys in the class. He was a jock through and through, with a reputation as a total meathead. But she tried not to judge—art class was for everyone, Mrs. Lamb always said, and everyone was for art class. If Brad had depths he didn't show off outside the football field or the wrestling mat, then good for him.

"What?" she asked.

He tilted his easel so that she could see it. His canvas was blank white, except for a leaking, spattered blob of red paint in the center, as though the flag of Japan had melted, then quickly refroze. It looked like a ketchup stain.

"It's part of my punctuation series." Brad's tone was serious, but his expression was of barely restrained laughter. "This one is *Period*. Get it?"

If she said no, he would chortle at her stupidity. If she said *yes*, he would no doubt guffaw and ask, *Are you getting it right now?*

She availed herself of the third option, the only palatable one: She shook her head minutely, then turned back to her own easel, ignoring him, pretending as though it had never happened.

His snickers and whispered attempts to snag her attention again made it difficult, though.


She was usually thrilled to see Dean when they made their daily connection between fourth and fifth period. Today, though, she was still thinking of Brad and his stupidity, and her impotence in the face of that stupidity. It just wasn't right that there could be stupid, cruel, careless people and no recourse for someone like her. She felt not happiness at the sight of Dean, but rather security and safety. She wanted him to wrap her in his arms and kiss her forehead.

But Dean took a step back when she closed in on him, glancing around for teachers.

"It's okay," she said, a little more grumpily than was strictly necessary. "We'll just get a warning."

Still, he held her off at arm's length. "I don't want to get in trouble."

It made sense, but she didn't really give a damn about making sense right now. She wanted comfort; it was being denied to her. Her temper flared, higher, then hotter than the moment required, stoked since the moment in art class. "Are you suddenly ashamed to be seen with me?" she demanded.

"What? No!" Dean seemed horrified by the mere suggestion.

She knew, deep down, that she wasn't angry at Dean. She was angry at Brad. At herself. And taking it out on Dean, even though she should have known better. Still, it welled and thrashed within her, and it needed an outlet, and here was Dean, who was safe, who would listen, who would take it and still love her.

"I mean, you haven't even asked me to homecoming yet and it's coming up and I have to buy a *dress*, Dean!"

Dean blinked, then stared. His expression, so blank as to be unsettling, slowly transformed into bemused guilt, as though he'd been driving on a highway and suddenly found himself on an unpaved back road. How, his expression screamed silently, did I get here?

"Of *course* we're going to homecoming together. I didn't think I had to ask. I'm sorry."

"You just..." She cast about in frustration. All the anger and hurt she'd collected, pointless and aimless and ill-timed, but still extant. It all had to go somewhere and do *something*; it couldn't just dissipate. "A girl likes to be *asked*, Dean."

With a slow nod, he took her hands in his own. Not a drop of sarcasm or patronization spilled from his lips as he said, "K. T., I would love to go to homecoming with you. Will you go with me?"

She nodded because of *course* she nodded, smiled at Dean, and leaned in to kiss him. He let her.


"Watch this," Jay was saying. They'd been talking about *Miami Vice*—sometimes it seemed like all they *could* talk about was *Miami Vice*; she'd watched it a couple of times with Dean and just couldn't understand why they liked it so much—and something about cocaine.

Now Jay had two little packs of Smarties, which he was unraveling, spilling the candy discs out onto the table. Brian chuckled as Jay separated out the white ones, sweeping the rest out of the way.

"Like this, okay?" Jay took the knife from his lunch tray and ground the Smarties into white powder.

"Jay...," Kim said.

"Who you talkin' to?" Jay asked, scowling. "I ain't Jay." He pronounced the *J* like they did in Spanish class, forcing out a harsh and overdone accent.

"Say hello to my little friend," Brian said in the same accent.

"That's *Scarface,* not *Vice*," Marcus complained.

Brian splayed his big hands out on the table. "Whatever," he grumbled under his breath. A part of Kim felt bad for Brian—the other guys always seemed to find fault with him. But she also disliked the way his eyes roamed her body with a hungry abandon, darting away long after she'd already noticed, as though he thought it didn't count as long as he shifted his gaze *eventually*.

But in the meantime, Dean seemed not to notice Kim's hand on his thigh as he stared across the table, almost disbelieving what he witnessed as Jay put his milk straw to the table and proceeded to snort the powdered Smarties.

"One hunnert percent pure...," Jay started, then cracked into his normal voice as he howled, "Oh my God! That *burns!*"

With a shriek, Jay jumped up from his seat, hopping up and down, shaking his head with animal ferocity. Marcus and Brian and Dean were no help, giggling and chortling at the sight before them. Even Antoine, who usually seemed so reasonable and stoic and responsible, had cracked a grin.

"What's going on over here?"

It was Mr. Hindon, the new school librarian. Everyone called him "Twitchy" because he was always squinting his eyes and wriggling his nose.

"We're okay," Dean assured him.

"Jay just got some bad coke," Brian said between low chuckles. "Must've been cut with rat poison."

Twitchy glanced at the white powder, then at Jay, who now executed a painful series of spastic dance steps, bouncing from table to table as he hollered in self-inflicted agony. The librarian sighed and rolled his eyes.

With Twitchy doing nothing and the whole room just watching in goggle-eyed amazement as Jay floundered around, Kim hopped up and ran to the water fountain with her bowl of soup. On the way, she dumped the soup in the trash can, then quickly rinsed it in the fountain before filling it.

With all eyes on her, she approached Jay and held the bowl out. He glared at her until she shoved it under his nose and said, "You have to flush it out."

He jammed his nose in the bowl and pinched one side closed, then drew in a harsh and blubbery breath through the open nostril. An instant later, he reared back, choking and gasping. Ropes of snot shot out of his nose, spattering into the bowl.

A thunderous round of applause went up from the collected lunchers.

Jay wiped his nose on his sleeve and turned to behold his audience. His eyes watered, swollen red like two Easter eggs set into his face, but he was grinning.

"Cocaine is the best!" he shouted to even more earsplitting applause.

Twitchy blew the whistle he wore around his neck as lunchroom proctor, and eventually everyone calmed down. Jay returned to the table and a welter of back slapping and handshakes, while Kim inched over to the trash can, careful not to let Jay's mucus water slosh over the edges of the bowl and onto her hand.

She had just dumped the bowl into the garbage when she became aware of someone standing near her. Turning, she beheld what had to be a freshman—upper-lip peach fuzz and pre–growth spurt height.

"Excuse me," he said to her, very earnestly, "but I wanted you to know that we took a vote…"

Here he gestured to a table nearby, where a group of similar freshmen waved happily to her.

"…and we think you have the best ass in this entire school," he finished, nodding very soberly.

He was a pimply little nothing, and she smiled at him and thanked him. Her pants felt even tighter, as though they'd spontaneously shrunk a size in the moment. She waved weakly to the table and offered a little smile—the boys there went wild.

She walked back to her table, keenly aware of the eyes like hands on her rear. She knew she should have been bothered by it, but all she could think was *I wish Dean would do something about it.*

**18**

# THE PRESENT: ELAYAH

Elayah pulled back the living room curtain and looked out to the driveway and the sidewalk. A group of reporters had gathered there as though they were waiting in line for the new iPhone.

Dad was getting ready to pull a double shift. There had been a plan: Since the doctors didn't want Elayah back in school yet, Mom was going to take Elayah to work with her. Elayah had protested this scheme but had lost out. She knew Mom needed to go back to work, and she also knew that there was no way in the world her parents were ready to let her stay home alone.

"People got nothing better to do?" Dad grunted.

The story of Elayah, of the time capsule, of the attack, had gone national and stayed national. Even though the podcast had started without any sort of comment from Elayah, she still received DMs from Indira at NPR, increasingly chirpy and insistent at the same time. And every day brought new people to town, like the self-styled "social investigator" she'd discovered in her Insta mentions, a white lady in her fifties who claimed to be able to solve crimes by "analyzing sociological data and extrapolating from known factors to arrive at unknowns."

Whatever *that* meant, she was in Canterstown, poking around, along with more like her.

"This is ridiculous," Dad growled. "Should have bought that gun. Mom talked me out of it...."

Her dad, she realized suddenly, was getting older. Her parents had a tendency to stop everything and hold her at arm's length, rhapsodizing about how big she was, how mature, how much older. This had been going on as long as she could remember, to the point that she wondered what exactly about parenthood caused the very specific brain damage that made parents forget that kids were *supposed* to get older, more mature, etc., and why should that be a surprise?

But truly surprising was noticing in the opposite direction, gazing at her father and beholding the tight gray coils scattered in among the black hair cropped close to his skull. The threads of silver along his sideburns and even speckled in his stubble on days—like today—when he did not shave.

*Black don't crack*, but there were signs of aging beyond the superficial. Her father's eyes seemed tired. His gait was slower.

Her dad had never seemed so old to her. She knew that the world moved on and that people aged and that people died. But her dad was just barely over fifty, which seemed both ineffably old and wholly young at the same time. He'd changed so little in the years since she'd become truly aware of him as a person, as a human being separate from herself. Photos of the two of them when she was a baby told the story—Marcus Laird had aged well, if at all, since the birth of his only child. In her more mordantly humorous moments, Elayah wondered whether somewhere in Mexico, Uncle Antoine was aging twice as fast, a surreal twin-centric version of *The Picture of Dorian Gray*.

But now...

"It'll be okay, Dad," she promised him. She both feared and yearned for a gun in the house.

Her dad had to go to work. Her mom was on the phone, explaining the situation to her boss. The reporters had spooked her folks, so now Mom would stay home with Elayah. Again. She could tell from Mom's tone of voice that her boss was being compassionate, but that the well of kindness was running dry. This couldn't go on forever. Her teachers were emailing assignments and lecture notes, but at some point, life had to start again.

She checked her phone. In and among the strangers commenting about and to her, the new folks trying to slide into her DMs, she caught messages from people she actually knew, kids at school.

**is @elayahlairdrox ever coming back to school?**

**I heard she still can't talk**

**news says she's "under watch"**

**what does that mean?**

**it means she's not over watch** 🙄

**I would never go out in public again just stay in my bed forever**

**lol she got STABBED IN BED you doofus!!!** 🤭🔪🛏️

Elayah bristled at that one. She scrolled back in her own feed. The last thing she'd posted to Insta had been a screen grab of the *Loco*'s front page with the very first—innocent, anodyne—story and tags that read #almostfamous and #frontpage.

Now, as her parents huddled behind her, discussing, she made her way into the garage, where the stuff from the time capsule still lay out on the tarp as she'd left it the other night. A part of her was surprised to see it, surprised that the police hadn't take it all as evidence.

She held her phone out to catch herself at arm's length. The photo looked not quite as dramatic as she'd hoped. She appeared wan and ashy, the stitching at her neck a bright purple against her skin. The lighting in the garage left much to be desired.

Without allowing herself any time to think, she posted it to Insta: **Still here #nofilter**

# LIAM

Pop had gone back to sleep after waking to make breakfast and coffee for Dad, as always.

*I don't trust Dad with the bean grinder*, he'd confided to Liam once. *He overgrinds.*

He'd enunciated *overgrinds* with a note of sheer horror in his voice.

As he knotted his tie in the living room mirror, Dad kept an eye on a YouTube clip of some conspiracy theorist explaining how "the Canterstown time capsule is just the beginning; the wrath of the eighties is coming!"

Dad practically snarled at the laptop. "This kind of crap doesn't help. It lures crazy and desperate people out of the woodwork. Sends a bunch of false clues and bad leads flying around. I mean, what the f…" He drifted off, as though just remembering that Liam was in the room.

"Dad, I know the *F* word," Liam grumbled. "I know both of them, actually."

Dad snorted. "Okay, well, let me know when you learn the third one. That's when you can start using them."

"There's a *third*…?" Liam stammered, perplexed as Dad headed back into the kitchen to top off the coffee tank. A burble of laughter told him he'd been punked.

When he emerged from the kitchen, mug steaming once more, Dad gave Liam's black eye another once-over, then left for the office. Liam had at least ten minutes before he had to bolt for school. He fired off a text in the group thread he had with Jorja, Marcie, and El.

**u guys see some of this crazy stuff?**

Marcie came back almost instantly: **your dad must be** 🤖

Jorja: **twitter says reporters still at school too**

El just sent a picture from her front yard. Liam inhaled deeply at the sight. Reporters at school, reporters at El's…

**this is what you get for dropping a surprise album**, he texted.

😂 😂 😂 said El, and Liam felt good.

# ELAYAH

Marcie had a job three days a week after school at a place in Finn's Landing called Boogie Woogie. It was one of those indoor playgrounds for little kids, and there was an entire preschool's worth there that afternoon. Something like thirty four-year-olds and some younger siblings capering and screaming as they flopped on bouncy houses, slid down slides, and chased one another from the vending machines to the restrooms and back again. Marcie rode herd on it all with nothing more than a whistle and her voice.

It was almost impossible to overhear them, Elayah thought, given the yelling kids and the hum of the inflatables. Not a bad place to conspire.

She had been manic all day, eager to hear from Liam about his 💀 ❓ night at SAMMPark. Being trapped at home while the others were at school had been torture. She still couldn't believe her mother had finally capitulated and let her out of the house, but Elayah's cabin fever was obvious and completely sincere. Mom recognized that. Besides, what could happen to her at Boogie Woogie? Collision on the inflated slide?

"Tell us about last night," Elayah implored Liam.

"What happened last night?" Marcie asked, then blew her whistle and pointed. "Hey! Down the slides on your *tush*, not your stomach!"

"And does it have to do with that shiner Liam has refused to talk about all day?" Jorja narrowed her eyes until she looked like the squinting emoji.

Liam shrugged and told them all the whole story, beginning with Elayah's Insta DM and ending with his joke to his dads that morning about a masturbation injury.

As he spoke, Marcie and Jorja both widened their eyes like owls on speed. Marcie had to divert her attention to a cluster of kids who were trying to fit their heads into the push-open drawer in one of the vending machines, but when she returned, she went right back to looking over at Jorja with disbelief etched into every line of her face.

Elayah gnawed at her lower lip. Yes, she had known that her plan with

Liam had been stupid and foolhardy, but she didn't realize it was *so* stupid and foolhardy.

"You weren't supposed to *fight* the guy," she admonished Liam when he finished.

"That part just sort of happened," Liam said. "But look, the good news is that it wasn't any of our parents. I got a good look at the dude—he was, like, in his late twenties, early thirties. Blond. No beard. Never seen him before. Not a parent. Not a friend of a parent."

"He could be an accomplice," Elayah said.

"You think our parents have accomplices?" Liam recoiled as though he'd just touched an electric fence. "We're not talking master criminals here. After thirty-some years, one of them has a henchman sitting around, just in case?"

"Think it through," Jorja said, arms crossed over her chest. "The accomplice wouldn't have to know anything. You can just go on Craigslist or TaskRabbit and hire someone to go to the park at night and pick up a package."

"Can we get back to how ridiculous this was?" Marcie asked. "I mean, I get Liam doing something this impetuous, but El? Come on! And—hey!"

Marcie excused herself to go tend to a group of kids who'd hit on the bright idea of lifting up a friend and throwing him over an inflatable barrier into a bouncy house. This had disaster written all over it, even to Elayah's unpracticed eye.

"Any other surprises for us?" Jorja asked while she was gone.

Elayah hesitated before speaking up. She still wasn't 100 percent certain she'd actually seen someone lurking out in the backyard. Even bringing it up risked making it real, as though she could conjure a nightmare into the waking world just by recalling it.

But these were her friends. Her *best* friends.

Jorja's expression turned from annoyed outrage to puzzled consternation when Elayah told them about the shadowy figure. Marcie returned, caught the gist, and took her hand.

"What time was this?" Marcie asked without even looking over at her. She was scanning the room for further toddler crimes in progress.

"Twelve thirty–ish." She checked her phone and scrolled to see what time Liam's text came in and woke her. "Twelve thirty-seven, to be exact."

"It couldn't be the same guy, then," Jorja mused. "You fought him at a little past midnight, right, Li?"

"Yeah."

"There's no way to get from the statue to the street and then to El's in a half hour." Jorja seemed sure of it.

Elayah was less certain. "It's only twenty minutes to the park. If he ran to his car after the fight..."

"And then scaled your fence?" Marcie sounded doubtful, taking Jorja's side. "It's awful tight."

Liam cleared his throat. "El, you're not even sure you actually saw someone, right?"

Had she? Elayah replayed the moments in her mind, but found nothing new or dispositive in her recollection. It had been late. She'd been both exhausted and amped at the same time.

When she didn't answer right away, Liam went on: "You know what it probably was? Some reporter, scoping out the house, looking for a good photo. Something like that. I can tell my dad—he's been pretty tough about making sure the press doesn't cross property lines."

"Don't say anything," Elayah replied quickly and a little more sharply than she'd intended.

With an eye roll, Liam said, "Is this more of the *I don't trust—*"

"No. But like you said, I'm not sure I saw anything. So why make an issue of it?"

Jorja leaned against an inflatable slide, stumbled, managed to avoid falling down entirely. "Because we're all sort of losing our minds? Not sure how to talk to our parents?"

It was a rare admission of vulnerability from Jorja. Elayah shot a glance over to Liam, expecting him to do one of those brotherly shoulder strokes or something like that. But before he could even move toward Jorja, Marcie—Marcie!—put an arm around Jorja's shoulders and hugged her briefly.

"My dad called last night," Marcie said quietly. "He calls once or twice a week. And I could barely talk to him. I just kept thinking, *Was it you? Did you hurt someone?*"

"Or are you covering up for someone who did?" Jorja asked it not rhetorically and not even aimed at Marcie. She clearly—miserably—was thinking it, too. About her father.

Elayah's phone vibrated for her attention. Probably her mom, checking up for the umpteenth time.

"Excuse me," a somewhat harried mom said, approaching Marcie. "My little guy went up the slide there and is afraid to come down. Could you...?"

Marcie nodded and smiled and went off to retrieve the kid. Elayah hauled out her phone to assuage Mom and froze at what she saw.

**Let's try it a different way this time.**

# 1986: DEAN

Scratching away with a pen on a sheet of flimsy airmail stationery on a Friday night, Dean occasionally stopped to consult the English-Spanish dictionary he had open on his desk:

*How is your sister?*

*¿Cómo está tu hermana?*

*The weather has been very nice here. How is it there?*

*El clima ha sido muy agradable aquí. ¿Cómo está allí?*

"What are you doing?"

Dean startled, almost ripping the thin paper beneath his pen. Jay had materialized from nowhere and now leaned against the doorframe leading into Dean's bedroom. Dean hadn't even heard the doorbell ring.

"I'm writing to my pen pal," he told Jay.

"You have a pen pal?" Jay's tone folded astonishment and disgust into a single question.

"So do you," Dean snapped back. "The one we were assigned in Spanish."

Jay gaped at him. "From last year, you mean? You're *still* writing to him? Wow!"

"I actually like Pedro," he told Jay without a hint of the shame he knew his friend sought. "We both like comics."

Jay shrugged as though disappointed in the answer but satisfied with the tone. "I never even wrote to mine. He sent me a letter, but I never read it. It was just a stupid extra-credit assignment. How was she going to know we did it—follow us to the post office and watch us mail each letter?"

At that, Dean tossed the pen across the desk, letting it roll until it fetched up against the bulk of his chemistry textbook. Jay lived life by one credo, which—boiled down to its essence—was *Don't do anything that's inconvenient or not fun.* The rest of the world didn't work that way, but Jay was smart enough, his parents permissive enough, that he could get away with it.

"Whatever. I'll finish it later. Let's go."


Friday nights, Jay made the rounds, starting at Dean's house—Dean always rode shotgun; he'd known Jay the longest—then circling around to pick up the twins, then getting Brian last. Bri always bitched about being the last to be picked up and having to cram into the back seat. Jay and Marcus took turns mimicking his discontent until he finally shut up.

With the start of the new season, they'd recently enacted a new ritual for Fridays: heading to Jay's for *Miami Vice.* This way, they could figure out the winner of the death pool in the moment. Jay's parents had converted their garage into a huge TV room, with a massive fifty-inch reverse-projection TV taking up half a wall, external speakers, and a semicircular sofa. They would load up on bags of chips, soda, and a bowl of M&M's, then watch *Vice* and keep careful count of the bodies.

When the show ended at ten—and they doled out the contents of the pot to the winner—the night stretched out before them. Jay, the oldest of them all, had his full adult driver's license, plus his own car, so he was the permanent driver for the group. They could pool a few bucks to defray Jay's gas costs, then spend the night in his car, going wherever they wanted, doing whatever they wanted.

Regardless of their final plans, though, they always—*always*—had to be in the car at midnight for the weekly "In-A-Gadda-Da-Vida" on WKOR, "the station that rocks backward!"

Now Jay piloted them around Canterstown, cruising up the main drag to the factory, which hovered into view as they crested a hill. The Wantzler factory anchored the horizon, its black bulk a stamp on the purple-blue night sky. There were no windows—or at least very few—so it gave off no light, only glowed at its base from the lights in the employee parking lot. The factory ran twenty-four hours a day to meet demand, its smokestacks purling gray against the sunless sky, disgorging new clouds like sacrificial offerings. Everyone in the town was connected to the factory in some way or another. When not running the board of ed—a part-time job if ever there was one, apparently—Jay's father was an engineer who designed the machines Wantzler used to manufacture cassettes. Brian's mother was secretary to the factory's director of operations. Dean's dad worked down in Baltimore but had spent six years as some sort of director for Wantzler.

"We could drive around the parking lot at the factory and see how long it takes for Fatso to run us off," Brian suggested.

*Fatso* was Martin Fratelli, two years their senior, and a former heavyweight wrestling champ in high school. He'd never managed the transition to college and had remained in Canterstown, where his great muscular bulk had managed a different sort of transition, settling around his waist. He worked nighttime security at the factory.

"Nah," said Marcus. "Pops is working night shift this week. I don't need the hassle."

The twins' dad was a shift supervisor. Possessed of a keen sense of justice and fairness, Mr. Laird felt compelled to assign himself the worst shift at least once a month as a show of solidarity with those under him.

"Then what?" Jay complained. When Jay had a task to focus on, there was no one better to have on your side—he was dedicated, brutally efficient, and utterly unmovable from the path to his target.

But when Jay had no target in his sights, boredom swamped him quickly and easily, drenching him in fractiousness and puckishness. Bored, distractible Jay was the worst kind. Most of the trouble Dean had gotten into in his life was the result of something into which Jay had dragooned him while in the throes of desperate ennui.

Brian tried again. "I heard Jenny Miller is having a sleepover with a bunch of the girls from drama club."

Marcus groaned. "If you say the words *panty raid*, I'm gonna kick you out of the car."

"I just—"

"It's not like in the movies!" Marcus yelled.

Dean sighed. Marcus and Brian argued about this all the time. Brian insisted that girls' sleepovers were like the one in *Animal House*, and Marcus swore up and down that they were just a bunch of girls sitting around in pajamas with junk on their faces, eating ice cream and listening to old David Cassidy records.

Before the argument could get too heated, Dean jumped in. "I have an idea," he said quickly. "It's a little weird, though."

When no one objected to *a little weird*, he went on: "Wouldn't it be weird to follow a pizza-delivery guy all night?"

"You mean, call for a pizza, then follow him back to the house?" Marcus said. "That sounds lame."

"No," Dean told him. "I mean just follow him everywhere he goes, all night long."

Flipping down the visor, Dean used the vanity mirror to check out the back seat reaction. Antoine had mastered the art of turning a shrug into a facial expression. Marcus looked somewhat doubtful. Brian appeared nonplussed.

But it was Jay's car, and all that mattered was Jay's opinion. With a curt, triumphant nod, Jay flipped a uey in the middle of Founders Street. It was late Friday night and there was no traffic in either direction, but the guys in the back seat still yelped in mingled and joint outrage and surprise. Dean grabbed for the armrest and held on for dear life.

Moments later, they were parked—lights off—in a small lot just off Center Street. Before them lay a three-store "shopping center" that included a (closed for the evening) dry cleaner, a (closed for the evening) optician, and Nico's Pizza, one of three pizzerias in Canterstown and the only one that delivered.

"Who farted?" Marcus demanded.

A brief argument ensued, ending when Jay cranked down his window a couple of inches to let in some fresh air.

"This is boring," Brian suggested a few silent moments later. Marcus grunted in agreement, and Antoine actually deigned to speak: "I agree."

"It won't be," Jay promised with an air of absolute, impossible, and unearned conviction.

Quite against every rational impulse he possessed, Dean believed Jay. He didn't know why. Jay sweated confidence, emitted it like radiation, glowed with it. His persuasive powers were natural and reflexive and difficult to combat.

Soon someone emerged from Nico's bearing a thermal pizza pouch. He was in his twenties, lanky, with a scruffy beard and a faded red Nico's ball cap perched on his head. He climbed into a slightly battered, late-model blue Datsun and pulled out of the parking lot.

After a pregnant pause, Jay cranked his Chevette's engine and followed.

Dean leaned forward in anticipation. In anticipation of precisely *what* he could not identify, but he figured something would happen. Something interesting.

No commentary drifted forward from the back seat. The peanut gallery, for now, remained silent.

Jay proved to be an excellent tail; he kept a couple of car lengths back, following almost lazily as the pizza guy cruised up Center. When he signaled left to turn onto Grady Street, Jay waited until he'd completed his turn and could no longer see the Chevette in the rearview before signaling his own turn.

When they came around the corner, though, Jay nearly slammed on the brakes. The Datsun was parked only a few yards in from the corner, its lights still on, sidled up against the curb at the foot of a shallow slope that led to a well-lit Victorian. The guys in the back seat shouted in surprise, but Jay recovered well and simply kept going, as though he'd always intended to chug down Grady.

"That's Brad Gimble's house," Dean said.

"Gimble the Dimble," Marcus offered.

"Gimbo el Dimbo," Brian added.

"Gimble the Simple," Antoine said into a moment of silence, a slight upturn to the corner of his mouth.

It wasn't a perfect rhyme, but it was still *perfect* and they all laughed.

As they passed the Datsun, the pizza guy climbed out and leaned in for his pizza, oblivious to them.

"Boooooring!" Brian chanted as Gimble's house shrank in their rearview.

"Where's the beef?" Marcus demanded in an aggrieved, elderly falsetto.

"It'll get better," said Jay. "I promise."

*How did* he *know?* Dean wondered. This whole stupid idea had been

Dean's stupid idea, and he hadn't even been entirely certain what he hoped would come of it. But now Jay had taken ownership of the notion. Which was good because the heat was off Dean to make it something interesting. But also bad because Jay had no boundaries and tended to take things too far.

Jay hung a left at the next intersection and drove straight back to Nico's. They beat the delivery guy—probably haggling over his tip—and parked in the darkest part of the tiny lot.

A few minutes later, the delivery guy returned, parked at the front door, and ambled inside.

It was twenty after ten.

Nico's business must have centered primarily on late-nighters, because starting about fifteen minutes later, the delivery guy bolted out the door, commencing an hour-long burst of activity. He started stacking up the orders, hustling three and four of them at the same time. Nico's had a thirty-minutes-or-it's-free guarantee, so he leadfooted it through the dark streets.

The guys followed him each time. Against all odds and against every conceivable likelihood, the night became fun and somewhat exciting. Jay used the sparse traffic to hide, playing an automotive game of cat and mouse. He'd let the delivery guy get far enough ahead that the others thought they were sure to lose him, then suddenly pull around a car and make a turn and—*mirabile dictu!*—there was the Datsun, chugging along.

They wove a complex skein through the streets of Canterstown that night, from the factory-adjacent near-shanties all the way up into the winding hills over town, where the private school kids lived their manicured-lawn lives. Sometimes they'd trail him back to Nico's; other times they'd peel off early and get back to the parking lot before him, to lie in wait.

Right up until eleven, he was consistently busy. He rarely even turned off the car upon his return to Nico's, leaving the keys in the ignition and the engine running as he dashed in, then careened back out with an armload of pizzas, subs, cans of soda.

Nico's closed at midnight on the weekends, and by a few minutes after eleven, things slowed down. The guys followed him on a lazy, twisty route through the hills over town, back behind the high school. They were the only two cars on the road, so Jay was hanging back, though not as far back as Dean would have liked.

The radio blared. Bruce Cockburn sang about the rocket launcher he wanted.

"'...*had a rocket launcher,*'" the guys sang along, "'*some son of a bitch would...!*'"

Jay punctuated the word *die* with a bash on the steering wheel. Dean's heart skipped a beat, then double-timed as he realized how close Jay had come to hitting the horn.

The delivery guy pulled over to the curb at a smallish Tudor house. He had a single pizza and three Cokes, attached to each other by a six-pack's plastic loops, which he dangled from his free hand as he bounded to the door.

"Hey, this is Lisa McKenzie's house," said Brian, cupping imaginary breasts before him.

An appreciative sigh filled the car. Jay coasted to a stop two houses away and killed his headlights.

The delivery guy spent a moment at the door with someone who was not Lisa McKenzie, but who appeared to be her equally well-endowed mother. Then, tucking some bills into his pocket, he ambled back to his car.

"This is officially getting boring," Brian said. "Are we done?"

Dean opened his mouth to agree with Brian, but just then the pizza guy pushed off the curb, did a *Dukes of Hazzard*–style dive into his car and peeled wheels, blasting away from the curb and hurtling over the rise and down a hill, out of their sight.

"What the—" Dean didn't get the sentence out. Jay floored it and hit his headlights.

"What are you doing?" Marcus cried from the back seat, crushed between his brother and Brian as the car twisted around a bend. The delivery guy's taillights pricked the darkness too far ahead.

"Slow down!" Dean yelled. The roads back here juked and jived like a sleeping cat's twitching tail.

"Gotta catch him," Jay said.

"We know where he's going!" Brian yelled.

They emerged to a streetlight-lit intersection. The light turned red as they approached. Dean was certain that Jay was going to blow through it, but at the last possible instant, he slammed on the brakes, shrieking to a smoky, squealing stop at the line. In the distance, the Datsun's taillights winkled once, then disappeared from sight.

"Damn!" Jay punched the dashboard.

"I think he knows," Dean said.

"Game over," Marcus called from the back seat.

"Over?" Jay's knuckles whitened on the steering wheel as he waited for the light to change. "Since when?"

"He caught us," Brian offered. "It's over."

"Says who?" Jay jumped the light by a half second, blasting through the intersection just as the light turned green overhead.

"No one wants to get in trouble," Marcus cautioned.

"No one's getting in trouble," Jay assured him. "He doesn't know who we are. All he's seen is our headlights in his rearview."

That was a good point. Back at Lisa McKenzie's house, they'd been half a block away in the pitch dark. The pizza-delivery guy might have an idea of the general size and contours of the car, but otherwise he knew nothing. He certainly couldn't have discerned the license plate or even the make and model. And the rest of the night, all he'd've seen would've been Jay's lights.

"Let's head down to Finn's Landing," Brian offered. "There's that one place that stays open late. We could get some smokes."

Dean didn't really smoke—every now and then a hit off a joint Brian purloined from his mom's stash—but that sounded a lot better than continuing the pizza game.

"I could go for a Coke," Marcus chimed in.

"Better than sitting around here," Brian said.

A general murmur of agreement clouded the confines of the Chevette as they returned to the center of town. But Jay shook his head. "No. Not yet."

The four others all groaned audibly as Jay pulled into the Nico's parking lot. The Datsun was parked at a slight angle before the store, its lights dead.

"What are we doing back here?" Marcus said ominously.

"Jay. Come on." Brian shifted uncomfortably in the back seat.

"Bad idea," Antoine advised. The car fell silent in the aftermath of a rare Antoine pronouncement.

But Dean was riding shotgun and had known Jay the longest. It fell to him.

"This is getting boring," Dean said. There was no sense appealing to Jay's sense of self-preservation—he had none. He feared neither physical harm nor punishment of any variety. But he lived in total terror of being considered dull or uninteresting.

"We're almost done," said Jay, gripping the wheel. He'd cut the lights but left the engine idling.

In the back seat, Brian clucked his tongue irritably.

"We're almost done," Dean said soothingly. "Everything's okay." If Brian lost his temper, it would take them forever to settle him down. He was slow to anger, but once the rage hit, it hit hard.

It was closing in on midnight. Dean reasoned that there was an excellent chance that they were already done, but even as he thought it, the world proved him wrong. The delivery guy ambled out of the pizzeria with an overstuffed thermal bag and a two-liter Diet Coke tucked under his arm.

The Datsun backed out of its spot, executed a three-point turn, then drifted past the Chevette as it prepared to turn out onto the street.

At the exact moment the driver was about to turn, Jay flipped on his headlights, pinning the driver's side of the Datsun in bright light. Thrown into stark contrast with the surrounding dark, they all got a good look at the driver as he raised one hand to shield his eyes, his face twisted into anger and shock.

"What are you doing?" Dean punched Jay in the shoulder to get his attention, but Jay only leaned forward over his steering wheel, staring straight ahead.

The delivery guy had been halfway into his turn and had no choice but to commit. He turned out of the cones of light Jay had thrown on him and went up Center. Jay floored it, tearing off after him, barely checking his mirrors as he pulled out onto the road.

Marcus swore loudly and profoundly in the back seat. "What are you *doing*, man?"

"I said: We're almost done." Jay spoke through gritted teeth. Dean wondered how stupid it would be to open his door and roll out of the car like Remo Williams.

*How stupid? Try, like,* totally *stupid,* Dean thought in his sister's Valley-est of Val-speak.

"Hang on...." Jay muttered, almost as though he resented needing to say it.

To keep up with the delivery guy, who had just executed a perfect right turn onto Bay Street, Jay had to tap the brake and spin the wheel hand over hand. Dean winced with the g-forces, and Antoine yelled out in protest as his twin and Brian crushed him against the inside of the door.

"Just pull over!" Dean pleaded. "Come on, Jay!"

But Jay had already hit Bay and floored it in order to catch up to the Datsun, which now was definitely exceeding the paltry twenty-five-mile-per-hour limit posted on Bay Street. The road twisted like a phone cord, and in a moment the Datsun's lights disappeared around a corner.

Jay took the corner at forty, this time throwing Antoine and Marcus into a howling Brian. Dean's head thunked against the passenger-side window.

"Jay!" Dean cried out. "Just *stop it!*"

Bay rose into a series of hills and turns like a spiral staircase, becoming Gill Drive. They'd caught up to within sight distance of the Datsun, which outpaced them, taking the corners with aplomb. Dean thought of Steve McQueen in *Bullitt* and grasped for the handhold in the armrest, holding on for dear life as he braced with his other hand against the dashboard. Jay clearly wasn't going to stop until he'd . . .

Until he'd what? Dean thought he knew: This would be the last delivery run of the night, and having started this whole mess, Jay was constitutionally and psychologically incapable of letting it go until the delivery guy clocked out and went home. Come hell or high water, Jay would see that last delivery.

And then what? Follow the guy home? One last menacing cruise before calling it a night?

*I thought this would be stupid,* Dean thought. *I was right. I just didn't know how.*

"Slow down," he pleaded. "Just a little."

Over a sharp rise, the Chevette actually left the road for an instant. Groans exploded from the back seat, and Dean's stomach lurched with that weightless, almost-but-not-quite-diarrhea sensation.

From here, Gill became a series of not-at-all-gentle turns wending down the hillside toward Grove Road. The Datsun accelerated into a curve ahead of them, disappearing from view.

Jay gunned it as he took the curve. The back seat boys crushed poor Antoine again. Dean, well-braced, managed to stay in place.

"Holy—!" he exploded as they came around the bend.

They were practically atop the Datsun, which had slowed once taking the curve. Jay slammed on his brakes as the Datsun crept forward ahead of them. The high-speed chase had suddenly become super slow. They inched along at something like fifteen miles an hour, no more than a car length behind.

"What's he *doing*?" Brian asked.

Dean was wondering the same thing. The hair on his neck erected. He didn't like this. "Go around him," he told Jay.

"Dean's right," Marcus vouched from the back. "This ain't good."

But Jay couldn't be dissuaded. His stubbornness had always overridden any common sense, and tonight was no exception. Despite the chorus from the back seat and the passenger seat, he grinned and turned up the radio. AC/DC offered up dirty deeds, done dirt cheap.

The Datsun slowed even more. Jay softly goosed his brake, keeping a car length behind.

Brian started cussing. A lot. Dean had never heard him cuss so much.

"Take out your tampon," Jay snapped over his shoulder. "It'll be fine."

Before Brian could retort, Dean slapped Jay's arm to get his attention and pointed through the windshield.

The Datsun had stopped. Pulled over in front of a dark house.

Jay braked, stopping in the middle of Gill, the nose of his Chevette pointed down toward town.

"Now what?" Brian's voice foamed with injury and satisfied anger.

"I don't—"

Jay broke off suddenly as the driver's side door to the Datsun opened. The delivery guy hopped out of the car, bearing a baseball bat. He slammed the door and bounced on his toes in the middle of the street, waving threateningly with the bat.

"Come on!" he yelled. "Come on!"

Jay started to giggle. It was contagious—Dean found himself chuckling, too. The three in back hadn't caught the disease yet.

"Get. Out. Of. Here." Antoine.

"You wanna mess around?" the delivery guy shouted, brandishing the bat. "Get out of the car, you pussy!"

He took a step toward the car. Dean wondered if he could read the license plate. The guy didn't seem to be in a state of mind to memorize a string of letters and numbers, in any event.

While it felt risky to tear his gaze away from the man with the bat, Dean knew that he had to check in on Jay. When he looked over at his friend, though, Jay was half-bent away from him, scrabbling under the driver's seat. A moment later, his left hand came up bearing a long hunting knife.

"Jay!" Dean yelped. "Man!"

"Jesus!" Marcus swore from the back seat. "Put that away!"

"Jay..." It was Antoine. And, wow, had they heard a lot from *him* that night. "Don't be foolish."

"This is just so he knows we're serious." Jay's words were calm and rational, but his expression rode the line between chaos and passivity.

The three in the back could only hear him—Dean could see, too. "Jay, man, let's not get out of control."

The delivery guy took a couple of more steps closer, his baseball bat now clutched in both hands, swinging back and forth.

"Hit your brights," Dean blurted out.

Jay, for a miracle, listened, clicking his high beams on. The delivery guy staggered, caught in the intense glow. He released the bat with one hand, shielding his eyes.

"You want me?" the guy shouted. "Come *get* me!"

Dean's eyes flicked from the knife to the bat. And he was keenly aware that the only thing keeping them from running this guy over was the fact that Jay's left foot was still on the brake.

"The coolest thing in the world," Dean said, each word falling into place without a moment's thought or consideration, "would be to peel out backward and do a bootlegger's turn."

Jay's eyes—squinted, narrowed, fixated on the delivery guy—widened in recognition and delight.

The delivery guy trotted forward a couple of more steps. Too close now. Too damn close...

And then Jay threw the Chevette into reverse and slammed on the gas. With a high-pitched howl, the car leapt backward, scooting up Gill.

The delivery guy jumped back, stumbled, fell to the ground, dropping his bat. Jay hooted laughter. He turned in his seat, craning his neck to check through the rear window, his knife hand the only one on the wheel. As they neared the crest of Gill, he cranked the wheel left and the Chevette spun drunkenly, its rear wheels bumping up onto a nearby curb.

"What the hell was *that?*" Now that they were out of danger, Brian was annoyed.

"Hang on," Jay mumbled. He shifted into drive and stomped on the gas. The car bounced forward, the rear wheels ripping the grass strip between the curb and sidewalk to shreds. Then the car was oriented properly, heading up Gill and back toward Bay. Jay was leadfooting it again, channeling his best Duke cousin, but Dean couldn't help checking the side mirror. There was nothing there but blackness.

"You think he'll follow us?" Marcus asked, voicing Dean's unspoken worry.

As if to answer, Jay tugged the wheel, turning them onto a minor residential street, then wove an intricate pattern of lefts and rights down random roads until they found themselves spat out onto Center near the county line.

If the delivery guy had been inclined to turn the cat and mouse game on its head—to make Jerry into Tom, as it were—then he'd've had a tough time figuring out where they went. There'd been no headlights behind them, so Dean decided they were safe.

Unless Jay decided to . . .

But no. He was driving north along Center, the opposite direction of Nico's.

They drove without speaking for a few minutes, listening to Rowdy Randy, the nighttime DJ on WKOR, as he mocked a 7-Eleven cashier who'd called in.

And then Jay dropped his knife back under his seat and sucked at his palm. "Nicked myself when I turned the wheel," he explained, very mildly.

"You all right?" Dean asked.

Jay held up his hand. A long scratch ran in a straight line down his palm. "It's fine. It's not even midnight. What now?"


They drove down to Finn's Landing and found an open convenience store. Everyone loaded up on chips and sodas. Brian ambled back toward the magazine section and stared at *Sports Illustrated* for a long time.

"We're ready!" Jay hollered to Brian.

"Give me a minute!" Brian hollered back.

They bought their junk and went out to the parking lot, loitering against the car as they peeled open bags of chips and popped soda-can tops.

"What's the deal with the knife, Jay?" Marcus asked, almost casually.

Jay shrugged. "Just in case."

"That's like my deer knife," Dean told him. "You think you're gonna have to..."

Jay, ignoring him, got in the car and cranked the engine. Music bubbled out from the open windows. Dire Straits, playing "Money for Nothing." Jay and Marcus duetted in a high falsetto, singing, "*I want my! I want my! I want my MTV!*"

Dean blocked it out. He hated this song. A few moments later, Brian emerged bearing a gigantic soda, a pack of Twizzlers, and a flat paper bag.

"What did you buy?" Marcus asked as Brian slid into the back seat, pushing the twins closer together. "I bet it's *Playboy*."

"More like *Playgirl*," Jay taunted, to general laughter.

"Shut up," Brian told them, struggling momentarily with Marcus, who half-heartedly tugged at the paper bag.

"I want to see what turns on gay guys!" Marcus laughed as he spoke. "Come on!"

"Get off!" Brian finally shoved Marcus in the shoulder and tucked the bag between himself and the car door for safety.

"'You can hang out with a gay person,'" Marcus said in his best Eddie Murphy impression, which was quite good. "'You can play tennis with a gay—'"

"'I kid the homosexuals a lot,'" Dean broke in, in a not-nearly-as-good Murphy. "'Because they're homosexuals.'"

Jay gunned the engine. Rowdy Randy scratched a record and played a fanfare and announced, "Your Friday night 'In-A-Gadda-Da-Vida'!" to much hooting and hollering in the car. Even Antoine perked up considerably and actually smiled as the song's bass guitar cranked through the first few thumping bars.

Dean allowed himself a small smile and gazed out the window as the familiar song pounded at his ears. Everything was perfect.

Wasn't it?

# 20

# THE PRESENT: LIAM

**Let's try it a different way this time**, the message began. It was, of course, from another burner account. **Everyone wins.**

Boogie Woogie was clearing out as dinnertime neared. Fish sticks and chicken nuggets were in high demand from the masses of kids exiting the building. Marcie had to clean and disinfect the playing surfaces, but she listened as El read them the message.

It went on to promise $5,000 in cash in exchange for "items in your possession." He even went so far as to say that El could choose the meeting place and time.

"This is a man who's willing to deal," Jorja mused.

"This'll go faster with some help," Marcie pointed out, brandishing a canister of bleach wipes.

They all pitched in, wiping down every visible surface as they discussed the message.

"How much is $5,000, really?" Marcie asked. "Don't get me wrong—I'd love to have $5,000. But is that really a fair trade for helping someone get away with murder?"

"We're not actually going to do this," Liam reminded her. "We don't even have the knife."

"Yeah, but what happens when we don't?" El asked. "First he came to my house and tried to take it from me. Then he tried to get me to give it up. Now he's trying to buy it. What's next? Is he going to knock down my door and threaten to shoot my mom? Or just grab me off the street one day?"

"None of that's going to happen," Liam promised, knowing he couldn't guarantee it. His voice went hollow and hard.

"What if we go on the offensive?" Jorja asked. She'd stopped wiping things. Not that she'd been doing a great job to begin with.

"Meaning what?"

"Meaning..." Jorja's face had that expression she got sometimes when she knew she was about to say something outrageous, but she planned to convince you anyway. "Meaning what if we agree to meet...but it's a trap?"


On the one hand, Jorja's idea was crazy illegal.

Which was actually a point in its favor. Liam's entire life had been rigorous instruction in right and wrong, and the notion of doing something absolutely insanely illegal sort of appealed to him.

On the other hand, though, it was dangerous and risky.

Jorja, determined to out–Stephen King Stephen King, had done some research online about hostage taking for a creepy short story she'd posted on Wattpad. (And how messed up was that? Well, at least Jorja would be the one on an FBI watch list, not Liam.)

"We wouldn't need much in the way of gear," Jorja explained. "It's actually easy to kidnap someone. We can do it with things from home for the most part. There's four of us. Liam fought the guy alone and was fine—with four of us, we can take him down, easy."

El vacillated, talking herself into and then out of it.

"I mean, I want to know what's going on here," she said, "but I don't want to hurt anyone. And I don't want to break the law."

"These people broke the law to get to you," Marcie pointed out, far more enthusiastic about the idea than Liam would have predicted. "Don't you want to finally clear this up, once and for all?"

"My dad has a Taser," Jorja told them. "I'll sneak it away, and within a couple of hours, we'll know everything. Problem solved; problem staying solved."

Ultimately, Jorja's supreme confidence and the lure of putting an end to the drama that had begun with her throat being slashed tempted El over to Jorja's side.

Which left Liam. Odd man out. As always. It was three against one, but this wasn't a pure democracy. He had a trump card to play: He could always just go tell his father what was going on.

*I'll tell my daddy!* It was his own voice, echoing from childhood. Running to tell a parent was beyond juvenile—it was cowardly.

"Okay, I'm in."

Jorja rubbed her hands together. "Great. Let's plan."

It was disturbing how easily Jorja cobbled together a kidnapping plan. It took her less than twenty-four hours. Then again, she was a writer wannabe who spent most of her time daydreaming creepy scenarios involving the ghosts of vengeful murdered wives, abused children wreaking havoc on their parents, and more. She was almost giddy at the prospect of doing it for real.

Elayah had messaged the mystery man with instructions to make the swap the next day, one hour after sunset. It would be fully dark by then.

They staked out the spot long before the sun went down. It was on the edge of town, opposite the factory about as far in the other direction as you could go and still be in Canterstown. Even so, the tips of the smokestacks peeked up over the horizon, solid black nubs jutting up from the earth, like zipper teeth missing their mates.

A two-laner of old blacktop had once been the primary conduit from the center of town to the closest highway. Shops and houses along that road commanded a premium. But then a million years ago, the Cross-County Expressway had been built, and suddenly that two-laner became obsolete. School buses still trundled along to shuttle kids from one end of town to the middle school, but other than a few locals using it when the CCE was backed up, it was typically empty. The stores had closed up, and the houses belonged to retirees and other folks who couldn't afford to move elsewhere.

They had—well, *Jorja* had—picked a spot near an old billboard that still advertised a new season of *ER* with ragged, peeling paper tiles. The lights had burned out long ago.

El and Marcie were stationed in a copse of trees with a pair of binoculars;

if things went dreadfully wrong, they would call the cops, consequences be damned.

Liam and Jorja took up positions equidistant from the billboard, lying in the tall grass. They wore all black, including balaclavas to hide their faces. Liam couldn't believe they were actually doing this. It was insane, and he nearly called it off a half dozen times.

Every time, he thought back to El in her hospital bed that night. The hitch in her breath. Every time, he sighed and settled in.

**everyone ready?**

It was Jorja. Playing general.

Marcie and El answered in the affirmative. Liam tapped out, **this cruise SUX.**

The idea was that the guy would arrive, go to the billboard, and take the package they'd tied to the post. It contained nothing more than a couple of old paperbacks, but it was just the bait. To get him into position. He was supposed to leave an envelope full of cash, but they suspected that wasn't going to happen. He would take the bait and run.

Or at least, he would *try* to run.

The sun dipped low. Liam's legs fell asleep, and he twitched to wake them up.

He dozed. He was aware he was sleeping, but he was also aware of his surroundings. The waving grass around him. The darkening sky. He thought of El, crouched in the trees with Marcie. Then he just thought of El and he turned warm.

👀 **up**

The vibration of Jorja's text shook him out of midfantasy. A low rumble sounded off to his left. He checked through the grass—a car pulled up near the billboard.

A man got out. Liam was pretty sure it was the same guy as yesterday, this time wearing jeans but the same black overcoat and black hat.

The car took off. The man waited until it had disappeared in the distance before he approached the billboard.

**now?**

**wait**, Jorja sent back.

The man stepped around the post, located the package. Liam had double-knotted it with a complicated sailor's knot he'd learned on YouTube. The man struggled with it.

**go**

Liam leapt up and charged the man. There were about ten yards between them; he covered the distance in a dozen big, loping steps, coming up on the guy's blind side.

Jorja had risen up from her hiding spot at an angle to the man and was spotted as she closed half the distance. The man uttered a wordless cry and yanked at the package, tearing it loose from the post. He probably thought he had a few seconds to pull a weapon or run.

He never saw Liam, who came up behind him and slammed into him with his shoulder, knocking him off his feet and sending him sprawling to the ground. The package flew from his hands and fell into the grass.

"Wait—!" the man exclaimed, holding up both hands, but by then Jorja was there with the Taser. She jabbed it at the guy, mistriggered. The Taser arced into the open air, and the man rolled over, kicked out.

Liam caught the foot and twisted, spinning the man over onto his stomach. Jorja straddled the guy's back and jammed the Taser into the back of his neck. A sizzling sound filled the air, and the man offered one explosive, truncated syllable of pain before slumping, unconscious.

Jorja turned to Liam, grinning. Her breath came fast, like Liam's, a series of gleefully satisfied huffs and pants. "See?" she said, brandishing the Taser. "Easy!"

**21**

# THE PRESENT: ELAYAH

Half a mile down the road, where the buildings faded into the background, only a single structure stood within sight, a ramshackle concrete cube with a faded red sign mounted above its single door.

PSYCHIC ADVICE, it read, along with a phone number that had been disconnected before any of them had been born.

For at least a hundred yards in every direction, there was nothing but overgrown grass and weeds.

For years, they'd school-bused past this building, ancient even when they were young. The jokes about a psychic going out of business flowed naturally, fast and furious like rapids. Even kids could see the irony.

This was where they took the man. Marcie had scouted out the place earlier in the day. It was empty inside, the windows papered over. Dust lay thick on the floor and on what had once been a sales counter.

There was an archway that led to a back room, but that, too, was empty. Not even ghosts haunted this place, just bad ideas.

Was this another bad idea?

She didn't know for sure.

They propped the man up against the wall, then zip-tied his wrists behind him, around a drainpipe exposed through a break in the wall. Liam tugged on the pipe a couple of times and pronounced it still sturdy.

Jorja had brought a large backpack, from which she'd produced not just the Taser and zip ties but now also a blindfold, which she tied around the man's eyes.

"Remember, when he comes to: no names," she told them. "And don't talk unless you have to."

The psychic's abandoned office swirled with dust and decades of pollen. There was no light here, but Jorja once again dug into her bag of tricks and brought out a small LED lamp that lit the place up, throwing harsh shadows around the tiny room. They danced over their captive's unconscious form.

Despite herself, Elayah found the moment haunting and intoxicating. This man—this helpless, confined man—was somehow connected to the knife across her throat. The spilled blood. Maybe he *was* the man who'd cut her.

Liam shook his head. "Guys...this is crazy."

"I want to know what he knows," she told Liam. "This is what we have to do. I could have been killed. I think I deserve some answers."

Marcie grinned. "And as soon as he wakes up, we're gonna get them for you."

Something about that grin scared the hell out of Elayah. Marcie had been her best friend forever; they'd shared *everything*. And yet she'd never seen this side of her.

They quickly frisked the man. As suspected, there was no envelope full of cash. "A liar, in addition to his other sins," Marcie commented.

"Nothing in his pockets except for this." Jorja waved an iPhone at them. "No wallet. No keys."

The man stirred. Groaned. His shoulders flexed for a moment as he reflexively tried to move his arms, but his wrists were bound together, then zip-tied behind him to the pipe. Elayah bit her lip, waiting for him to speak. Waiting for his voice.

*Don't scream.*

She would know the voice. Below the blindfold, his clean-shaven cheeks glowed with sweat, blotched with dirt, but he had no beard at all.

*Could have shaved.*

She couldn't take it any longer.

She lunged toward him, lips parting, ready to shout, "Who are you?" but in the same instant Jorja grabbed her from behind and yanked her back. The shout became a wordless gasp.

It was loud enough. The man's head snapped up at the sound of her gasp, rotating his obscured eyes in her direction. She experienced a trill of fear in her lower abdomen, like being stabbed in her gut with a sharpened icicle. He couldn't see her, but her amygdala didn't know that and it shouted *Fear! Danger!*

"Who's there?" he asked, and in that instant all the fear bled away, seeping out her pores like cold sweat.

It wasn't the voice with the knife. It wasn't *Don't scream.*

"Who's there?" he asked again.

Marcie put her hands on Elayah's shoulders and steered her away from the guy.

Jorja typed into her phone and then held it up. "You don't need to know who we are," said a synthetic voice. "We don't want to hurt you. Tell us who sent you and why, and we'll let you go."

The man said nothing. He simply "peered" around the room some more, twisting his head this way and that, trying to find an angle from which he could see from under the blindfold.

"If you tell us what you know," Jorja's phone said, "no harm will come to you."

The man did not quite chuckle, but his throat rippled in something like amusement. Or maybe it was resigned disbelief.

They gathered in a corner, where they could whisper without being overheard.

"I say we introduce him to a knife of our own," Marcie said calmly, and reached into her purse.

# LIAM

It wasn't the biggest knife Liam had ever seen, and it wasn't wickedly, intentionally lethal like the knife they'd found in the time capsule, but it was big enough and sharp enough to shock him.

"What the hell, Marse? Why do you even have that?"

Marcie shrugged as though explaining why she had a tin of Altoids in her purse. "Just in case."

"Just in case? Just in case?" Liam thought he might be hyperventilating but couldn't stop. "Were you worried someone was gonna bring an Easter ham without telling you?"

"Calm down," Jorja told him. "I'm sure she's thought this through."

"What, are we gonna torture the guy?"

"It won't get that far." Marcie's tone, distressingly imperturbable, evoked choosing between the four-pack and the six-pack of nuggets at McDonald's, not opting for war crimes. "All we have to do is put it up to his throat. Let him know we have it. He'll crack."

And wow. Marcie. Calm, cool, collected Marcie. The first one to lose it. He would not have bet on that.

"This might work," Jorja interjected with infuriating calm. "We need answers. He has them. It's simple math. We won't actually *hurt* him."

"And what if he still won't talk?" Liam asked. "Are you gonna cut him open to look for what he knows?"

Marcie folded her arms over her chest, the knife glimmering against the hank of red hair that fell over her shoulder. "I don't like *any* of this, but this guy either tried to kill El or knows who did. We didn't start this."

Liam's throat bobbed as he tried to swallow. He couldn't believe *he*, Liam, was the responsible one, outvoted by the others. Black was white; up was down; ketchup was mustard. The world no longer made sense.

"He doesn't have a wallet or any ID on him, and we can't break into his phone." Jorja handed it to Liam. "If you know some hackers, call them. Otherwise, let's see what we can see."

"Who's actually going to do this?" he asked. "Not me. El?"

Elayah had been silent during the entire conversation, staring at the knife in Marcie's hands. It took another "*El?*" for her to snap out of her fugue state and shake her head slowly.

"No. I don't...I don't trust myself."

Well, hell. He never imagined in a million years that Elayah Laird would worry about going all *Hulk smash* on someone.

"I'll do it." Marcie drew herself up to her full height, the knife still clutched in one fist. "He hurt my best friend. Or he knows who did. I have *zero* problem with this."

"Don't actually cut him," Jorja cautioned.

"I'll be careful," Marcie promised.

Which wasn't exactly the same thing.

Liam thought everyone seemed a little too eager, but he also knew that he was outvoted. He stepped back, turning the phone over and over in his hands.

Marcie crouched near the hostage and patted him on the knee. Liam's stomach tightened. That knee pat bothered Liam for some reason he couldn't identify . . . until he did.

Patting the guy on the knee was a humane gesture. It acknowledged the man's humanity. And yet Marcie was still about to treat the guy like a cold side of beef hanging from a slaughterhouse hook. Somehow it would be less nauseating if Marcie just treated the guy like a thing, not a person.

Jorja stood nearby and used her phone app to talk.

"Let's start with something easy. Your name."

The man said nothing.

"There are two ways to do this," the phone went on.

*Oh, God, don't say a hard way and an easy way*, Liam thought.

Jorja's phone said exactly that. Liam groaned and turned the man's phone over again. It was a pretty new one.

"Who are you? Who sent you?"

The man shook his head and sighed. "Come on. Let me go. We can still make the swap."

Clearing her throat meaningfully, Marcie laid the knife against the man's leg. "I'm giving you one last chance. And then I'm going to cut. I'm not telling you where or how deep. You'll find out soon enough."

"You're kids, right? You're not going to hurt me."

Jorja's eyes lit up, and she typed quickly on her phone screen.

"Haven't you read the science on the teen brain? Our heads aren't quite right. Not until we turn twenty-five. Until then, the prefrontal cortex is still mushy. Consequently, we lack planning capacity. And impulse control. Who knows what we might do to you? You like cutting up girls? You like working for people who do?"

The man stiffened, though whether at the accusation or at the touch of the knife, it was impossible to tell. He might not have entirely believed Jorja's soliloquy, but he didn't entirely disbelieve it, either. "Let's just finish this up and be out of each other's hair, okay?" he suggested.

Marcie seemed to consider this, and for a moment, Liam thought she might agree.

And then, without a word, Elayah stepped over to Marcie and grabbed the knife.

# ELAYAH

The knife caught the cold white light of the lantern and warped it along its shiny surface. A smear of silver. A fun house mirror.

Elayah had watched the whole thing at a remove. It felt unreal, but at the same time *too* real. That heightened sense of surreality that comes in deep, deep dreams.

As she watched Marcie, she suddenly wanted the knife in her own hand. Her palm itched for it. In a single, unbidden instant, Elayah understood the term *bloodlust* in more than an academic sense.

Yes, she knew she was in a fragile and precarious state after what had happened to her. One of the doctors in the hospital had—out of Elayah's earshot, or so she'd thought—advised her parents to have Elayah see a therapist. That night, when her parents—again, thinking her out of earshot and again, wrong—spoke, they spoke of health insurance and what it didn't cover, and why was the insurance company's website so damn difficult to navigate, and that's exactly what they *want*; they want you to give up, Dinah!

She wanted the knife and she wanted to cut. To hurt. To inflict harm. It made no rational sense, but this was beyond rationality. She wanted it. To balance the scales. She'd been hurt, so someone else needed to be hurt.

This man before her probably hadn't been the one who'd cut her. It wasn't just the voice and the lack of a beard—*Shaving cream and a razor, ever heard of it?*

a persnickety voice in the back of her head asked—but some ineffable, unquanti-fiable sense that extruded from her beyond the usual five. Her mom might have called it *woman's intuition.* Her grandmother—Dad's mom—would have called it *heavy gut. I know what I know,* Nana was given to say. *I know it in my heavy gut.*

Elayah didn't truck with mysticism or the vaguely sexist notion that women had an intuitive understanding of the world to compensate for logical short-comings. But as she took the knife from Marcie, felt its heft, its weight, she knew what she did believe in: common sense. Righteousness. Responsibility.

The knife felt good and right in her hand.

Standing with it, staring straight ahead at the man. Maybe he'd cut her. Probably he hadn't. But it didn't matter. He was *here.* He was *now.* Guilty or not, he abutted the sin at every border.

Her throat burned. Her eyes flared wide, then narrowed, her breath com-ing hot and hard and fast.

"Tell. Us," she rasped in a voice not her own, and the next thing she knew, she brought the knife up in a wide arc that made Marcie jump back. Jorja shouted out; Liam uttered a wordless, strangled syllable.

But she blocked it all out. The world blurred and smeared around her, funneling into a single tunnel of clarity that centered on the bound man.

She slashed down with the knife. Felt something solid that yielded, then a cry of pain, but it wasn't enough.

Liam was there. She struggled against him, but he was too strong. His fingers found the underside of her wrist and pressed—hard. The knife fell from her nerveless hand.

"Get her out of here!" Jorja yelled. "Get her out of here!"

# LIAM

With Marcie's help, he managed to drag El out of the room and into the tall grass behind the building. El was screaming. Garbage syllables.

Fragments of curse words. Tears spattered the air around her as she jerked her head back and forth.

"You're okay," Marcie swore over and over. "You're okay."

"I'll never be okay!" El yelled, breaking away from Liam's grasp. "I can't even sleep in my room! I can't even close my eyes in my own bed! Because of him!"

Marcie did what Liam could not—she hugged El, enfolding her loosely in her arms, then spoke softly into her ear.

"I just want everything to be normal again," El sobbed. "And he wasn't going to tell us *anything*, so I wanted to *hurt* him, to *make* him talk and…"

Liam watched as El trembled in Marcie's arms, whether from rage or shock, he couldn't tell.

Reaching into his pocket, he retrieved the guy's phone. It was a newer model and it had been turned off, so the face recognition didn't work when turned on—it demanded a pass code Liam didn't have. But the lock screen…

He showed the phone to El. "This is who you attacked," he told her.

The lock screen showed the time and date, but more crucially, it showed a picture. The man they'd abducted. Arms around a young woman with hollow eyes who smiled a deep, exhausted smile. In her arms, she cradled a swaddled infant.

A father.

"Ah, crap," Elayah said. She disentangled herself from Marcie and pressed a palm to her forehead. "Crap. I…I'm sorry, guys. I just…I just lost it there. I just…"

"We understand," Marcie said without checking with Liam first. But, yeah, he supposed he understood.

"I felt…" El shivered. "I felt the knife go *in*. Did I—"

Liam checked his phone, which had just buzzed. "Text from Jorja. You slashed up his leg, is all."

"I'm starting to see how it could have happened," she said.

Marcie and Liam exchanged a glance. "What do you mean?"

"Whatever our parents did. Whatever they covered up. I get it. It's so easy."

22

# THE PRESENT: ELAYAH

Back inside, Jorja knelt, wrapping a white gauze bandage from her backpack around the man's upper leg. Red dots peeked through the gauze. Elayah watched and felt nothing but the hollowness of self-recrimination, the sensation of knowing you owe someone an apology but being unable to give it.

The emptiness filled quickly with a war between her anger and her fear of that same anger.

They huddled briefly in a corner. Jorja ran a white noise app and left her phone at the man's feet to cover their conversation.

"Can we all agree this is a bad idea now?" Liam asked.

"I'm not ready to concede that," Jorja announced with placid calm, as though she hadn't just bandaged a freaking *knife wound*. "If anything, he'll be more afraid of us now."

The logic was unassailable and grotesque.

"How badly did I cut him?" Elayah's own voice echoed in her ears.

"It was pretty deep," Jorja said after a moment's hesitation. "But nothing I couldn't bandage up. It's not like he needs stitches or anything."

"Thank you, Doctor." Liam's sarcasm made Elayah's stomach lurch.

Jorja arched an eyebrow. Summers, she was a camp counselor and had passed multiple first aid courses with flying colors. They all knew she could assess and bandage a wound. Other than the eyebrow, though, she let Liam's snark go unanswered. It wasn't the time.

"We shouldn't be fighting among ourselves," Marcie reminded them. "We need to learn whatever it is he knows."

Jorja glanced over at the man on the chair. "We already know this for certain: He's not a Craigslist find or a TaskRabbit. He would have started spilling whatever he knew already."

"He's clearly a ninja." Liam's acerbic tone made Elayah's head hurt.

"That's not what Jorja's saying," she snapped at him. "She's saying this guy is clearly loyal to whoever sent him. You don't buy this kind of loyalty online."

Liam held out his hands, palms out. "Whoa. No need to gang up on me."

"Jorja's right," Marcie said. "El did us a favor—he's gotta be scared now. So let's see what he'll tell us." She took the knife from Jorja and marched over to the man, first stooping to shut off the white noise. Then, with a calmness and aplomb that made Elayah's throat pulse again, Marcie laid the flat of the blade against the man's collarbone.

"Who sent you to the statue and then to meet with us tonight?"

The man gritted his teeth. Even with his face half-covered, he was clearly in pain. Tears dripped out from under the blindfold, and beads of sweat dotted his temples. "I'm not telling you anything," he managed after a moment. "You're the ones who know everything already."

Marcie held the blade steady. Turned to face the others. She mouthed, *WTF?* What did *that* mean?

# LIAM

He hasn't seen any of us," Liam said as they huddled again in the shadows and beneath the umbrella of the white noise. "We can let him go or just scoot and call an ambulance to come get him—"

"He's gotta know I'm involved," El pointed out. "How hard would it be to figure out who my friends are?"

"It's all speculation," Jorja said, waving off the mere notion of any sort of threat. "He can't prove anything. We all just deny it. He's not bleeding out or anything. His wound has clotted already."

"Great, so we only hurt the guy a little bit," Liam said. "This is still kidnapping and assault, plain and simple. And I hate to break it to you, but just because we're under eighteen doesn't mean we're gonna get off. In Maryland, they send cases like this straight to criminal court."

El regarded him as though he'd just recited the first chapter of *The Westing Game* from memory. (Her third-grade talent show talent. Needless to say, she didn't win.)

"Oh, come on!" Liam exclaimed. "My dad's the sheriff! Of course I know that!"

"Maybe..." El worried at her lower lip. "Maybe it's time to back off."

Marcie and Jorja both shook their heads. "No way," said Marcie.

"We're in too deep now," Jorja added. "The only way out is through. We've already kidnapped the guy. Now we *have* to see this through. It's our only option."

Liam sighed. "There's got to be another way."

"I don't know if there is," Marcie said. "This is our best chance to figure out what's going on."

"He's not talking. Unless you're willing to start cutting things off..."

El spoke into the silence Liam left at the end of his declaration. "And the science is pretty clear: Torture doesn't actually work. Not really."

"What if we let him go?" Marcie asked suddenly.

"Finally, someone is talking sense!" Liam exclaimed.

"Follow me here," she said, speaking quickly before Jorja could interrupt. "What if we cut him loose and then follow him? At some point, he's going to return to whoever hired him or whoever he's helping, right?"

Expecting Jorja to protest, Liam was surprised to find her eyes wide with interest and possibility. "I could order some gear off of eBay. We could put a tracker on him...."

"We're not waiting for you to get stuff sent to you from eBay," Marcie said gently.

"We should do this tonight," Liam said. "Now."

"Not tonight," Jorja said. "We leave him here tonight. Let him stew for a while. Then we reinterrogate him in the morning and cut him loose whether he answers our questions or not."

El heaved out a sigh. "I'm not on board with leaving this guy here all night long. He could get away. Or something could happen to him."

Deep inside, Liam felt relief that El was now starting to think of the guy as a person, not a human pincushion. "I'll stay with him," he said. "I'll come up with an excuse. It's not a school night; no big."

Jorja agreed with a shrug. "But look," she said, "we swear. Right now. No matter what happens, we never talk about what we did tonight."

Three hands piled into the center. El held back.

"This is what they did, isn't it? Our parents. They did something bad, and they covered it up."

"We don't know that for sure," Liam said gently. "Maybe they were covering for a friend. Or maybe this is more complicated than we think."

She sighed and put her hand in the middle. "Okay. I swear."


As soon as they were gone, Liam marched back into the building and stood before the man, arms crossed over his chest. A part of him—a louder and more persuasive part than he liked to admit—wanted to start pummeling the man and not stop until the guy either talked or couldn't talk. This man was connected somehow to El's night of terror, to the mystery that had brought them all here, to this ridiculous and frightening and dangerous pass. Beating the man within an inch of his life would satisfy some dark and barbaric instinct.

Yeah, for El's sake he wanted nothing more than to bash the man's head against the wall until it cracked open. But instead, he picked up the knife where Marcie had left it on the nearby counter. "Okay," he said, making his voice husky and whispery. "I'm going to cut you loose. When you hear the door close, you can take off the blindfold and leave."

He took a deep breath and slipped the blade of the knife between the man's hands, where they gapped just enough to leave room to cut the zip tie.

"Remember," he went on, "I still have the knife. And you're injured. If you try anything, it won't end well for you."

He began to saw away at the zip tie.

"Thank you," the man said, his voice cracking with relief and sincerity.

Shaking the tiniest bit, Liam broke through the zip tie. He figured there was about a fifty-fifty chance of the guy actually adhering to his guidelines. And he knew he wouldn't really stab the guy. So the whole situation was fraught. He was bluffing with not much of a hand. This could all go wrong so quickly and so badly.

The man sat perfectly still. Liam jammed the knife through his belt and backed out the door, keeping an eye on the hostage, who did not move, not even as Liam edged out the door.

# 1986: JAY

Unable to tolerate prattling Miss Leister in Brit lit, Jay decided that he would just bail on reading chunks of *The Canterbury Tales* in Middle English (*not* Old English, the way some idiots kept saying). His A was guaranteed anyway. As soon as the bell rang, he dashed out of class and ducked into the lavatory, where he fumbled in his backpack for a pad of hall passes. He ripped one off and quickly filled it in, signing it illegibly. That was the key to a good fake hall pass—an unreadable signature.

Exiting the lavatory, he nearly collided with Dean, who was ambling along, his backpack heavy, a brace of comic books tucked under one arm. "Want to skip Leister and all her *whan that Aprill* crap today?" Jay asked.

Soon, they were both headed toward the cafeteria, then turning left to make a loop around toward the auditorium. As long as they popped into Brit lit before it ended and flashed their passes, they'd be all right.

As they passed the auditorium and turned toward the hallway that led to the outer doors for the 4-H greenhouse, Jay paused at the case that held the Cup. Dean didn't realize until he was halfway down the hall, then turned back and waved furiously for Jay to join him. But Jay ignored him, staring at the Cup.

Dean returned to his side, and Jay, without a word, stepped to one side and pried open the door to the auditorium. The chamber was dark. He tilted his head to Dean and then slipped inside.

"If we get caught in here...," Dean said.

"We won't. Stop being a grandma."

They felt their way down the left-hand aisle. Backstage, they flicked on one of the lights, a pale, dull yellow for the stagehands to see by while the principal preached the gospel of utter boredom or the drama club put on one of its twice-yearly plays. Jay dropped onto a rolled-up carpet; a puff of dust erupted like a cartoon fart.

Dean waited a moment, then, with a shrug that could have been intended for Jay or for himself, joined Jay on the carpet. "What's up, Doc?"

"You think Brian jerks off too much?"

Dean spluttered laughter. "Why are you even *thinking* about that?"

"He's always asking me to buy porno magazines for him. And I do. And then he wants new ones."

Dean considered this. "Wow, is he wearing them out or something?"

They exchanged a look of disgust at the idea.

"He just looks at a lot of porno, is all," Jay said. "A lot."

Dean gazed at him, eyebrows hunched in thought. "You didn't bring me here to talk about Brian whacking off."

"My mom's in the hospital." As soon as he said the words, Jay regretted it. It felt like deliberately stripping off armor just as you were about to joust. It had tumbled out of him, a moment of unchecked, brute honesty that would never have happened with someone else. He hoped Dean hadn't heard.

But Dean was sitting right next to him, those stupid comic books tucked under his arm. Why did someone as smart as Dean read that junk?

"What happened?" Dean asked.

"Nothing happened." Jay shrugged. He had to slough it off now, skin himself, let the ragged, scaly remains of his vulnerability float tattered in the wind while a newer, stronger flesh lay bare.

"C'mon." Dean's blue eyes had clouded, swamped by trouble. Dean was like a girl that way—he actually cared about this stuff. Maybe that was why Jay had let his guard down.

"She's depressed."

Dean blinked a few times. "I don't get it."

Heaving out an exhausted sigh, Jay shook his head. "It's not like...like she just feels bad or whatever. It's like a disease. In her head. But not like she's crazy or anything," he added quickly.

Dean nodded slowly. "I'm sorry, man. I'm really sorry."

"Whatever." Jay stared ahead, seeing nothing. Mom had been a wreck for a while now. Most days, she didn't even rouse herself from bed, and on the days she did, she usually just lay on the sofa. Not even watching TV—just lying there. It reminded him of the day after John Lennon had died; he'd come home from school to find Mom on the sofa, sobbing, *The White Album* clutched to her chest like a life preserver in the North Atlantic Ocean. Nothing he'd said or done could shake her loose for the rest of the day.

And now...well, recently it had been as though Mark David Chapman was going around killing a different Beatle every single day, then moving on to the Stones, the Monkees, and every other band Mom loved. Every day was a day of mourning. Every day was a disaster of epic proportions, the Dearborn house gone funereal and near silent with the vast stillness of Mom.

Then she went into the hospital. And the silence just grew. Jay came home from school. Dad came home from work...some nights. Other nights, he had board stuff. Or he just...didn't come home. Not until Jay was already in bed.

"Are you okay?" Dean asked.

The consolation, the concern, the goddamn *pity* in Dean's voice—they were the straw that broke the camel's back. Jay flashed a tight, dishonest smile. "I'm fine. Hey, we should come back here tonight."

Dean goggled at him. "Just the two of us?"

"Sure. Why not?"

"I thought we weren't going again until the end of the semester. To change our grades."

Jay grinned. It was as honest and as true as what he'd said about his mother. "I'm gonna tell you something...."

# 24

# THE PRESENT: ELAYAH

After a fitful night's sleep in Mom's bed again, Elayah waited impatiently, glaring at reporters through her living room window until Jorja and Marcie showed up in an Uber. She ran from the house to the car, where Jorja already had a door open. They took off before a single reporter could get to a car to follow them.

She'd spent the night in and out of sleep, her dreams haunted by shadowy figures in a murky fog. Every time she awoke, she lay still in the darkness next to Mom, half expecting the door to explode open with cops serving a warrant for her arrest. She couldn't help thinking they'd done the wrong thing—beyond even the kidnapping. They should have let the guy go. It had gone too far, and they should have just let him go.

They rode in silence, not wanting to say anything incriminating in front of the Uber driver, a sixty-something grandmother who chattered the entire time about her grandchildren, pictures of whom festooned the dashboard of her ten-year-old Miata. Jorja asked her to drop them off a few blocks away from PSYCHIC ADVICE.

"So that there's no digital paper trail connecting us to this place," she explained after they'd disembarked and watched the car trundle off into the distance.

They hiked half a mile to the building and stepped inside. It took a moment for Elayah's eyes to adjust to the gloaming within. She noticed two things. One, the spot with their hostage was empty.

Two, the delightful smell of coffee filled the room.

"What the hell, Liam?" Jorja screamed.

Liam perched on the old counter. A box of Dunkin' coffee sat next to him, along with an open box of donuts. "Oh, come on. I brought coffee and donuts. You can't be *that* pissed."

"You let the guy go!" Marcie exclaimed. "That wasn't the plan."

"Sure it was. I just did it early."

Elayah pushed past Jorja and Marcie and stood before Liam. It took her far longer to speak than it should have, gazing up into his eyes, which flicked back and forth as they gazed back, as though he were trying to conjure words of his own.

She spoke first, though: "Thanks. You did the right thing." *When I should have,* she did not add.

Then she broke off a piece a chocolate donut and popped it into her mouth.

"We had an agreement," Marcie said again, her voice hot.

"Don't worry," Liam said with a saucy grin that made Elayah weak. Fortunately, chewing the donut gave her something to do in the moment. "I followed him."

The man had limped, going slow, Liam told them. He followed at a safe distance. A mile down the road, where it intersected with Route 54, the road that led south to Brookdale, the man waited for the late-night traffic to abate, then staggered across 54 and turned onto Gilbert Street. Liam was just wondering how long the guy planned to hobble along on that bad leg when he walked up a driveway, grabbed a spare key from a fake rock in the flower bed, and let himself in.

The address was 147 Gilbert Street. Liam noted it and went home to sleep.

"And then," he finished, breaking a sour cream donut in half, "I woke up early and laid in a supply of coffee and donuts. Because I love you guys. Bonus: I was back home in time to fist-bump the dads good night."

He jammed half the donut into his mouth and offered the other half to Elayah. When she demurred, he shrugged and somehow managed to cram that half into his mouth, too.

"So we just find out who lives at 147 Gilbert," Marcie said, "and we've got...well, something at least."

Jorja was already fiddling with her phone. "According to real estate sites, that house hasn't been on the market in close to twenty years. Our guy would have been a kid at the time."

Elayah did a reverse address lookup on whitepages.com and came up with the name Lisa De Nardo. Then she scooted over to Facebook. Lisa De Nardo's profile was locked down pretty well. No photos visible, but they did note that she graduated from Canterstown High in 1987. Same year as their parents. Other than that, they landed only her maiden name, McKenzie.

They went to Elayah's house. Both of her parents were at work—Dad on a weekend shift, Mom making up time at the real estate office.

Mom's yearbook did indeed reveal a Lisa McKenzie, an attractive blond with a dome of too-sprayed hair and a wide smile.

"Let's go see her," Elayah said.

Liam and the others exchanged a look before Marcie spoke. "Are you sure? We don't know what we might find. The guy from last night is working with her."

"This could be some crazy-ass *You* stuff going down here," Liam warned. "We got *way* lucky yesterday. Pop always says luck is like salt in the shaker— you eventually run out, usually when you need it the most."

"Why is it about salt specifically?" Jorja asked, her brow furrowed. "I mean, you could say that about any ingredient, really."

Liam goggled. "Is that what you got out of that?"

Elayah threw her hands up in the air. "Guys!" The previous day's adrenaline had run out long ago. Her rage and her violence had burned themselves out, leaving a fine ash of determination. She felt close to the end of this and wanted to get there. Now.

"What if *he* answers the door?" Liam asked.

Jorja shrugged. "He never saw any of us."

"He might have seen my face at the statue the other night," Liam reminded her.

"I don't remember my parents ever talking about someone named Lisa," Marcie said, screwing up her expression into her deep-thinking face.

"Me neither," Liam offered. " 'Hello, Ms. De Nardo,' " he went on in an overly bright voice, " 'did you go to school with our parents and murder someone in 1986?' "

"We'll be a little more subtle than that," Marcie observed dryly.

Elayah stomped her foot for attention. "This isn't a debate. This isn't even a discussion. I'm going. You all can come with me or not, but I'm going. Maybe Lisa De Nardo can put us on the right path."

"Well, then I'm going with you," Marcie said.

"Me too," Jorja said quickly.

Liam sighed. "Okay, okay. I'll drive."


Lisa De Nardo's house was an off-white Tudor with a bright red door on a smallish lot in a neighborhood of similar houses. It also had a sign in the front yard that read #MAGA 2024 in white text on a red background.

"This is gonna go well," Liam muttered.

"You didn't mention this," Jorja said, sounding very inquisitional in that moment. Sometimes her dad's lawyer spirit possessed her in the weirdest ways.

"It was dark. I didn't notice it."

"She might be one of those nice racists," Marcie said with an air of perfectly feigned innocence.

"You ready, Marse?"

They had agreed that Marcie would lead the questioning—adults really, really liked her.

"I'm ready."

"Let's just do this and get out of here," Elayah grumbled.

De Nardo answered the door on the first ring and—much to Elayah's despair—could not have been sweeter to them as she listened patiently to Marcie's spiel. The woman was tall and curvaceous—*buxom* floated up from the depths of Elayah's unconscious vocabulary—with frosted blond hair tied back in a ponytail. She could have been a friend's older sister, and Elayah had to remind herself that she (A) was her dad's age and (B) had a damn Trump sign in her front yard.

Elayah studied De Nardo carefully as Marcie explained about the attack, looking for any hint of recognition or knowledge, finding none. Either Lisa De Nardo was a good actor or she really knew nothing about the man with the knife.

"I'm so sorry for what happened to you," she said, wincing at Elayah's exposed neck.

"It wasn't your fault," Elayah told her. "But, Ms. De Nardo, if we could just ask you a couple of questions…it might help lead to the arrest of the person who attacked me."

It was the thinnest of possible premises, and somehow De Nardo fell for it. She insisted they call her *Lisa*, then let them inside. The living room into which she led them was all dark wood accents juxtaposed to bright yellow furniture. It worked.

"Have a seat." Lisa gestured airily to the sofa and an overstuffed armchair. "I work from home, so if anyone asks, I was at my computer the whole time, right?" She dropped a wink that goosed a conspiratorial grin out of Elayah, who then immediately reproached herself for responding at all. #MAGA 2024. Right.

"We just have a couple of questions," Marcie said, clearing her throat. She held out her phone and flicked through the apps for a moment.

"I'm sorry," Lisa said, "but wow. Except for the red hair, you look so much like your mom did at your age. It's crazy."

Marcie cleared her throat again. "I do?"

Liam, next to her on the couch, elbowed her in an absolutely unsubtle way. Elayah and Jorja locked eyes and groaned, but Lisa just chuckled.

"No, it's okay. We all have lives to get back to. Fire away, kids." She had swung a chair out from the nearby dining room and now sat down, crossing her legs. Elayah noticed Liam noticing and experienced a hotter flush of anger than she would have expected. Yeah, yeah, Lisa De Nardo was a MILF for sure, but they had all seen the damn sign outside!

"You said I look like my mom," Marcie began. "So you knew her? You knew all of our parents?"

Lisa threw back her head and laughed a little too throatily. Elayah was getting a serious creepy vibe from her now. No one had to break out that level of flirt-laughing for high school kids.

"We all knew each other. It was a small school. Still is, I guess? Anyway, sure, I knew them. Didn't really pal around with them or anything, but I had a couple of classes with your dads…." She pointed to Jorja and Liam. "And *everyone* knew the Laird twins. Black Lightning!"

With a dazzling smile, she turned to Elayah, who smiled tightly in return.

"I was there junior year when your dad and your uncle broke the county record for the fifty-meter relay. Wow, what a moment!"

"It was the hundred," Elayah told her.

"Was it? I guess that's twice as impressive!" Lisa's laughter tinkled musically, and Elayah decided she hated this woman with every bone in her body.

"So, did you put anything into the time capsule?" Marcie asked, getting them back on track. "Or did you witness anyone putting anything into the time capsule?"

Lisa frowned. "What time capsule?"

"The one in the news. The reason we're here."

With a heavy sigh and a little shake of her head, Lisa backed off her frown just the slightest. "I get my news from Newsmax and the radio."

"This was in the *Loco* last week," Marcie tried. "A big story."

"I don't have much use for the mainstream media," Lisa sniffed.

"It's just the *Loco*." Liam couldn't keep a note of condescending sarcasm out of his voice, but it apparently sailed right over Lisa's head.

The story had also been on ABC, CNN, NPR.... But those, of course, would just be fake news, to be avoided at all costs. Elayah gritted her teeth together, but Marcie came to her rescue, jumping in and offering a quick sketch of what had happened: the burial of the time capsule in 1986, last week's excavation, followed by the attack. She left out the knife and its wrapping and the note, still in accordance with the sheriff's orders, but came down hard on the attack in Elayah's room.

"So what we're wondering," Marcie finished up, "is what could have been so important in there that someone would kill for it. We have a picture of the contents...." She nudged Jorja, who sheepishly stumbled over to the other side of the room and showed her phone to Lisa.

Elayah had a sudden hunch. "Ms., I mean, Lisa, may I use your bathroom?"

"Of course." She pointed out the door.

Elayah went into a small powder room just off the kitchen. She turned on the sink to cover any noises and began pawing through the medicine cabinet. Nothing jumped out at her.

Under the sink was a small pail filled with cleaning supplies, an open box of tampons, and a bottle of soap refill. There was also a first aid kit. Elayah opened it. It had clearly been used, but there was no way to tell when or how. Nothing incriminating.

She shook her head at her mirror image and flushed the toilet just to make it seem real, and that was when she caught a glimpse of the trash can.

White gauze.

Spotted with blood.

She took a deep breath, resisting the urge to pound out of the bathroom, waving the bloody gauze and screaming, "You know! You know!"

Instead, she took a few pictures of the gauze, then calmly walked back out to the living room, where Lisa was just finishing looking at the photos on Jorja's phone.

"I'm really sorry," Lisa was saying as she handed the phone back. "None of this is ringing a bell for me at all. . . ."

"Is there anything you *do* remember?" Marcie raised an interrogatory eyebrow at Elayah, who thought less than a second and nodded. They had agreed they wouldn't push hard unless they had to.

Well, they had to.

"Nothing that someone might want to hurt someone over?" Marcie continued. "Because we have reason to believe you might have been involved."

Lisa's neck stiffened, and her countenance changed in an instant, going from "cool mom who might just be willing to give you some over-the-shirt action" to "stone-cold beeyotch."

"You have reason to believe, do you?" She smiled without mirth. "I don't rightly care what you have reason to believe. You come into my home and accuse me of trying to hurt this girl?"

Taken aback, Marcie floundered for a moment. "That's not what we're—"

"We're not accusing you of anything," Liam interrupted, physically pushing Marcie back against the sofa as he leaned forward, blasting Lisa with his best, highest-megawatt smile. It was, Elayah surmised, something like watching an irresistible force meeting an immovable object as two very attractive people stared each other down.

Lisa cracked first, though not along the fault line they'd wished for. "I think you kids should go. I don't know anything about what your parents were up to back then. I didn't even know they buried a time capsule."

"But—" Liam said.

"No. Time to go." And this time it wasn't hot older lady to studly young man. This time it was grown-up to kid. Against which there was no defense or rejoinder.

# LIAM

**E**vidence. Finally, *evidence*. And El had just walked away from it.

"You could have said something," he said for the third time since they'd vacated Lisa De Nardo's house. "She knows something! Why didn't you text us?"

They were stopped at a red light. He took advantage of the moment to slam his palms against the steering wheel to vent his frustration. Bloody gauze. *Bloody gauze!*

"Settle down," Jorja told him from the back seat. "What were we going to do? Flash our badges and read her her rights?"

"You could have *taken* it!" Liam ignored Jorja's jab.

"Touch someone else's blood? Gross," said Marcie.

"Come on. That would be tampering with evidence," El said with maddening poise. "And what was I supposed to do, wad it up and shove it in my pocket? That's not contaminating it or anything."

"She's involved!" Liam howled, slamming on the gas as the light changed. He was in no mood for intolerably, infernally placid rationality. Elayah had found actual evidence and then let them just walk away. He wasn't used to being pissed at El—he'd actually never in his life been pissed at El—but this was a special occasion for sure. "It was the guy. I saw him go in there with my own two eyes."

"Whoever he is, he can't be her husband," Marcie said, scrolling her phone. "Too young, for one thing."

Liam figured that a lot of young dudes would be happy to be married to a hottie like Lisa De Nardo, but he wisely kept that thought to himself.

"Could be a son?" Elayah offered.

Marcie chewed at her lower lip. "All I'm finding for De Nardo on Facebook is two guys in college. Too young and neither one looks like the guy we saw last night."

"Guy we *kidnapped* last night," Liam reminded her.

"It's a dead end," Jorja said. "She kicked us out. We need to find another angle."

There was a murmur of agreement from Marcie, then a nod from El.

Liam couldn't believe it. *They had their first real evidence!*

"Are you guys nuts?" he demanded, making a left at a stop sign. "You're giving up on her? I didn't even want to do this! I didn't even *want* to get involved, but you guys pushed me. *You* guys wanted to torture the dude. *You* guys wanted to do all of this, and now you don't want to do the work? Fine! I give. Let's just call it a day. Let's just pick the easiest answer, right? Let's say El's *uncle* whacked someone and skipped town, which is nice and neat."

No one spoke for a moment. Liam replayed what he'd just said and realized . . .

Yikes. That was pretty likely, actually.

"That's not funny, Liam." Marcie had pressed against the door, arms folded over her chest, not even bothering to look at Liam in the rearview.

"I didn't—"

"Take it back, Liam," Jorja said, quiet, but firm. "Right the hell now."

El said nothing. She gazed out the window as Liam drove, pointedly ignoring him.

He hadn't really *meant* it. It had been a joke. A bad one. He'd stepped right on Sacred Uncle Antoine. It was stupid and now El was ticked off. He had to say something to make it better.

"Look, it *can't* be El's uncle. Like he's been reading the *Loco* down in Mexico and saw the story and teleported up here in time to cut her throat? Get real."

"Enough," El said. She wasn't looking at him. His joke couldn't actually end up being the truth, could it?

Silence from El was twice as deep and twice as long as silence from anyone else. Unbearable. He had to keep talking. "I say it's the dude, and we should go back there and make the MILF tell us what she knows."

"I said enough!" El twisted in her seat, fixing him with a glare. "Shut up already!"

Liam's heart pumped too fast. His fingers shot pain up his arms as he gripped the wheel even more tightly. He dared slide his eyes sideways for half a second to scope out El's anger, but she wasn't even looking at him anymore. She was staring down at her phone, her cheeks darkened and her lips thin against each other.

"What's wrong?" he asked with more venom in his voice than he truly intended. "Did you miss a Portkey Portmanteau or screw up a Confoundable?"

El shook her head, and he noticed the tears at the corners of her eyes. Every joke in him died in that moment.

"Rachel. She posted another story." El dropped her phone, screen down, in her lap and glared out the window.

Marcie was already on it from the back seat. "Girlfriend is way too thirsty," she said, skimming the web.

"Please don't do that," El told her.

"'Time Capsule Cache Still Not in Custody!' Oh, Jesus..."

"It's never gonna end," El said quietly.

"'Sources inside the sheriff's department...'" Marcie began quoting from the story. "'Contents of the time capsule have not been impounded or otherwise taken into custody, and so remain with their original possessor....'"

"At least...at least she didn't use your name," Jorja offered.

"Doesn't matter," El muttered. "Everyone knows the stuff's at my house." She slammed her head back against the headrest.

*She's never gonna sleep again,* Liam thought, and gripped the steering wheel tightly. His sense of humor and his sense of the absurd *and* his sense of outright idiocy all failed him—he could conjure no joke, witticism, or snark that could allay her fears, put her at ease, balm her inner wound.

"I'm not the source, if that helps," he blurted out.

His comment was bad, his timing worse. They'd just pulled into El's neighborhood. She thumped the side of her fist on her armrest and said, "Pull over, asshat."

An apology was in order, but Liam was genuinely terrified that something that true and heartfelt would necessarily come with an admission of undying love. Completely without intention or forethought. It would just *happen*.

So he pulled over. And he let her out about three houses down from hers. Marcie hopped out, too.

"Stay until we get inside," Marcie said darkly.

"Well, duh."

"You don't get the presumption of common sense anymore." Jorja's voice sounded so much like Dad's in that moment that Liam almost double-checked the rearview.

He had a hundred comebacks. But Jorja was right and he deserved it, so he bit his tongue and kept watch on El and Marse by the light of his high beams until they were inside.

# ELAYAH

The last time Marcie had spent the night was on Elayah's sixteenth birthday. There'd been six girls visiting the Laird house that night, sucking up Dad's bandwidth and devouring every scrap of food in the place. It had been amazing, and then two days later the county went on COVID-19 lockdown and Elayah had spent a couple of weeks wondering if she'd given anyone the virus at her party, or if anyone had given it to her. In the end, two girls came down with it and both pulled through fine, but the juxtaposition of the party to the lockdown and illnesses had killed any desire for sleepovers for Elayah.

She knew Marcie wouldn't say it, but this scheme seemed to be the perfect way to get Elayah sleeping in her own room again. With Marcie nearby, she bet she could do it.

Dad seemed ill at ease with Marcie in the house, but he and Mom did that nonspeaking parental communication thing they did, and he smiled tightly and asked how her parents were as they sat down to dinner.

Marcie had no problem chatting *ad infinitum* with her parents, which did a good job of hiding Elayah's own reticence. She imagined that if the situation were reversed—if she were spending the night at Marcie's—that *she* would be the one blathering on and on with Kim, wallowing in small talk, and *Marcie* would be the sullen one at the table, trying not to glare, wondering, *What did you do? What do you know?*

*Does the name Lisa McKenzie mean anything to you? Do you know a blond guy in his late twenties or early thirties who's going to be limping for the foreseeable future?*

After dinner she and Marcie retreated to her bedroom, which felt brighter and airier already. Marcie was a pretty good actor—she didn't betray any nervousness or anxiety about being at the scene of the crime.

They spent some time on Insta, absorbing the usual gossip. Marcie filled Elayah in on the who, what, where, why, and when of school so that she'd be caught up when she returned after the weekend. She really appreciated it. She was tired of being "the girl who got attacked." She was ready to be herself again. Ready to return to school and her life.

Her hand went to her throat. Maybe she would wear turtlenecks for a little while.

Marcie noticed the movement. "Does it still hurt?"

"A little. The stitches are supposed to dissolve on their own. The doctor says I might have a little scar, but it shouldn't be too bad."

Nibbling at the cuticle on her left thumb, Marcie got around to asking, "What was it like?"

They hadn't talked about that night. Not in any detail.

Elayah didn't want to relive it to the degree it would take to give a fulsome answer. "It didn't even hurt at first." She shrugged. "Then it hurt a *lot*."

"How was Liam that first night in the hospital?" Marcie grinned wickedly. The easy questions had been asked, apparently.

Elayah's cheeks and forehead flushed with acute heat, the internal combination of well-aged passion and brand-new anger. "Can we at least *try* to pass the Bechdel Test tonight?" she asked. "Especially after that comment he made about my uncle?"

Marcie held her hands up, palms out in surrender. "Okay, no more Liam talk. Got it."

With that subject off the table, they realized simultaneously that there was really only one other to discuss.

"So…," Marcie eased into it. "Uh, do you think your uncle maybe *did* have something to do with it?"

Did she *think* it? It had been her second thought upon seeing the knife and realizing its possibilities. The worst part about that possibility was that it was probably the best-case scenario. It would mean that everyone she knew personally was innocent.

Her *first* thought had been that Antoine himself had been killed back in 1986. He'd never abandoned his twin, his family, leaving them to decades of heartache, mystery, and hurt—he'd been murdered.

But there were the postcards.

"It makes sense that it has something to do with him, right?" she said to Marcie. "Uncle Antoine did something back in 1986 and ran off to Mexico. It's right there."

"That might not be what happened," Marcie said with a solidity and a confidence that made Elayah love her even more. "There's De Nardo. And this other guy. Who knows?"

"I never knew him. It's not like finding out he killed someone would wreck my relationship with him or anything."

Marcie groped for Elayah's hand, but she slid it away before Marcie could get there. Elayah didn't want to be comforted any longer. She didn't want to be coddled and protected.

Someone had come into her bedroom, her safest place, and put a knife to her throat. Something was happening around her that she could not entirely perceive, like a bad odor that starts as a whiff, then grows in intensity. Impossible to ignore and impossible to track down.

"What are you thinking?" Marcie asked gently.

"Honestly? I'm thinking about my uncle's postcards. If it weren't for them, I could just tell myself someone killed Antoine back then, and I wouldn't have to think that maybe *he* did it."

"Yeah." Marcie considered. "What *is* in those postcards, anyway? What did he say?"

Elayah shrugged. "I'll show you."

Mom and Dad were still downstairs. Elayah stole into her parents' room with the long-practiced silence of a child whose father often slept days when on night shift. She slid to the floor and shined her phone's flashlight under their bed.

A long, flat plastic tub reflected part of the light back to her. She rolled it out just enough to lift the lid. Mementos. Mom kept swearing that someday she would assemble an album. A shadow box. An étagère. Day after day, year after year, they remained under the bed.

The postcards—eleven of them in total—were rubber-banded together in a corner of the tub. She took them, returned the tub, and went into her bedroom.

Marcie had taken the desk chair. Once, Elayah would have flopped onto her belly on the bed to examine the postcards, but the bed still coruscated with bad energy and ill remembrances. So she unbanded the stack and spread out the postcards on the desk in front of Marcie, snapping them down image-side up as though she were a blackjack dealer.

Marcie had never seen the postcards before. She treated them with a quiet reverence that Elayah had once possessed as a child. Now, though, they were just one more old family artifact that meant nothing, certainly less important than her dad's old track trophies.

"Do you think the police will actually get this guy?" Marcie asked.

*Which guy?* Elayah wondered. The guy who'd cut her? The guy they'd kidnapped? The guy who did something to someone back in 1986? There were too many people, too many possibilities.

She knew Liam's dad. She'd grown up around him, spent a lot of time with him as a kid, before all the parents sort of drifted apart. Even though he was a cop, she liked him.

But she also knew that the Canterstown Sheriff's Department wasn't exactly S.H.I.E.L.D. Or even the FBI. There was a chance this crime—these *crimes*, she amended, touching her stitches briefly—would never be solved.

She went cold at the thought. Marcie noticed the shiver.

"It's going to be okay," she promised Elayah.

Elayah eyed the bed. Just an ordinary bed. It looked more like a torture rack to her.

"I know it will be," she lied to her best friend.

They turned to the postcards. The first one was blank-faced, a generic airmail postcard that—the theory went—Antoine had purchased in the US before crossing the border.

The rest of the postcards were from sites in Mexico City and a place called Temoaya. They called up Temoaya on Google Maps—it was about two hours outside Mexico City. Google Earth showed them what it looked like. Did Antoine still live there? Was Antoine even alive?

Marcie said little. She seemed to understand intuitively that this was fraught and tenuous territory.

Elayah flipped over the first postcard. Uncle Antoine's printing was sloppy, almost juvenile. Her image of him was always of a teenager, even though she knew he was Dad's exact same age.

Mom, Pops, Marcus—

I'm sorry, but I can't explain this right now. Maybe later. I'll try. I've gone away. I have to do this. Please don't try to find me. I love you all, but I can't be home right now.

Love, Antoine

She'd read it before, of course, filching the pack of cards from her parents' room, poring over each and every one. It had been a while, though. And it had always felt like reading excerpts from an old Victorian novel, from back when a novel was really nothing more than a fictional biography. Her ninth-grade English teacher, Ms. Burke, had explained the origin of the novel this way: "These weren't considered fiction the way we think of it today. The very first novels were biographies; they just happened to be biographies of people who had never existed."

She flipped over the last card, this one postmarked from Temoaya in September of 1987, almost a year after Antoine disappeared.

Mom, Pops, Marcus—

My Spanish has improved a lot since coming here. I think in it now. Don't use my English much—it's a little weird writing this to you!

*I'm working in a bar (they call them "las cantinas" here), doing odd jobs, sometimes tending bar. I only speak English when there are tourists in town, but that's not often. Everyone treats me well here. I have a little apartment to myself and it's nice.*

*I'm doing well. I hope all of you are well, too. Once I'm fully moved in, I'll send my address.*

*Love, Antoine*

That was the last they'd heard of him.

Emotions surrounding Uncle Antoine—his disappearance, his vacancy, his mere existence—resisted easy quantification for Elayah. She had a sense that she was supposed to feel an emptiness, an Antoine-shaped hole in her life, the way her dad clearly and harshly missed half of himself. But she'd never known him. Never seen him other than photographs and a single, grainy home video shot by her grandparents with a janky, old 8mm camera in 1976. And in truth, one little kid looked like another, especially when they were identical twins.

Still, he was gone and he was blood, and she felt something, even if it was only perplexity and an almost frangible sense of abstract loss.

"Wow," Marcie breathed. "This is…" She trailed off and said nothing else.

"I think there was something in the yearbook about him, too." Elayah sneaked back into her parents' room and snagged her mom's senior yearbook. In her room, she and Marcie flipped through it until they found a section in the back labeled *Gone, But Not Forgotten*.

The first page was an *In Memoriam* for a kid named Bradley Simon Gimble, who had apparently died in a car accident. Sad, but irrelevant to them.

They turned the page and there he was: Uncle Antoine. Eternally young, in black and white. Because apparently color printing was too difficult for the eighties?

**Antoine Louis Laird.** *'Toine. Black Lightning.*
*Antoine's disappearance shocked the Canterstown com-*
*munity. He had planned to attend Howard University after*
*graduation. We all miss him, none more so than his twin*
*brother, Marcus. Wherever you break the tape, Antoine,*
*your hometown crowd is still cheering for you.*

"That's nice," Marcie said. "I wonder who wrote it."

"I don't know." Elayah flipped back through the pages until she found
her dad's photo in the senior section. There he was with that greasy hair, otherwise identical to Antoine.

**Marcus Louis Laird.** *Marco. Black Lightning. University of Houston–*
*bound! Lewis and Baptiste!*

"That's weird," Elayah muttered.

"What?"

"My dad didn't go to University of Houston. He went to Howard."

"Like Antoine planned to."

"Yeah..."

Elayah stared at the page, her brow furrowing. Something...something
tickled the back of her brain. Puzzle pieces wanted to slip into place, if only
she would let them.

Her dad talked about Howard a *lot*. He talked about Houston when he
mentioned his childhood track heroes, but never talked about wanting to go
there.

Marcie watched her, clearly wanting to ask a question, but just as clearly
respecting Elayah's need to process on her own. Instead, she turned to the
postcards and skimmed through the ones they'd skipped over. Meanwhile,
Elayah stared at the picture of her father, the smile, the hair, the almost-
familiar squint of the eyes.

She wondered how her life might have been different had Uncle Antoine
never run off to Mexico. If she'd grown up with him in her life. A duplicate
Dad. She wished that had been the case. How different would the world be?

Or at least her little piece of it.

"Hey," Marcie said. Quietly. To herself.

"What?" Elayah asked.

"I…" Marcie hedged. "I'm not sure, but…"

She pulled out her phone and tapped into Photos, where she pulled up a picture of the note they'd found in the time capsule. Then she laid her phone next to Antoine's first postcard.

Elayah leaned over, peering from the phone to the postcard and back. And then she saw it.

Both began with the words *I'm sorry*. And to her admittedly untutored eye, they looked the same.

Gnawing at her lower lip, Elayah skipped back and forth between the two. Were they? Were they the same?

She had a sudden inspiration and took a picture of the postcard's text. Then she opened that picture and the note in a photo-editing app, placing them each on separate layers. Manipulated the images until they were the same size. Then she overlaid one on the other.

Oh, God.

Without a word, she held out her phone to Marcie, who leaned in to scrutinize it. She spent more time than was necessary to realize the obvious.

"They're the same. I mean…there's little tiny differences, but it's different paper, probably different pens, but they look the same. They overlap almost perfectly."

Precisely what Elayah had thought. She appreciated that Marcie had taken more time than was necessary, pretending it was a tough call. But facts were facts. It was as obvious as the air she breathed.

"Uncle Antoine wrote the note. He's the one who killed someone."

"Who?" When Marcie spoke, Elayah realized that at some point they'd both begun whispering. "Why?"

"I don't know.…" She glanced at the yearbook again. Her dad's picture. Black Lightning. Lewis and Baptiste. University of Houston.

*Duplicate Dad.*

She'd thought it moments ago, and for some reason, now it echoed, coming back like a bad sequel no one wanted.

*Duplicate Dad.*

Something nibbled around the edges of her thoughts.

*Houston and Howard. Howard and Houston. Black Lightning. Houston and Howard. Howard and Houston.*

And then a new voice in her head: *Anyway, that's how your dad and I got close. Love close.*

Mom.

*Love close.*

Oh.

It was beginning to make sense. She resisted it, but it clamored in her head, singing out its truth.

Oh, *God*!

Elayah's guts, already tangled and taut, loosened and pulsed. Without a word to Marcie, she leapt up and ran to the bathroom down the hall, fell to her knees at the toilet, and threw up with an abandon she hadn't experienced since she was a kid. It felt like it took forever to void her stomach, and even when it was empty, her throat continued to constrict, dry heaves, the painful cut pulsing with heat.

The mystery wasn't really a mystery at all. It was a puzzle, a puzzle with only two pieces: who killed and who died.

And Marcie was there behind her, rubbing her back, her shoulders. Elayah slumped against the cool porcelain of the toilet and spat bile into the bowl. Marcie tore off some toilet paper and held it out to her.

Elayah wiped her mouth and finally looked up at her best friend.

"I think I know what happened," she said. Tears gathered at the corners of her eyes, and she wiped them away with the heel of her palm.

*My dad is Antoine. My dad is Antoine.*

It made sense. It made absolute perfect sense.

The decision to skip University of Houston and go to Howard. That had been *Antoine's* plan, not Da—Marcus's.

Marcus. She had to think of him that way now. She'd never known Marcus. Marcus died thirty-five years ago. Her father was Antoine, the man she'd been told had disappeared.

It fit. It fit so perfectly that she couldn't believe she'd missed it. Mom had told her: She and Dad had been casual, not serious... *until Antoine disappeared.* What if that was because Marcus was literally a different person afterward? Antoine had killed Marcus. Taken his place. Maybe because he'd always been in love with Mom? Oh, God...

Dad/Antoine had had access to the time capsule. It all fit.

"We need to go to your house," she told Marcie.

"What?"

She thought of her father—of Antoine—downstairs. A murderer. On the sofa. Arm draped around Mom's shoulders.

"I just can't stay here. I'll explain when we get to your house."


Once safely ensconced behind the door of Marcie's bedroom, they called the others into a Group FaceTime.

She laid it all out. Hoping against hope that one of them would tell her she was crazy, would point out some flaw in her theory that would make it impossible. Jorja, she was certain, would find a flaw. Jorja would make it all unhappen.

"The only part I can't figure it out is the postcards from Mexico," Jorja mused. "But the handwriting matches. So maybe he wrote them here and then mailed them to someone in Mexico to send back. To cover his tracks."

"Can we get a sample of your dad's handwriting?" Marcie asked suddenly. "Just to be sure?"

"Handwriting changes over time," Liam said. "That's what I've heard, anyway. I don't think it would match after thirty-some years." He paused, and when he spoke again, there was honest grief in his voice. "I'm really sorry, El. It looks like your dad was involved somehow. But maybe it's not as bad as it looks. Maybe someone attacked *him* with the knife...."

"You'd think he would remember something like that," Jorja sniffed. "Seems more likely he's covering up—"

"God, Jorja!" Marcie exclaimed. She put her arm around Elayah and squeezed against her. "Shut up, okay?"

Abashed, Jorja busied herself with something off-camera. Liam gazed out from the phone's screen, melancholy.

Jorja had failed her. Her dad was Antoine. She knew it. She could feel it. The other details all swam in a dense fog, but that one stood out clear, like a buoy caught in a lighthouse's beam.

"Now what?" Elayah whispered.

"This is sort of out of our league," Marcie said quietly. "It's getting complicated."

"My dad can—"

"No." Elayah cut Liam off. "How are we supposed to trust any of them? I want the truth, not what they *want* us to know."

Liam opened his mouth to protest, then shut it.

"We need someone else who can get information," Jorja supplied, speaking a bit hesitantly after Marcie's chastising. "We've done everything we can on our own."

"Like hire a private detective?" Marcie asked.

"Oh yeah, they're all over Canterstown," Liam snarked.

While the three of them batted ideas and sarcasm back and forth, Elayah brought her knees up to her chest. She couldn't go to the police. She couldn't go to her parents. And her friends wanted to help but couldn't.

And out there—somewhere—someone was willing to hurt her. And she had no idea if he would try to again.


In the middle of the night, she awoke for no reason. Marcie slept soundly beside her. She fumbled for her phone in the dark to see what time it was.

The photo app with the handwriting samples was still open. And the handwriting still matched. That was incontrovertible. Indubitable.

He was her father, but he wasn't who she thought he was. What did that mean? Was she at risk? She didn't want to imagine that, but if her father had killed his own *twin* . . .

What was she going to do? What the hell was she going to do?

Sobbing silently next to Marcie in the dark, she clutched her phone to her chest as though it could serve as armor. But nothing could protect her when she didn't know from which direction the attack would come.

Her phone buzzed. Wiping her eyes, she forced herself to look at the screen.

And suddenly she knew *exactly* what the hell she was going to do.

# 1986: DEAN

Jay, it turned out, had been going into the school almost every night since that first night. Alone.

At first, Dean was horrified. Every time they went into the school, they increased the risk of being caught. They'd agreed that first time that they would only do this together. Safety in numbers. More eyes and ears on the lookout for danger.

But then Jay explained what he'd been up to: recon. Over the course of those nights, he'd painstakingly identified the doors that matched each and every key on the ring they'd duplicated. His key ring, unlike Dean's, was now meticulously labeled. Main office. Janitor's closet. Kitchen. Nurse's office. And so on.

In the process, he'd also uncovered other sets of keys that opened other doors. Lockers. Cabinets.

"We can go anywhere," Jay told him, eyes dancing with excitement. "We can go *anywhere*, man!"

Dean tried mightily to imagine where in the school he would want to go and came up empty. It was just *school*.

"Sometimes," Jay told him, "you do a thing just because you can."

It was hard to argue with that.

"It'll be worth it," Jay promised.

The thing about Jay was this: When he promised something, it almost always came true.

He and Jay went alone that night. As though unlocking the door to his own house, Jay opened a side door and let them in near the science wing. He wore a backpack filled with a glassy clinking noise; when Dean had inquired as to its contents, Jay had gazed at him inscrutably and said nothing.

They wended their way through the dark, silent corridors, preceded by the funny yellow cones of their flashlights. Jay pointed out doors Dean had never noticed before, like the one nestled between a drinking fountain and a girls' bathroom. That one he actually unlocked, revealing a tiny closet crammed with mops and a wheeled bucket. Nothing to write home about, Dean thought, until Jay cleared the implements away and ushered him in.

There was room for only one person, so Dean stood there and obeyed as Jay told him exactly where to look. Two small holes at roughly eye level resided beside a shelf bracket, nearly invisible in its shadow. You could look right into the girls' room. One of the janitors had done this.

"But why?" Dean asked.

"To see tits!" Jay erupted, as though Dean's sheer idiocy had lit a fuse in him.

Dean pondered this. He couldn't imagine girls going into the bathroom and taking off their shirts and bras in the middle of the school day. Especially right at an opportune moment when the mops would be out in use. It made no sense.

But it didn't have to. He shrugged and stepped out of the closet. "Is this why we came here?"

Jay grimaced with the frustration of a man who has been trying to make a point and can't find the right words. The two of them restocked the closet, locked it, and proceeded down the hall.

They trotted up a flight of stairs to the second floor. The business classrooms, with their computer terminals, were off to the left, the SGA office to the right. Where it had all started.

"Up ahead," Jay told him.

Another door that Dean had never noticed, this one tucked into an alcove near the teachers' restroom. Dean expected another janitors' closet and maybe a peephole into the bathroom, but instead he beheld a narrow flight of stairs rising up into darkness. The air within was slightly stale and humid.

The school was only two stories tall. And they were on the second floor already.

"Where do these stairs go?" Dean asked.

Jay grinned wickedly. "They go up."

At the top of the stairs, there was another door. Jay pushed it open, and a blast of cooler, drier air hit him. They were outside. On the roof of the building.

"Voilà!" said Jay.

Dean had had no idea. Of course, it made sense that there would have to be some way to get to the roof, for maintenance. He'd never really thought of it before.

"Pretty cool, right?" Jay asked as they wandered the perimeter.

The school wasn't all that high, but Dean felt a sort of imperious power as he strode the rooftop. A combination of unearthed knowledge and unexpected perspective. The parking lot, from here, lay like a black blister on the surrounding green skin of grass. The football field seemed small, hemmed in by its ring of bleachers. Off in the distance, a copse of trees now at eye level, when usually they loomed from a hilltop.

"I was talking to Brian—"

"Why?" Jay interrupted with a smirk.

"Stop that. We pile on him too much. It's not right."

Jay shrugged. "He's just so…" He faded off into nothing, then rallied. "He's so needy. Like he wants everyone to like him. Like he's afraid of them not liking him."

*Them* in this case meant *other people*. People not in their group. Who were, therefore, irrelevant in Jay's worldview.

"So? Don't you want people to like you?"

With a snort, Jay shook his head. "Who cares? I have enough friends. Life's not about who you know—it's about what you do."

Somewhere in the cracked mortar between those two notions, Dean felt there was the glimmer of an idea, a revelation, an epiphany. But he couldn't suss it out.

"Anyway," he said, after giving it some thought, "I was talking to Bri, and he said we should bury the time capsule there." He pointed out to the trees.

"Why there?" Jay asked, as though the fact that it was Brian's idea made it less palatable.

"For one thing, it overlooks the school. And he said there are covenants on that land. He says no one's allowed to build there for something like a hundred years."

Jay shrugged and stopped as they turned from the eastern side of the school to the northern. From here, the lights of town twinkled like earth-bound stars in the distance, barely visible over hills and treetops. With most of the town obscured and only the lights visible, it was almost beautiful.

"Here." Jay crouched and hauled two beat-up lawn chairs from under a mounted air-conditioning unit.

They settled into the chairs, and Jay rested his backpack between his feet and unzipped it, revealing four bottles of beer.

"To friendship," Jay said, and it was the most sincere thing Dean had heard in a long time from his friend. So sincere that at first he doubted it and thought it must be a setup for a joke.

But Jay's expression was utterly guileless in that moment. Dean clinked bottles with him and popped the top, then took a long pull. He actually hated the taste of beer, but there were no other options.

Wordlessly they drank, staring up and out. Wisps of cloud cobwebbed the sky, leaking threadbare light from the moon and stars.

"I haven't told anyone else about my mom," Jay said. "Mum's the word."

"Of course." But Dean knew that the secret wouldn't remain so for long. Word would get out. There was something wrong with Jay's mom. That kind of secret was perishable; it had a shelf life.

Dean reached into the backpack for another beer and yanked back his hand at the touch of sharp, cold steel. A line of blood spilled out red below the second knuckle on the inside of his left index finger. He sucked at it to stanch the flow.

"What the hell?" he asked.

Jay rummaged in the backpack and handed him another beer, then held up the hunting knife he'd had stashed in there as well.

"I thought you left that in your car." The bleeding seemed to have stopped. He used the opener on his key chain to pop the new beer.

"I've been carrying it around since then. You never know."

"Never know what?"

Jay's shrug no doubt was intended to evoke an air of mystery, but it had the opposite effect. Dean could tell that Jay knew exactly why he now carried the knife everywhere.

"Just in case," Jay said, and leaned back in his chair, dropping the knife almost idly into the backpack.

TRANSCRIPT BEGINS

INDIRA BHATTI-WATSON, HOST:

This is *No Time Like the Present*, an NPR podcast. I am Indira Bhatti-Watson, reporting from Canterstown, Maryland.

(SOUND BITE OF MUSIC)

BHATTI-WATSON:

Days after her assault, Elayah Laird returned to Canterstown High.

(CROWD NOISE)

BHATTI-WATSON:

Escorted by deputies, Ms. Laird walked from her father's car to the school door. Reporters shouted out to her as she made her way to the building.

VOICES:

—know who attacked you?

Over here, Elayah! Look over—

—any sort of comment—

After digging up—

—over *here,* look this way—

—time capsule with—

For God's sake, look *this way*—

Have the police informed you of—

—any way to tell if—

—for just a second, over here!

BHATTI-WATSON:

Conspiracy and speculation, like nature, abhor a vacuum.
With few facts to go on and no information forthcoming from
the sheriff's department, the air around Canterstown has
filled with innuendo, punditry, and hot takes.

JONATHAN WELLER, MECHANIC:

Ask me, it all has to do with the *Challenger* explosion.
That was in eighty-six, too. And it never made no sense
to me.

CURTIS REINHOLT, CPA:

Let me get this straight: The girl's father buried a time
capsule back in eighty-six, and now *she* just happens to
be the one to dig it up? And then she gets her throat cut?
Something's going on, right? You have to ask the father. It's
always the man in the house.

ZACHARY HINDON, HIGH SCHOOL MEDIA SPECIALIST:

Marcus Laird and his brother were something like local
celebrities back then. They were the fastest relay team in the

county, and they would have proved to be the fastest in the state, I bet.

BHATTI-WATSON:

Would have. Perhaps. But Antoine Laird went missing in the fall of 1986, at the same time the time capsule was buried. Another tidbit of information in this case that has spun out theories by the locals and captured imaginations nationwide. There seem to be overlapping puzzles, or perhaps puzzles that share pieces, and none of them are anywhere near complete.

The entire town has been caught up in the fervor of the mystery of the time capsule, turning Canterstown into what some are calling a tragedy circus. There are exactly two hotels in town: a somewhat shabby Holiday Inn and an even shabbier El Car Motel, which we've learned is willing to rent by the hour, though it does not advertise this fact. Both are packed to capacity.

Beyond town, you'll find a few bed-and-breakfasts catering to those passing through on their way to more picturesque locales. Bigger chain hotels loom the farther east and south one goes, but the press—always seeking advantage and a short drive—has begun offering cash to rent people's homes.

CONSUELA KENT, NBC NEWS:

Look, my producer said, "Stay close to the action." So that's what I'm doing.

BHATTI-WATSON:

And recently a local listed her two-bedroom Colonial on Airbnb and received an astounding $680 for a week. This has kicked off an Airbnb frenzy. Extended families packed into one house in order to rent out others. Friends crashing on couches in order to sublet apartments and old row homes.

As we of the press settle in, spending money, the three local diners have seen booming business. In a town that was suffering the ravages of wealth inequality, even before the COVID-19 recession, the circus—tragedy or not—is a welcome infusion of financial largesse.

MARK SMITH, PROPRIETOR, MARK'S DINER:

I hate what happened to that poor kid, but damn if it hasn't been good for my bottom line. Refill?

# 1986: KIM

Kim had a plan.

Saturday night, her parents had a wedding to attend. She would be home alone. Except not.

No skulduggery required in this case—her mother in particular worried with the same ease with which most people breathed, and the idea of her only daughter home alone terrified her. When Kim suggested that Dean could come over to keep her company, Mom had almost wept in relief.

This was going to be the night. No question.

She wore a skirt without leggings. Considered wearing nothing underneath, a notion that caused fear, shame, and exhilaration to well up in her as though pumped into a single fountain. She settled for her skimpiest underwear, frilly things she'd bought on a dare at the Victoria's Secret in the mall.

For her top, she wrestled with options, finally deciding on a button-up IZOD shirt in mint green, the sleeves rolled up. It was almost shapeless, but it would be easier to take off than the tight turtleneck she'd also contemplated.

After her parents left, she went into the kitchen, where Mom had left her a twenty, and made a quick call before returning to the living room, where Dean was watching TV.

"I ordered pizza for dinner," she told him.

An innocent enough statement. Pizza, so far as Kim knew, was harmless. She and Dean had eaten pizza together a million times.

But he suddenly looked ill, his face gone pale, his eyebrows jumping out in stark relief from the utter whiteness of his skin.

"From Nico's?" Strangled, he could barely get the words out.

"Where else?" she asked. What a ridiculous question. There was a Domino's over in Finn's Landing, but they never delivered out this far. Besides, Nico's was so much better.

For a moment, she thought Dean might throw up. His entire face twisted, seeming to collapse around and into his lips, which had pinched into a tight rictus.

"Are you okay?"

Dean stroked his temples, as though attempting to smooth out whatever jagged concerns had clotted there. "I'm fine. I'm fine."

It was as though he'd said it twice to convince both of them.

*After dinner it'll all be different. He just needs something to eat. And then we'll go into my room and everything will change.*


# DEAN


That night, damn them, Nico's was as good as their thirty-minute guarantee. They'd been making out on the sofa, and when the doorbell rang, he startled, his arm spasming and almost smacking into Kim, who ducked just in time.

"What is *with* you?" she asked.

"Nothing!" he exclaimed far too loudly.

"Can you get the pizza?"

Quite against his will, his eyes widened. He struggled to narrow them. "Me? It's your house."

She tilted her head. "I'd just feel safer if you got the door. It's dark out."

Dean ran through a million scenarios in his mind, tacks he could take, strategies he could employ. Lamely, he spilled out, "It's just the pizza guy."

"Exactly. So here." She held out a twenty-dollar bill. "We'll have dinner and then maybe something special for dessert."

Dean's heart hammered. Was that a double entendre? He was pretty sure that was a double entendre.

The only way to get out of this was to absolutely refuse to answer the door. But that would mean a fight with Kim, and he didn't want to fight with her, especially when he wouldn't be able to explain his recalcitrance. It was one thing to argue from a position of strength, with a solid rationale serving as both sword and shield. Quite another to stand in the arena with nothing between you and the enemy but your underwear. Which is exactly how he would feel refusing to answer the door without a good reason.

So he took the twenty and headed to the door. What were the odds, he heartened himself, that it was the same pizza-delivery guy? Pretty slim, no doubt.

It was the same pizza guy.

He actually saw the car, the beat-up Datsun, before he saw the guy. Opening the door, he beheld the car, idling at the curb down the slight grade of Kim's front lawn. The pizza guy was crouched, plucking something from the doormat.

"Dropped the receipt," the guy said somewhat apologetically, straightening. He grinned sheepishly and held out the slip of paper, as well as the pizza box.

Dean stared at him. The voice was the same, but different. Now deferential and relaxed, as opposed to the previous week's aggressive rage. The face, placid.

Dean's eyes flicked to the car. That baseball bat, he was certain, was still in there, probably nestled in the little crook between the driver's seat and the door. For easy access.

"Uh, is this right address?" the guy asked. Dean hadn't moved to take the food or the receipt. The pizza-delivery guy craned his neck to double-check the wrought iron numbers mounted next to Kim's front door. "Thirty-seven. This is Fairpoint Street, right?"

Dean nodded mutely, taking the receipt between numb fingers. He couldn't feel the paper. Nor could he feel the cardboard of the pizza box or the heat radiating through its bottom.

He managed to remember to hand over the twenty, shifting the box to his receipt-bearing hand for a moment. The guy dived into his pocket for change, but Dean shook his head and waved it off.

"Thanks!" said the delivery guy. It was a nine-dollar pie. Something like a 110 percent tip.

The guy flashed a quick grin and flicked the bill of his cap with one finger in salute. "Have a great night."

Dean said nothing. Stepped back inside and nudged the door shut.

*He didn't recognize me.*

Deep breath.

*Of course he didn't recognize me. Our headlights were on. It was dark. All he saw were light and shadow. Especially when we hit him with the high beams.*

He brought the pizza up the stairs to the living room, paused at the top of the staircase, then ducked into the dining room to peel back the curtains and peer out into the darkness. The delivery guy had just closed the door to the Datsun. After a moment, the car pulled away and disappeared around a bend.

A hand on his shoulder goosed him like a golf club to the ass. Almost dropping the pizza, he spun around, knowing his eyes must be wild. Kim held her jerked-back hand as though she'd just touched a beehive.

"What is *wrong* with you?" she asked.

"Nothing." The lie corroded his tongue as it oozed from him. He wiped beads of sweat from his hairline. He held up the box. "Let's eat."


After they ate, Kim went into the bathroom and wasn't back by the time Alex Trebek announced Double Jeopardy. Dean called out to her and heard her respond from somewhere farther back in the house than he'd expected.

Picking his way through the hallway, he once again marveled at how familiar her house had become to him. Almost as familiar as his own. He knew the people in the framed photos along the wall, the family members both living and not, and thought of them not by their names, but by the same familial sobriquets as Kim—Grandma and Grandpa, Aunt T, Uncle Bumps, and all the others. They had become an extension of his own family.

The hallway was dark. He went on to the end of the hall. A flickering light drew his attention to Kim's room, to the left.

She lay on the bed, buttons of her shirt undone into the depth of her cleavage. The flickering light was from her nightstand lamp, which she'd covered with a red scarf.

"Hey," she said.

Dean swallowed. "Uh, hey."

"We don't have to be downstairs on the old sofa," she told him. "Or worry about my parents."

Dean nodded, swallowing again. "Are you sure?" he asked.

She shifted on the bed, making room for him, her answer the blank space awaiting his occupation.

His legs rigid and rubbery at the same time, Dean stepped over to the bed and sat down, his back to her.

"I'm not sure," he said after a moment.

The shift of her body jostled the mattress, tilted him slightly. Her hands touched his shoulder, kneaded.

"It's okay. I'm sure. I know I said I wanted to wait until marriage. . . ."

"You did. And I don't want to take that away from you." He fixed his gaze straight ahead on a hook she'd screwed into the wall. Several medals on ribbons hung from it, her various blue-ribbon awards for marching band competitions.

"You're not. It's my decision. I'm ready."

The medals reflected the reddish, muted light, their gold surfaces gone dull in the crimson glow.

"I don't know if I am," he said at last.

The mattress shifted again, tilting him back slightly as she pulled away from him. When he craned his neck, she was rocked back on her heels, staring down at her hands in her lap, the right scraping at the nail polish on the left.

"Hey." He took her hands, pulled them gently apart. "It's not about you. It's all me. I've had it in my head that this wasn't going to happen and then . . . it's just an adjustment. Plus . . ." He took a deep breath. He had to tell her. "Plus, there's something else. I'm a little mixed up tonight."

She tossed her hair; it moved as one piece, almost like a hat or helmet. "Why?"

"It was the pizza guy," he began.

He told her about that night, but he didn't tell her everything. He didn't tell her about the baseball bat. Jay's knife. Some things seemed too far.

And besides, her reaction to what he thought of as the least objectionable and most mundane parts of the story was enough. He'd thought that the idea of following the pizza guy was stupid and pointless, but also harmless.

Kim, though, actually gasped at even that minor infraction. "What were you *thinking*?" she demanded. "This is what you guys do on Fridays?"

"Look," he said, moving on quickly, shifting the conversation from his own stupidity to his very real fears, "I don't think he recognized me, but I keep thinking…what if he did? What if he wrote down your address? Or just kept it from the receipt? What if he thinks I live here and he's going to show up after his shift and do something stupid?"

"Stupider than spending hours on a Friday night driving around following a pizza-delivery guy?" She'd buttoned up her shirt at some point and now folded her arms over her chest as though to say, *You can't touch and you can't even look anymore.*

Dean pinched the bridge of his nose. "Kim…I'm serious."

"So am I." She swung her legs around, hopped off the bed, and marched out into the hall.

# KIM

Her mother had told her—so *many* times, it seemed—that girls matured faster than boys. But Dean, smart and clever and kind, seemed so much more grown-up than the other boys her age that it was easy to dismiss her mother's admonition when it came to him.

She'd forgotten, though, that Dean-with-her was a different creature than Dean-with-the-guys. *That* Dean was susceptible to whatever hormone-induced outrages boys managed to conjure among themselves, like a masculine version of a witches' coven, invoking foolishness and stupidity and banal cruelty in lieu of something useful.

*There is nothing more dangerous than an angry man,* her mother had once warned her. *Except for one who's bored.*

Dean caught up to her in the kitchen, where she'd gone after leaving her bedroom.

"You should call the store," she said, rummaging in a drawer, "and apologize."

Dean blinked at her. "What?"

She turned and held out the Nico's menu she'd dug out of the kitchen junk drawer. "Call. Apologize."

Dean laughed. "No way."

His laughter hurt more than if he'd struck her. It reduced her. It demeaned her. Anger was one thing, mockery quite another.

"I'm not joking, Dean." She let her voice rise into the registers of outrage she rarely permitted herself. "You did something stupid and you should apologize for it. We're not kids. We're practically adults."

"You don't have to shout," he told her, taking a step back, out of the kitchen and into the dark hallway, where shadows swaddled him. "Don't get so emotional about this."

In response, she snatched the handset from the phone mounted to the kitchen wall.

"Fine. *I'll* call." She tapped out the number on the handset and held it to her ear.

"Don't!" he yelped. In half a second, he'd bridged the space between them and seized the phone, ripping it away from her and slamming it back on the base with a hard plastic *clack* and a distant, hollow ring.

"Look, I'm sorry," Dean said, palms raised. "But we can't just—"

"Go home," she said.

When he hesitated and opened his mouth to speak again, she screamed it, and the scream felt good, felt powerful.

"Go!"

Dean nodded and mumbled something, then backed away toward the stairs and out the front door.

**27**

# THE PRESENT: ELAYAH

Her first day back at school had been hell, pure and simple. All things considered, holding a clandestine meeting that afternoon seemed safer and more pleasant.

They met in Brookdale, not Canterstown, where hopefully they wouldn't be identified by any random passersby. Liam had agreed to her scheme only if he could be present. She wasn't sure if she was still angry at him or not, but he could call his father at any moment and end all of this, so she suffered his presence.

They arranged the meeting at the creatively named Burger Joint. She and Liam took a table together with an easy line of sight to the door and sat next to each other so that Indira Bhatti-Watson would have to sit across from them.

Indira looked nothing like what Elayah expected. Her voice through Elayah's earbuds had been all cigarette rasp, whiskey-smoothed into something sensual and clear. Elayah had expected someone older, maybe in her thirties, with smoky eyeliner and full red lips and a come-hither vibe.

Instead, Indira Bhatti-Watson was almost a pixie, topping out at five three, max. She wore her black hair in a messy bun, streaks of yellow and pink and blue ribboning through it. Her left earring did not match her right earring. Like, at *all*.

She spied Elayah immediately and slid into the seat across from them.

Indira's eyes shone with excitement and glee, and she started babbling with neither preamble nor introduction.

"I'm so glad you agreed to meet with me," said the husky siren possessing the body of Indira Bhatti-Watson. "This is great! It's so great. I mean, I came here because of what happened to you and the whole idea of uplifting a story about a woman of color, and then when I couldn't talk to you, I just really sort of fell in love with the idea of the story of the *town itself*, its history and how it's changed, but I always kept the other stuff on a low boil, you know? That's what my mother says: a low boil. Anyway, I—"

"You said you knew something about my uncle," Elayah interrupted. She knew the type; if she let Indira go, the woman would yak until the heat death of the universe.

**I have info on your missing uncle** was the exact formulation of Indira's last DM, the one that had caught Elayah's attention at Marcie's in the depths of her despair. And in an instant, she'd known exactly what she had to do.

For days now, targeted because of what they'd dug up, she'd labored under the misapprehension that she had nothing else to offer or to surrender, that her only poker chip was the junk her dad and his friends had consigned to an airless vault under the ground thirty-odd years ago.

But that wasn't true. Yeah, there was a crazy man out there trying to get back what was his, and that crazy man might even be her own father, but there were also crazy *reporters* trying to get something else only she had: information. It was time for some quid pro quo.

(When she'd said exactly that to the others during the school day, Liam had essayed a weak joke about calamari that had flopped badly. And, damn it, sort of endeared him to her.)

"This is not, actually, your worst idea ever," he'd eventually conceded.

"If we can exploit the resources of a news-gathering organization," she'd told him, "then maybe we can figure out what's going on. Or at least prod someone else into figuring it out before the guy with the knife comes back."

There was Rachel, of course, who was easy-access, but she was small-time. Local. What assets or resources could she bring to bear?

Indira was perfect. Backed by NPR, which was big-time enough to count. And she was young, so neither she nor Elayah would likely have an advantage in outwitting each other or screwing each other over.

Indira tapped her bitten-down fingernails on the chipped surface of the table. "I really do know something about your uncle. What are you willing to do in return?"

"What do you want?" Liam asked in his gruffest tough-guy voice, the one he'd used junior year in the drama club's production of *Twelve Angry Jurors*. Its reappearance almost surprised her into laughter, but it made Indira jump, so she suppressed her reaction.

"It's an even trade," Indira said, blinking her long lashes and pulling back from the table, bracing herself against it with her palms at the same time as though to hold on during a tornado. "I tell you about your uncle; you tell me what the police won't let you tell the press about the time capsule."

Elayah favored Liam with a meaningful look. She wanted it to appear as though the two of them were considering something, but in reality, she was just stalling because she'd already made up her mind. It seemed like a good idea not to just jump on the opportunity.

"I want information," Indira pressed. "Specifically, confirmation." She consulted her phone for a moment before looking up.

"So, in the article that we believe prompted the attack on you, you say that there was evidence in the time capsule. You say you're not allowed to say what it is, but that 'We know what you did.'"

"I was misquoted. Sort of."

Indira grinned lopsidedly. "Was the evidence a knife? Can you confirm that? Because we have a source inside the sheriff's department telling us that blood test results were recently received from the state police lab on a large hunting knife."

Did Indira know who Liam was? She gave no indication—no special dart of her eyes toward Liam when she mentioned the sheriff's department—but she could just be a really good actor. Liam, for his part, covered up his sudden shock by diving into a hamburger with gusto.

Elayah weighed the possibilities here. She was desperate for help, and desperation made for a poor bargaining position. Still, someone had invaded her home, and she had good reason to believe her father wasn't who he claimed to be. Liam's dad seemed out of his depth. She had to do *something* to put the pressure on.

Mental coin toss. Heads, confirm; tails, no comment. The coin wobbled in the air and never landed because this was a really, really stupid way to decide something.

"It was a knife," she said, then hurried on to cover the sound of Liam nearly gagging on a quarter pound of beef and bun. "And it looked to me like there was blood on it. We think someone was killed with that knife and then it was sealed up in the time capsule to get rid of it."

Licking her lips, eyes thrilled, Indira leaned forward, closing in to conspirator's distance. "Do you have a picture?"

"What have you got for me?"

"Right. Your uncle. Antoine Louis Laird." Indira didn't even look at her phone to refresh her memory. "Since he disappeared in eighty-six, it made sense that he might be involved in whatever happened. Maybe even instigated it. So I did some digging, and guess what? Customs has no record of an Antoine Laird crossing the Mexican border in 1986 or 1987."

Her blood freezing enough to cause her skin to crackle, Elayah could not speak. Of course not. Of course there was no record. Because he wasn't Antoine to begin with and he'd never gone to Mexico because her dad had killed him.

"So what?" Liam had her back. Pushing for more. "He might have used a fake name. Or crossed illegally."

Indira shrugged. "Sure. I guess so. But isn't it weird that a kid from the middle of nowhere—apologies—with no access to anything like Google back then would know how to fake a passport? Or cross the border without help?"

"He could have figured it out," Liam said.

Indira sighed. She'd lived up to her end of the bargain. "That picture?"

Collecting herself, Elayah flashed her the image on her phone. "That's all you get for now. Maybe you can track down some more info for me and then you can have the pic." She paused for a dramatic beat. "And I'll also tell you about the note we found with the knife."

Indira's entire face seemed to widen in absolute shock and jubilation at this news. She actually made a little squealing noise as she drummed the table lightly with her fists.

"Okay. Okay, great. Deal."

"One more thing," Elayah told her. "You might want to dig up whatever you can on a woman named Lisa De Nardo. Maiden name McKenzie."

Indira arched an eyebrow. She said nothing as she tapped the name into her Notes app.

Elayah managed to hold it together until Indira cleared the door of Burger Joint, but then she buried her face in her folded arms on the table. "Oh man," she whispered. "It's true, isn't it? Antoine never went to Mexico because Antoine is my dad and he killed Marcus so he could be with my mom and the only reason I exist is because—"

"Hey." Liam put a hand on her shoulder and stroked, gently. At any other time, the shock and pleasure of his touch would have made her flinch, but in this moment, the news about Antoine still ringing in her ears, she barely felt him at all.

# LIAM

They agreed to meet up with Jorja and Marcie at Jorja's house to debrief. Liam parked in his driveway, which abutted Jorja's property. He cut the engine and then died immediately when El put her hand on his.

He hadn't expected it. He thought she was still angry at him.

"Hang on," she said.

*I love you, too,* he almost said aloud.

"You think I was stupid, telling her that stuff about the knife, don't you?"

So the hand touch wasn't a confession of true love after all. And truly, he thought it wasn't the smartest move to tell Indira about the knife, but he was more concerned with the fact that the reporter seemed to have a mole in the sheriff's department...a phrase he never thought he'd construct without a concomitant image of an actual, physical little burrowing mammal tunneling its way under the building where his dad worked. But these were weird, mysterious times.

"You did what you had to do," he told her, and tried not to let his grief show when she took her hand away. "I'm gonna skip this"—he gestured next door, indicating Marse and Jorja and the discussion they were to have, recapping the meeting—"and see what I can figure out at home, okay? It's getting late. Dad'll be tired. Maybe I can get him to say something he wouldn't normally say."

El pursed her lips and tilted her head, examining him from a new angle. He hoped it was a flattering one.

"Yeah, sure," she said, and patted his hand, killing him all over again.

# ELAYAH

Jorja's dad gave her a big hug when she walked in. The first time she'd met him, as a kid, he'd done the same, and it had sort of creeped her out; she generally didn't like people who were handsy. But Jorja's dad was a hugger. He hugged the mail carrier, for God's sake, when the guy came to drop off catalogs and bills and junk mail. He did complicated handshakes with the kid ringing him up at the register in the grocery store. He hugged his clients when he got them acquitted and especially when he didn't.

And he hugged Elayah upon seeing her for the first time since the attack, then whispered, "I'm glad you're okay. We've all been worried sick."

The hug bothered her anew, as though she'd never gotten used to it in the first place. *Did you know? Are you covering it up?*

"Thanks," she said, breaking the clinch, avoiding his gaze. "Where's Jorja?"

"I think she's in the back room with Marcie. You know the way."

She'd spent a lot of time in Jorja's house. She felt no compunctions whatsoever about grabbing a cookie off a tray in the kitchen on her way through the house to the back room.

As she rounded the corner, she almost choked on a chunk of chocolate. Marcie and Jorja stood in the center of the back room, arms around each other, kissing.

Elayah froze. They weren't just kissing—they were *kissing*. Jorja's hands were exploring every inch of Marcie's ass, and Marcie was pressing herself tight against her. The distance between them was atomic, if that. This wasn't the first time they'd done this. Or if it was, they were moving a lot faster than Elayah would have.

"Wow," she said out loud before she could stop herself.

The two of them froze mid-tongue-swapping. One eye from each of them rotated in her direction, and then they burst apart from each other.

"I mean, wow, this cookie is *sooooo* good," Elayah said unconvincingly.

"Hi!" Marcie said brightly, completely unaware that her lipstick was smeared over half her cheek. "Glad you're here! Right, Jorja? Jorja?" Without looking in her direction, she flailed a hand, smacking Jorja's arm.

"Um, oh, hi…," Jorja mumbled, embarrassed, wiping the residue of Marcie's lipstick from her mouth.

Oh. My.

**28**

# 1986: MARCUS

Marcus woke in the middle of the night from a dream of fire.

He often dreamed of fire. Sometimes it was just a campfire, and he sat there, watching its flicker and its crackle, the sparks fitful and brief.

Other times, he held a torch, stood in a shifting bubble of glow. Was there something in the murky dark, something hunting him? Or was he the predator, seeking, prowling? It depended on the dream.

Still other times, like tonight, the fire was everywhere. All consuming. All around him. Everything within sight had gone aflame. Above the roar of the fire, he heard a voice like his own, and because it was a dream, he'd forgotten he had a twin until it was too late, until the voice cried out with a final, choked-off burst of agony and recrimination and he remembered—*how could he have forgotten?*—that he was a twin, that there was another half of him in the world, another half of him out in the blaze, set alight like birthday cake candles, unable to extinguish by blow or by wish, and he called out to Antoine, his breath plucked from him by heat, his voice reduced to a hacking whisper as he jerked awake in bed, one arm flailing out to slap against the headboard.

The *thap!* of his hand on the cheap pressboard echoed for a moment in the stillness of the room. His own breathing settled into its natural rhythm, then hitched in his chest as he held it, straining his ears.

The room's silence roared at him, lashed at him. It was too quiet.

Anytime he awoke in the middle of the night, he sought out the soft, subtle, and familiar hiss-rasp of 'Toine's sleep breath. His twin slept flame-less sleeps, never rousing during the night. Antoine's presence had been a security blanket since the womb, and Marcus liked to imagine the feeling was mutual, as so many of their feelings were.

But now, in the quiet of his held breath, he heard nothing. Blood hummed and pulsed in his ears. Through the door and down the hall, the refrigerator cranked to life and started running.

Marcus let out his breath and swung his legs out of bed. Once, there'd been a gap between his bed and his brother's. Now, the gap had become a precipice, a stretch of emptiness all the way to the wall. Antoine's bed was now ensconced in the little room over the stand-alone one-car garage that held not a car, but rather boxes of junk, the scattered remains of old toys, and bags of trash to be set out for collection on Tuesday.

A fear he knew to be irrational—a lingering remnant of Antoine's fire-cloaked dream scream—swarmed his heart like a cold vapor. He stood and went to the door, peering down through the dark hallway. Through the win-dow there, he could see the edge of the garage and the window above.

" 'Toine?" he whispered, foolishly expecting a response.

Marcus wondered if this, too, was a dream, if he'd dreamed that he awoke from the fire dream, if expectation of Antoine's presence was simply a continuation of the first dream's tragedy.

He pulled on his robe and crept down the hall to the back door, then padded across the scraggly grass of the backyard to the garage. He needed his brother. Antoine had given no reason for his decision to move out of their room, had spoken little, as was his habit now. Antoine's silence be damned—on the track, Marcus needed the slap of the baton in his brother's hand, and on a night like this, he needed the comfort of his brother's presence. This was the deal with twins. They had to be there for each other. It wasn't optional.

The stairs creaked horribly on the way up. The handrail was wobbly.

He didn't bother knocking. Antoine would be asleep. Marcus just wanted to see his brother. Like always.

He opened the door. His eyes had already adjusted to the darkness on his way over from the house.

Antoine wasn't there.

**29**

# THE PRESENT: LIAM

Liam let himself into the house. They'd met with Indira at around dinner-time, and now it was getting dark. He had homework to do and could not conjure an instrument small enough to measure his desire to do so.

Pop's car was gone; he would be at the restaurant. Dad's was in the driveway, though.

And Dad himself was passed out on the sofa in the living room. He'd been pulling double shifts for days now, compensating for the deputies tasked with handling visiting press and such. He had no overtime budget to speak of, and since the sheriff was not eligible for overtime pay, he had the joy of working extra hours to keep the books balanced without sacrificing safety. Nowadays, he didn't get home until past midnight most nights.

Yay for being the boss! It all made Liam's plan to live a life of as little responsibility as possible *very* appealing.

He stared down at his sleeping father. Now what was he going to do? He'd planned to pump Dad for any progress on the case, counting on annoying him into letting something slip. Sometimes that worked.

But now, watching him sleep, a wave of pity crashed against the shore of resolve, breaking it like packed sand. Let the poor guy sleep.

That was when he noticed the laptop. It was almost but not entirely closed, resting on the coffee table an arm's stretch away from Dad's slumbering form.

Was that light gathered in the crook of the not-shut computer? Was it still on?

He nudged the lid open a little more and stooped to look at the screen. It was still on. And it showed Dad's desktop.

His father was absolutely fastidious about password protection and locking his computer, but he must have dropped off thinking he'd shut the lid all the way. And the automatic sleep timer hadn't kicked in yet.

*You're not going to do this, Liam. Even* you *aren't that stupid.*

He skated his fingertips across the trackpad. That would keep it awake for a few more minutes.

Worrying at the corner of his mouth, he decided the hell with it. The laptop glowed up at him as he spun it to face himself. His dad's email was already open, and there was a nice, juicy one about halfway down. It was from the Maryland State Police crime lab. Liam licked his lips and skimmed Dad's sleeping form for a moment. Then he quietly double-clicked the email.

*Dear Sheriff Blah Blah...Attached please find...requested report... summary...human blood...*

Human blood.

Liam's throat clicked audibly as he swallowed.

*Handwriting analysis...separate email...*

Rocking back on his heels, Liam pressed his thumb and forefinger to the bridge of his nose. Human blood.

On a hunch, he checked the date of the email and his temper flared. It was from days ago. Before he'd cajoled Dad into talking about the blood on the knife. Dad had known it was human blood, but he'd told Liam the results were *inconclusive. Probably deer blood.*

Even angry, Liam was smart enough not to do anything stupid like forward the email to himself, but he quickly took pictures of the screen with his phone, then shut the laptop and headed to his room to think.

# ELAYAH

**M**arcie had another shift at Boogie Woogie, so they congregated there.

"So why is your dad lying?" Jorja asked with all the penetrative glare and intensity of a TV district attorney.

"He might just be holding his cards close to his chest," Marcie suggested. She'd returned from wrangling a five-year-old who had stuffed the princess castle full with every plastic food toy from the fake grocery store. It had taken a good ten minutes to unclog the castle. "He's still figuring it out, and he doesn't want to talk about it."

"He also probably doesn't entirely trust me," Liam admitted. "He still thinks I was involved in leaking the story to the *Loco* that started this whole thing."

"But look, at least we *know* something now." Marcie held up her phone, where she'd synced the data from her iPad. She'd been keeping a running list of clues, suspects, and other evidence as they uncovered them. Elayah couldn't bear to read it. It was all bad news. Her dad was a killer, a fratricide. And there was a good chance everyone else's parents were covering it up.

"What do we actually know? A list of facts isn't knowledge if nothing comes of it." Jorja's voice was gentler than usual, even in reproof. Elayah noticed it—did Liam?

After she'd caught Marcie and Jorja making out (the session was, she decided, too hot and heavy and involved way too much hand movement to be mere *kissing*), there had been some fumbling and stammering all around before Jorja suddenly—read: conveniently—remembered that she had to take out the trash. Tucked away in the back room, Elayah and Marcie had circled each other warily at first, two prizefighters assessing each other for weak spots, for vulnerabilities.

And then Elayah gave up and said, "Girl! What the hell!"

Marcie blushed.

"I don't get it. Are you..." It seemed ridiculous to have to ask her best friend about her sexuality. They'd spent so much time talking about boys.... Marcie had always agreed—enthusiastically!—when Elayah waxed rhapsodic about Liam's pulchritude. Elayah had never detected even a hint of anything but Straight Girl from Marcie, not in all the years they'd been friends. Was her gaydar really *that* bad?

Marcie shook her head fiercely. "Gay? Bi? I don't know. I think I'm…" She drifted off for a while, her expression shifting from contemplative to dreamy. "I think I'm just Jorja-sexual."

"You and Jorja. When did that start?"

Marcie's blush deepened. "While you were in the hospital. She came over to my place and we were talking, and the next thing you know, I was all over her."

"All over Jorja." It still didn't compute.

"I think I was just like…my best friend is in the hospital because some lunatic slashed her throat, and holy crap the world's a mess, and I just suddenly needed to taste her tongue like my life depended on it, and I just did it." She said it all in one breath, her chest now heaving as she caught up. The blush had become the flush of memory. "I've always kind of…I thought it was just a girl crush for a while. But it never went away. Because she's just *so* Jorja, you know? Just unapologetically Jorja and the rest of the world can go to hell, and I…I don't know. I guess I'm into that. And she's into me. Which works out well."

"Wow." Elayah couldn't think of anything else to say.

And now here they were, standing around Boogie Woogie, where Marcie once again ran off to pry a kid away from the fire extinguisher. Three of them knew a secret.

All four of them wanted to know another secret entirely.

"Okay, so we can't say one hundred percent it's murder," Marcie challenged on her return, dragging Elayah's thoughts back to the moment, "but we know there's human blood on the knife now. So there was at least a struggle."

"Do they know whose blood it is?" Elayah asked.

"It's not like there's a database of blood out there," Liam said.

Jorja perked up. "Actually—"

"Don't get started," Liam told her. "I know this one. There's ViCAP and CODIS, but they're not comprehensive. The blood on the knife doesn't belong to anyone in the system."

"Which it wouldn't, if the guy died in 1986." Jorja managed to sound triumphant in this pronouncement. As though summarizing for an imaginary, spellbound jury.

Elayah quirked her lips. "It doesn't matter. We know who the victim is."

"We don't know for certain." Marcie this time, defiant and protective. Elayah appreciated it, but Marcie's optimism was beginning to feel forced and unrealistic. "Maybe they fought and Antoine ran off."

Elayah shook her head sadly. "I know you're trying to spare me thinking about this stuff, but there's no record of him entering Mexico."

"You really gonna trust decades-old government records?" Liam scoffed.

"We need more information before we know anything at all for sure," Jorja said, gamely picking up on Marcie's glass-is-half-full vibe.

"We know about the handwriting," Marcie said, matching the enthusiasm of her girlfriend? Friend with benefits? "We could also do something with blood type, right? According to the report from the state police, the blood on the knife was AB. We can narrow it from there just by asking our parents for their blood types."

"Why don't we just open our own DNA lab and really go to town?" Liam joked.

"I bet that Indira lady could get us into a DNA lab," Jorja mused.

"That's actually a great idea." Elayah perked up. Until this very moment, she hadn't realized it, but there was a tiny part of her that wasn't convinced her dad was a killer. DNA could prove it one way or the other. And at least then she could stop speculating. At least then—either way the cards fell—she would *know*.

"You're forgetting, geniuses—we need the knife in order to get a DNA sample."

They all turned to Liam. Jorja and Marcie groaned at the exact same time, which made Elayah wonder what *else* they did simultaneously. And, oh, that was so *wrong*! What kind of person thought about her friends having sex? Ick.

"It's something to keep in mind," Elayah said finally. "If we can get any kind of DNA, Indira might be able to help."

"I just want to say one more time—"

"We're not going to your dad, Liam," Marcie said before Elayah could. "We don't know how involved he is."

Liam shrugged. "Fine. But from where I'm sitting, we're out of leads, out of ideas, and out of possibilities."

Elayah hated to admit it, but he was right.

**30**

# THE PRESENT: ELAYAH

She swore she would at least *try* to sleep in her own bed, in her own room, by herself. She left the door open, which she hadn't done since the idea of privacy first invaded her thoughts in fourth grade. She needed to get past this, to transition from victim to survivor.

Her best efforts and intentions sufficed not enough—an hour after confirming her own exhaustion, she still lay awake, the covers too heavy when on her, her body too exposed when uncovered. With a sigh of resignation and annoyance, she hauled herself out of bed and padded down the hall. Her parents' door was ajar, a blend of pragmatism and fear. No light glimmered within. Mom was alone in there, Dad at work.

Warm milk. That was what she needed.

As she approached the top of the stairs, though, she heard something. Froze in the dark.

*He's back.*

*He's not back, El. It's Antoine. Dad. Whoever. He's home early.*

Who was he talking to?

She crept down the stairs, skipping the spots that she knew creaked. Halfway down, the bluish light of an iPad made her come up short and crouch, as though the uprights of the banister offered any sort of shielding from view.

But her dad wasn't looking in her direction. He was leaning forward in his favorite armchair, staring down into his iPad, where Liam's dad loomed in FaceTime.

"...anything at all. I'm desperate here."

"Marcus, I swear to you: You will be my first call as soon as I know anything."

"I mean, how the hell did a *knife* get in there?"

"Marcus, man, seriously—I'm on it. We're working every possible angle."

"My little girl can't sleep." Dad's voice was almost plaintive, the closest Elayah had heard to lachrymose since she'd busted her knee playing soccer as a kid. A kick gone awry, the ball tripped her up, and a goalie's foot knocked her kneecap off-kilter, almost snapping it loose from its tendons. The pain, expansive and bright, had exploded out of her in a high-pitched wail.

Dad had charged across the field, shoving parents and kids and the ref out of the way, collapsing at her side and scooping her into his arms as she screamed in pain. He'd been both a comfort and a fright, his words soothing, his tone terrified.

She dug her fingernails into her palms. He was her *father*. Every memory and every cell screamed out for him and to him, but she couldn't stamp out the image of him driving a knife into his own twin. Desperately and brutally, she yearned for it not to be true. There had to be an explanation.

"She can't sleep," Dad went on. "We have to figure this out."

"I will, Marcus. I promise you."

Dad nodded and said nothing for a moment. Then, suddenly, he said, "What about, you know, Peej? He had a knife like that, remember? Didn't he?"

"We *all* had knives like that. But, yeah, I think Peej had one."

Peej? Who was Peej?

"So? Have you talked to him?" Dad said.

The sheriff snorted. "'Hey, Peej, how you doin'? Remember that knife you had thirty-five years ago? Where is it?'"

"Damn it, don't laugh!" Elayah recoiled a bit at the anger in her father's voice, so seldom heard.

"I'm sorry. Look, it's not like back then. We're not all together all day, every day. Peej is...you know. And a lot happened back then—"

"No kidding."

"Yeah, look—"

"What about him and Katie, remember? Huh?" A sneer surfaced in Dad's voice. "I know you remember *that*. What about *that*?"

"We were kids," Liam's dad said with a touch of *I'm a cop* in his voice. "We all did a lot of very stupid things, Katie included. Do you really think one of them killed someone over it?"

"No. Don't be ridiculous. But look—a lot of weirdness happened, right? Something went down that we didn't know about."

Liam's dad suddenly looked off to one side. "Marcus, I have to go. I'm working this. I swear to you. We'll figure it out. All of it. Take care of your family, and let me take care of the rest."

A moment later, the iPad screen went back to the FaceTime interface. Elayah crouched on the steps, staring at her dad as he stared blankly at the iPad until it went to sleep on its own.

# 1986: KIM

The day after her fight with Dean, Kim went to church with her family, as she did most Sundays. She'd been attending First Lutheran as long as she could remember—Reverend Parker was like an uncle to her, and she always enjoyed the time spent in the murmuring quiet of the nave.

This Sunday, though, she was out of sorts. The argument with Dean, his anger, her own exasperated disappointment: These emotions clashed, jousting for a pointless victory, eventually fusing into a hot, heavy ball of lead that sat in her belly like the first aching hours of her period.

When the service was over, she emerged blinking into the autumn light, glad for the release. Sitting in the pew had felt like punishment for the first time in her life. Restless and aimless, she'd wanted nothing more than to fling her limbs about her, to pull at her hair, to leap into the air. To *do*. To *feel*.

"Free at last, free at last," said a familiar voice. "Thank God A'mighty, I'm free at last."

It was Jay, dressed in tan slacks and a blue blazer, his tie burgundy and nubby, squared off at the bottom like Alex P. Keaton's. He approached her from behind as she lingered near the door to the church. Her parents were still inside, chatting with Reverend Parker and some other parishioners.

She shouldn't have been surprised to see Jay; his parents occasionally guilted or otherwise cajoled him into joining them on Sundays.

"It's just an hour," she told him, a little more frostily than she'd intended.

He shrugged; he appeared for all the world to wish he had a cigarette to light at that moment, leaning against the doorjamb with a relaxed insouciance, his grin lazy and unfocused.

"I have better ways to spend an hour. Wouldn't you rather be with Dean?"

Now it was her turn to shrug. They hadn't spoken since the previous night. She didn't know when they would speak. Or what they would say.

Just then, a kid strode by, his poorly knotted church tie tugged loose around his neck. As he passed them, he turned back for an instant, his eyes traveling up and down. Kim's jaw tightened. She wore a simple black dress, lace sleeves, hem below the knee, but the kid acted as though he were scoping her out on the beach in a bikini.

Worse yet, she recognized him.

"That's him," she mumbled.

Jay perked up a bit, glancing around. "Who? Who's him?"

Embarrassed that she'd spoken aloud, Kim knew she had no choice but to answer.

"That's the kid who told me I had the best ass in school. The freshmen voted." She strove for neutrality in her voice, but some awkward, mutated Siamese twin of anger and pride shambled forth instead.

Jay checked over her shoulder, scrutinizing the runty little pimply pipsqueak. For a moment, she thought he was going to march down the church steps, stride over to the kid, and hit him. The idea thrilled and repulsed her.

"Take it as a compliment," he said instead. "And he has no shot with a girl like you, so you win."

She didn't know exactly what *a girl like you* meant. What kind of girl was that? Was she? Both comments were supposed to be compliments, she knew, but they didn't feel that way. Still, Jay smiled as he spoke, and for once there seemed to be nothing devious or ulterior in his expression.

"Well." There was nothing more to say. Jay was Dean's best friend, and so, through some transitive property of relationship algebra, he was Kim's friend, too, but she really had nothing in common with him other than church and Dean.

"Well," she said again, "I should get going. I have to finish up a project for social st—oh no." For in that moment, she realized that she had left her social studies notebook, along with all her project notes, at school on

Friday. She'd spent Saturday planning and preparing for her night with Dean (an effort both silly and tragic in retrospect), figuring she would use Sunday to complete her time line of the Underground Railroad.

But the notebook was at school, and the project was due second period on Monday. There was no way to finish it on time. She could ask for an extension, throw herself on Mrs. Lawson's mercy, and hope for the best....

As she worried at her lower lip, her distress snagged Jay's attention. "What's wrong?"

She told him. Jay once again appeared to wish for a cigarette to dangle from his lips. He'd always had a James Dean sort of carriage, married to a casual insolence that was potent but impersonal. He didn't hate you; he hated the universe into which he'd been born.

"Where'd you leave it?"

"I'm not sure. Somewhere between fifth period and last bell, I must have left it on a desk or something. It could be in trig, band, or history."

Jay grunted at that and stared off into the distance. With a little cast-off shrug, he fixed his eyes on her. "We're friends, right? I can trust you, right?"

She'd never known Jay to ask for trust. For that matter, he'd never called her a friend before, either, but he no doubt assumed the same transitive property she'd assumed.

Still, she answered in the affirmative for both.

At her assent, his face split into a broad and genuinely happy grin. "Great! Can you be ready in an hour?"

"For what?" she asked, perplexed.

"You'll see," he said mysteriously. He had no cigarette to flick into enigmatic darkness, but as he wandered away, she imagined he had.


Jay picked her up at her house an hour later.

He said nothing as he pulled up, simply drifted to a stop in front of her house and waited. She tugged open the door to his car and slid in. She'd never been in Jay's car before. It was cleaner than she'd expected, with a faint odor of french fries and hot dust.

"Where are we going?"

"To get your notebook."

Soon, they pulled into the driveway encircling the school. Instead of turning into the student parking lot, Jay drove through the bus pickup area and made a right, cutting through the faculty lot, then followed a small, one-car-wide strip of pavement around the back of the building, where two lonely parking spots abutted the school near a dumpster.

What was going on? Was there someone working on a Sunday who would let them in?

Jay killed the engine and waited a moment before hopping out. "Come on," he said to her when she didn't move.

Clambering out of the car, she rushed to a gray door set into the redbrick facade. Jay had practically run there, and she followed his lead for no reason she could identify.

A moment later the door opened. A jangling cluster of keys hung from the lock.

"Where did you get those?"

Jay ushered her into what seemed to be a workroom of some kind. There were metal shelves against the walls, loaded down with tools, rows of rough brown paper-towel rolls, and more. "Got the keys from Dean," Jay told her.

Dean? But—

Well, wait. Dean was the SGA vice president. Maybe that's why he had keys to the building?

Sure. That made... It made *some* kind of sense.

Didn't it?

Maybe.

But why had he never mentioned it to her, then?

The room was dark, lit only by the rectangle of the open door, which Jay soon shut. She didn't have time to think any further—before her eyes could adjust to the dark, Jay took her elbow and led her through the workroom and out another door into the hall. Dim light filtered in from windows at either end of the hall. They were somewhere near the gymnasium, if she had her bearings right. It was easy to forget how massive the building was. On an average school day, she hustled to and from the same six classrooms and the cafeteria.

"Pretty cool, right?" he asked.

Her brain and her dry mouth said no, but the rest of her body begged to differ. She had to admit to the thrill of being here when she wasn't supposed to be. Her vision seemed clearer, her hearing more alert. Even smell was enhanced—chalk dust from the distant eraser trays, janitorial disinfectant.

Above it all, the awareness of Jay close by, too confident and too relaxed. He'd known exactly where to park, to keep his car obscured from casual view.

"How often do you do this?" she asked.

He grunted. "Dean didn't tell you?"

"No."

Jay nodded in satisfaction, but his eyes betrayed a small wonder. "Let's get your notebook."

They tried the band room first. It was locked, but Jay had a key. He lingered in the doorway, watching idly as she checked her band locker, then her desk. When she found nothing, she made a cursory check of the entire room, on the theory that someone else had seen the notebook and tucked it away. The whole time, she was aware of his eyes following her. Unlike the pimply freshman, his gaze was unworrisome and benign. Let him look. It was Jay.

"Not here."

He nodded. They headed to the math wing, where she had trigonometry. Her desk was empty, as were all the rest. Once more, she did a quick recon of the entire room, just in case.

"You sure it's not just in your locker?" he asked her as she joined him at the door.

"Positive."

In her social studies class, they hit pay dirt. The notebook—a green marbleized cover with HISTORY stenciled on it in purple ink—lay on Mrs. Lawson's desk. Someone must have turned it in to her after finding it.

She snatched up the notebook and breathed easy for a solid ten count.

"Let's celebrate," Jay said brightly. "I'm thirsty. Let's get a Coke."

Without waiting for her assent, he led her to the teachers' lounge, unlocked it, and flipped a light switch. It was dingier than she'd expected, with a worn sofa and a cheap set of plastic chairs ringing a scarred linoleum-topped table. A corkboard pinned with notices hung between a refrigerator and a Coke machine.

Jay rocked the machine back and forth until it almost fell over on him. He braced it for a moment, then wrestled it back into place. With a hollow, clanking complaint, a Coke can clunked down into the dispensing slot.

Jay handed the can to her. "I'll get another one."

She demurred. "No. We can share. It's okay."

They sat on the sofa and shared the Coke, taking polite sips, as though neither one wanted to drink the last of it.

"Thanks for helping me," she said, handing over the can.

Jay offered a one-shoulder shrug. "Sure."

The silence seeped into the room like fog, swaddling them in seconds. Kim couldn't bear it. "I...I didn't see your mom in church today."

She'd meant it as a casual icebreaker, but Jay's jawline visibly tightened, and she pressed herself slightly against the arm of the sofa, as though that could provide protection from his anger.

He swigged from the can. "So, Dean told you."

"Told me what?"

That look of bewildered wonderment from earlier returned to his face, stronger and more prevalent now. She'd never seen Jay confused by anything; he projected absolute confidence at all times. Total control.

Handing over the can, he clasped his hands together and stared down at them in his lap. "My mom's in the hospital. For depression."

Kim held the Coke can like something that had died. "Depression," she said.

"It's not like..." His fingers twined around each other so hard that they went alternating white and bright red. "It's not like she can just get happy, okay?"

"No, I get it." She set the Coke can down on the floor and put a hand on his shoulder. He flinched. "My cousin had...was...had depression. Was depressed. He, uh..."

Jay turned to her. "So you get it?"

She nodded.

He stood and ran a hand through his brush cut hair. "Man. It's like I've been walking around with something in my backpack for months and couldn't take it out. Dean really didn't tell you?"

Dean hadn't told her a lot of things, apparently. One part of her was angry at him for holding out, but another part understood his loyalty to his friend.

"Dean's pretty good at keeping secrets," she told him, standing. "I'm really sorry about your mom. I'm glad she's in the hospital, though. Getting help. That's a good thing."

"No one understands." Jay didn't—couldn't?—look at her. "People are all like, *Can't she just get over it?* But it's not like that. It's something in her head. Something's wrong in her head. But when you say that, people think she's crazy. When they first told me, that's what I thought. I thought, *My mom's nuts.*" He ground his fists in his eyes.

Kim stood close to him and touched his elbow. He was so much taller than she was. "It's going to be okay. She's getting the help she needs. It's okay."

He dropped his hands loosely at his sides. No tears dropped from his eyes, but crescents of them clung to the undersides of his lids. She took note of his lashes. Why did boys always have such astonishingly, effortlessly beautiful eyelashes? It was unfair.

"Thanks," he said. The word cracked halfway through, became a husky whisper.

He leaned in close, but not too close. She remembered something Dean had said once: *Jay is all balls and no dick.* By which he'd meant this: *Jay will take any risk you can imagine, as long as it doesn't make him vulnerable.*

But now, in this moment, he *was* vulnerable. Whether he knew it or not. It had perhaps snuck up on him, tripped him from behind when he least expected it, and he was lost and flailing.

He was never going to do it, so she did, extending up on her toes to press her lips against his. Unlike Dean, he shaved every day, his smooth chin and upper lip a contrast to the rasp of his dry lips.

Unmoving, he let her kiss him. She used her lips to pry his open, seeking his tongue with her own. When the tips of their tongues touched, the sparked circuit electrified something within him, waking him from his statue-like stupor. He enfolded her in his arms, thrusting his tongue into her mouth, aggressive and needy, so unlike Dean's delicate probings.

The sofa was behind them, and then it was under them.


She had been told it would hurt. She'd been told there would be blood. (Hers, of course—*Only women bleed*, went the song.)

Neither turned out to be true. There had been no blood at all. Oh, there'd been some discomfort at first as he'd entered her, a sense of distending that was both familiar and unfamiliar at the same time. She never really saw his penis in all the hurry, but she certainly felt it. It felt enormous, but there was no way to be sure.

And then his first thrusts had been increasingly uncomfortable until she put a hand on his shoulder and pressed slightly, slowing him. He obeyed wordlessly, and she settled into his rhythm.

It was good, but not great. She knew that the first time wasn't supposed to be terrific for women, so she had no high expectations.

It took longer than she thought, but then his arms convulsed around her with surprising and frightening strength and he groaned as though in pain. For a fleeting instant, she thought he'd hurt himself somehow, but then she felt him ejaculate inside her, a sensation that shocked her more than his sudden death grip on her. No one had ever told her she'd be able to feel that.

*I could get pregnant.*

But she'd just finished her period. She thought she was probably safe. Probably.

In any event, there was nothing she could do about it now. It was done and over with. She knew where there was a clinic, if it came to that.

Collapsed atop her, he withdrew suddenly, and the loss of his weight and his penetration felt like new breath. She pulled her legs together and up, tucking them under herself as she sat up. Her underwear hung from one foot.

In a cloud of flustered chaos, he scrambled at the other end of the sofa, zipping up his pants, tucking in the tails of his shirt. He didn't look over at her.

She had to know.

With the least needy tone she could adopt, striving for utter neutrality, she said, "How was it? For you?"

Buckling his belt, Jay didn't look up at her. "It was good," he said. He could have been describing a Whopper.

"Good," she said. And meant it.

"We can't tell Dean," she added a moment later.

Now he looked over to her, his eyes clear and bright. "Right. I wouldn't."

And then, after a pause: "I won't."

She nodded, lips set in a thin line of grim gratitude. It was difficult to project thanks and understanding with your underwear crumpled at your feet, looped around one ankle, but she did it nonetheless.

# 1986: KIM

**M**onday morning, Dean sought her out in the library. She was there to renew her copy of *Jane Eyre*. Twitchy stamped the book and handed it back to her with a spastic little smile.

"Can we talk?" Dean asked with an urgency that was whispered yet fierce.

She wondered if he knew. Had Jay kept his word? Had he said nothing?

She'd spent the previous night and most of the morning wondering if she could truly trust Jay. Pondering, too, how she had changed.

Or, more accurately, how she had not.

A virgin no longer, she expected some difference in the world just beyond her fingertips. She had been prepared for either a brighter world, open to possibility, or a dimmer, grimmer one, with expectations and hopes ground underfoot like a glimmering cigarette.

But she felt no different, and the world boringly turned in its courses as always, the sun rising in the east and setting in the west.

Virginity, she decided, was a scam. She had lost nothing the previous day that mattered except maybe a dollop of her self-respect.

But now she was face-to-face with Dean, and she knew she could not expect him to adopt her attitude. He would feel betrayed. Because he had, in fact, been betrayed.

Twitchy had faded back into the woodwork as librarians were supposed to. She led Dean toward the stacks, and they huddled together in the lee of the Dewey decimal system. She couldn't help but think of *The Scarlet Letter*. A creeping blush of self-recrimination seeped like lava along the back of her neck and up to the tips of her ears. Had Dean seen Jay already? Had they spoken last night?

"I'm really sorry," Dean told her, hands crammed into his pockets. He wore black slacks with a crisp pleat, a bright yellow collared shirt, matching yellow socks, and black loafers. "I made a mistake. It was really stupid. Two mistakes, really, and they were both really stupid."

She knew what he meant without needing further explanation: the original mistake of following the delivery guy and then the mistake of snatching the phone from her so violently.

But she knew something else, too, something she hadn't known Saturday night: She knew what it felt like to err so grievously, what it felt like to steep in a gaffe, the clammy crawl of its steam on your exposed skin. She had lost her virginity to her boyfriend's best friend. She'd done it willingly. Hungrily, even. Multiple layers of betrayal, stacked atop each other. Even Hester Prynne would cluck her tongue, no doubt. Jay was no Reverend Dimmesdale.

It could have been worse, she supposed. It could have been Brian.

"It's okay," she said, and some part of her thought that maybe she could absolve herself, too.

"It's not. You're right—I'm going to call Nico's and apologize to that guy."

Kim choked out a cough in order to throttle the laugh that wanted to burst from her throat. "No," she said into Dean's alarmed surprise, "no, don't. Don't bother. No one came to my house. It's all over now. Just...don't."

He tilted his head and beheld her with a mix of bemusement and gratitude. "Are we..."

"We are." She lifted herself on her tiptoes and pecked him on the lips before Twitchy could see and stop her.

She convinced herself that that kiss made it all better, like toddler scrapes and baby bruises.

# Ep. 005

TRANSCRIPT BEGINS

INDIRA BHATTI-WATSON, HOST:

This is *No Time Like the Present*, an NPR podcast. I am Indira Bhatti-Watson, reporting from Canterstown, Maryland.

(SOUND BITE OF MUSIC)

BHATTI-WATSON:

The trail seemed cold. The interest and the mood of the reporters who'd flocked to Canterstown on the promise of a juicy story about a teen girl, a mystery from the past, and danger in the present were waning. As the case stalled and the sheriff's office continued to issue no comment in the name of protecting the investigation, reporters started to grumble to themselves and to one another that the window of opportunity had closed.

And then it happened. It happened at the perfect time, as though it had been scripted.

Just when the reporters were getting bored. Just when the editors and podcast producers and section chiefs were looking at their budgets and deciding that there was no story in Canterstown. Time to pull out. Leave some business cards behind just in case something pops, but otherwise, move on to the next tragedy, the next trauma, the next drama.

It happened.

Violence and fear at Elayah Laird's house. Another late-night police visit to a house that had already suffered enough. A new mystery.

And no one left town.

TINA SEDGWICK, DAY CARE OWNER:

I guess I had sort of forgotten about it. I mean, there weren't as many stories coming out, and I figured everything was winding down and it would be one of those things where years later, we'd know what happened. But it looked like there would finally be some peace and quiet again.

BHATTI-WATSON:

But that was not to be.

**33**

# THE PRESENT: ELAYAH

For the first time since the attack, Elayah not only slept that night in her room, by herself, but also with the door closed. She considered this a personal triumph.

It took her a long time to fall asleep. Her mind whirled: with the mysterious Peej and equally mysterious Katie, with Liam, with her dad and her uncle, with the man at PSYCHIC ADVICE, resolutely saying nothing even after Elayah attacked him.

*You're the ones who know everything already.*

What did *that* mean, anyway?

It hadn't been that many days ago. It felt like a lifetime. But not in a good way. Not in an *I've almost forgotten about that bad thing I did* way. More like in an *I've had so much time to marinate in my own badness from that thing I did* way.

She hadn't hurt the man because she wanted information; she'd stabbed him because she *wanted to*. Because she wanted to balance the scales somehow, blood for blood, pain for pain.

It was the first time she let herself think it. She would have kept stabbing him if the others hadn't stopped her. That man with a wife and a baby. Without even knowing if he'd done anything to deserve her wrath.

*I can't be that person. I don't want to be that person.*

Was it in her genes?

She promised herself she would do better. And then she counted backward from one hundred in her head, a trick she hadn't used in years, but by the time she hit seventy-nine, she was mixing up numbers and the next thing she knew, she'd drifted off.

Only to be awakened by a crashing sound.

A moment later, she heard her mom shriek: *"Marcus! No!"*

Elayah's mind screamed for her to run to the door, to throw it open. But her body had yet to figure out where it stood on the whole fight-or-flight proposition, and while it worked through its menagerie of hormones and other assorted chemicals, it froze her in place, the sheet pulled to her chin, her head twisted doorward so hard that her muscles throbbed.

A moment later, another shout, this one indecipherable. And then her mother bashed through the door, swinging it shut behind her and locking it.

"Someone's in the house!" her mother whisper-cried. She pulled Elayah from the bed and dragged her into the closet, where the two of them huddled on the floor.

"Your father went after him." Mom was shaking, her body vibrating against Elayah's, as though she were sitting on a dryer. "Oh, God. Damn it, Marcus. Damn it, damn it, damn it."

She could barely touch the numbers on her phone, the only light they had in the closet.

"Hey, Siri, call 911," said Elayah, and her own phone, charging on the nightstand a couple of feet away, chirped to life.

Mom dropped her phone and started laughing, which turned into crying, which turned back into a sort of laughing hiccup as they clutched each other in the darkness.

# LIAM

Liam sat up in bed, back propped against the headboard, forearms resting on raised knees. He stared into the darkness until it wasn't dark any longer, his eyes adapted to the meager glow leaking in around his blinds from the outdoor lights and the little blue LED on his phone-charging pad.

Motes and colors danced in the darkled room.

He could turn on a light. He could just close his eyes and go to sleep. But no, not Liam.

It was a stupid thing to do, sitting up in the dark. Which was perfectly on-brand because Liam was a stupid thing, too.

*She's still angry about what you said about Antoine. She can't stand you. Which makes two of us. At least we have* that *in common.*

With an angry growl, he swung out of bed and started pacing back and forth in his dark room. There had to be a way to fix this. It was El. He *had* to fix it. Because he didn't deserve her, but he was a man obsessed and obsession didn't cling to inklings of entitlement. Ahab didn't really *deserve* the whale, right?

Or maybe he did. Liam hadn't even bothered with the Wikipedia entry on *Moby Dick*. Life was too short and the book was too long. He had a solid C in English lit, so that was fine.

Argh! He shook his head fiercely. This was his problem. He couldn't focus. There was a knock at his door.

Which . . . it was, like, two in the morning. What the hell?

Pop eased the door open and didn't seem surprised when he saw Liam standing in the middle of the floor rather than asleep in bed.

"No one sleeps in this house any more," Liam cracked weakly. "We're like the house where sleep goes to die."

"Dad just called," Pop told him. "There's been another break-in at El's house. I thought you would want to know."

# ELAYAH

The two of them got the all-clear from the sheriff himself, who stepped into Elayah's room and hunkered down before sliding open the closet door. "It's all right," he told Elayah and Mom. "It's all over."

Elayah didn't want to step into the room. She also wanted to launch herself into the sheriff's arms because the man had a *gun*, and right now that seemed supremely important. She realized that this must be how white people felt about cops all the time, even the ones they hadn't known from kindergarten potlucks.

Dad was in the kitchen, making a pot of coffee and grumbling to himself under his breath. Mom ran to him and they held each other.

"It's really okay?" Elayah had said nothing as Liam's dad walked them to the kitchen.

"The guy never got into the house," the sheriff said calmly.

"He was in the damn garage!" Dad shouted.

"I guess that's technically the house," the sheriff allowed. "But he never got into the house *proper*. I think he was after the time capsule stuff. I don't think he wanted to hurt any of you."

"Are you *crazy*?" Dad slammed his mug down on the countertop, and it actually shattered right there in his hand. Mom squeaked out a shocked little mew and fetched up against the wall. Dad seemed not even to notice.

"This is the guy who came into my house and slashed my little girl's throat!" Dad went on. As though it somehow strengthened his point, Dad motioned for Elayah to come stand by him.

She wasn't about to do that. Not with his anger purling off him like fog from some dark, foreboding swamp.

Instead: "You're bleeding," she said.

"What?" He looked down at the alien appendage grafted to the end of his arm. "What the hell?"

Elayah slipped away down the hall to the bathroom. There were bandages in the medicine cabinet there. Antiseptic and Neosporin under the sink. She thought of Lisa De Nardo's bathroom. Her heart thrummed; her blood raced. She didn't know what she was feeling, but she knew it was strong and forceful and untamed. Fear, still draining through her. Shock and surprise. Worry. Love, for her mom. And, yeah, she thought, for her dad. Who might have maybe possibly killed his own brother, but the level of utter rage boiling from him in the kitchen—his voice clear even down the hall—could not be feigned. No one was that good an actor. His fear for her life and his zeal in protecting it were real. That still meant something.

She marveled at her hands, which did not shake as she collected supplies. When she returned to the kitchen, Mom was dumping the broken pieces of mug into the trash while Dad kept yelling at Liam's dad.

"Antoine had the right idea!" Dad ranted, unstoppable even by the balm of Mom's hand on his shoulder. "This town's never been worth a damn. We all shoulda left a long time ago. What the hell?"

"Marcus, man, please calm down—"

"Please calm down? Please calm *down*? Be straight with me, man—if we lived over in Cobb's Point, you'd've had someone sitting on this place twenty-four seven, wouldn't you?"

Cobb's Point was an elevated enclave on the west side of town. *Elevated* in more ways than one. It was literally higher than the rest of the town, sitting on a bluff that overlooked Canterstown. It was generally richer.

And whiter.

The sheriff's jaw tightened. Finally, he said, "This town's only been getting Blacker for twenty years, Marcus, and somehow I keep getting elected sheriff. What's that tell you?"

Dad spat out a *"Ha!"* and made a curt, cutting gesture with his hand, as though the very notion were too risible to contemplate, much less rebut.

"And one other thing: I'm here to serve and protect, but if you tell me to 'be straight' again, we'll have a problem."

Dad ground his teeth together. "Screw you. You know I didn't mean it that—"

"Enough." Liam's dad cut him off with a single raised index finger. "I can't stand here all night and do this with you. I have to get my team to work."

"That'll be a sight to see, I'm sure," Dad snapped, and turned away.

Elayah brushed against the sheriff as he turned to walk out. His eyes, hard and icy, softened at the sight of her. He actually touched his fingertips to the brim of his hat, as though he'd stepped out of a Western.

"El," he said, and walked out of the kitchen, down the hall toward the front door.

Elayah stood there with the bandages and the antiseptic and the antibacterial cream, worrying at her lower lip as she watched her parents, her mother trying to calm her father, her father trying his best not to snap at her for it.

She'd witnessed this waltz before. With a heart-skipping resolve, she put the medical supplies on the counter and dashed down the hall after Liam's dad.

She caught up to him on the front stoop, tugging at his elbow, a move which she belatedly realized was probably quite foolish given he was armed.

But he just twisted around, regarding her with those same gone-kind eyes. "What is it, El?"

"I just..." She shook her head, then shook it again. The words had seemed so easy, so inevitable on her short jaunt down the hallway. Now they wouldn't come.

She froze there, caught between the hard truth that this was all her fault, that she shouldn't have talked to Rachel...and the harder truth that even though he'd gone to school with her parents, the sheriff was still a cop, a white cop, and she couldn't be sure she could trust him any longer.

"El? Is there something you..."

They both turned toward the road at the sound of a car approaching. Once again, neighbors had turned out for drama at the Laird house, and Elayah was glad to have the sheriff standing between her and the cameras.

The new car was Liam's, but he wasn't at the wheel. Before the car even drifted to a stop at the curb, the passenger door flew open and Liam leapt out, hit the ground at a run, and charged over the front lawn in a straight path to Elayah.

"Of course," his dad muttered.

Liam's dad might as well have been invisible and intangible for all Liam took note of him. Instead, he took the stoop steps two at a time and bounded to her side in an instant. Then, as though he'd hit a wall, he stopped dead in his tracks, two feet from her.

"El..." His voice strangled itself in his throat, like a baby throttled by its own umbilical cord. "El, I'm so sorry."

Sorry for what? It almost didn't matter now. She nodded, numb.

The sheriff sighed, clapped a hand on Liam's shoulder for a paternal beat, then trotted down the steps to wave off the onlookers and the first reporters.

"Let's get you inside." Liam guided her in and closed the door. Elayah stood there in the foyer with him, staring down at her hands.

"I don't know what to do," she said. "I don't know what to *do*."

"We'll think of something," he told her. She knew it was a lie; she chose to believe it anyway.

# 34

# 1986: KIM

They stood in Brian's garage and stared.

"It's a lot bigger than I thought it would be," Kim said at last.

Dean paced slowly around the time capsule. The thing was three feet tall and more than a foot wide. Much larger than they'd anticipated.

"It looked smaller in the catalog," Brian admitted. "We could always send it back and get a smaller one."

A general murmur of agreement cluttered the garage for a moment.

"No," Jay said. "No. Lookit: If we send it back, that's at least a week. Then two weeks for a new one. By then it'll almost be Thanksgiving. The ground will be too hard to dig. We'll have to wait for spring. Let's just do this now." He thumped the top of the time capsule, which rang dully. "We can just put more into it, is all."

Marcus nodded. "Yeah, that makes sense."

Everyone waited for him to look to Antoine for agreement and confirmation—the twins never did anything without handcuffing themselves together first—but an awkward moment passed, and Marcus defiantly did not so much as glance in Antoine's direction.

Kim cleared her throat. "I agree with Jay." Her voice squeaked a bit.

"Well, let's start gathering our stuff, then," Dean said, adopting a commanding tone. "We'll do it the day after homecoming, right? That's a week."

"Six days," Marcus corrected.

There was general agreement at this. Then Jay added, "We should put something in as a group, too. Like, something from school."

"What do you mean?" asked Brian.

Jay shrugged. "I was thinking of something like the Cup."

The Cup. Formally known as the Steingard Trophy. A sixteen-inch-tall goblet of hammered copper with a black band around its rim, chiseled with the names of four local alumni who'd died in World War I. It represented the high school's 1972 football victory over hated rivals the Riverdown Rafters. The two schools had passed the Cup back and forth for decades, beginning in 1943, the year of their mutual foundings, with the Rafters topping the rivalry at seventeen wins and years of possession. But the rival high school had been shuttered in the summer of 1973, and so had never had the opportunity to reclaim the Cup. Riverdown had more victories, but Canterstown would own the Cup forever.

"It's in the display case," Dean protested. "They're not going to let us just walk in there and take it."

Jay chuckled painfully, as though dealing with his mental inferiors suffused him with both amusement and injury. "They don't have to let us. We have the keys."

The boys all went silent. Antoine studiously pursed his lips and stared up at the joists in Brian's garage as though scrutinizing the structural integrity of the roof had been his true reason for coming to Brian's house. Marcus's eyes widened, and he actually took a step back from Jay. Brian swallowed and grinned uncomfortably.

And Dean twitched his lips and hissed, "Jay!"

"It's okay," said Jay, his voice laconic, untroubled. "She knows."

Dean goggled. Kim shot Jay a fierce look.

"I helped her get some homework," Jay said. "It was fun, right, Kim?"

Kim ground her teeth together at his smile. "Yes."

"So let's immortalize the Cup," Jay said, spreading his arms wide to encompass legend, myth, history. "It'll vanish. It'll be a mystery. And fifteen years from now, we'll dig up the capsule and—"

"Go to jail for theft," Marcus said dryly.

"The statute of limitations will have run out by then," Jay said, sniffing the air as though he'd detected an offensive odor. "I checked. Besides, by then I'll be a cop and I can take care of it. Come on. It'll be great."

As with all Jay's suggestions, this one was agreed to, though with a little more grumbling and a little less enthusiasm than usual.

They made plans for the burial, and then—as the twins and Dean left, and Brian went inside the house—she lingered long enough to catch Jay alone. He had remained behind and was measuring the opening of the time capsule with a tape measure.

"What the hell was that about?" she demanded.

"What was what about?" His feigned innocence might have fooled someone else, but not Kim. The corners of his mouth trembled with the urge to turn up in a self-satisfied grin.

"You told . . . We said we weren't going to tell Dean."

"I didn't tell him about *that*," he said, coming down too exaggeratedly on the word. If anyone else had been within earshot, they'd've known exactly what *that* meant.

"Just be careful what you say."

"I'm always careful about what I say," he told her with finality.


Later, she pondered that. And the hell of it was this: That was true. Jay never said anything without a reason.

*It was fun, right, Kim?* That was what he'd said. And of course he hadn't been talking about the break-in. Did he want more than just that one time from her? Was he going to hold that secret over her head, use it to have another taste of what he'd had in the teachers' lounge?

They had a secret between them.

Secrets bound people together, she knew.

She was bound to Jay now. Inextricably. In a knot that bristled with thorns. King Alexander, she remembered, had forgone untying the Gordian knot in favor of cutting it open instead.

She was going to marry Dean someday. Her bones sang that to her when she thought of him; her core went liquid and warm. He would write, and maybe she would have a gallery somewhere that she could run part-time while raising their kids.

Jay was Dean's best friend. He would be best man at the wedding. He would visit them in their home. He would come to Fourth of July barbecues.

And he would know. He would know that he could end it all or have it all.

A familiar feeling came over her, an almost tangible sensation of something viscous and slightly cool on her flesh. It was the way she'd felt when the pimply freshman had "complimented" her ass. It was the way she felt every time she caught Brian's eyes on her.

And now she felt it as she thought of Jay and what lay between them.

Benjamin Franklin had said something about secrets once. She remembered it vaguely, could pick out the outline like the haze of headlights in fog, but not its full shape.

Her dad had a copy of *Bartlett's Familiar Quotations* in his den. She sat at his desk and flipped through, paging along patiently until she found Franklin's section.

There. There it was:

*Three can keep a secret, if two of them are dead.*

On the wall behind her father's desk was a glass-front case in which he kept his hunting gear. Two polished rifles, the wooden stocks oiled and gleaming. And there, at the bottom of the case, resting on a bracket like an afterthought, a straight length of steel with a black handle. Her dad's hunting knife.

Sometimes you untied a knot.

Sometimes, like Alexander, you found another way.

**35**

# THE PRESENT: ELAYAH

They were in panic mode now. The second break-in at Elayah's house was two too many. She was kept home from school *again* and spent the day stewing until her friends got home and checked in on their group text.

Liam: **i still think Lisa knows something**

Marcie: **well she's not talking so**

Liam: **anything from Indira?**

Elayah: **not yet. we have other names to go on. who's peej? who's katie?**

Jorja: **check the yearbook. find them. we go talk to them.**

Marcie: **make it a race. go get your parents yearbooks and . . . !**

Elayah already had Mom's at hand. She flipped it open, knowing that Marse and Liam and Jorja would soon do the same.

She thought maybe *Peej* was shorthand for initials: P. J. Maybe. But the only person she found with those initials in the class of 1987 was someone named Paul Jamison. Who—a quick web search told her—died in 1991 in Operation Desert Storm.

Jorja: **I can't find my dad's yearbook. I don't know where it is.**

Jorja: **And now that I think of it, I don't think I've ever seen it before.**

Elayah snapped a pic of her mom's cover and sent it to Jorja to help in her search. SLEDGEHAMMER PRIDE! the cover proclaimed in thick, wavy black letters. Hand-drawn, as was the cartoony representation of a sledgehammer, speed lines indicating it being swung with great force. It resembled the Wantzler logo, which was no coincidence. Then she dived back into the class of 1987.

Jorja pinged occasionally to update them. She was having no luck finding the yearbook. **I bet my dad didn't keep it.**

Liam: **mute! unsubscribe!**

Elayah blocked it out and pored over the yearbook. Peej was a wash, but they had a little more luck with the mysterious Katie.

There was only one Kathleen in the senior class: Kathleen Rourke. She had hair blown out and sprayed into wings, thick eyebrows, and the older-than-eighteen look everyone had in those old black-and-white yearbook photos.

They checked the usual places: Facebook, whitepages.com, some other sites. It wasn't hard to find Kathleen Rourke. She still lived in Canterstown, over on Bay Drive.

Liam: **are we really doing this?**

Marcie: **yes**

But she also texted Elayah separately: **are u sure?**

**absolutely**, Elayah sent to the group.

She spared one more moment to flip to the memorial page for Uncle Antoine. Or Uncle Marcus. Whichever he turned out to be. She was no longer as certain as she had been—her dad's paternal protectiveness made sense whether he'd killed his brother or not (she was still his daughter, after all), but something in his fury echoed with sincere effrontery. He didn't act like a man whose chickens were coming home to roost.

She gazed at the photo for a moment, and then her eyes drifted over to the opposing page. She blinked a few times. It took a moment for her brain to catch up to what she was seeing; it resisted interpreting the input, as though too confused by its existence.

Also listed as *Gone, But Not Forgotten* was Jorja's father.

With his close-cropped hair, he actually looked a lot like Jorja at that age, which convinced Elayah even more than his name printed in black-and-white below the photograph.

Patrick Jason Dearborn.

*Peej? Is that you?*

She snapped a quick picture of it and texted it to the group along with the only emoji that captured her mood: 🗿

*   *   *

On the way to Kathleen Rourke's house that night, they discussed the mystery of Jorja's dad.

"I never did find his yearbook," Jorja told them.

"Because he's gone," Liam said. "Not forgotten, just gone. So he never got one. Sayonara, Peej."

"It's some kind of prank or joke." It was Jorja speaking, but she was clearly aiming to convince herself.

"Right. The yearbook staff just decided to stick your dad in the section for dead and missing kids." Elayah didn't know *what* the deal was with Jorja's dad's consignment to the *Gone, But Not Forgotten* section, but she didn't think it was a joke.

"I'm sure there's an explanation," Marcie said consolingly, and patted Jorja on the arm.

"A joke." Jorja spoke almost inaudibly and folded her arms over her chest, staring moodily out the window.

Liam's phone announced that their destination was on their right. Kathleen Rourke lived in a somewhat dingy little cottage halfway down the block. The yard was mostly weeds, and the surface of the driveway crackled with fissures. A single dim bulb hung over the front door.

The reporters who had been clustered like soldier ants at El's house had now spread out, roving Canterstown in ones and twos. With no information forthcoming from the Laird house or the sheriff's department, they'd begun interviewing anyone they could find in town who'd graduated in 1987.

Which, perhaps, is why, when they rang the doorbell at Kathleen Rourke's house, the light on the stoop went out and a voice from within cried, "I told you all: Leave me the hell alone!"

"Ms. Rourke!" It was El who stepped forward and leaned in close to the door. "It's Elayah Laird. I Facebooked you!"

Nothing.

El pounded on the door. "Go check your Facebook!" she yelled. "We're not reporters."

After a moment, the door opened a crack and a single eye peered through at the four of them clustered on the stained concrete stoop. "Oh, Lord," said a hushed, incredulous voice. "You're the girl. The one who got stabbed."

"Can we come in?" Elayah asked. She pitched her voice a little lower and huskier than usual. Put a hand up to her throat. Playing the sympathy card.

And playing it expertly, because Kathleen Rourke opened the door wider and hustled them inside, saying, "Quick, quick, quick. Before more damn reporters show up."

Elayah tried not to gawk once they were inside Ms. Rourke's house. Her Facebook profile (set to public—old people, amirite?) had indicated an interest in Hummel figurines and rabbits, but that didn't prepare Elayah for what was clearly an obsession.

Porcelain rabbits perched on every elevated surface—the coffee table, the end tables on either side of the sofa, the walnut-stained shelves mounted along each wall, the mantel over the fireplace. Bunnies, bunnies, everywhere. Bunnies up on their haunches, bunnies in repose, bunnies flopped atop one another, bunnies in jackets and spats, bunnies in evening gowns. Bunnies with pointed ears and bunnies with drooping ears.

"Do you have a pet rabbit?" Elayah asked politely.

"No." Ms. Rourke sighed. "I'm allergic."

She was about Elayah's dad's age. No, actually, take that back: She was pretty much exactly her dad's age. They'd graduated at the same time.

But while her father had grown older, Kathleen Rourke had just grown old. Her blue eyes glimmered dimly from a wrinkle-cracked pair of sockets. She looked more like Elayah's grandparents than her parents. Life had not been kind.

Though life had not been kind, Ms. Rourke was. She bade them sit on the sofa and in the easy chair (Elayah took that), then sat primly on an ottoman, her legs outstretched, ankles crossed.

"Is this about the time capsule?" she asked without preamble. "Of course it is. What else could it be? I didn't put anything in it. I barely remember hearing about it. Saw the pictures in the paper, of course. Lot of junk, if you ask me." Her eyes skipped over to Elayah. "But I guess it was more than just junk."

"How did you know our parents?" They'd agreed that Marcie would do the talking again. She had her phone out, a list of questions they'd all contributed open in the Notes app.

Rourke's expression settled from interested to confused. "I don't believe I did," she said.

Marcie licked her lips and chided herself under her breath. Then, to be sure, she quickly introduced everyone and explained who had whom for parents.

"No, no, I understood," Rourke said. "But I don't really remember having much contact with them. I was sort of a jock back then. A tomboy. I don't think we're supposed to use that word now. I'm sorry."

"It's okay," Marcie told her. "Did you know someone named Peej?"

They didn't even wait for the answer—her look of honest bafflement told the tale.

"You said you were a jock," Marcie went on. "Did you know the Laird twins at all?"

A fond smile creased her face at the mention of the twins. "Black Lightning. Pride of the school. Fastest four legs in the county. But I played basketball, not track and field. I think one of the twins was in my...chemistry class?" Squinting into the past, she sought confirmation. Couldn't find it. "I'm not sure."

"So you didn't know any of them?" Jorja jumped in before Marcie could follow up. She sounded antsy. Impatient. Elayah willed her to chill out.

"I knew *of* them, of course. Especially after..." Rourke paused, as though wondering if she should proceed, and then continued, her voice gathering steam with a *damn the torpedoes* timbre. "After what they did. You *do* know about what your parents did, right? How they broke into the school?"

"Wait, they did what?" Elayah sat bolt upright.

Rourke nodded. "It was a whole mess. They only really caught one of them, but things leak out....It was sort of an open secret that they were all involved. They had to be; your folks were all thick as thieves back then." She paused, lost for a moment in her own skin. "They still close?"

The four friends exchanged looks between them. Liam shrugged.

"Not like in high school," Jorja offered.

Kathleen sighed heavily and seemed so much older, as though the hope of their parents remaining "thick as thieves" had been one of the primary sparks animating her. "Too bad. They always tell us that high school will be the best four years of your life. But they don't bother to tell us that you shed it, like—"

"The school," Marcie prodded. "They broke in?"

"Oh, right. It was homecoming, I guess. I was at the dance. And then suddenly there's police cars in the parking lot, lights spinning. By Monday, word had spread that there'd been a break-in. And then...I was in...math? Calculus, I guess. With your dad." She pointed to Liam. "He got called to Admin in the middle of class. We all knew what it was about."

Liam's expression said it all: He couldn't imagine his father—his *cop* father—breaking and entering.

"What happened then?"

Rourke squinted again, this time tilting her head to the ceiling. "It became a sort of a joke. 'Keygate.' Someone was expelled....I'm sorry, I don't remember much more. It was a long time ago."

"Did anyone call you Katie back then?" Marcie asked.

"No. I was always Kathy or Kath. Why?"

Marcie shook her head and did her best to plaster a pleasant smile on her face. Her best wasn't all that great.

"No reason. Did you know anyone named Katie?"

Rourke favored them with a befuddled look, the same way Elayah's grandmother looked when her phone asked for her password.

"Thanks for your time," Elayah said hurriedly, for Jorja was already on her feet and headed to the door.

# 1986: DEAN

Rules.

Rules made things simpler, Dean had deduced at a young age. When you followed the rules, even if you did the wrong thing, you could still at least proclaim, *I followed the rules*. And people generally had sympathy for you in that case.

One reason he liked being with Jay, he knew, was that Jay broke the rules. Being in Jay's presence gave Dean the vicarious thrill of breaking rules, but with the sense that someone else had done it first or worst. It was like when his father sped on the highway—Dean's dad always made sure someone else was going even faster. *If the cops are going to get someone, it'll be the guy going faster than me*, his dad's theory went.

Dean's relationship with Jay was similar. Jay broke the rules first and fastest; Dean could watch and assess the danger, then follow if it seemed safe or bail if it didn't.

But there were times—like now—when he couldn't let someone run ahead of him and test the waters. Now, in this moment as in so many others recently, he had to break the rules all on his own.

The only advantage to insomnia that he'd identified was this: He possessed an expertise of the nocturnal rhythms of his house. Jenny crashed early, exhausted from college and her job at the record store, falling asleep at an enviable ten o'clock almost every night. Nothing could wake her.

Mom and Dad sometimes stayed up late to watch Johnny Carson's monologue; Dean could hear Ed McMahon's baritone guffaws through their door down the hall if he opened his own bedroom door. Dad's snores provided a handy method of determining when they were asleep. Once Dad was out, Mom never stirred, either.

On this night, Mom and Dad had closed their bedroom door at eleven; ten minutes later, the familiar, broken snorts of Dad's sleep breathing echoed down the hall.

Dean waited another half hour, just to be safe. Then he crept out of his bedroom, down the hall. Past his parents' room. The night was cool, but he wore shorts, a T-shirt, and a light blue windbreaker. His hair, washed, was lank and brown, spilling over his head like unkempt blankets on a bed. It was strange to go out without his hair slicked back, without the hard armor of Dep shellacking it to his skull.

He snatched up his shoes and padded outside onto the front porch. A single yellow bulb illuminated the front of the house, and for a horrible moment, he was and felt utterly exposed. Trees on either side of the property line blocked him from sight in those directions, but directly across the street, the Seavers had a light on in one of the upstairs windows. They had a new baby; they never slept.

Slipping on his shoes, Dean double-knotted them, then bounced up and down on his toes for a moment. Insomnia didn't mean *not tired*. It just meant *can't sleep*. He should have been exhausted, tossing and turning in late-night frustration.

Instead, a high electrical current whistled in his nerves, sparking at the tips of his fingers. He was Lightning Lad and Thor combined; he could light up a city if you plugged him in.

He inhaled, then exhaled, then started running.


The school was, technically, within walking distance of Dean's house; it's just that the walk—roughly twenty minutes—was considered too long by whatever metrics and analysis the county board of education used to determine such things. As a result, Dean took the bus to school on days when he couldn't hitch a ride with Jay or borrow Mom's car.

He jogged along Founders Street, turning left onto the access road that wound its way through an empty field, coming up on the science-wing side of the school, opposite the main entrance. As he closed in, the school came into greater focus, and he spied a figure loitering by one of the side doors, a slim black figure against the red brick.

People liked to make jokes about Antoine and Marcus being difficult to tell apart. Which was ridiculous because for one thing, they wore their hair very differently—Marcus's was what he called *relaxed*, glistening with something like Dean's own signature gel. And Antoine's was cut into a high-top fade. You'd have to be blind not to know who was who.

Even without the haircuts, though, he couldn't imagine how someone could mistake them for each other. Their identical faces betrayed emotions, thoughts, notions, realizations with utterly distinct miens; Marcus's eyes widening in surprise, while Antoine's remained the same, tilting his head instead. Each had a signature poise; the way they held their limbs was so manifest and particular to each twin. And their voices, the rhythms of their speech . . . nothing alike at all.

*What'd I tell you?* Dean remembered his dad saying one time, nudging Mom with an elbow. *They all* do *look alike! Oh, come on, honey—it's just a joke!*

Dean gritted his teeth and cast the memory from his mind as he got closer to the school. His breath was coming hard and hot now, his lungs burning. How did the twins do this for *fun*?

"How do you guys do this for fun?" he asked as he slowed to a halt by the school. Panting.

"All depends on what you're running from," said Antoine.

"Or to?" Dean asked.

Antoine shrugged. Dean fancied himself an accurate translator of Antoine's silent communiqués, but he couldn't decipher this one.

"Have you been here long?" he asked Antoine.

Antoine shook his head.

They unlocked the door and went inside. Together, they navigated the halls and the stairs. Dean led the way. On the second floor, they located the appropriate alcove, and Dean unlocked another door, then trotted up the revealed stairs. Soon, they were outside on the rooftop.

"Here it is," Dean said, gesturing to the encircling night with a hand sweep.

Antoine planted his fists on his hips and gazed around. There was a mild haze in the air, a smoggy, translucent, almost invisible gray that clung to the night; it lent the stars and the moon fuzzy halos.

Dean held his breath. When he'd first come up here with Jay, he'd been nearly poleaxed by the sight, by the spread and sprawl of the trees and fields, the dim ribbon of factory smoke rising in a wavering column in the distance. No specific or unique element stood out; it was merely a matter of new perspective. And perhaps of the proscription of the discovery, of finding the stairs, of standing where students certainly were never intended to stand.

At the end of the day, though (for it was literally the end of the day, midnight nigh), it was just a rooftop. It was just the same view as from the second-floor chemistry lab, only raised by a few feet.

"It's beautiful," Antoine said into Dean's self-doubt. And he turned and flashed a grin, wide and toothy and explicit. "It's really beautiful, man. Up here, it just all seems different, you know? Like it's part of a different world."

Dean had felt exactly the same. He hadn't realized it until Antoine gave it voice.

He came over to Antoine's side; their shoulders brushed against each other. He took Antoine's hand in his own and they stared out at the moon together. It was waxing gibbous, almost three-quarters full, a pregnant, gleaming bulge.

After a moment, they kissed. It was light and there was no desperation or need, just quiet want and a longing that had lingered but was, for now, fulfilled.

# THE PRESENT: LIAM

S ettle down, Jorja Jean." Liam deliberately dropped in her middle name. They'd called her *Jorja Jean* until somewhere in sixth grade, usually in a singsong voice. He thought it might take her back, calm her down.

It didn't. The whole way back to El's house in the car, Jorja fumed about what a waste of time the visit had been.

"It's not a waste," Marcie told her. Liam stole a glance in the rearview. Marcie patted Jorja's hand, and she didn't pull it away. "We learned our parents broke into the school at homecoming."

"No, we learned that she *remembers* it being our parents," Jorja said with petulant ire. "She could be wrong. Or it could have involved *one* of our parents."

"We'll find out," Marcie said.

"Why does it matter? They broke into school. If it was a really big deal, don't you think we would have known about it already?"

"Maybe something happened when they did," El said from the passenger seat next to Liam. She was gazing moodily out the window as the nighttime blurred by. "Maybe something worth killing for. They buried the thing a week later."

And, she didn't add, her uncle ran off to Mexico at the same time. Or was murdered. One or the other. Too many coincidences to be just coincidences.

"It's pretty weak sauce, if you ask me," Jorja said.

El huffed out a piqued breath. No one spoke.

"I'm sorry," Jorja said after a moment.

No one said anything.

"I'm a little…" She fumbled in her pocket for something. A square of paper. She unfolded it into what looked like a letter and handed it over to Marcie, her expression miserable.

"I found it when I was looking for Dad's yearbook. In the little storage space under the basement stairs, in a box of old high school and college junk. No yearbook, but…" She gestured to the paper.

"Holy crap," Marcie said, and handed it up to El, who scanned it quickly. She whistled low and long. "These are committal papers, Jorja."

"I know."

Committal…?

Oh. Oh man.

Liam pulled over to the side of the road. This required his full attention.

Jorja's dad did time in a mental hospital.

With the revelation, Jorja sort of broke down. Marcie tried to comfort Jorja in the back seat, with El turned around so that she could offer sympathy.

Never before had Jorja seemed so vulnerable and so overcome.

"It was my dad, wasn't it?" Jorja said.

Liam skimmed the paperwork, figuring it would be too highbrow for him, but it was actually cut-and-dried. Jorja's dad had been admitted to Sheppard Pratt down in Baltimore in January of 1987, less than three months after the time capsule had been buried, along with its secrets and mysteries. He'd been released that summer, in July.

Other than a statement that both the committal and release had been at the behest of his father, Jorja's grandfather, there was nothing else to go on.

"My dad did it," Jorja said, and hitched in a breath. Liam thought for a moment that she might start sobbing. "Whatever *it* was."

"We don't know that," Marcie told her, clutching her hand.

Liam thought of his own dad's admonition about "crazy people." He held the letter loosely and stared ahead down the road. In the distance, the factory—always the damn factory—loomed.

It couldn't be his own dad. Liam knew that for a fact. And he desperately didn't want it to be El's dad—he liked Mr. Laird, for one thing. And he more than liked El.

Marcie's dad was sort of a dick, but he was never around, so it didn't matter one way or the other. Given a choice between ruining Marcie's dad's life and ruining Jorja's, well . . . it wasn't a hard choice.

But then again, it wasn't his choice to make.

"I can't believe this is happening," Jorja whispered.

Liam did a double take as Marcie took Jorja's face in her hands and kissed her passionately on the lips. He exchanged a glance with El. A glance was all it took for him to know that she'd already known about Marse and Jorja.

Of course. Odd man out again. Emphasis on *man*.

"I guess that's one way to shut her up," he cracked.

El and Marcie stared daggers at him, but Jorja blubbered laughter, howling until tears streamed down her face. Her mirth broke the others' sternness, and Marcie and Elayah both chuckled.

*Most people with mental health issues are victims, not perpetrators.* That was what Dad had said. It popped into Liam's mind as though it had just been spoken.

"Maybe your dad didn't do it," Liam said. "Maybe it was done *to* him."

No one spoke. He couldn't blame them—no one was used to Liam saying anything remotely profound. Or even interesting.

He twisted around in his seat. Jorja gazed at him with hope in her eyes.

Liam was unaccustomed to being taken so seriously. A thousand jokes popped into his head, each one calculated to burst the bubble of solemnity in the car. But it wasn't time for that.

"We're still blind here, guys," he said. And the truth of it pressed down on him. The helplessness weighed a ton. "We don't know what happened. We know that someone connected to Lisa is trying to find out. Maybe Lisa herself. And we know our parents were involved. But we've been thinking they did something wrong. What if they were the victims? What if something horrible happened to your dad, Jorja? Something so awful that he spent the last half of his senior year in a mental hospital? And our parents knew what it was, but it was so bad or so tragic that they did what we did the other night: They swore never to tell."

"And they literally buried it," El whispered.

"Right."

"We have to go to him, don't we?" Jorja asked after a moment.

Marcie put her arms around her and kissed her temple. "We'll all go with you."

"Absolutely," said El, reaching into the back seat to put her hand on Jorja's.

He nodded and stretched his own hand back there. "Yeah," Liam said. "Sure."

# 1986: DEAN

Their first kiss had been stolen, passionate, electric, stumbled upon at Jay's eighteenth birthday party two weeks after the end of junior year. Jay's parents had supplied a cooler of beers, with an admonition that everyone was limited to one apiece. Dean, having had one already, decided that it would be a minor infraction to slip out into the garage and have a second. Jay's parents, after all, were already breaking a rule. So it was okay for him to break one. Or so the logic went.

Antoine had beaten him to the cooler and stood there, a beer in one hand, his other tucked behind his back.

"This is the last one," he said with a shrug of apology.

Then, as though to compensate Dean for the stricken look on his face, he showed his hidden hand.

"Look what I found." Antoine's grin was wide. Too wide. It stretched the corners of his mouth in a way that appeared painful. It didn't touch his eyes.

What he'd found was a copy of *Playboy*, which he held open to the center-fold. Miss May 1982 gazed out at them with blue eyes, reclining on a bar counter, a glass of wine in one hand.

Dean licked his lips and paged slowly through the magazine with Antoine. They settled onto the cooler, using it as a seat. It pressed them close together, and he was aware of the familiar—from Kim—sensation of another body's heat. Unfamiliar, though, was the hard, unyielding press of Antoine's shoulder and arm, the lean muscle. The strength and the power.

Too, there was the scent of Antoine's sweat. The garage was un-air-conditioned, verging on sweltering in the June heat. Yet still they sat, so calmly, paging through the magazine, pursuing the obligatory ritual of absorbing each naked form as the curl of slick paper revealed it. Golden-toned leg after golden-toned leg, pink-tipped breast after pink-tipped breast.

Sweat collected on Dean's upper lip. He was so hard. Unbearably hard. No photo spread had ever done *this* to him, made him so painfully erect and aware.

"Do you…" He had to say something. His head swam in the humidity; naked body parts seemed to caper in the air. "Do you like Black girls better than white girls?" he asked Antoine, and felt like an idiot as soon as the words were out of his mouth.

Antoine paused mid–page turn. The leaf fell over, revealing nothing more enticing or titillating than the second part of the interview with Billy Joel. Dean wished for something—anything—to happen, for some outside force, some external element, to interrupt and throw a scrim over the stupid, *stupid* question he'd just asked.

But the universe chose not to intervene, and instead the only sound was the dry crinkle of the page turning. More Billy Joel. An ad.

"I don't like…" Antoine broke off, not lifting his eyes from the cramped columns of text before him, staring down as though all the answers in the universe were encoded in the words of the Piano Man.

"Hey," Dean said, trying to be comforting. Comfort seemed necessary in that moment. He put a hand on Antoine's shoulder.

Antoine wrenched his gaze away from the magazine in his lap, turning to look at Dean. Their eyes locked.

A bead of sweat lingered in the divot of Antoine's upper lip. The philtrum. That was what that little depression was called—the philtrum. The word raced around and around in Dean's head. Philtrum. Philtrum. Philtrum philtrum philtrum *philtrum.*

Not sure why, Dean reached out and wiped away the bead of sweat, blotting it with the pad of his thumb against Antoine's upper lip. He felt moisture and the bristle of Antoine's fuzzy, nascent mustache. Something like terror flared in Antoine's eyes. Fire burned there.

Dean leaned in to quench it. He shut off his thoughts and pressed his lips to Antoine's.

The first time Dean kissed Kim had actually been the opposite—*she* had kissed *him*, leaning in and up as they sat on her sofa together, the only light coming from the TV. She'd been snuggled up to him all night, stroking his arm, walking her fingers along his shoulder, playing with his hair. Something incipient burgeoned in each touch, and when she'd eventually kissed him, he hadn't even been surprised.

*You weren't getting any of the hints,* she'd mock-complained later, *so I had to make the first move.*

And here he was, in Jay's garage, making the first move for the first time. The cushion of Antoine's lips, and then the soft click of them parting. The next thing he knew, they'd touched the tips of their tongues, and Dean's throat trembled with an involuntary groan. He was so hard. Harder than he'd ever been before. It was as though his cock had been cast in concrete.

Bringing up his hands, he framed Antoine's face and pulled him in closer, thrusting his tongue into Antoine's mouth. Devouring him from within. Antoine grunted with pleasure and grabbed Dean's wrists, holding his hands in place. The *Playboy* fell from Antoine's lap and rustled to the floor in a heap.

The kiss became more fervent. Antoine's hands slid up Dean's arms to his shoulders, then around to the back of his neck, gently holding him in place.

Kim usually took charge. Kim usually pried open his mouth, launched her tongue inside, and played thirty-second notes as though he were a woodwind. Now he was the aggressor. He was attacking Antoine, unable to restrain himself, and Antoine wasn't resisting in any event.

Eventually, they separated, pulling apart by mere inches, inhaling each other, eyes drilled and fixed. Dean's chest heaved. He was aware of Antoine's fingers, still curled around his neck, cradling him. He'd never felt safer.

"What did we do?" Antoine asked between gulps of air. "What did we just do?"

Dean leaned in close and brushed his lips against Antoine's. "This," he said.

*   *   *

Shortly thereafter, Antoine's speaking tapered off. When he was alone with Dean, he spoke, but still not as much as before. Dean asked him about it only once, and Antoine's response had been equal parts painful truth and severe reproach:

"I just can't talk when everything I say is a lie."

Dean had never thought of himself as a homosexual. He thought he knew what homosexuals were—men who thought they were women, who wanted to be women, so that they could be with other men.

Dean had no confusion about who or what he was. He was a man. He aspired to look like Sonny Crockett, not Marilyn Monroe. He liked the stubble that peppered his cheeks and chin after a day without shaving. He liked the square, straight lines of his body.

In the days after his encounter with Antoine in the garage, his perceptions began to change.

Antoine had spent winter break of junior year in New York City with a cousin attending NYU. He'd returned to Canterstown with a cheap faux leather jacket bought from a street vendor and a wealth of knowledge gleaned from magazines purloined from Manhattan's sketchiest bodegas.

"Don't listen to the idiots around here," Antoine told him. "Being gay doesn't mean you want to be a girl. It just means you like guys."

That simple revelation had been a shift for Dean—a true realignment of his personal mental tectonic plates. He had been unable to let go of the notion that *like guys* and *want to be a girl* were synonymous, were like matched socks that just had to be worn together or not at all.

His Sunday-night sessions with Dr. Ruth began to take on a new character. Whether by coincidence or message from the divine heart of the universe, her callers began to transition from girls moping over their boyfriends and guys trying to figure out what made women happy in bed to a steady march of gay men working through their own sexualities. For the first time, he heard discussion of "being gay" as a good thing, a positive thing, a *normal* thing. In those calls, Dean began to see the shape of a world that could be his. The ground quaked and the earth moved and the plates adjusted themselves; the idea took root, and suddenly he couldn't *not* imagine the world and himself as they were. The idea of *being gay* transmogrified, melting from impossible and alien, and then reconstituting itself as not only normal, but also absolutely *natural*.

One night he even stood in the family room, alone in the dark, hand hovering over the light blue phone extension on the side table. He would call Dr. Ruth. He would say:

*Hi, Dr. Ruth. I'm seventeen and I think I'm gay and I have a girlfriend, but I'm sort of cheating on her with a guy. And I'm probably too young to be in love, at least that's what my dad says, but I feel so much and it's so strong and I don't know what to do or what I am or who I am.*

And he imagined Dr. Ruth purring back at him in that German accent that couldn't possibly be soothing and yet somehow was:

*Zere is nossingk wrong vit you. Being gay is just how you vere born. Virst you must accept yourself, und zen you may ask ozzers to accept you.*

Then she would probably try to walk him through *coming out*, as she'd done with other gay callers. That, he knew, just would not happen. He couldn't tell anyone. His father would have none of such talk. His mother would be devastated.

Jenny...

*Maybe* he could tell Jenny. Maybe. The Jenny of a year ago, definitely. She might not have understood, but she would have kept his secret unto death. Of that much he was certain. But this new Jenny, this Valley girl who'd inhabited the body of his big sister like an invasive spirit—he couldn't be sure about her. She might tell the world in a burst of brainless euphoria, just to see what happened.

*Being gay* felt like it could be natural. *Coming out* felt impossible.

Antoine, similarly, had no one to turn to. His parents hewed strictly to the teachings of the ministers at their church, who infrequently but vociferously railed against the "plague of the homosexual, who seeks to turn our eyes away from God and God's plan for us."

It sounded awful. Dean's parents wouldn't tolerate homosexuality, but at least they never talked about it, and they didn't make him go to a church that fulminated against it.

And as for Marcus...

"I can't say anything to him," Antoine lamented one night.

They'd begun sneaking out a couple of nights a week, stealing time from the black blank in which the world slept, liberating them for precious hours at a time. Usually Antoine jogged to Dean's house, and the two of them would make quiet circuits of the neighborhood, stealing down the half-paved road that led to a new development, where no one would see them holding hands or kissing.

But as the weather turned and the dark morning hours chilled, they realized they needed shelter. And so they discovered an abandoned house in a development midway between their houses. A sign advertised it for sale, but the yard was thickly overgrown, marking it unoccupied, isolated, ignored. And a notice on the door declared it condemned, scheduled for demolition.

They covered the basement windows with tar paper and brought flashlights and sleeping bags, then spent the drowsy time between one and three in the morning kissing and probing, desperate and eager and anxious to try more.

"He won't understand?" Dean admitted to a level of confusion. The twins were identical—if being gay was something genetic (and Dr. Ruth assured him it was), then didn't that mean Marcus should be gay, too?

"I don't think he'll deal well," Antoine said. "He'll think it means *he's* gay, too."

Exactly. Dean frowned. This was one of those areas where he knew his curiosities needed to be tamped down, that his thirst for answers did not outweigh Antoine's tolerance for emotional pain. Such territories—including the issue of race—were fenced off for now, NO TRESPASSING signs displayed conspicuously.

Over the darkled, hijacked morning hours, he and Antoine explored both each other and what they had become. Or were becoming.

They told no one. Of course not. And Dean was too close to Kim to break up with her. *Break* being such a brutally appropriate word. There was a bond between them, and he could not imagine the pain of severing it. They'd been friends since first grade, then more as time went on. They had planned to marry, which once seemed so far off, but now seemed imminent. After college, they'd said. A little more than four years from now. Back then, high school felt like it would take forever, but here they were, almost at the end of it. College would swim by like a dolphin, and then . . .

And then what? Would he still have Antoine? Just as he couldn't imagine leaving Kim, so, too, could he not conceive his life without Antoine. Antoine, who had opened him. Antoine, who had filled him.

"I don't know what to do." It spilled from him, his voice a hoarse whisper, a broken bottle lost along the highway, dim and gray with road dust. His entire body felt old, racked. Shame, fear, and longing tickled along his spine and then stabbed forward, spearing his heart, choking it.

Antoine wrapped his arms around him. They were entangled in a blanket Dean had brought from the linen closet, one no one ever used, one no one would ever miss. Until the presence and the pressure of Antoine's body chilled it, Dean hadn't realized that he'd been trembling, shaking and shivering as though flu-ish.

"Be you," Antoine whispered in Dean's ear. "Just be true and be you."

The problem, Dean knew, was that he had no idea who he was.


Kissing Antoine on the school roof now, his thoughts drifted to Kim again, and he suppressed them with savage deliberation. The days afforded precious few opportunities for Antoine and him to cleave to each other; he would not allow the exigencies of the daylight world to intrude on their night-swaddled second lives.

They pulled out Jay's hidden chairs and sat closer than Jay and Dean had, fingers lazily intertwined. Clouds warped the sunless sky overhead.

"We should go away somewhere," Antoine said out of nowhere.

"What do you mean? On vacation?" *How would* that *work?* Dean wondered.

A shrug. "Maybe. Or maybe for good."

*For good.* "What do you mean?"

Antoine licked his lips. "What's keeping us here? Think about it. School? Who cares about school? Plenty of people get by without school."

"Our families," Dean said. And it was crazy that he even had to say it.

"No. You think they would understand this?" He gestured back and forth between them. "How can you be loyal to them if they won't be loyal to you? We've talked about that. Look, I'm closer to Marcus than . . . I mean, genetically. Biologically. I'm so close to him. But even he wouldn't understand. He makes the jokes, too, you know."

Dean flushed. He, too, had made jokes about homosexuals. It was safer that way. It was armor.

"Where would we go?" he asked. It couldn't happen, but there was no harm in imagining it, right?

Antoine stared up at the stars, thinking. "Just away. Somewhere where we can be us."

Dean had trouble imagining a world in which *that* could be possible. A world in which there were no stares or giggles or meaningful clearing of throats. When he watched Crockett and Tubbs on *Miami Vice*, those tight-as-brothers cop partners, one Black, one white, he thought that maybe that was the most he could hope for. Dr. Ruth could say that it was okay to be gay... and it could even actually *be* okay to be gay... but the world was the world.

*Somewhere where we can be us.*

Dean shook his head. "Right. Where's *that*?"

"New York. San Francisco. Big cities, Dean. It's different in the cities. Trust me."

Dean wondered if that could possibly be true. And if so, what exactly did it mean?

He had become, of necessity, two people. For sixteen hours on most days, he was Daylight Dean: Kim's boyfriend, Jay's best friend. Comic book reader and writer-in-training. He rarely spoke to Antoine because Antoine rarely spoke at all.

Then, for eight hours or so on some days, he became Nighttime Dean: Antoine's... what? What exactly was he to Antoine? What was Antoine to him? *Boyfriend* sounded wrong. *Boyfriend* was what he was to Kim. *Boyfriend* implied *girlfriend*.

He didn't know. There were a great many things he didn't know. Sometimes Dean felt as though his life had become a space shuttle, soaring into the upper atmosphere, and he could only cling to it from the outside, holding on for dear life against the g-forces and the wind shear, praying to God that it wouldn't blow up and send him spiraling down to his death like Christa McAuliffe and Judith Resnik and the others.

"I do trust you," he told Antoine, tightening his fingers on Antoine's in solidarity. "Absolutely. But we can't just *go* to a big city."

Antoine laughed. He laughed infrequently these days, never in the day-light with the others. Dean surmised that he might be the only one to hear Antoine's laughter, it plausibly being denied even to Marcus.

"Why can't we?" Antoine asked. "The world is bigger than this town and the factory. You want to be a writer, right? You think you can be rich and famous writing about Canterstown?"

For the first time since their first kiss, Dean experienced a frisson of anger toward Antoine. His writing was sacred and holy and his alone. It was not to be questioned.

"We've got time to think about this," he told Antoine. "I don't want to worry about it right now."

Antoine absorbed that. "Okay. So after graduation, then. But that's not as far away as you think. It's October. It'll be Thanksgiving and then Christmas. And then second semester will race by. We'll be done and even before then, we have to make big decisions. Life decisions."

Dean knew. He had the Princeton application on his desk at home, along with a stack of three more: Rutgers, Boston University, and Western Maryland College as his safety school. With Jay planning on bumping all their grades, he wasn't worried about his GPA, but he *was* worried about his essays, which confounded and bemused him. How could he sum up who he was and what he wanted when he had no idea who he was? And when *what he wanted* was both within his reach and also impossible?

"We've made the decisions," Dean pointed out. All of them knew one another's plans: Jay would head to College Park just to get through college as quickly as possible on his way to being a police officer. Brian was bound for either College Park or the University of Connecticut, depending on financial aid. Kim was going to Western Maryland. And Black Lightning were already being courted by a dozen schools, though they'd planned for two years to go to the University of Houston, like their heroes Kirk Baptiste and Carl Lewis.

"I'm not gonna go to Houston with Marcus," Antoine said, as though he'd tuned in to the radio frequency of Dean's thoughts and picked up Dean's most immediate transmission.

"What?" Dean gaped at the announcement. Perhaps even more than their first kiss, it disrupted every notion of Antoine he'd constructed in his imagination.

Antoine sucked at his lower lip for a moment, thinking. "I need to be somewhere where I can be me. I'm thinking Howard."

Dean had never heard of Howard University. Antoine explained that it was a Black college in Washington, DC, originally chartered by Congress after the Civil War. It had provided an education to thousands of freed slaves in its earliest days and had grown to become an important and respected institution for Black students.

"You could go, too," Antoine said excitedly, as though just realizing something important. "They actually have special minority scholarships for white kids. Isn't that wild? And we could be ourselves. We could be *real*."

"I don't want a minority scholarship," Dean said. "You want me to be, what, one of maybe a hundred white people in the whole place?"

Antoine laughed mirthlessly. "Dean. Come on, man. Right now I'm one of maybe ten Black kids at our school. You can handle it. Trust me."

Groping for words, Dean could not meet Antoine's eyes as he spoke. "I'm not even sure I want to go to college." He was admitting it out loud for the first time ever. "It's what my parents want. And my grandparents. But I sort of want to take a year off and work on my writing. But I don't know what my dad will say."

"Screw your dad," Antoine said with bright urgency. "You want to work on your writing? Come to Howard with me. We'll get an apartment off campus. I'll go to school and you'll write. It'll be great. We'll be free. We'll be out of this crappy town and away from everyone. We can do it, Dean. You and me. Together."

During his soliloquy, Antoine had taken Dean's hands in his own and ended up partly crouched on the roof before him. It almost looked as though he were ready to propose, and the very thought caused bubbles of amusement to burble up from his gut, bubbles that quickly burst into drizzles of acid when he thought one step further.

Proposing.

Marriage.

He could never marry Antoine. They could never have a life together.

Gay people couldn't get married. Or have kids. And he wanted those things.

He was pretty sure he wanted those things.

"I don't...I don't know."

"Then forget college. Forget it all," Antoine said, his voice rising in excitement, his breath coming fast. "We could go to Mexico."

"Mexico?" Dean shook his head like a swimmer rising up from the water. "*Mexico?*" Antoine might as well have suggested the moon or Mars. They all started with *M*, and they were all equally reasonable.

"Sure." Antoine tightened his grip on Dean's hands, his excitement mounting with each syllable out of his mouth. "No one knows us there. No one cares who we are. What we are. We'd just be two American dudes showing up. I have some money saved up. You do, too, right?"

Dean, in fact, had money in a bank account that he had never touched. As well as a stack of savings bonds from his grandparents, birthday gifts given reliably and predictably every year since his birth. For college expenses.

"American money goes real far down there," Antoine said with the confidence of someone who had researched it. "We could coast for a while, get the lay of the land."

"And then what? When the money runs out?"

Antoine shrugged. "We'd get jobs doing translation or something at a resort. We both speak Spanish pretty well."

"*Un poco,*" Dean hedged. They both had straight As in Spanish, but what did that really *mean*? Other than ordering in the language when his parents had taken him to Tio Pepe's for his birthday, he'd never tested his Spanish in any sort of real-life environment.

And besides...why was he even *thinking* of this? He wasn't moving to Mexico!

"Antoine, this isn't happening."

"You could write." Antoine said it in a sly tone of voice that Dean usually associated with his twin, and the combination was jarring, unsettling. "Think about it—you go down there with your American bankroll, and we get a little place, and you have something like a year to do nothing but work on your writing. It would be an adventure," Antoine went on, his speech accelerating, as though velocity counted as much as logic in the game of persuasion. "Like Hemingway, right? American expatriate. Teen author in a foreign land...think about it."

Dean *had* thought about it. He'd often considered just skipping college entirely and knuckling down on his writing, but the reaction from his family would be devastating. Whenever he brought up writing as a career, the response typically ran to something like this: *Well, you're very talented, honey, but that's not a surefire way to make a living. You should have a fallback position, just to be practical.*

College would put off for four years the need to decide on that fallback position. College would give him four years of security while he tried to get something published.

"Every suggestion you make," he said slowly, "involves me following you somewhere."

Antoine opened his mouth to speak, then closed it. Then drew in a deep breath and tried to speak again before finally scrubbing his hands up and down his face and saying, "No. No, man. I'm trying...I'm trying to work out a scenario where you're happy. You don't *want* to go to college. You don't *want* to keep going out with her, right?"

Dean bristled. "She has a name, man. You know that."

"She has tits, too," Antoine shot back. "So what?"

Dean's jaw locked into place at an angle. For a hard moment, he couldn't speak. Words foamed at the back of his throat like hot soda bubbles. They'd never argued before. Never raised their voices to each other. He couldn't believe this was happening.

"It's not about that," he managed to spit out, his voice strangled and raw.

"Then what's it about? You know what she's called? You know what gay people call the girl you go out with so everyone thinks you're straight? A *beard*. She's not your girlfriend, Dean—she's just your beard."

*Beard.* It was such a reductive, insulting term. It made Kim seem like a disguise he slapped on when he needed to go out, unsuspected and surreptitious in the bright, straight world. But she was more than that. Kim was his friend, his *good* friend. They'd told each other secrets. They knew each other in ways no one else did.

Except...

Maybe...

Antoine.

"It's not that simple," Dean said. His throat had opened up; the bubbles gurgled and burned his throat on their journey down. "I can't just..." *Abandon her* lingered on his tongue and refused to emerge. He knew Antoine's rejoinder without hearing it: *Abandon? So what are you going to do? Stay with her? Marry her? Live a lie just so that you don't hurt her feelings?*

And yes, damn it, that had been the plan. That had been the plan, and he'd been fine with it until the moment in Jay's garage; until the kiss, he'd done a good job of suppressing and ignoring that other part of himself. He'd pretended not to feel his blood rise during *Conan the Barbarian* when Arnold Schwarzenegger rippled and flexed his way across the screen. He'd convinced himself that he wanted to *be* Sonny Crockett, rather than the truth, which was that he wanted to dive into Don Johnson like a cool pond on a hot day, swim in the man's stubbled, chiseled body, run his tongue and the tips of his fingers along every inch of him, sink his teeth into his shoulder, his thigh.

He wanted nothing more than to be with Antoine. But he also needed...

Safety?

Security?

He needed to fit in. To belong.

He couldn't figure out how to have both.

"I can't just make these big decisions right now. Be patient. Please."

Antoine, still hunkered down before him, gazed steadily into Dean's eyes, the moment distended and protracted. There was nothing but the warm brown of Antoine's eyes, the wide black discs at the center. And then Antoine smiled softly and cupped Dean's face with his hands.

"Of course," Antoine said. "Of course."

"We'll figure it out," Dean told him, even though he wasn't sure how.

They kissed under the waxing gibbous moon. Everything was okay when they kissed. When they kissed, nothing else mattered in the world.

# 39

# THE PRESENT: ELAYAH

Mom was working late, catching up on everything she'd missed out on while babysitting Elayah. So as bedtime approached, it was just Dad and Elayah in the house.

It was time. They'd all agreed—it was time to talk directly to their parents about what had and hadn't happened. No more *It was a long time ago.* No more *Don't worry about it.*

In the morning, they would question Jorja's dad. And track down Liam's dad and Kim, both working nights. Come the weekend, they'd go down to Finn's Landing to talk to Marcie's dad.

But in the meantime, here was *her* dad.

They ate warmed-up leftovers—chicken tortilla soup, always better the second night—and watched a little TV. She turned off her brain, let the screen flash and babble before her, interrupted by Dad's occasional grunt or guffaw, and before she knew it, he was yawning his way toward the stairs.

Perfect timing. Catch him off guard.

"Dad, can you tell me about Keygate?"

Dad startled, one hand on the banister. He turned to her, his eyes wide. "Keygate? Holy...where'd you hear that?"

"It's mentioned in your yearbook."

And it was. Now that she had the word to home in on, Elayah found references to it scattered throughout the yearbook. Nothing in any bios or official text, but on some collage pages, the words *key* and *gate* had been placed in proximity, as had pictures of keys and gates, or combinations of the words and images. Elayah had worked the yearbook staff long enough to read between the lines: Word had come down from the administration that there was to be no mention of what would have been a scandal. So the yearbook staff in 1987 had made as many oblique references as humanly possible. It was practically a moral imperative to slip such things past the watchful eyes of the school administrators.

Dad grimaced. "It's late. I'm too tired for stupidity. Maybe tomorrow."

She'd had a feeling he might say that. "Okay. I'll just wait up for Mom, then."

Dad was three steps up before he twigged to the subtext of her comment. "Oh, hell no!" he said. "Don't go bothering your mother with that nonsense."

Sprawled out on the sofa with her phone, Elayah pretended to be intimately involved in something on Instagram. "I'm sure she remembers everything."

Dad groaned and made a show of stomping down the three steps. He stood before her and planted his fists on his hips. "Fine. You win. What do you want to know?"

She spent another half second scrolling, then locked her phone and slid it into her pocket. "Just everything."

They sat across from each other at the kitchen table, and he told her exactly that. Or at least as much as he could remember. One of them—he couldn't remember which—had access to a key grinder. Another was trusted by the teachers to borrow keys. And so they'd copied the keys to the building.

Elayah was in something like shock. Based on Kathleen Rourke's admittedly faded recollection, she'd expected a story of homecoming night. A prank gone awry, maybe. She hadn't expected to hear about multiple break-ins, a plan to change grades, a search for a *swimming pool*, of all things.

"I don't understand how you got away with it for so long," she told him. "What about alarms? Cameras? Security systems?"

Dad snorted as though he'd inhaled a peanut while watching something hilarious. "In 1986? In a school? Elayah," he said with great restraint and patience, "we are the reason schools *now* have cameras and alarms and security systems."

"Peej," she said. "That's Jorja's dad, right?"

He nodded. "Yeah. Started going by his initials back in law school, I guess. Maybe college. Not sure."

"What about Katie?"

"Katie?" He seemed puzzled.

*You said her name your own damn self the other night!* she wanted to scream. But she also didn't want to admit that she'd been eavesdropping.

"You knew someone named Katie back then. Who was she?"

"I can't tell you what I don't know."

"But what happened? How did all this lead to the knife and someone getting killed?"

Dad reached across the table and took her hands in his own. She flinched at his touch and he withdrew, his expression aggrieved and dazed. "Baby girl...nothing. Nothing at all. You're chasing shadows. Worse yet, you're chasing *old* shadows. We broke in and we did stupid things and we got caught and it ended. But none of us killed anyone. None of us died."

Elayah pulled her hand away and stroked one finger lightly along the path of stitches on her throat. "But something happened, Dad. You either don't remember or you're not telling me. *Something* happened."

Sagging in his chair, Dad contemplated his hands, empty on the table before him. "I don't know what to tell you. I'm not lying. Nothing happened. I swear it."

More than anything, she wanted to believe him. It's not that she didn't. Or couldn't.

It wasn't even that the yearbook entries and the handwriting match made her suspect every last thing she knew about her own father.

It was that the knife in the sheriff's custody and the line across her throat and the memory of the blade at her neck didn't allow her to believe.

She made one last attempt: "What about Jorja's dad? Why was he in Sheppard Pratt?"

Her father steepled his fingers before him and sighed deeply. "Baby... that's not for me to say. You'll have to ask him."

Elayah nodded. "I will."

# LIAM

They went to Jorja's dad's office the next day during lunch period. The county public defenders had a small storefront in Finn's Landing, a two-block walk from the courthouse. Jorja's dad had seniority, so he actually had a tiny office of his own, and he sat at a smallish desk behind an older model iMac. His desk blotter bristled with Post-its. Other than his nameplate—P. J. DEARBORN—the desk was clear. Almost too neat.

"Hey, gang!" he said brightly as they entered. "A little off-campus lunch trip? Short a few ducats, sweetheart? Let me see...." He delved into his pocket for his wallet and started riffling through bills.

"We're not here for lunch, Dad." Jorja's voice was dull but resolved.

There was no point in dragging it out. Jorja slapped the committal papers down on her father's desk and stood there holding Marcie's hand. Liam wondered what that felt like, holding the hand of someone who meant something to you? Would he ever get there with El?

He shook an imaginary Magic 8 Ball. *Outlook not so good.*

Jorja's dad slipped his wallet away and glanced at the paper as though it were a lunch menu and he'd eaten a big breakfast. Then, seeming to realize exactly what it was, he froze. His expression locked into place, still that goofy Dad grin. As the moments passed, the grin corroded into a sickly grimace. He covered the paper with his hand and stood up abruptly and shouted, "Where did you get this?"

Bruce Banner turning into the Hulk caught all of them off guard. Jorja and Marcie took a united step back from the desk. El, standing next to Liam, gasped loudly.

Liam's fists clenched. Some instinct deep inside his bone marrow was ready. And it was ridiculous because this was *Jorja's dad*, the Cub Scout S'more King and the worst Little League coach in the county.

"Where did you get this?" he roared, now holding up the crumpled paper in his fist. "Where were you poking around? Who the hell do you think you are? All of you!" As he said this last, he finally directed his attention away from his daughter, firing a scathing glare at the other three.

"Dad, I just want to know—"

"You have no *right* to go through my things!" Mr. Dearborn yelled. "These things are private!"

Jorja yanked her hand away from Marcie and folded her arms over her chest, refusing to budge again. "I want to know what happened. I deserve to know. I'm your daughter."

Jorja's dad crushed the paper into a ball and hurled it angrily at the wastebasket in the corner of his office. His rage threw off his aim; the wadded-up sheet hit a windowsill, bounced off, and landed in the middle of the floor.

"Get back to school *now*," he seethed. "And we'll talk about respecting people's privacy tonight when I get home. Believe me."

"Who's Katie?" Jorja asked. Liam's estimation of Jorja rose a notch. At this point, with Peej's seething anger clouding the room, Liam would have just left, had it been *his* dad. But Jorja gamely took another shot. "Who's Katie, and what did you do to her?"

Peej went purple. Liam thought it very possible that he would do a real-life reenactment of the exploding-head emoji. No joke.

"Go. *Now*."

Two generations glared at each other. Jorja had no choice—with no cards to play, she folded.

"Fine, Dad," she muttered, and turned around. "Come on, guys, let's go."

# ELAYAH

Since they were in Finn's Landing, they had lunch at Wally's restaurant. The hostess recognized Liam, sat them immediately and brought out free off-menu appetizers: Liam's favorite potato skins and boneless "nuclear wings."

"We still don't know if he's the criminal or the victim," Jorja said, licking nuclear sauce from her fingers. Elayah couldn't even *look* at the wings without her eyes watering. "If he did something or if something was done *to* him."

"You think he knew Lisa De Nardo back when she was Lisa McKenzie?" Marcie asked.

"I don't think either one of them would answer that question right now." Liam dipped a wing in ranch, then plopped it atop a potato skin before eating both.

"There's no way we're gonna make it back before lunch is over," Elayah warned them.

Liam shrugged. Jorja and Marcie did, too. Well, as long as everyone was on the same page.

Her phone rang as their server brought out bowls of chili.

"Lisa De Nardo," Indira announced without salutation. "Born Lisa McKenzie. Graduated 1987 with your parents."

"This is stuff we know." She mouthed *Indira* to the others, who perked up immediately.

"Married in 1996 to Edward De Nardo. Divorced in 2007. Three sons—"

"No, two sons. We found them on Facebook."

She could almost hear the smile in the pause on the other end of the line. "No. Three sons. You found the two named De Nardo. But there's a third son. Peter McKenzie, born in December 1987."

"Peter McKenzie," she told the group. Liam and Jorja held up hands slick with sauce. With a knowing sigh, Marcie dived into her purse for her phone.

Elayah did some quick mental math. That made Peter McKenzie ten years older than the older of Lisa De Nardo's other two sons. And she would have been only eighteen or so when he was born. Right out of high school.

Wait. If he was born in December, then she would have gotten pregnant back in—do the math—March. Right?

She thanked Indira, promised to get back to her with the photo of the knife. This new information seemed significant. Lisa McKenzie would have gotten pregnant while still in high school. Which was hardly unique in this town, but still…that first son had been born out of wedlock and had his mother's last name. So there'd been no father as far as the paperwork was concerned.

Why not?

Marcie held up her phone, showing her the Facebook profile for Peter McKenzie. His profile photo was the same one as on his phone's lock screen, right down to the adorable newborn baby.

As she panned the phone around the table, Liam coughed gently into his fist, then wiped sauce from his hands with a Wet-Nap. "I guess we're not going back to school at all, huh?"

# 1986: JAY

Jay had already read ahead three chapters in the chemistry textbook, so he was bored out of his mind as Mr. Chisholm droned on and on about moles and significant digits. School was just a wall, like in the song. *We don't need no education....* Those little British brats were right: His schooling was interfering with his education. The structures and the strictures of school chafed at him. And when he chafed, everything became an irritant. Especially Jism, who tried too hard to be one of them. He thought being twenty-three made him a peer.

Jay glanced two rows over at Lisa McKenzie, who was drawing something involving wide loops in her chem notebook. From here he couldn't tell what, but he knew it wasn't a molecule or an electron shell. More likely a big goofy-looking heart with *Mrs. Lisa Chisholm* calligraphied into it. With an arrow through it.

Lisa was passably cute. Quiet. She hadn't always been so. Back in middle school, in a language arts class, Jay had cracked a funny joke right before class started. Lisa had glared at him witheringly and snapped, "Grow up, Jay."

And he'd replied, instantly, the rejoinder welling up from some dark and perfect pit of revenge, "Grow *out*, Lisa." Which had sparked even *more* laughter, settling the argument perfectly.

She'd had the last laugh, though—flat-chested Lisa McKenzie *had* grown out, quite impressively, almost as though she'd only needed Jay's admonition for it to happen. Still, Jay would never give her a second look if it weren't for the whispered rumors that she and Jism were secretly getting it on. She was six years younger than him, which wasn't so terrible, he figured. Jay's mom was five years younger than his dad.

But it nagged at him. Not the age difference. Not really. It was the secrecy that nibbled at the edges of his consciousness. He didn't like it when people tried to hide things.

Why? Well, he wasn't going to go there. He had a theory, but he didn't like what it said about him, so he stuffed it deep down, piled plenty of memories and traces of old thoughts over it, and didn't allow himself to consider it.

He realized in that moment that the class had gone quiet. Even Jism's voice had fallen silent. Jay blinked and focused on the world around him, emerging from the hollows of his own thoughts. All eyes were on him, and Jism stood at the head of the class, arms crossed over his chest, the hint of a smirk on that California surfer-boy face.

Jism always had just the right amount of tan. Jism never burned in the sun. Jism was no taller than Jay, but his shoulders were broader, his waist narrower, his chest more expansive, which everyone knew because he wore his collared Canterstown High coaching-staff polo shirts one size too small.

He had a sweep of dirty blond hair that was in a perpetual muss.

"Jay?" Jism said, and from his tone and his deportment, it was obvious that this was the second time he'd said it.

Jay croaked out a polite, "Yes?"

A waterfall of titters spilled out from the class, splashing down the aisles and across the rows. Jay shot a look to his left and down—Dean was shaking his head minutely.

Across the way, Lisa had a hand over her mouth as she giggled. *What else do you do with that mouth?* Jay thought savagely. And a brief tableau of the possibilities flared before him, flustering him even more as Jism opened his stupid mouth filled with stupid perfect white teeth and said, "Thanks for that, but I was asking you for the answer."

The answer to what? He flung his gaze from the chalkboard to the opaque projector, seeking some hint as to what the question might be in the first place.

There were sodium ions on the board. Chlorine on the projector. NaCl. Salt?

"Salt," he said with as much dignity and authority as he could muster.

More laughter. Harder and more aggressive. The leader seemed to be Brad Gimble, who sat two rows down and had turned in his seat for the show. Everyone else was chuckling, but Brad was outright guffawing, doing everything but pointing right at Jay as he laughed.

Why the hell was a dunce like Gimble even *in* this class? Jay clenched his jaw. The laughter became static. His vision narrowed to the sight of Jism, who now observed him with smarmy, self-satisfied regard.

"Close," Jism said after a beat to allow the laughter to drop slightly. "But I was looking for 'Avogadro's number.'"

The laughter ratcheted up. Jay's cheeks flamed, and he wanted to rip them off his face.

Jism permitted another few seconds of laughter, then called for quiet with both hands, patting the air downward before him. When he had the class under control again, he nodded briefly to Jay.

"I know you're smarter than everyone," Jism said in a tone of voice that belied the sentiment, "but it still helps to pay attention, right?"

The red-hot shame flaming in Jay's cheeks grew hotter. He said nothing, merely looked down at his notebook. The page for this day was fresh and blank, with only the date written in the corner.

Conscious of every eye in the room on him, he picked up his pen and, with meticulous focus on the page before him, wrote *Salt*.


Jay slammed his locker shut. The door rebounded, slapping itself open; he slammed it again, this time kicking it for good measure. Dean stood nearby, watching. There was a long list of things Jay hated in the world—school, teachers, Democrats, commies, more—but at the very top of that list was embarrassment.

"Who does he think he is?" Jay hissed at his locker door.

"What's wrong with him?" Brian asked from the other side of the locker aisle.

"Seriously," Jay said. "Who the hell does he think he is?"

"You weren't paying attention," Dean said lightly. "Forget about it. It's no big deal. No one cares."

Jay turned and fired laser bolts from his eyes down the narrow aisle of lockers. At the other end, Brad Gimble was spinning the dial on his combination lock.

"*He* cared."

Brian cut his eyes left and snorted. "Gimbo? So what?"

"Totally," Dean agreed. "I don't even know what he's doing in chem with us. He's a meathead who only knows two words: *Foot. Ball.*"

No reaction from Jay.

"Take the SAT?" Dean went on. "He can't even *spell* SAT."

That joke wrestled a chortle from Jay, but below the chuckles, he was running calculations.

"You busy tonight?" Jay asked.

Brian licked his lips. "I'm free!"

God, not Brian. Jay shook his head. "Sorry, man. This is a two-man job."

Dean considered. "Okay."

# 1986: MARCUS

Training for the spring track season didn't start until the ground thawed during second semester, but Black Lightning had always maintained a rigorous regimen even in the off-season. Like the post office, they delivered no matter the weather, practicing sprints and relays in the rain, snow, and blazing heat. One day, they'd chased each other around the track through a phalanx of fog so thick and dense that it felt like needles in their eyes, barely able to see each other in the murk and gray.

Since moving into his own bedroom, Antoine had not joined Marcus for their usual thrice-weekly after-school training. Marcus figured Antoine was running on his own, either over at the junior high school track or out on the road. Maybe *that* was what he was doing on the nights he disappeared from his bedroom.

If so, fine. He was tired of babying his melancholy twin, of beseeching Antoine to open up and just *talk*, for God's sake. Ever since he'd come back from New York City and his visit with cousin Duane in the winter of junior year, Antoine had begun closing off, clamming up. It had hit its nadir (or its zenith, perhaps, depending on how you assessed it) right after Jay's birthday party that summer. From that point on, Antoine barely spoke at all, even in private. Even to Marcus.

*Well, screw him, then*, Marcus thought.

He'd done sprints and a few bounding drills, along with some high knee work for speed. Now, dripping with sweat, he headed to the locker room. School was out, but the football team was still crashing into one another out on the field, and Coach Kline said it was fine for Marcus to use the locker room while football was in practice.

He chuckled to himself as he jogged from the track to the school door, thinking of how easily he could get into the school at any time, with or without Coach Kline's permission.

The locker room should have been empty, save for the gym bags left behind by the football team. But instead, he was surprised to see Antoine sitting on one of the benches, leaning forward with elbows on knees, his fingers steepled before him.

"What up?" Marcus asked with a little more asperity than he'd intended.

If Antoine noticed, he didn't show it. "We need to talk."

Snatching a towel from the shelf to his right, Marcus snapped it open and wiped the sweat from his face. "I've *been* talking. *You* need to talk."

Antoine shrugged noncommittally, now staring at the drain set into the floor. "Okay. So I'll talk. College."

"Are you worried? How are your grades?" Once upon a time, he wouldn't have needed to ask. But when midterm progress reports had been handed down, Antoine hadn't bothered sharing his. "Don't worry about 'em. Jay's got that on lockdown. All we have to do is *run*."

Pursing his lips, Antoine shook his head. "I don't know."

"You been training? Scouts from Houston aren't gonna like it if one half of the Laird twins is out of shape. They want us both. We have to be ready."

Shaking his head again, Antoine stood up, still not looking at Marcus. "That's what I want to talk to you about. I don't know about running anymore."

Stated so plainly and so baldly, it could be nothing more than a joke, so Marcus treated it as such, offering a hollow chuckle. "Yeah, right. Because two Black kids from Canterstown have so many options—"

"That's another thing," Antoine interrupted. "I'm not just Black. I'm African American. *We* are."

"Afro what?" Marcus snort-laughed. "What the hell is *that*?"

"I heard it when I was in New York. It makes sense."

"I'm so tired of your crap," Marcus said with a long-suffering sigh. "You spent one week in New York, and suddenly you think you're better than everyone."

"Not better. Just enlightened," Antoine said, a note of urgency creeping into his voice. "Why should we be defined as the opposite of white people? Why should we be defined by our skin color at all? We're not our skin, Marcus. We're people. With a history and a culture."

Marcus flapped his hand dismissively. "When you start talking like this..."

"What? You've been riding me for being quiet all this time. Now you're riding me for talking?"

"You're serious, aren't you?" Marcus felt as though—impossibly—he were seeing his twin for the very first time. It was disorienting and more than a bit horrifying, this familiar face rendered so suddenly and absolutely unfamiliar. "You're really thinking of quitting track? Are you nuts?"

"I've been thinking about a lot of things," Antoine told him with infuriating calm, as though he considered Marcus a child. "And I've decided some things for myself. For myself, for once. Not for us. For the first time in my life, I'm thinking of *me*. Can't you get that?"

Marcus leaned in close. "We had a *plan*, 'Toine. We were going to Houston. Black Lightning. Everyone was on board. Mom and Pops. We had scouts in the stands. They want *us*. Not you. Not me. *Us*. Now you're backing out? Punking out?"

"Not punking out," Antoine said, almost completely disconnected. "Realigning. Who benefits when we run, Marcus? Think about it."

"We do!" Marcus yelled, gesticulating wildly. "We win!"

"No." Still that same placidity. "*They* win. *They* benefit. We run, they win."

"White people," Marcus said sardonically, now folding his arms over his chest.

"Yeah. And good for them. Fine. But I don't have to play the game. We run. We get, what, a sponsorship? We're going to be the Michael Jordan of track and field?"

Marcus bristled, his back teeth coming together tightly. They'd talked about just such a scenario, and goddamn it, Antoine had been excited by the very idea he now mocked, his voice larded with sarcasm.

"Maybe Adidas or Nike pays us to wear their shoes?" Antoine went on. "You think they're gonna pay us anything more than a pittance compared with what *they* make from having us show off their shoes? Huh? No. They'll give us a little bit and take the rest. We put on the shoes and do all the work, and we run our asses off, and young brothers everywhere decide to wear those shoes and be like the Laird twins, be like Black Lightning."

"Exactly!" Marcus shouted. "You don't want that?"

"And it's white people who benefit, man!" Antoine's facade of cool finally cracked. "They take all the money! They just *rent* our Black bodies instead of buying 'em outright like they used to."

Marcus took a step back as Antoine lunged toward him during his outburst. He didn't fear his twin—they'd never fought physically, had rarely ever fought verbally until recently—but seeing his own face, his own body hurtle toward him like that was off-putting.

He understood Antoine's point. And it wasn't a bad one. But as best as Marcus could tell, the game was rigged against them and there was no option not to play. Which, really, is what Antoine was proposing: Fold their hands, put their cards down on the green-felt table, and walk away from the poker game.

But just like the lottery, no matter the odds, if you didn't play, you could never ever win.

"Where have you been going?" Marcus asked. "I know you leave your room some nights. What are you up to?"

"I...there *is* something else," Antoine said, his voice quieter now, the seething notes fading back into calm.

"What?" Marcus asked. Something *else*? Something *else*?

Antoine fidgeted for a moment, pulling at his own fingers, gnawing at his lower lips. "Naw," he said finally. "Nothing. Never mind."

"Never mind." Marcus shook his head. "You drop all this on me and you want me to walk away with *never mind*? Really?"

"Nothing else to say," Antoine told him.

"You better have something else to say! We had a *plan*, 'Toine. We were going to Houston together. Run the relays. Make the Olympics. Help out Mom and Pops. You remember that?" He tilted his head as though the new position would dislodge memories stuck somewhere where his twin couldn't access them. "Pay off the house, maybe. Get Pops out of the factory. And now you just up and decide you're not doing any of that and you have nothing else to say? For real?"

Antoine pursed his lips and hung his head. But no matter what Marcus said or how he said it, nothing could get his twin to speak again.

**42**

# THE PRESENT: ELAYAH

She pounded on the door to Lisa De Nardo's house until her fists went numb. And then Liam took over.

"We know you're in there!" Elayah yelled. "You work from home!"

"Guess we'll just start knocking on your neighbors' doors!" Jorja cried out as loudly as she could.

The door swung open with such force that Liam nearly stumbled in. Lisa De Nardo glared at them. She wore a V-neck sweater with a daring décolletage and was flushed with pink anger all the way down to her cleavage.

"Get off my property!" she hissed, eyes darting up and down the street.

"Not until we've spoken," Elayah told her.

"I don't have to—"

Marcie pushed between Liam and Elayah and held up her phone, with the photo of Peter McKenzie.

Lisa ground her teeth together, threw the door open wide, and stepped aside.

This time she didn't offer them seats, so they stood in the living room.

"What do you want with Peter?" she asked, folding her arms over her chest. "He's been through enough."

"You saw him the other night, didn't you?" Elayah asked.

"Yes, okay? Peter came here. Out of nowhere. Bleeding." She sniffed and her face went hard. "I bet you all did that to him. Why would I tell you anything? Why shouldn't I just call the cops?"

Elayah had nothing there. Fortunately, Liam jumped in. "Maybe because if you call the cops on us, we'll call the cops on him? And we can prove that he tried to buy incriminating evidence *and* that he assaulted me in SAMMPark. So, like..." He spread his hands in a *whattayagonnado?* gesture.

"We're minors," Jorja said. "He's not. If you want to protect your son, tell us what you know."

Lisa thought this over, pondering, her eyes darting from them to the ceiling as she considered. Elayah's trust in Lisa De Nardo was attenuated and slight, a filament suspending an anvil. But any information was better than no information. Even a lie, she reasoned, might eventually lead them to the truth.

"I don't see how I have a choice," Lisa said finally. "Don't go to the police, okay? He's just getting his life together. The baby. Working with his father. Leave him alone. Please."

"Who's Peter's father?" Elayah asked. "Is it Patrick Dearborn? P. J.? Were you ever called Katie for some reason?"

Lisa blinked at each question, jerking her head back as though evading repeated physical blows. "What?" she asked.

"Yeah, what?" Jorja asked.

Elayah felt guilty for springing this on Jorja, but she hadn't wanted her friend to talk her out of making the accusation. It made sense. They knew "Peej and Katie" had gotten up to something. And Lisa had ended up pregnant in early eighty-seven. Peej had been in Sheppard Pratt, but there were such things as visitations and weekend passes.

"Is your middle name Kathleen or something like that?" Elayah pressed.

Lisa batted away the questions. "I can't believe you, just marching in here and asking personal—"

"I don't give a damn about your *personal* anything!" Elayah roared, shocking not only Lisa but also the friends arrayed around her. "Someone came into *my* house and cut me open in *my* bed, and that person knows *your* son, so start talking!"

The room vibrated with her anger. Lisa De Nardo's jaw dropped and hung there.

"We sorta can't control her," Liam said conversationally. "Ask your son."

Lisa's jaw finally found its proper alignment again, and her lips pressed together in mute, impotent anger. "I can't believe I'm telling you...."

"Just do it," Elayah said.

"Rip the Band-Aid off," Jorja advised.

"Not her dad," Lisa said, waggling a hand at Jorja. "Someone else."

"Who?" Elayah asked.

"Martin Chisholm," Lisa said.

She said the name as though it meant something. As though she'd said *Barack Obama* or *Brett Kavanaugh.*

Martin Chisholm.

"Wait," Jorja said, suddenly standing very, very upright. "Martin Chisholm? The guy on TV? Running for the General Assembly? The school superintendent?"

"Yes."

"I...I don't understand. Why would he be after the—"

"He did..." Were those tears in Lisa's eyes? Damn it, Elayah did *not* want to feel sympathy for this woman, this woman who was just *fine* with being grabbed by the pussy. Elayah thought of the #MAGA 2024 and how much she disliked this woman, of her hungry eyes on Liam, of Liam's appraisal of her.

"He was my science teacher. And...we did something we weren't supposed to...back then."

Cold, invisible mummy rags wrapped around Elayah from every direction.

"We, uh..."

Elayah didn't need the next word. She didn't have to hear it, and it didn't even matter what the word was.

"...dated," Lisa finished.

Oh, hell no. The *word* did matter, it turned out.

"What accent is that?" Elayah asked, struggling to keep her voice from breaking into lethal shards of anger. "When you say *raped*, it sounds like *dated.*"

"He didn't rape me, little girl. I'm not a *victim.* It was completely consensual." At the suggestion that she was a victim, Lisa had regained her composure, her strength, and her snotty attitude. "It was a different time. It was barely even a secret. We went out in public together sometimes. I don't expect you to understand."

"I understand you were a minor and he wasn't."

"Never mind." She waved her hands. "Forget it. Forget it all. And forget I gave you his name. Now get out of my house. I can still call the police for trespassing."

On the way back to the car, Liam kicked the #MAGA 2024 sign, splintering its wooden stake and knocking it off-kilter.

"So now that makes sense," Jorja said. "He got his son to try to recover the evidence. Because you wouldn't trust someone you hired, but you'd trust your own son, right?"

Elayah had a thought. After the second break-in, the police had boxed up and carted away the stuff in the garage, leaving the empty tarp in a heap on the floor, but objects didn't exist only in physical space any longer. They were digital as well. Elayah had taken a *lot* of photographs of the time capsule's contents.

Including the envelope. The blue one she'd noticed on that first day, jam-packed with arousal. Elayah had photographed the outside and each page of the letter.

Sure enough, when she pinch-zoomed the last page, it was signed "*L*" in a flowery script.

As they got into Liam's car, she read the letter out loud to them. The temperature in the car climbed, and she found herself idly considering Liam. Damn, that boy!

"Well, that's it," Marcie said. "We've got him."


The police arrested Martin Chisholm the next day at his campaign headquarters. In his late fifties, he had the robust appearance of a man much younger, his hair still thick and insouciant, his jawline firm beneath a full beard. He made for excellent photos and videos as he was marched down the steps of his headquarters in handcuffs, guided by the sheriff and a deputy to a waiting cruiser.

Elayah had given Indira a heads-up the night before, alerting her to Chisholm's guilt and begging her to be discreet. Indira promised she would be and was as good as her word: She just happened to be at Chisholm's headquarters when the police arrived and was first on the scene to record his protestations and denials.

The denials didn't last long. Presented with the envelope containing Lisa's love letter, Martin Chisholm confessed.

The full story came out months later, at trial, but Liam's dad took pity on Elayah and drove over to her house to fill her in shortly after Chisholm had been booked and locked up pending trial. He brought with him a large cardboard box filled with the contents of the time capsule. Except for the blue envelope, of course.

He sat across from her at the kitchen table, her parents flanking her, and explained that the statute of limitations for statutory rape had expired long ago. But they could and would prosecute him for breaking and entering, as well as threatening and attacking Elayah.

Chisholm had seen the report in the *Loco* about the time capsule. And the pictures. Including the blue envelope, which would have been familiar to him, even after so much time had passed.

And then when the follow-up story hit, with Elayah claiming, "We know what you did...."

He snapped. He saw his political career, his entire *life* going up in flames. He'd gone to her house, figuring that if he could retrieve the envelope and destroy it, maybe he could still rescue himself and preserve his viability....

Something tickled at the back of Elayah's mind, something that felt as obvious as the sheriff's hat, resting on the table between them. Something she should have known already.

But Liam's dad kept talking. Lisa De Nardo was already inundated with press requests. Elayah felt bad that she'd brought the wrath of the fourth estate down on her, Trumpy or not, but there was nothing she could do about it.

"So," Liam's dad finished with a quirk of lips that was almost but not quite a smile, "I'm not happy that you went off and got involved, but I am happy that we can put it all behind us now."

Yes. Mystery solved. After thirty-five years.

Except...

"The knife," she said as the sheriff stood and plucked his hat from the table.

"I'm sorry?" he asked.

"The knife. I..." She licked her lips. It had just clicked for her, and she felt like an idiot for not realizing sooner. "There's still the issue of the knife, right? It wasn't in the photos that the *Loco* posted online. Because you already had it by then."

Her dad had risen to walk the sheriff to the door. He turned back to the table now, then glanced over at the sheriff. "Dean?"

"I don't see where you're headed with this," the sheriff said.

"Don't you get it?" Elayah's frustration at her own stupidity bubbled out, her voice taking on an aggravated tone. "We thought the guy who broke in was looking for the knife. But Chisholm couldn't have been—he didn't see a picture of it. When he... right before he... he said to me, *Where is it? I know you... I saw it. Where did you put it?* He was talking about the envelope. Because he couldn't have known about the knife."

The sheriff's expression was that of a man who has stumbled home, exhausted, only to find that a pipe has burst right over his bed.

"El, the knife is... seriously, like I told you from the beginning, the knife is nothing. It's a gag or a fluke. But this, this Chisholm case—that's real. And I'm grateful we got the guy."

"Never did like him much," Dad said.

"We know there's human blood on it, though," Elayah pressed. "But it can't have anything to do with Chisholm. So..."

Liam's dad nodded wearily. "Look, the man who tried to hurt you is locked up. Get some sleep. At last." He turned to her parents. "Marcus. Dinah."

And then he was gone. And it was just her and her parents and a safety that felt hard-earned and fragile.

# LIAM

Liam sat on the sofa, channel surfing without actually seeing anything on the TV. It was just a rapid-fire slideshow of colors and patterns to him. All he could think about was El and Martin Chisholm and the envelope that had changed everything.

He thought of Lisa De Nardo. A nice-enough lady, for a lunatic. Pretty hot. And apparently molested by her teacher a thousand years ago. Who knew?

Dad burst through the front door, his face suffused with outrage in the instant he spied Liam. Before Liam could offer up something witty and deflective, Dad jabbed an accusatory finger at him. "You read my email!"

It was the last thing Liam expected to hear. Dad had been off to assure El and her family that Chisholm was in custody and not getting out anytime soon. For a half second, Liam was prepared to deny the charge—reflexively, hotly—but then he remembered: *Oh yeah. I totally did that.*

"She knew there was human blood on the knife!" Dad went on stomping into the living room, the handcuffs on his gun belt jingling in a very not-jolly way. "There's only one way she could have found out: You! You hacked my email."

Liam didn't want to tell him that it hadn't even required hacking. And being on the defensive with Dad rarely worked. "You told me it was incon-clusive! Deer blood!" he shouted, rising from the sofa. "You lied to me!"

"You're damn right I lied to you!" Dad shouted right back. "Because I didn't think I could trust you with the information, and holy hell, Liam, I was right!"

Neither of his fathers had ever struck him, but Liam knew in that moment what it would feel like if one of them had. The sting of it. The red moment of surprise.

"This isn't new for you!" Dad went on, in a rage. "You've been told since you were little that I do things that are confidential and important, that you can't go poking around, that you have to know when to keep your mouth shut. And you *still* went ahead and told Elayah and God knows who else a piece of information that is very, very important and needs to be kept quiet!"

"Why?" Liam demanded.

"You don't get to ask that question!" Dad thundered. "This has nothing to do with you. This is my *job*, not a game for you and your friends!"

Liam clenched his fists and unclenched them. For a blistering moment, they stared at each other. And then Dad uttered a wordless cry of frustra-tion, slapped the wall with one hand, and spun around to stalk off into the kitchen.

*Think it through. Think it through. Don't go off half-cocked. What should you do next?*

He had no answers, so he stomped into the kitchen. Not really sure why or what he hoped to accomplish, but he wanted to stay on the offensive.

In the kitchen, Dad stood at the fridge, his head bowed so that his forehead rested on the stainless steel door. All the anger and fury had drained out of him, and if that fridge hadn't been holding him up, Liam suspected his father might have collapsed in a heap on the floor.

Damn. Sheriff was never supposed to be this kind of gig.

"Hey, Dad?"

Dad slowly turned to Liam, his eyes wide, blank, and questing. His voice was slow and shaky. "I'm doing my best, Liam. I swear to God. It's all...it's all too much."

"Oh." Liam was not prepared for this. Not at all. Pop showed vulnerability, sure. Not Dad. Dad knew about body armor. Dad had a gun. Dad solved other people's problems all day long.

With a heavy sigh, Dad wandered over to the table and slumped into a chair, pinching the bridge of his nose as though he could chase away a headache that way. "I'm sorry I yelled. That's not who I want to be. Just...this case...I'm trying."

"I know." Liam slid into a chair opposite his father. They didn't have the kind of relationship where Liam would take his dad's hand in a moment like this. "I'm sorry I looked at your email. It's El, Dad. I was kinda desperate. But you've never even known what desperate feels like."

Dad snorted. "I know this will come as a shock to you, but I had a life before you came along."

Liam let his jaw drop as far as it would go. "What? Wait, are you saying I'm *not* the center of the universe? You've been lying to me all these years?"

" 'Fraid so, buddy. But don't blame me—it was Pop's idea."

Dad chuckled hollowly, then scrubbed his hands down his face. Staring down at the table, he opened his mouth to speak, then stopped, then started again.

"This is going to sound horrible, but...when you were born, I told Pop that I prayed you would be straight."

Liam grinned. "Hey, prayers *do* get answered!"

Dad shook his head. "It's not funny. It was awful. Why should I have to pray for something like that? But it's been hard. . . . It *is* hard. Still. Even now. And I thought, *Even with two accepting parents to show him the way, his life will just be so much easier if he likes girls.*"

Abashed, Liam said nothing. It was the kind of statement that felt like a soft, hot lump of clay in his throat.

"Want to know something really ironic, Liam?" Dad went on. "When I finally came out to my parents, my *mom* was the problem. Your grandfather just nodded his head and—I'll never forget this—looked at me and said, 'Just keep being a good man, Dean.' It took Mom years to understand, to wrap her head around it. I think it was easier for Dad because he was less invested. He always kept Jenny and me at a remove. Like we were projects that were his responsibility and he took it seriously, but he had no emotional investment. Whereas Mom felt everything we felt. Mom still had this invisible umbilical connection. It was as though I'd told her I had terminal cancer. All she knew back then was AIDS and gay bashing and Matthew Shepard. And fear becomes anger so easily."

Liam opened his mouth to speak, but in that moment, the only thoughts that crashed around in his head and became coherent were about El.

*El, I have to tell you something. I know I've messed up. I know I've been a jerk sometimes. And I'm so sorry. So, so sorry. It's because I never let my guard down around you; I never let myself be real. Because I'm so scared that if I do, you'll know the truth: I am desperately, insanely in love with you, and I'm so scared that if you know that, you'll laugh. Or even worse, just say, "Well, that's nice." I can't imagine how I could live with that in my past, but I can't live without the possibility of you in my future, so I'm just saying it all now, and please don't laugh and please don't say, "Well, that's nice."*

*Oh, God. That's what I'm going to tell her. The next time I'm alone with her. I know it. Oh my God.*

"Liam?" Dad said.

"I—"

Dad's phone interrupted. It was the theme song to the old Superman movie from when he'd been a kid. Liam had watched it with him roughly 1.3 million times.

"Yeah?" Dad asked the phone. As Liam watched, his face drained of all color. "Oh, crap. Okay, I'll be right there."

# Ep. 009

TRANSCRIPT BEGINS

INDIRA BHATTI-WATSON, HOST:

This is *No Time Like the Present*, an NPR podcast. I am Indira Bhatti-Watson, reporting from Canterstown, Maryland.

(SOUND BITE OF MUSIC)

BHATTI-WATSON:

We're bringing you this special episode because there's some breaking news. As we reported yesterday, the Canterstown Sheriff's Department issued and executed an arrest warrant for Martin Gregory Chisholm, the Lowe County superintendent of schools and a candidate for the Maryland state senate. Chisholm, we learned, allegedly had an affair with an underage student that began in 1986, and evidence of that affair was concealed in the unearthed time capsule that prompted this podcast. In an attempt to reclaim that evidence, Chisholm allegedly threatened the life of seventeen-year-old Elayah Laird, slashing her throat, then allegedly returned to her house days later to break into the garage.

But now, Chisholm's defense attorney has produced evidence that at least one of these crimes may be off the books. Video of Chisholm attending a campaign rally on the night of the garage break-in has surfaced, and it may turn out that it was impossible for Chisholm to have committed that particular crime, casting doubt on his culpability for the others.

As has been the case all along, the sheriff's department has refused to comment on the investigation, but our sources tell us that the county attorney will still pursue charges against Chisholm for the attack on Elayah Laird, though the video may give a jury reasonable doubt.

We'll have more in our next regular episode.

# 1986: DEAN

Around dinnertime, Jay picked up Dean. They sped over to Finn's Landing and got burgers and Cokes at the Burger King drive-through. Then Jay sped back to Canterstown, not speaking, sucking at his Coke with a manic intensity as he focused on the road ahead.

"Okay if I turn on the radio?" Dean asked, just to break the silence.

Jay shrugged. Dean hit the button and was greeted with a burst of static that slowly resolved into Peter Gabriel, caught midsyllable: "—out frontiers, war without tears." A good one. Dean relaxed in the seat and nibbled at his burger. Jay would talk when he was good and ready. Unlike Antoine, the problem wasn't getting him started—it was getting him to shut up once he got going.

They cruised along the main road, then took a series of turns that brought them deep into a new development. Jay hunted out a discreet parking space and had been parked for less than a minute when he croaked, "Ha!"

Dean peered out the window. He thought this place looked familiar. . . . Yeah, he knew it from the night they'd chased the pizza guy. This was . . .

Just then, from one of the houses, Lisa McKenzie skipped down the front steps. She'd changed her outfit since school, wearing an electric-blue double-breasted jacket over a matching skirt. From here, Dean couldn't tell what color shirt she wore beneath. Her hair was teased and sprayed higher than usual, falling on the sides in a rigid phalanx to almost touch the broad shoulder pads in the jacket.

She turned left onto the sidewalk and walked down the street.

"What are we doing here, Jay?" Dean usually refrained from adopting any sort of authoritative tone around Jay. It was just counterproductive. But now he needed answers, and he put some muscle into his voice.

"Nothing." Jay cranked the key and glided down the street, following Lisa at a distance.

"It's still light out!" Dean hissed, looking around wildly. "We can't do this again!"

"Stop being a grandmother," Jay shot back.

They drifted along at ten miles an hour, hanging back. Just when Dean was beginning to consider doing a *T.J. Hooker* roll out of the car, Jay braked and pulled to the curb.

Ahead, Lisa paused at a corner. A car stopped at the intersection, and she got in.

"Yes," Jay whispered, and began to follow.

"We did this already," Dean protested. "Come on, man." He thought of the knife. Jay's backpack was in the back seat, but was the knife in there or back in its place under Jay's seat? And why was he suddenly so worried about the damn knife?

Following the car with Lisa was both easier and harder than following the pizza-delivery guy. Easier because it was daylight out and there were more cars on the road to hide behind. Harder because...it was daylight out. And there were more cars on the road to lose Lisa behind.

But Jay channeled his inner Remington Steele with true aplomb. Silent, he steered through traffic, keeping an eye on the other car's rear bumper. It was a late-model Ford, painted a too-bright green. Pretty easy to maintain a line of sight to it.

As the sun dipped overhead and headlights began blinking open into the twilight, the Ford turned into a parking lot at a restaurant.

Jay tapped the brakes, slowing down, timing it perfectly so that just as his car drifted by the parking lot, the doors to the Ford opened and Mr. Chisholm emerged, then darted around to the other side to hold open the passenger door for Lisa.

With an excited squeal, Jay accelerated, cranking the wheel around the next corner, where he stopped at the curb, hitting his hazards.

"Holy crap!" Jay erupted once the car was still. "They *are* sleeping together."

Dean smirked skeptically. "They're having dinner, not sex."

"You think her parents know?"

"I don't know."

Overlooking the ennui in Dean's voice, Jay pressed on, refusing to drop the subject. "Why would they be having dinner? Teacher and student?" Jay tapped at the tip of his chin, thinking. "Do you think he could get in trouble for this?"

Dean shrugged. "I guess. But who cares?" Then he realized: "Are you going to say something to your dad?"

For several seconds, Jay contemplated this. "No. He's got his hands full with Mom right now. But someone should do *something*, right?"

"It's none of our business, Jay."

"It has to be *someone's* business. Why not us?"

Dean lightly thumped the side of his head against his window. "What do you want to do? Go all *Rockford Files* and sneak in there and take pictures of them eating dinner? Who cares, man? Who. Cares?"

Jay strummed his fingers on the steering wheel, staring straight ahead. Just then, a car behind them honked, first a brief blip of a sound, then a longer, protracted *BRAAAAAAAP!*

Flipping the guy behind them the bird, Jay killed his hazards and gunned the engine, peeling away from the curb.

"I care," he said.


They drove past Nico's. The flesh on the back of Dean's neck crawled until the neon sign disappeared in the distance.

It was darker now. Mr. Chisholm and Lisa would be tucking into their entrées. Did she call him Mr. Chisholm when they were alone at dinner?

He was surprised but not shocked to find them nearing the school. It was okay, he decided. A little time wandering the echoing halls, with nothing whatsoever to trigger his anger, would be good for Jay. Dean knew that Mr. Chisholm had—perhaps unknowingly, but maybe quite intentionally—skewered Jay through his core: his pride. Jay wasn't capable of shaking something like that off in one go—it would take some time.

Jay moved with purpose. He wasn't here to blow off steam or enjoy some solitude and some rooftop time with his best friend. He was on a mission.

Chasing after Jay, Dean soon found himself in the science wing, outside Mr. Chisholm's room. Jay patiently yet swiftly clanged through his keys until he found the right one and unlocked the door.

"What are we doing, Jay?" Dean followed Jay into the room. The lab benches sat cool and black, the Bunsen burners neutered and impotent. He suddenly flashed to a possible future: Jay turning on the gas to those Bunsen burners, letting it build up, tossing a match as he walked out of school.

No, no. That was crazy.

*Mine eyes have seen the glory of the burning of our school* went the old song, the one they used to sing while leaving on the last day each year, plunging deep into summer. *We have tortured all the teachers, we have broken all the rules....*

*Glory, glory hallelujah*
*Teacher hit me with a ruler*
*I been waiting at the door with a Colt .44*
*And she ain't my teacher no more!*

Just a song. No one was going to blow up a school. No one would shoot a teacher.

"Jay..."

"Take a chill pill," Jay advised. He threaded through the lab benches and plunked himself down in Mr. Chisholm's chair. "Let's see what Jism has up his sleeve."

There was no key on the ring to unlock the teacher's desk. Dean approached, curious. Was Jay going to just rip the damn thing out of the desk?

No. Instead, he opened one of the side drawers. This sort of desk locked only the middle drawer, the shallow one above the kneehole. The filing drawers on either side could open.

Jay eased the top right drawer out, then gestured for Dean to help. Dean crouched and supported the weight of the drawer—it was jam-packed with folders and papers, and it weighed a ton. Dean strained to keep it parallel to the floor as Jay felt around behind it. After a moment, Dean felt the tinny vibration of something clicking loose, and the drawer—hitherto attached to the desk—came free in his hands.

He almost dropped the damn thing. "Give me some warning next time," he chided, setting the drawer on the floor.

"What did you *think* I was doing?" Jay asked, his tone such a marvel of condescension that Dean could feel only astonishment, not anger.

Now the front of the desk had a massive, gaping wound. Jay poked his head into the empty square that had housed the drawer and then wormed a hand in there, too. Dean waited patiently.

"My mom has the same desk at home," Jay said conversationally, and then—as he manipulated something in there—the middle drawer clicked once and popped open a sliver.

The side drawer had been haphazardly packed, disordered. The middle drawer was meticulously organized, with pens lined up together in one nook, pencils in the next. A little well corralled a herd of paper clips, with a stack of note cards off to one side. In the very center of the drawer rested a square light blue envelope. Jay plucked it up. Another envelope—also light blue—was under it.

The envelope in Jay's hand was open, so they prized out its contents—a single sheet of paper with a blue-and-purple flower in the upper left-hand corner, crammed with tight, round female penmanship.

"Oh yeah...," Jay murmured, and skimmed the letter quickly.

Dean blushed as he followed suit. Lisa was not shy about expressing her appreciation for the pleasures she'd experienced at Mr. Chisholm's hands. Fingers, more like. And tongue. And, of course—

"The girth of you inside..." Jay brayed a long, wild, horsey laugh that jerked Dean away at least a foot and had him checking to make certain the windows were closed. Anyone anywhere in the building would have heard that.

"Are you seeing this?" Jay held up the letter. "Are you *seeing* this?"

"Yeah. You were right. They're banging."

"They're makin' bacon," Jay howled in a high falsetto. He thrust the letter at Dean and picked up the next envelope.

Just holding the letter made Dean feel dirty. It was none of his business. He glanced around for the envelope so that he could replace the letter, but Jay was already tapping the contents out of the next envelope. Another sheet of stationery. When Jay unfolded it, something fell to the floor at Dean's feet, and without thinking, he stooped to pick it up.

It was a Polaroid. Of Lisa McKenzie. She wasn't naked, but she wasn't exactly dressed, either. She wore a lavender bra that was almost see-through, her nipples dark smudges against the fabric, and a matching garter belt with stockings.

"Kim's hotter, right?" Jay peered over Dean's shoulder and spoke in an utterly neutral tone that still hinted at . . . something. Dean couldn't tell what. But Jay rarely if ever brought up Kim, rarely if ever discussed her appearance.

"We shouldn't be doing this." Dean itched to get the Polaroid out of his hand, but ceding it to Jay seemed like a bad idea. "He was a jerk to you, yeah. But come on."

Jay grunted noncommittally, still enrapt by the photo. Lisa was staring rather dully at the camera, arms at her sides. Dean had seen sexier poses in catalogs and bra ads on TV.

"We should get out of here." Dean spoke slowly. "If you're gonna do something, do it. But we shouldn't just be hanging out here, reading dirty letters to our chem teacher."

Jay's eyes never wavered from the photo; his fingers tightened on the envelope in his hand, crimping it at its pristine edges.

"He shouldn't have embarrassed me." A hoarse whisper. Dean knew exactly how much effort it was taking for his best friend to admit to that vulnerability, that frailty. That he gave a single solitary crap what anyone else thought about him.

"I wasn't hurting anyone." With what seemed both a physical and spiritual effort, Jay tore his eyes from the Polaroid, refocusing on Dean. "I wasn't hurting anyone. I wasn't doing anything. I just spaced out a little. He shouldn't have done that."

"Yeah, I know. I know, man." Still crouched by the chair, he stretched out his free hand and patted Jay on the shoulder. The big clock on the wall above Mr. Chisholm's desk clicked loudly into the silence, slaying seconds as they stared at each other.

Dean thought he'd counted thirty of the clicks. He plucked the envelope from Jay's nerveless fingers and tucked the Polaroid back inside. "Let's go, man."

Jay nodded, then sighed. "I'll clean it all up."

The shortest, straightest path from the science wing back to the car cut through the locker warren where Dean and Jay both had lockers. Jay led the way, Dean trailing behind, then almost colliding with him when Jay suddenly stopped short.

"I have to pee." Jay said it in an almost mesmerized timbre, his eyes unfocused and distant.

Dean sighed. The lavatories were maybe ten steps away. Why did Jay have to be so dramatic? He'd been borderline catatonic since they left Mr. Chisholm's room, his gait stiff, his demeanor blank. Now he stood limblocked at the edge of the locker maze, seemingly unable to take a step farther.

"Jay…"

"I have to pee."

"So take a piss!" Dean flung an arm out, pointing to the alcove that led to the men's lav just a few steps away.

Jay turned slowly, half facing Dean, then rested his palm against the closest locker. "This is Gimble's locker, right?"

It was. So what?

The empty space around them filled with the metallic shush of Jay's fly unzipping. Dean hopped back a step as Jay fished his penis out of his pants. The sacred Bathroom Rule was in full effect, even though they weren't standing at urinals; Dean averted his eyes. Jay's expression was still flat as he braced himself against the locker one-handed, fumbling.

Dean realized without looking to confirm: He was probing for one of the locker's vents.

Jay went still. His countenance relaxed as a hissing sound filled the air along with the slight tang of urine.

It took only a moment or two, and then Jay tucked himself back in and turned to Dean with a huge grin plastered across his face. They stared at each other.

And then Jay cracked up, laughing as though he'd just watched Eddie Murphy from the front row. Clutching his stomach, he howled, staggering backward and crashing into the other row of lockers.

Dean couldn't help it; he started with a soft grumble of mirth, then broke down into full-on hilarity.

They collapsed against each other, then sank to the floor, heaving and chortling until they managed to catch their breath and compose themselves. Dean wiped tears from his eyes.

"Well," Jay said with bright eyes, "I feel a *lot* better now!"


Back in the car, the adumbrative night protecting them as they pulled—headlightless—out of the parking lot, Jay suddenly said, "That pizza guy. Remember him?"

With a hollow laugh, Dean said, "Sure. We exchange Christmas cards."

Jay huffed a syllable of laughter. "Do you think we should do something about him?"

"Do something? Like what?"

"I don't know. I wonder if he saw my license plate."

Dean cleared his throat. He'd wondered the same thing. And the fact that so much time had gone by with nothing happening had imbued in him a confidence that they'd dodged any consequences of their actions that night. But all he knew for certain was that he'd dodged a bullet once. He didn't plan on putting himself on the firing line again.

**44**

# THE PRESENT: LIAM

Liam's lunch bag had never contained anything as prosaic as plain old peanut butter and jelly. Pop had always managed to jazz up anything he packed for Liam, and even though Liam was on the cusp of graduation, Pop still insisted on packing his son's lunch every day. Today was a nice, crunchy brioche with aged cheddar, horseradish, and prosciutto. Plus grapes, granola, and some funky crackers that looked as though they had spores on them but tasted amazing.

He was halfway through the sandwich when El arrived with the others.

"I figured it out," El said, plopping down her tray. It was taco day. Pop would have been horrified at what the school claimed were tacos.

"Figured what out?" he asked.

"We need the police records from 1986," she announced.

Wait, what?

"She's right, you know," Jorja said. "To see if anything weird was going on. That's the next step."

"Next step?" He managed to swallow the chunk of bread he'd been chewing through. "Next step in *what*? It's over."

Marcie blinked at him owlishly from across the table. "Didn't you watch the video of the Chisholm campaign event last night? It was on YouTube."

"Peter was there, too." Jorja leaned in conspiratorially, as though anyone around them cared to eavesdrop. "So he *couldn't* have been the guy to break into El's garage."

"And when I went through the box of stuff your dad brought over, guess what? One of the tapes was missing. Which means whoever broke into my garage—"

"*Not* Peter," Jorja said, as though he already needed to be reminded.

"—and took one of the cassettes. *That* must be the person who's connected to the knife," El said triumphantly.

"Or—and follow me here—someone at my dad's work dropped the cassette behind the fax machine."

El rolled her eyes. "When they took the stuff after the break-in—"

"*Second* break-in," Jorja added helpfully. Marcie nodded in solidarity.

"—they had to give me a receipt. I checked it. They only logged one cassette. There were *two* in the time capsule. So whoever went into the garage—"

"Not Peter," Liam said quickly, before Jorja could. Marcie scowled at him, but Jorja just shrugged and bit into a taco, which obligingly crumbled in her hands.

"—took that second tape. And that's the person we're after now."

Oh, holy crap. She wanted to keep going. She wanted to keep doing this.

It was *insane*. It was *over*. They'd gotten *so* lucky already. They could have easily ended up in jail for kidnapping Peter McKenzie. Now they should lie back, settle back into life.

"Guys, are you serious?" he asked.

Jorja looked at Marcie. Marcie looked at El. El looked at Liam. "Of course we are. We're not done."

"Well, I'm done. My dad ripped me a new one last night. And two is about all I can handle. Can you imagine if he ripped me a *third* one?"

El seemed shocked by this. Couldn't she just give it a rest?

Well, no. She couldn't. Of course not. She'd never been very good at giving things a rest.

Looking at her, he knew he would cave eventually. Might as well start now.

"Fine," he said. "How do you plan to get the records?"

"I saw online that you can request documents and stuff from the town. You just fill out a form."

"That'll make my dad happy. I'm sure he'll get right on it."

El frowned at that. She obviously hadn't considered who would eventually see that request.

"I bet Indira could do it," Marcie suggested.

Jorja's face lit up, and she leaned over to peck Marcie on the cheek. "Great idea!"

Liam mimed gagging. El was already on her phone, texting.

"You're just jealous," Jorja said smugly.

Liam laughed as though it couldn't possibly be true.

# ELAYAH

Turned out that as part of her ongoing research, Indira had already requested the police records and had had a bunch of interns scan them. El traded the image of the *I'm sorry* note for a link to a Dropbox folder containing the scans.

Mr. Hindon let them use the media center after school for a "research project" while he was reshelving and straightening up. The four of them spent the afternoon poring over the documents, sprawled out in various configurations across the room.

No one spoke. It was boring work, going through police reports from the weeks before and after the burial of the time capsule back in 1986. Most of it was "cat stuck in a tree" type of stuff, a hideously boring window into the place and time of their parents' youth.

Their parents' names never popped, not even once.

"What the heck does *WPWP* mean?" Marcie asked. She was the first person to have spoken in almost an hour.

"Don't worry about it," Liam said quickly.

"It's all over some of these," Marcie said. "I just want to know."

"I said don't worry about it." Liam sounded a little grumpy, which the others all took as the signal to badger the living hell out of him.

Eventually he cracked. "Okay, okay, fine! I'll tell you."

He took a deep breath and glanced at Elayah. "It's an old code that they used back in the day. It stands for 'wrong person, wrong place.' They, uh, they used it when they'd hassle Black people for being, you know…"

"For being Black?" Jorja asked.

Elayah shook her head. "For being somewhere they didn't belong," she said. "White neighborhoods."

No one spoke.

"Speaking of white hoods," Jorja said abruptly, "did you know there was a Klan rally in Canterstown two weeks after homecoming? Apparently, they used to happen, like, once a year. Some dude who owned a farm over near the water tower was a sympathizer and would let them use his field. Anyway, the sheriff's office had deputies staged there, and there's a report from an undercover officer."

"Two weeks after? Then the time capsule was already buried."

"It would be easy if it was Nazis," Marcie said.

"Whoa!" El sat up straight. "Look at this!" She waved her phone at them.

"Can't read it when you're waving it around like that," Liam told her.

She held it out steady so that they could look.

"Remember that guy Bradley Gimble?" she asked. "From the yearbook? The guy who died in a car crash? Says here that the crash was, like, a couple of days before they buried the thing."

Jorja and Marcie had leaned in close to scrutinize the phone.

"You know that place out on Route 9 where the road curves up around the bend? His car went off the edge and dropped—"

"That's impossible," Jorja interrupted. "There's that big stone wall there."

"*Now* there's a big stone wall there," El pointed out.

"This says he was drunk," Marcie said, scanning El's phone. "They found beer bottles in the car. Ugh—his throat was crushed by the steering wheel."

"That's interesting!" Jorja said brightly, clearly filing it away for future use in a story.

"Well, unless the knife was driving the car, I don't think it fits."

Jorja gave Liam her most withering look. Liam puckered up and blew her a kiss; she pretended to grab it out the air, examine it in the palm of her hand, then toss it over her shoulder with a shrug.

"It's just a weird coincidence, is all," El said.

"It's all weird coincidences," Marcie said. "The trick is figuring out what *isn't* a coincidence. Like...like this one here." She tapped at her iPad screen. "Does the name *Douglas Rumson* mean anything to any of you?"

They all pondered. Negative head shakes all around. "Nope," said Liam.

"He was twenty-two back in 1986. Worked as a pizza-delivery guy for some place called Nico's."

"My dad still talks about their pizza," Jorja offered.

"How *are* things at the Dearborn house these days?" Liam asked.

Elayah groaned. Marcie glared. But Jorja just shrugged.

"We don't talk," Jorja said soberly. "My mother tries to get us to communicate, but we're both stubborn. So there's nothing to say."

"Anyway...," Marcie said after they all realized Jorja had nothing else to add. "On this guy Rumson: About two weeks *before* they buried the time capsule, he says someone started following him around."

"Like, dudes in black trench coats?"

Marse shook her head. "Nope. It was a Friday night and he was at work, and someone in a late-model car started following him everywhere he went on deliveries that night." She paused. "It sounds really creepy from the way he described it."

"So..." Elayah tapped her chin, thinking. "So we know that a couple of weeks before everything went down that someone was sneaking around town, following this guy."

"How is this related?" Jorja asked. "I mean..."

"I'll tell you how," Liam said, sitting up. "Everyone keeps telling us, 'Oh, this was just a sleepy little town back then. Everyone worked at the factory and everything was fine, not like today.' But there was stuff going on, man! Knives and blood and car crashes and weirdos following pizza-delivery guys. What if it was our parents following the pizza guy? And what if they followed him another time and killed him?"

"Why?" Jorja asked.

"Who the hell knows?" Liam flung his hands as high as his arms would let him. "Come on! Something happened! Someone *bled*!"

Elayah elbowed him in the ribs, hard, then jerked her head toward the circulation desk, where Mr. Hindon had glanced up from his computer. "Keep it down. We're not alone."

"I don't see a Douglas Rumson on Facebook anywhere near here," Marcie announced, waggling her phone. "I checked every town I could think of. Nothing."

"Missing person report from 1986 for Douglas Rumson, maybe?" Elayah asked.

Jorja clucked her tongue. "Good idea. Let's look."

They returned to their screens.

# LIAM

They never found a missing person report for Douglas Rumson. Which didn't mean anything—it could have been filed in 1987 or never filed at all. Or lost in the intervening decades. Man, the passage of time was harsh.

El shook him off when Liam offered her a ride home. "My mom's picking me up." And then, almost as an afterthought: "But thanks."

He flashed a grin that felt painted on, a thin scrim of lie presented to the world to cover up the absolute fact that he'd screwed up with her, totally and completely. He'd waited too long. And then he'd made her mad. Lost any chance he ever had.

Ha. Yeah, right. As though he'd ever, *ever* had a chance with El.

Still smiling his idiot's smile, he bade her farewell and drove home.

*This,* he thought as he loped into the house, *is the last day of the beginning of your life. And the beginning of what historians will someday call* El-less Liam.

*I guess that would make me just plain Iam.*

There was something there other than a bad joke. Something about *Iam* and *I am* and being without El, but Liam knew he wasn't the one to figure it out. He stood there in the entryway to the house, the door still ajar behind him, trying to puzzle it out for so long that Pop poked his head around the corner from the living room.

"I've been sitting here waiting for the door to close."

Liam said nothing.

"Kinda still waiting."

Right. Liam shook himself and shut the door, then meandered into the kitchen. He was heartbroken and ruined, but he was also hungry because he was pretty much always hungry. Gotta feed the machine.

Pop followed him into the kitchen just as he opened the refrigerator. "You're about to perform some kind of culinary crime, aren't you?"

Liam frowned, leaning into the fridge's cool and glare. "Not if you stop me."

Knowing both when he'd been had and when he'd been beaten, Pop steered Liam away from the fridge with both hands on his shoulders, settling him into a chair. "Grilled cheese?"

"Two, please."

With a sage grunt, Pop hauled a block of cheddar out of the cheese drawer, scrutinized it like an old-timey prospector examining a nugget of gold from the river, then began grating it into a yellow pile on the butcher-block counter. As he worked, he said, "What's new?"

"Marcie and Jorja are hooking up, if you can believe that."

Pop did a pleased double take. "Well, that's sweet! Good for them. You don't seem particularly happy about it."

"Kinda could use my best friend these days, but she's too busy sucking face with El's best friend."

Shrug.

"You want to talk about it?"

"Not much point."

"There's always a point."

Liam groaned. He was hungry. Watching Pop take *forever* to carve fat slices of brioche was killing him.

"So here it is: A while back, I said stupid things to El and things are still kinda frosty, which is totally cool for her, but sucks for me 'cause I would like her not to hate me."

Pop shrugged with one shoulder as he assembled the pieces of the sandwich for the griddle. "Yeah, I guess your life is over."

"At last someone understands me."

"You know the frame in the dining room, the one of that Halloween when Dad and I were Lenny and Squiggy?"

"Yeah."

"Go get it."

The sandwich would take a couple of minutes, so why not? Liam fetched the framed photo. When he returned, Pop was assembling the makings for the second sandwich as the first one cooked on the stove top. Damn, how did he manage to make something as mundane as grilled cheese so mouthwatering?

Pop shifted the grilled sandwich to a plate, put the other sandwich over the heat, and presented Liam with the first half of his meal. Then he wiped his hands on a dish towel and popped the back off the frame Liam had brought in.

Under the first photo, the Halloween one, was a second one Liam had never seen before. It was his dad, younger, in high school, wearing a tux and standing very upright and very humorlessly with a girl of about the same age.

"Who's that?" Liam asked.

"Dad's girlfriend."

Girlfriend. Wow. Liam knew, of course, that his father had not really acknowledged or discovered his sexuality until partway through college—and a boyfriend named *Whit*, believe it or not—but it was one thing to know it; quite another to have evidence. It was difficult to tell if the girl with her arm looped through Dad's was attractive or not. All that 1980s stuff got in the way.

"Dad with a girlfriend. Sheesh. Does not compute."

"Don't look at me—he was already gay when I got to him."

Liam chewed through the sandwich. "I know you have a point here, but I'm too stupid to get it."

"You're not stupid, and I hate when you say that about yourself." Pop said it lightly, but with just enough spine that Liam knew he meant it. "You ride yourself too hard just because you have some friends who are smart*er*. Smart*er*, Liam. You're a smart kid. And even if you can't do differential calculus, you have other skills that other kids would kill for. Hell, I flunked algebra twice—once in high school, once in college. And then I went to culinary school instead and suddenly I wasn't a dummy; I was a genius."

The grilled cheese sandwich was just utter perfection. Just the right amount of cheese, melted just so, its texture velvety and smooth on his tongue. A little dash of pepper for heat. And the amazing bread, which Pop had baked from scratch last week—crusty and soft at the same time, in the same bite.

"Still don't see the point," Liam said, but he had to admit that the sandwich was beginning to make him not care about whatever the point was.

Pop pried the second sandwich off the grill with his pancake turner and slipped it onto Liam's plate.

"The point is this: When your dad was around your age, he thought he was straight and figured his life was going to look a certain way. He was wrong."

Chewing that over along with the sandwich, Liam shook his head. "I'm always going to be in love with El. Nothing will change that."

Pop sat next to him and put an arm around him. "And that's okay. But being in love with her doesn't mean you won't find happiness with someone else. And not for nothing, but you might be wrong about being in love with her. Or her hating you."

"I'm not wrong."

As he made his way through the second sandwich, he stared at the photo. He wondered what had happened to this girl. Dad had never mentioned her.

Was there something there? Who knew?


# ELAYAH


Marcie left school with Jorja, which wasn't a big surprise. Until Elayah realized Marcie had her extra-large purse, the one she used when she'd spent the night at Elayah's.

Holy crap. Was Marcie *spending the night* at Jorja's?

As the sky darkened and she waited for Mom to pick her up, Elayah composed text after text to Marcie, but sent none of them. It was tough, she realized, to find the right words to ask your best friend if she was getting Jorja'd on the regular.

Her focus turned to a frown when Dad's car pulled into the school parking lot. It was supposed to be *Mom*.

Life in the Laird house had settled into a flimsy ritual of school and work, a fragile, desultory performance in which the three actors played their roles by rote. Elayah went to school, came home, and finished her homework just as her father roused himself from sleep to prepare for his night shift. They spoke only as necessary. Mom observed it all, silent. She tried once to tease out from Elayah the nature of her and Dad's quiet disharmony but yielded nothing in the conversation.

Now, reluctantly, she threw her backpack in the back seat and climbed into the passenger seat. "Mom got held up at work," Dad said with forced brightness.

"Uh-huh," she said.

They glided back out onto the street. The school was set back far from any of the main roads, down a long, winding single-laner that wended through dying soybean fields and cornfields gone fallow. Someone, theoretically, owned all this land. Also theoretically, it had to be worth *something*. But it never sold.

"How are you doing?" It was Dad-code for *How's your throat? How's your soul?*

"I'm good." It was the same answer she gave every time, both positive and neutral at once.

"I'm glad you're getting out with your friends. How's Liam?"

She didn't feel like talking about Liam. Talking about Liam made her think of Marcie and Jorja, in each other's clutches. The press of them. The heat they must have felt. The light in Marse's eyes when she'd talked about it, the urgency in her voice.

Her anger at Liam had burned out days ago, and its residue of annoyance was blown away by her long-lived affinity to him. Every time she thought of him, she became less angry.

Liam. She wanted what Marcie had with Jorja. She wanted him against her. Wanted to wrap herself around him, but more than her yearning for him, she wanted to *be* wanted *by* him. She craved his urgency, his compulsion, his…his…*lust*, okay? She had little experience in this arena, but she knew from romance novels that, crushed to a man in an embrace, you could feel his hardness against you. She'd never in her life experienced that, but she knew she could and she craved it. She wanted the feeling and to know that she and she alone was the cause of the excitement, that she had summoned his arousal as though with a spell. She wanted to melt into Liam, to the point that all she wanted was to want, the word *want* over and over in her head, reminding her, at the last, of the other meaning of the word: privation.

And she lacked Liam, that much was true.

Drawing in a deep breath and relocating herself in the universe, she said, "He's okay, I guess."

Dad diverted his attention from the road for a split second to grace her with a skeptical eyebrow arch like the Rock.

She couldn't restrain a giggle from spilling out from between her lips. It was the first time since all this had started that she'd allowed herself to relax in her father's presence. It felt good. It felt right. She missed him, and suddenly she didn't care if he was Antoine or Marcus or Loki in disguise. He was her dad.

Dad paused at a stop sign, checked the intersection, then proceeded. "You're so obvious, it's painful, baby girl. You think that boy doesn't know you're into him? Who do you think you're kidding?"

"It's gross talking about boys with my dad."

"Hey, I was a boy once! I can give you the inside scoop! Help me help you, Elayah."

Their chuckles were interrupted by a loud, single *WHOOP!* Behind them, a red light spun into the darkening day.

"What the hell…?" Dad muttered, staring up into the rearview mirror.

It was a Canterstown Sheriff's Department cruiser, pulling up behind them, its cherry top lit. Dad spent a split second fuming, then signaled and pulled over to the side of the road. There was no shoulder to speak of—the road cratered off to the side, leading right into a decaying field. The car came to a halt with its passenger side tilted downward, tipping Elayah against the door.

"What the hell?" Dad grumbled under his breath, staring into the mirror. "What the hell?"

Then he suddenly seemed to remember that he wasn't alone in the car. With a queasily upbeat expression, he said, "Everything is going to be fine."

She swallowed hard enough to tug at the stitches. Sure, everything would be fine. Because routine traffic stops *never* went sideways.

The cop paused briefly at the rear of the car to stoop and peer through the rear window, assessing.

He approached from the driver's side. Dad had the window down already and his hands visible on the steering wheel.

"License and registration, sir." A Canterstown sheriff's deputy. Didn't look much past twenty-five. He wore the short-sleeve version of the uniform top, with tightly corded arms adorned with tattoos.

"I'm just reaching for my wallet," Dad told the deputy. He always put it in the little nook in the center console when he drove. Plainly visible and always in reach. "Do you mind telling me what this is about? Was I speeding?"

He hadn't been speeding.

Without thinking, Elayah said, "I can get the registration," and leaned forward toward the glove compartment.

"NO!" Dad shouted, turning to her. The deputy took a step back and put his hand on the butt of his gun.

"No one move!" he shouted. "No one move!"

Elayah froze in place, halfway to the dashboard. Dad had twisted in her direction, a veil of barely throttled fear and rage fallen over his face.

"Sir, I'm going to ask you to get out of the car."

"She was just getting the registration."

"Sir, this is now the *second* time I'm asking you to get out of the car."

Her father's fuming face was a wonder and a horror to behold. In that moment, she knew that if it were possible to kill someone with a thought, the cop would already be twitching his last moments of life on the road.

But Dad tamped it down. "Of course," he said. "I'm turning and coming out."

To Elayah, he whispered, "Don't move a muscle. It'll all be okay."

Keeping his hands in view at all times, he turned, took a deep breath, and opened the door. "I'm coming out now."

He stepped out of the car. She wanted to reach for her phone, to record what was happening. That was what you were supposed to do.

But her phone was in her back pocket. If she reached for it, would he shoot? Or would he see the phone and change his attitude, knowing he was being recorded?

*Don't move a muscle*, Dad had told her.


Dad drove in a cold fury, his eyes laser-focused on the road ahead.

It had been about fifteen humiliating minutes before the deputy allowed her dad back into the car with a stern warning to check his brake light, which was busted.

"A taillight," Dad mumbled. "All that over a goddamn *taillight*."

She'd been too afraid to move. Too afraid to speak up. Too aware of the deputy's gun at his hip, of the unwarranted but very manifest fear in his eyes, of the string of dead Black bodies punctured by police bullets that stretched so long and so wasted in her memory and beyond.

At the house, he immediately called the sheriff. A little while later, headlights sliced themselves into glowing ribbons through the slats in her blinds. Peering out, she saw a sheriff's department cruiser pulling into her driveway. A bump of fear knocked her heart off-kilter for an instant, and then Liam's dad heaved himself out of the driver's side, stood for a moment. Arched his back with a grimace. When he thought no one was looking, he allowed himself frailty, weakness. Haggard and haunted, he mounted the steps to the house and rapped on the door.

She left her room and stood in the shadows of the hallway as her father harangued and hollered at Liam's dad for a solid five minutes before even letting him speak.

"Marcus, I know you're pissed and you're not inclined to cut me any slack these days, but you know—you *know*—that this isn't how I run my department. You know that."

"I want his badge," Dad demanded. "At the very least, he needs to be on suspension or something. Right now. Right the hell *now*, Dean."

"I can't do that. I need all hands on deck. It's crazy right now. You know that better than anyone."

"So he gets to treat me like that, he gets to scare the living hell out of my daughter, and you're just going to let him get away with it?"

"Of course not. I'm going to talk to him—"

"Oh, you'll *talk* to him! Well, that's all right, then!"

The two men eventually not so much arrived at an armistice as wore each other out to the point of enervation, unwilling to surrender but unable to swing another punch.

She found Dad at the small dining room table, tapping away on her mom's laptop. A glance at the screen told her he was writing to the governor.

She sat across from him. He kept pounding at the keyboard, then abruptly stopped, turning to her. His body vibrated. Anger and impotence rolled off him in thick waves.

"Dad," she said, and the words began rolling out before she was entirely certain what she was doing.

But it was clear in an instant, in the space between her own heartbeats. He was angry. Outraged. Powerless. Full of self-loathing and no self-worth in this moment, berating himself for his failure to protect his daughter in so many recent circumstances.

And she knew that now was her chance, her chance to *learn*. His thoughts were brittle, his resistance weak. She hated herself for doing it, for exploiting his pain and frangibility.

But she had to do it.

To learn.

To know.

"Dad," she said, "what really happened back then?"

His sigh deflated him, his shoulders slumping, his chest caving in. He looked so much like her grandfather in that moment. He'd died of "respiratory complications" a year ago, a lingering remnant of the coronavirus. The sudden resemblance poleaxed her and she almost excused herself.

"Nothing happened back then that would have explained any of this," Dad told her. He closed the laptop and folded his hands over it as though praying to the gods of processors and RAM to bring him wisdom. "Everything was kids' stuff. Nothing serious."

"What did you guys *really* do in the school? When you broke in?"

He stuttered a laugh. "I told you, baby girl—it was nothing. Dumb stuff. We stole hall passes. We were gonna change our grades in the computer...." He groaned. "That was...that was the really dumb thing. We all sort of slacked off because we knew we'd end up with the grades we needed. And then that all came crashing down around us."

"Is that why you went to Howard instead of University of Houston? It was on your yearbook page. *University of Houston–bound.* But you went to Howard."

Stroking his jawline, he nodded, staring absently into the air. Present with her no longer, he was elsewhere. Else*when.*

"Dad?"

"We were supposed to go to Houston. Together. Our heroes were Kirk Baptiste and Carl Lewis."

She knew that. The part about Baptiste and Lewis, at least. Her dad had told her tales of them when she was young, spinning them out as folk heroes. Other kids had princesses and knights and superheroes—she had Kirk and Carl, the runners.

"And then things changed," he told her. "That's what happens. In life. Things change and you change with them."

He seemed to think he was finished, that she was satisfied.

*Are you Marcus or are you Antoine?* she yearned to ask. To demand. But that would put him on the defensive. He would clam up.

"Because...," she prompted.

With a groan in the back of his throat, he went on, dragging the words out slowly at first. "Howard wasn't even on my radar. Antoine brought it up, told me all about it. And when he left, I guess... We ran relay, sweetheart. We were a matched set. Houston was interested in the twins, you know? That ol' Black Lightning bolt had two forks in it, and they weren't as inter-ested in just one. We were more valuable together.

"So I changed my mind. Long after the yearbook deadline. I went to Howard because 'Toine had... Anyway, he was in Mexico, so I decided to..."

He broke off. She licked her lips, ready to goad him on again, but he was in his own zone now, spooling out the past.

"No, that's not true," he admitted. "That makes it sound like I thought it out, like I had a good sit and went through all the pluses and minuses and decided. It wasn't like that. It was from my gut, not my brain.

"I went there, and I learned more about what 'Toine had been telling me. I learned what it really meant to be Black in America." Here he paused. "I guess that's not true, either. I knew already. But growing up here, back then, I didn't know that there was a community. I didn't know about the great Black intellectuals, about the histories and traditions that came over on the slave ships. I just didn't know, because no one here taught it and my parents were too busy surviving. But then I went to Howard and..." His eyes widened, seeing something long gone. His tone became almost awestruck. "There were words and phrases to describe it all, an entire science and history to it. And for the first time, I really understood—in my head *and* in my heart—that I wasn't alone, that other people had had the same questions, the same rages, the same fears and wonderings. There was a way to put it all together, and I'd been trying to figure that out my whole life, but then I went to Howard and found out that other people had made a map for me. I just had to follow it."

"Did you?" she asked.

He inclined his head a bit, pursing his lips, his eyes growing larger for a moment, then smaller. "Best I could, baby girl. But this place kept calling back to me. There was your mom. And there was Antoine."

"But...he wasn't here any longer."

"No, but he had been. This was where I saw him last. And this was where I knew he'd come back. *If* he came back."

"Are you still waiting?" she asked, her voice smaller than she'd ever heard it.

"I told myself to stop waiting a long time ago. But I don't think I listened very well."

Suddenly, he grinned. A big, broad, happy grin that flabbergasted her with its joy and its presence.

"Hot chocolate?" he asked. "There's marshmallows, too."

"Yeah," she said, and then stopped because her phone was buzzing.

**can we meet?** asked Indira.

**45**

# 1986: DEAN

J ay's obsession with the Steingard Trophy had only grown since he'd first mentioned it that day in Brian's garage. He insisted on putting it in the time capsule. "We'll be legends," he promised. "We'll go down in history. When we dig this thing up fifteen years from now, we'll be in every newspaper and on every TV channel you can imagine."

Brian snorted derisively. "No one will care about this thing except for us."

"They'll care if it contains the Cup, missing for fifteen years!" Jay pointed out.

And there was something seductively authentic in his claim, a certainty that convinced them.

They had agreed to bury the time capsule the week after homecoming. That was the absolute latest they figured they could do it before the ground got too hard for digging. And they had to steal the Cup on a weekend, otherwise someone would notice immediately that it was gone.

The problem, Dean pointed out, was that homecoming itself was coming up this very weekend. In three days.

At the lunch table on Wednesday, they huddled together—even Kim, who had become more invested in this than Dean would have imagined—and discussed.

"We need to do it *during* homecoming," Jay said.

"Are you nuts?" Marcus asked. "The dance is *here*. The school will be full of people."

"It won't be *that* full," Brian said with vexation. "Not everyone is going to homecoming."

"Can't get a date, huh?" Marcus cracked. "Pour a beer in your hand; get your girlfriend drunk."

"Bite me."

"You'd like that, wouldn't you? A little nibble around the head?"

Brian cracked his knuckles and shot a fierce glare at Marcus, who pointedly ignored it.

"Knock it off," Dean said. "Shouldn't we wait until after the dance? Go in on Sunday?"

Jay shook his head fiercely. "They display the thing in the case during football season. And then it goes out to be polished and all that crap when the season's over. Last year, they took it right after homecoming, when they were cleaning up the school. We have to go *during* the dance."

"That's too dangerous," Kim protested.

Jay snorted. "Look, the dance is in the gym, right? So they close off the rest of the building, except for that little hallway from the gym to the bathrooms near shop. No one can get into the rest of the building."

"But we can," Marcus said, grinning.

"You guys are going to the dance." Jay pointed to Marcus, Kim, and Dean. "So it'll be me and Bri and 'Toine."

Dean bit his bottom lip and risked a glance over at Antoine, who studiously did not return the look, instead focusing on Jay.

"Are you sure you need all three of you?" Dean asked. "The more of you there are, the better the chance of being caught."

"I need lookouts." Jay clearly could only barely be bothered to explain himself. "Sound good?"

Marcus and Brian agreed immediately and enthusiastically. Kim said, "Sure." Because why not—she wouldn't be at risk.

Antoine, silent as always, simply put his hands on the table and nodded.

Which left Dean. He nodded, too, but by then no one really cared.

That night, he and Antoine met at their hideaway. They'd stocked it as well as they could. As the autumn nights grew colder, Dean wondered if he could sneak a kerosene heater in here.

"You don't have to go along with Jay's crazy plan," he told Antoine as they lay on their pile of sleeping bags, tangled together.

"It's not like I have a date for homecoming." Antoine's voice was light. Almost too light. As though he was trying too hard.

"Come on." Dean turned and leaned over to kiss his forehead. "It's not like—"

"I'm not saying we should go together." Antoine didn't pull away, but he didn't seem to acknowledge or even notice the kiss. "I'm just saying: I have nothing else to do."

Dean sighed and rolled onto his back. "Don't you think I'd rather be with you?"

"This isn't an argument," Antoine said mildly. "I'm just telling you how I feel and how it is."

"I want to fix it."

Antoine shrugged. "Remember the first time we broke into the school? You and I went off together, and we didn't even look for that damn pool. We were making out in the hallway, and we heard someone coming...."

Dean looked away. He remembered. He'd pulled away from Antoine so fast that, in disentangling himself, he'd knocked over Antoine, sending him sprawling to the floor.

His fear of discovery. He knew it lay between them sometimes. A third, unwelcome body. He understood.

Laying his head back, Dean stared up at the ceiling joists. This place would be knocked down, come the end of winter. Where would they meet then? Where would Daylight Dean have his moments of nighttime sunshine?

"Have you given it any more thought?" Antoine asked into the silence.

He knew what Antoine meant: running away together. San Francisco. New York. Mexico.

"I don't get how you can be so blasé about it," Dean said. "We wouldn't just be...it wouldn't just be putting distance between us and our families.

We'd basically have to shut them out entirely. They would never accept this." He traveled a finger back and forth between them.

"I know." Antoine leaned up on one elbow and rested a hand on Dean's chest. "If my family can't tolerate who I am—who I *really* am—then I don't need them. Or want them."

Dean shivered.

"It's getting cold here these days," Antoine said.

"That one window is drafty." Dean pointed. Where would he get a heater, anyway? And kerosene in an enclosed space was a bad idea. "I'll fix it. But that's not why...I can't believe you could just turn your back on your family."

"They've turned their back on me. Every Sunday in church. Every time Pops yells at a gay guy on TV. 'Get that queer crap off my TV!'"

Maybe...

Maybe Antoine was right. Maybe running away...

Maybe it would make their families reassess.

Maybe.

"I love you," Dean said.

"I love you, too." Antoine kissed his cheek. "We'll work it out. We'll figure it out. I promise."

46

# THE PRESENT: ELAYAH

One thing Elayah knew for certain was this: They were at an impasse. She was up for whatever Indira could offer at this point.

They all met the next day, right before school. It was two-shots-of-espresso in the morning, and Elayah was buzzed. Indira pulled up to the school in a rented minivan and let them all in.

Clustered around Indira's iPad, they again watched video of the campaign event that served as Martin Chisholm's alibi. Sure enough, there he was, glad-handing diners at a local restaurant, offering up an *Aw, shucks!* handshake here and there. Peter McKenzie was at his father's elbow the whole time. Where Chisholm's smile had the practiced sincerity of a politician, Peter's was strained and bad-CGI-fake.

"Are you absolutely sure?" Indira asked.

"I'd be more sure if I could see the bottom of his shoe," Liam cracked. The swelling had gone down, but he still had a slight red crescent that crooked down from his eyebrow. "But, yeah, that's him."

"Okay, I just wanted to be positive," Indira said, and slept the iPad.

"You think he knew his dad was a rapist?" Marcie asked.

"More relevant to our interests: Do we think he knew his dad slit El's throat?" Jorja continued.

As she did every time someone mentioned that night, Elayah touched her cut. She wondered if it would ever feel normal again.

"Okay, so…" Indira clapped her hands together once. "Just wanted to double-check that and also give you guys an update. We still haven't found Douglas Rumson. At least, not the right one. There's a bunch of them online, but so far not the right one."

"Maybe because he's dead?" Jorja posed.

"Or maybe he's just not on social media," Marcie said. "Some old people aren't."

"Look," Indira said pointedly, gazing at Elayah, "do you have a better image of the note? Something higher res?"

Indira had come up empty this time, but at least she'd tried. Elayah thumbed through her phone until she found the best picture of the *I'm sorry* note.

Indira studied it, pursing her lips. "Don't text it—upload it to my Dropbox. I want full resolution. I have a handwriting analyst I can use. They'll expedite it."

"Expedite what?" Elayah asked as she uploaded the photo. "We already compared it to the postcard."

"Yeah, but I want to compare it to publicly available samples of Chisholm's handwriting, just in case," Indira told her. "You guys might have been wrong."

"Won't his handwriting have changed over the years?" Jorja asked.

Indira shrugged. "Let's leave that up to the expert."

"Could you double-check it against the Antoine postcard?" Elayah asked eventually.

"Sure. But you know what would really be great? If we could get access to the knife," Indira went on. "We could run a DNA test on the blood. I have a lab guy who owes me a favor. We could compare it to each of your parents'."

"What would that tell us?" Marcie asked.

"If nothing else," Elayah jumped in, "it would tell us if one of our parents bled on the thing. Right now none of them admit to knowing about the knife."

"And if the DNA doesn't match any of them, it proves something else," Indira put in. "It proves that there's someone else who's involved and maybe your parents are in the clear."

"And if it matches El's dad…," Liam said slowly. "Doesn't that mean El's theory is right? Marcus is really Antoine? They're twins—they have the same DNA."

"Common misconception," Elayah said automatically. "Identical twins have super-similar DNA, but there *are* differences."

"It's a moot point," Jorja pronounced, "because there's no way for us to get access to the knife and the blood."

"We'll do what we can." Indira stood to leave. "I have a budget conference call in a few. I'll be in touch soon."

They piled out of the minivan just as buses began arriving in the parking lot.

Indira poked her head out the window. "Oh, also, consider this: How did Lisa's lust letter get in the time capsule in the first place? De Nardo wouldn't have done it. Chisholm wouldn't have done it. So who did?"

She grinned at them, and then she was gone.

Jorja and Marcie, holding hands, strode off toward the school as students began filtering in from buses and cars. Elayah stood frozen at the spot where she'd disembarked from Indira's ridiculous minivan, unable to move.

Who *had* put the love letter in the time capsule? Had it been the same person who put the knife in? Why?

None of this made *any* sense! The more she learned, the less she knew. It wasn't supposed to work this way!

"Hey, uh, El…"

Liam was still standing near her, hands jammed in his pockets. He clearly wanted to say something to her. She waited patiently, but he only stared at her, then dragged his attention over to the school, clenching his teeth.

Whatever he had going on in his head, she couldn't fathom it or fix it. She thought instead about the night of the second break-in. How her father had immediately charged into the garage. Wasn't that sort of crazy? Why would he run toward danger like that, with his wife and daughter nearby?

Unless it was an act. Unless he knew the person in the garage was an accomplice.

She shook her head. It was becoming too complicated. She was seeing connections where they probably didn't exist. Threats looming from every shadow. Next she would be one of those conspiracy nuts who thought the government was out to get them and that every politician was a child molester.

Martin Chisholm and Lisa De Nardo floated to the top of her thoughts. Well...

"So, El..."

She blinked back into the present. "What?" They had a couple of minutes before the homeroom bell.

"I...," he said.

She gave him a second or two to get to the next word, but nothing came out. His hands, now out of his pockets, actually shook.

"Are you okay?" she asked.

He grimaced and gazed into the distance for a moment, steeling himself. Then he returned his attention to her and said, "I have to... There's something I have to say to you. Can I say something to you?"

"Yes." Her voice sounded faraway, papery.

He licked his lips. A single second stretched to the breaking point, like putty.

"Actually, never mind," he said. "I'm not so good with words."

And he lunged forward, taking her face in his hands, kissing her with an ardor channeled from every extremity of his body, sluiced through every blood vessel, driving every last atom of passion and heat and life into his lips, which pressed into her own, reviving her, transferring to her. Her own body came alive, relit, hot again, her hunger and her glow feeding back to him.

It wasn't even a surprise. It was the opposite of shock. It felt like the most natural conclusion to the most familiar song.

"Are you kidding me?" she asked with soft wonder when they broke apart.

"I'm... I probably should have asked," he mumbled. "Was that wrong? I should have asked, right?"

Staring at him, she asked, "How long have you been wanting to do that?"

She watched him give up on doing the math. "Third grade...?" he said at last.

"What took you so long?" she yelled, then grabbed his face between her hands and hauled his lips back to hers.

47

# 1986: DEAN

On Friday night, the Canterstown Sledgehammers narrowly defeated their rivals to the south, the Brookdale Bobcats, with a field goal in the last thirty seconds of the fourth quarter. The next night, the SGA's homecoming committee threw open the doors to a gymnasium reconfigured by crepe paper, banners, and gel lights borrowed from the drama club into a glittering dance hall that almost—*almost*—didn't look like a high school gym.

Decked out in a tuxedo that appeared to have been cut from a sheet of pinstriped tinfoil, Marcus danced with Dinah, the two of them grinning into each other's eyes as though nothing else existed in the world. But dancing with Kim, Dean found his thoughts roaming—as they often did now—to Antoine.

He was not so foolish as to imagine a time when he would dance like this with Antoine, but there had to be a way to balance out the halves of his life. A way to reconcile Daylight Dean with Nighttime Dean. Could he really live the rest of his life as this bifurcated creature, this bizarro version of Jekyll and Hyde?

"Ow!" He'd stepped on Kim's foot.

"Sorry."

She grinned up at him with an expression that said, *Oh, my man.* "We're getting you some dance lessons before prom, mister."

Prom. Oh, Lord. "Maybe take a break?" he said. "Get some punch?" And without waiting for an answer, he disengaged and headed for the food table.

# BRIAN

The ride to school occurred in near silence. Brian was used to Antoine's reticence, but Jay said nothing other than the occasional monosyllabic grunt when answering a question.

*Did you bring the duffel bag for the Cup?*

*Yuh.*

*Did you bring gloves so we don't leave fingerprints?*

*Yuh.*

Jay drove with a grim intensity, a monofocus that Brian found deeply concerning. But Antoine, in the back seat, said nothing. And Jay said nothing.

So Brian said nothing.

They parked in the student lot, which was packed with the cars of those attending the dance. This way the car wouldn't stand out in one of the other lots. But as soon as they got out, they headed not for the entrance near the gymnasium, but rather the side door that opened into the social studies wing. It was farther from the display case, which was only a few yards in from the main entrance, but the big double doors at the front of the school seemed too dangerous.

In silence, they entered. Antoine faded back against the wall, keeping an eye out as Brian and Jay navigated the hallway to the display case.

And there it was. The Steingard Trophy. Brian had to admit he felt a thrill at the idea. In fifteen years, they would dig up the time capsule and reveal the greatest practical joke in the history of Canterstown. That might not be much, but it would be *something*. After graduation, he would leave this town knowing that he'd left his mark. Even if the rest of the world wouldn't know until September of 2001.

He chuckled to himself. By then they'd all be flying around in hovercars and vacationing on the moon. Cool.

He prepared to head down to the language arts wing and take up his post there, but Jay was standing before the case, staring straight ahead.

"Hey, man," he whispered. Sound carried in these wide, empty halls, lined with cinder block and linoleum. In the distance—down one floor and on the other side of the school—he could hear music from the dance. "Dancing in the Dark." That girl was hot.

"Jay? Man?"

Still Jay did not move. Staring straight ahead.

Brian closed in on him. Looking over Jay's shoulder, he could make out his reflection in the display case's glass doors. Tears dripped along his cheeks.

"Um." Brian didn't know what to do. What did you do when a guy was crying?

And then Jay slammed the edge of his gloved fist against the display case and howled like a wolf cut off from its pack.

# 48

# THE PRESENT: ELAYAH

She wandered the halls between classes in a daze. She'd kissed Liam. He'd kissed her. They'd kissed each other. And wow, oh wow, oh wow.

Marcie. She should have texted Marcie immediately, but she'd been so blown away, blown apart, that she'd been unable to think straight or focus. Her mind was a playback loop of the kisses, overrunning and overpowering every other thought as though she'd drifted off to sleep. Her classes were background noise. The world thought everything was normal. The world thought nothing had changed.

Stupid world.

She'd thought up some extremely naughty combinations of emoji to send to Liam and was in the process of deciding if she dared do it—too soon?— when she spied an incoming message from Indira. She tapped on it and her heart sank.

Indira: **No match between Chisholm and the note. Double-check confirms note and postcard in same handwriting. Sorry.**

So that much was definite, at least. Whether Antoine or Marcus, the same person had written the note and the postcards. Meaning there was a damn good chance that her father or her uncle had killed someone with that knife.

The glee and giddiness of the kiss could not stand against the steamroller of that news. Elayah crumpled against a wall, staring at the screen and the two sentences that would—she knew—absolutely destroy her family one way or the other.

Marcie spotted her from down the hall and raced over, her expression panicked. "Bathroom. Now."

They slipped into the closest lavatory and crammed into a stall together. And then, without preamble, Marcie produced from her backpack a copy of the 1987 Canterstown High yearbook.

"Was looking through this in study hall. I have news."

"Yeah, me too," Elayah mumbled.

Either ignoring her or not hearing her, Marcie planted her butt on the toilet and opened the yearbook.

"I realized who Katie is. We had it all wrong. It's not a Kathleen or a Catherine. It's my mom."

*That* made Elayah stand up straight. "What are you talking about? Your mom's name is Kim."

"Yeah," Marcie said morosely, "and her maiden name was Tate. And I remember her telling me there were like ten other Kims in her class, so they called her Kim T. And…" She twisted the yearbook around so that Elayah could see it, pointing at the picture of her mom and the line of text right below it.

**Kimberly Alice Tate.** *Kim T. K. T. Love you, Dean!!! Western MD or bust! Marching band 4ever!*

"K. T.," Elayah whispered. "Katie." She smacked her forehead. "Duh."

*Peej and K. T.* That was what her dad had said to Liam's dad on FaceTime that one night. Now they had "Katie."

"What did they do?" Elayah asked. "Did you text her about it? Did you ask her about Jorja's dad?"

Marcie curled into herself, folding her body over the yearbook as though to block it out of reality. "No. I can't do this. It's crazy. It didn't seem real before. But now—"

"Now that it might be your mom, you mean?" It came out nastier than Elayah had intended. But given everything she'd been through, given how insanely, terrifyingly *real* this had been for her since the first night, she discovered that she could not muster so much as a scintilla of empathy for her best friend.

Marcie grunted, closed the yearbook, and muttered, "Sorry."

It had been personal for Elayah almost from the beginning. Just the synchronicity of her uncle's disappearance with the time capsule's burial. Only now, she thought, maybe it wasn't mere serendipity. Maybe there was correlation.

Maybe there was causation.

She showed the text from Indira to Marcie. Soon, they were wrapped up in each other, huddled as though against the whole of winter.

"You think my mom did something bad?" Marcie asked.

Elayah ruminated on that for a while before the only worthwhile and sober answer occurred to her:

"I hope not."


Only DNA, she realized, could solve this problem. They'd discussed it before, but now they had exhausted all their other avenues. DNA would at least eliminate some possibilities.

**we need dan from our parents**, she texted.

**dan?** Liam asked. 😛 😛

**DNA damn autocorrect**

**easy enough**, Jorja responded.

Marcie: **what will we do w it?**

**Indira has a lab she can use**

**then what?** Liam that time.

She gnawed at her lower lip and didn't respond. He wouldn't like the answer.

When she saw him in the halls after last bell, she told him: "We need the knife. To compare the blood DNA to our parents'."

"Oh, sure," he said, chuckling. "They let you check evidence out with a library card."

An idea had occurred to Elayah. It was the sort of idea that you knew was awful but barged its way into your thoughts nonetheless.

"What if we took a page from our parents' book—"

"Nope!" Liam backed away abruptly, colliding with some freshmen who scampered away in fear. "Nope! No way!"

"—and broke into the sheriff's office and took a sample from the knife?" she finished.

"No!" Liam stomped. "No way. Not gonna happen. Are you nuts? The building is staffed twenty-four seven. And the knife is probably in this vault they have, which is pass-code protected, so there's no key to duplicate in the first place."

"Can you get the code from your dad?"

Liam folded his arms over his chest. "You're talking about breaking and entering, theft, obstruction of justice, tampering with evidence, interfering with a police investigation, *and* pissing off my dad, most of which are big deals. *Not* happening. Haven't we done enough crazy stuff for one semester?"

"Liam—" Elayah began.

"No." She was shocked at how defiant he was. "Besides, getting DNA off the knife doesn't matter. We'd still need a sample from Antoine to compare it to, and guess what? No way to do that."

A bit red-faced from his heated rejection of the plan, he bobbed his head, took a deep breath, and said, "Sorry, El. Really. It's too far."

He was right, and she hated him for it, and she also half hoped he would jump forward and start making out with her. Sure, it would make everyone else in the hallway uncomfortable, but that was what she wanted anyway.

Liam sighed. She knew he couldn't say no to her. Not entirely.

"We can't get the blood from the knife, but we have the report. The one I took pictures of that told us it's AB. I can give that to Indira. That's something, right?"

She smiled at him. Life was good again.

Now their mission was simple: Get DNA samples from the parents who'd buried the time capsule.

It was easy enough. A strand of hair from a brush here, a used Q-tip there…Liam walked them all through some basics of evidence collection, relying on half-remembered comments from Dad and a couple of YouTube videos.

None of the evidence they gathered would ever stand up in court, but at least it could point them in the right direction.

They delivered their DNA bounty—a motley collection of used tissues, hair, Q-tips, and an old toothbrush—to Indira at a coffee shop in broad daylight. The meeting seemed to call for something more clandestine, but even punctilious Jorja had to admit that absolutely no one in the place so much as glanced in their direction.

"How long will this take?" Elayah asked.

Indira shrugged. Today, she wore a blue patterned scarf with another set of mismatched earrings. "However long it takes. I'll let you know."

Such a promise was eminently reasonable and understandable. That didn't stop it from aggravating the living hell out of all of them.



While they waited for the results of the DNA, they decided to focus on the mystery of Peej and K. T. With Kim's two jobs—one of which was an unpredictable Uber schedule—it had taken them this long to find a time when they could get to her. And even Marcie agreed that it was time to get some answers from her mom. The four of them went to Marcie's apartment together.

As they entered and paused in the narrow little entry hall, Elayah had the oddest sense of . . . whatever the opposite of déjà vu was. She had been to Marcie's mom's home roughly a jillion times, but now she experienced the sensation of entering for the very first time. An impression of familiarity overtook her, swiftly overwhelmed by the certainty that she'd never been here before. She shivered; Liam put an arm around her.

Marcie's mom had an hour before she was due to fire up the app and go Uber it up. They found her in the kitchen, stirring sugar into a steaming mug emblazoned with the slogan MAMA NEEDS HER COFFEE. Marcie had bought it for Mother's Day one year. Elayah had been with her.

Were they really about to interrogate her?

"Hey, Mom, what happened with Jorja's dad?" Marcie asked.

*I guess we are!*

Marcie's mom did a double take. "Nice to see you, too, sweetheart. I thought you were over at Jorja's, but it looks like you brought the whole crew." She gestured for Elayah to come to her, which Elayah dutifully did, accepting a tight one-armed hug and a kiss on the forehead.

"I'm so glad you're up and about, honey."

Elayah tried not to let her affection for Kim interfere with her quest. "Thanks. But if you could answer Marcie's question…"

Kim leaned back against the counter and kept stirring her coffee, staring into its depths as she spoke. "Teaming up on me. This is about the time capsule. All that stuff. Right?"

They all four nodded mutely. Liam just had to chime in: "This is what we do now, apparently."

With a groan and a sigh, Kim pushed past them—gently—and went into the tiny, cramped living room. Growing up, Elayah had found Marcie's life somewhat magical. With divorced parents, she had two of everything: two bedrooms, two TVs, two living rooms, two kitchens.…But as she'd gotten older, she'd realized that such mystical bifurcation came at a cost—combining Marcie's two into one still would not have equaled Elayah's mundane singleton lifestyle. Marcie's life was less than the sum of its parts.

They followed Kim into the living room. The TV—muted—showed someone furiously whisking a bowl of what appeared to be cookie dough. Kim was addicted to cooking shows, the more outlandish, the better.

Kim sighed as she sank into an overstuffed armchair that faced the TV, swiveling it to face the four of them.

In all the years Elayah had known Marcie, the decor, the furniture, the framed photos on the walls—none of it had changed. Not a whit. As she settled onto the sofa, she knew that if she flipped the worn, lumpy cushion, she'd espy the faint borders of the stain she'd caused at age seven during a sleepover. Chocolate milk met damask; chocolate milk won.

Kim stared at them. "Peej," she said, a rasp of memory in her voice. "You guys just had to go dig it all up, didn't you? Everything that was supposed to stay buried."

Was it an admission of something? It felt like an admission of something. Elayah had slept in this woman's home, eaten her cooking, used her shampoo, borrowed her *tampons*, for God's sake.…What had she done?

"Maybe you guys shouldn't have buried it in the first place," Jorja said with a level of snark Elayah found shocking in a girl talking to her girlfriend's mother.

But if Kim was annoyed or offended, she did not show it. Instead, she merely smiled and said, "Has your dad ever showed you his senior yearbook?" Regret and satisfaction blended in her voice, satisfaction taking the upper hand, if only slightly.

Jorja blanched, then recovered. "He doesn't really keep stuff like that."

Kim smirked knowingly. "Ask him about it," she said. "It's not for me to say."

"We know about Sheppard Pratt," Jorja said with as much dignity as she could muster.

"Mom, come on," Marcie complained. "We're just trying to—"

"Trying to do Dean's job for him?" Kim shook her head and finally sipped the coffee, which must have been awful, judging by the expression on her face. "Look, I get it. The tables are turned. Suddenly you guys get to look through all our dirty laundry. You think one of us did...something. What kid wouldn't want to slap their parents back for all the slaps?"

"My parents don't believe in corporal punishment," Jorja said somewhat officiously.

Kim sighed with her entire body. "I wasn't being literal, Jorja. Jesus." She slurped some more coffee, then stared down into the murky depths of her mug. "We did some things," she said after a moment. "I did some...I did some stuff I'm not proud of. But I don't think...I don't think we hurt anyone."

"Did you know Lisa De Nardo?" Elayah asked. Marcie, next to her on the sofa, had gone mute. She clutched Elayah's hand with the desperation of abused puppies.

"Who?"

"McKenzie," Liam jumped in.

"Oh." Kim shrugged. "Sure. Not well, but, yeah."

"Did you know about her and Martin Chisholm?"

Kim burbled laughter. "No one *knew* anything. Rumors didn't get hashtags and GIFs until a few years ago, guys. People saw things. People talked. We knew, but we didn't *know*."

"And no one went to the police." Elayah's outrage spilled out like bile.

Every time she thought about Lisa De Nardo née McKenzie in the hands of that rapist while no one lifted a finger to help her, her indignation flared anew. "No one did anything."

"He wasn't that much older than us. No one thought much of it."

Elayah couldn't accept that answer, but she had no response other than to light her hair on fire and dive-bomb Kim while screaming at the top of her lungs. She settled for squeezing Marcie's hand instead.

"How did Lisa's note end up in the time capsule?" Jorja asked. "It had to be one of you who put it in there."

"Beats the hell out of me, Jorja." Kim seemed almost cheerful in her ignorance. "It was a long time ago, one, and two, do you really think I would notice a little bitty thing like that? That damn time capsule sat in Brian's garage for at least a week, and they never locked it. Any one of us could have gone in there and put the envelope in there. Or done it the day we buried it while we were digging the hole and not paying attention."

"Brian? Wait. *Dad?*" Marse sat up straighter.

"Sure. Your father kept the time capsule in Nana and Poppy's garage."

"So he could've put in the note or the knife or both," Jorja mused. "He had access."

"We *all* had access," Kim said wearily. "That's what I've been trying to tell you. Dean's no dummy—if this was easy to figure out, he'd've done it by now."

"Can we go back to Mr. Dearborn?" It was the first time Liam had spoken in a while. He stood behind Elayah, his hands resting lightly on the back of the sofa. When she twisted around, she saw a thoughtful, focused expression aimed unerringly at Kim.

Slip the boy some tongue and suddenly he's all *True Detective*. Who knew?

"He goes by P. J. now," Liam went on, "but you guys used to call him *Peej*?"

"Patrick Jason," Kim said, nodding. "He never liked *Patrick*. Once he was in law school, he decided to be P. J., so we started calling him Peej. But for a couple of years there in high school, he went by Jay. Using his middle name before he settled on initials."

"My dad didn't kill anyone," Jorja said hotly. "He's a defense lawyer, for God's sakes."

"Yeah, and when we were kids, he thought he was going to be a cop," Kim shot back.

"Really?" Jorja's temper cooled instantly in the wake of this pronouncement. "*My* dad?"

"Sure. And Dean was going to be a writer." She passed a hand over her eyes. "We made mistakes. I . . . I cheated on your dad, Liam. With Jorja's dad. That's the big secret, okay? Are you happy now?"

Liam stiffened. "*You* were my dad's girlfriend?"

"Yeah. I thought we . . ." A sound halfway between a laugh and a sigh emanated from her. "We were going to get married. That was the plan. But then, you know." She shrugged.

"My dad didn't even know he was gay until college," Liam protested. "He met this guy named Whit—"

"I don't know about that. When we broke up, he . . . It was after Christmas break. Right before Peej was sent away. Look, that year a lot changed. Everything changed."

"Because of the time capsule. And Uncle Antoine."

Memory, Elayah knew, could be sunshine, and memory could be a blade. Kim winced with the pain of remembering. "I wish it was just that. I wish I could tell you that poor, sweet Antoine ran off and we all changed. But we were changing before that. Like you guys are right now. And we were figuring it all out.

"Let me tell you something: You're all smart and talented kids, and you've been told that most of your lives. We were, too. And we all ended up stuck here, except for Antoine, who got out while the getting was good. Smart and talented isn't enough."

"Then what is?"

Helplessness radiated from her eyes as she spoke: "I don't know. If I did, do you think I'd still be here?"

# 1986: DEAN

Dean delivered a cup of punch to Kim and then—without even actively deciding to do it—lied and told her he needed to use the restroom. He left her there on the edge of the dance floor and walked briskly to the gym door, then down the corridor. Past the girls' bathroom. Past the boys' bathroom. To the spot where the galvanized steel security barrier had been unfolded from one wall and locked into place on the opposite wall, barricading away the rest of the school. He leaned against the wall and lightly thumped the back of his head against it.

What was he going to do? What was he going to do with his life?

Prom. Jesus, he'd completely forgotten about prom until Kim brought it up. It had been tough enough coming to homecoming with her, knowing how much it hurt Antoine to see them together like this. In six months, how much closer would they be? He wanted them to be so much closer, and it would hurt so much more to watch Dean go to prom with her.

What could he do? What *should* he do? Why couldn't it be easy? Why couldn't the world just accept him and Antoine as they were? And not the world of San Francisco or New York, not the world of far-off cities he'd never been to. The world of Canterstown. The world of his family and Antoine's family and their church. Who were they hurting? They weren't hurting *anyone*. They weren't doing anything wrong. They were just trying to be together and be true, but the world kept telling them *no*.

"Hey." Kim approached from down the hall. "Everything okay?"

He had become so practiced at the lazy, easy smile. "Yeah. Just catching my breath for a second. You're tiring me out."

She pressed herself against him, kissed his jawline, then leaned up to whisper in his ear, "I *want* to tire you out."

A hot pulse thrummed along his rib cage. His stomach flopped. Kim put a hand on his chest.

"Guys!"

And the crashing sound of a body hitting the security barrier, which rattled in place.

It was Brian on the other side of the barrier, eyes wide and wild. "Guys, there's a problem with Jay! He's losing it!"

With as much care as the impulse allowed, Dean pushed Kim away. "What do you mean?"

Brian fumbled with his keys and scanned the barrier for the keyhole. As he did, he spoke rapidly. "He started banging on the glass. Said something about his mom. . . . She was in the hospital or something—"

"Was?" Dean asked.

Brian found the right key. Slammed it into the lock. "Yeah. Was. She's dead, man. She killed herself this afternoon."

Dean's heart lurched as though his body had been yanked on a tether attached to a jet. He heard Kim gasp but scarcely registered it.

"Where's Marcus?" Brian asked as he unlocked the barrier.

"With Dinah. No time to get him. Or explain any of this to her. C'mon."

Between the two of them, Dean and Brian hauled the barrier open enough for Dean to fit through. Before they could close it again, Kim squeezed through, too, carefully pressing her dress close to her body so as not to catch it.

"You don't have to come—" Dean started.

"He's been a wreck for a while because of this," Kim said. "She's been in the hospital for weeks and—"

"How did you know that?" Dean regarded her with a quizzical expression.

Kim strove to keep her face neutral and succeeded. For the most part. "We talked. When he let me in the school that one time."

With a cluck of his tongue, Dean nodded, as though tasting a new meal and unsure of its flavors. He swallowed it, though. They relocked the barrier behind them and followed Brian through the hallways to the central entrance.

It was worse than Dean had feared. Jay stood in a circle of broken glass. The display case doors had been smashed to pieces and glittered all around him like a fallen halo. As they watched, he reached into the case, withdrew a framed photograph, and dashed it to the floor at his feet. From the amount of debris around him, he'd been doing it for a while.

The Cup, ironically, was untouched.

"Jay!" Dean stage-whispered. "You have to stop this, man!"

"What year?" Jay asked no one in particular, staring straight ahead at the broken glass of the case. "What year was she born? I can't remember. I can't remember!"

He spun around, glaring at Dean with wild eyes. "If I can't remember, how will anyone know? How will they know what to put on the stone?"

Dean hesitated. His best friend's face, flushed and pale at once, bright red broken by speckles of white, loomed at him. Nothing made sense anymore.

"I'm gonna bring the car around," Brian said. "Someone's gonna hear this, and we gotta get him out of here."

Dean nodded permission and Brian ran off. Dean and Kim came up on either side of Jay. Dean didn't want to risk a touch—it might set him off.

Kim was not so concerned. She put a hand on Jay's shoulder. "I'm so sorry, Jay. I'm sorry she's gone."

Jay didn't flinch. He sniffled back tears and growled, "She's not *gone*. She *left*. There's a difference."

"She was sick. She didn't know—"

"Yeah, man." Dean leapt on the idea. "She never would have left. You know that. It was in her head."

Jay laughed bleakly and took a wooden plaque from the case. "Who cares?" His voice was hoarse and dead at the same time. "Who cares about any of it? She's dead."

He smacked the plaque against the wall once. Twice. Three times. It made a sharp, loud cracking sound each time, echoing down the halls. On the fourth blow, the plaque broke in half with a disappointingly dull snap.

A terrible light blazed in Jay's eyes, candles set aflame with pain and anger. "We should burn this place down. We should burn this whole town down. No one would miss any of it."

Dean and Kim locked eyes in fear. Jay did not make idle threats. He meant every word of it. In a day or an hour, he might not, but at this moment, he had every intention of setting fire to the whole town. Dean wondered if Jay had matches on him. He wondered if he was going to have to fight his best friend.

The rhythmic pounding of feet dragged Dean's attention away from Jay. Antoine dashed around a corner and skidded to a halt before them, his eyes wide, his breath coming in huffs.

"Police!" he gasped. "Coming in! Now!"

Dean's heart free-fell into his gut. What the hell were they going to do?

"Jay, the cops are coming." He infused as much authority and stability into his voice as he could, pushing through the panic and the heat of fear. "Brian's getting your car. We have to go. Now."

With one hand, Jay pushed Dean away. Kim's hand on his shoulder didn't seem to bother him.

Dean was torn. He had Kim hanging on to Jay, Jay refusing to move, Antoine standing there with fear in his eyes. . . . He could run, but how could he abandon his best friend?

Down the hall, voices. The police.

Dean hadn't brought his keys with him to homecoming, but Brian had handed his set off when he ran for the car. Dean flicked through them and found the key to the nearby storage closet. The encroaching voices and the sound of heavy footfalls made his decision for him.

"Stop screwing around, Patty," he said, hoping that the use of Jay's hated childhood nickname would shock him out of his trancelike state of methodical violence.

Jay didn't so much as budge.

Fine. Jay was on his own.

He grabbed Kim's hand and gestured to Antoine. They dashed down the cross corridor, and Dean discovered his hand was remarkably steady as he unlocked the storage-closet door. They were within eye- and earshot of the display case. The storage closet was packed with boxes and cleaning supplies. Antoine went in first and pressed himself into a corner. Dean pushed Kim in, then stepped in himself. He could swear he heard a clear voice—"You! Stop!"—as he closed the door, praying the hinges wouldn't squeak or squeal.

He managed to ease the door closed without a sound.

In the dark, a hand groped at his. Kim. He squeezed tightly.

"We just have to be quiet," he whispered to her.

Breath sounded all around him. He knew the cadence of Antoine's respiration. He closed his eyes against the dark, swallowed. Breathed through his mouth to be quieter. 'Toine's breath and Kim's seemed to roar at him like bull elephants.

They heard the police yelling at Jay. Heard more crashes and smashing as Jay ignored them.

A steadying hand on his shoulder. Antoine.

Yelling again. *"Stop! Down on your knees! Hands where we can see them!"* All the stuff they'd ever seen or heard on *Miami Vice* or *T.J. Hooker*. Not entertaining now.

He heard Jay laugh and expel a breathtaking string of curse words. Then a scuffle. Then a sudden quiet.

Kim squeezed harder. Behind them, Antoine muttered something under his breath, and Dean wanted to tell him to be quiet, but saying that would defeat the purpose.

Were those footfalls outside the door? Was that the squeak of a shoe?

Any second now, he knew, the police would open the storage-closet door. Any second now.


Monday morning came. Dean could not be certain if he awoke from a fitful sleep in which he dreamed he was awake or if he'd never slept at all. One seemed as likely as the other, and his exhaustion offered no answers. He stared up at the ceiling, his radio alarm clock chattering away at him.

No one had opened the storage-closet door. They'd escaped. He'd tried to call Jay all day Sunday. The first several times, no one answered. At around two in the afternoon, Jay's dad picked up and said that Jay was not available, would not be available, and stop calling, please.

Dean thought about Jay's mom. He didn't call back.

Now Jenny pounded at his door. "Like, totally wake up!" she complained. "Turn that off!"

Normally when she banged on his door and beseeched him to turn off the rock, he would crank it up. Anything to blast the Valley girl pop out of her head. But this morning, he could not be bothered—he slapped his hand out, shutting off the radio.

He dragged himself through the rote necessities of the morning—a piss, a scrub of his face, a pass with his toothbrush. With perfunctory efficiency, he slicked back his hair into its gleaming, immobile crust.

Since he was running late, he had the perfect excuse not to eat breakfast. When he arrived at school, he was shocked to find Jay there, hanging out with the twins near the school store.

"What happened?" Dean asked in a whisper, sidling up to the trio.

Jay shrugged. His voice, too, was hushed, but not as dramatically as Dean would have thought for someone dragged out of the school by the cops a couple of nights ago.

"They brought me over to the sheriff's. Called my dad. Then they let me go with him and said someone from the school would talk to me."

Dean couldn't believe it. For this he'd lost two nights of sleep? He glanced over at Antoine, but Antoine did not look back.

First period was calculus. Jay sat two rows over from Dean and seemed absolutely at peace until the PA burbled, "Patrick Dearborn, please report to Admin."

A murmured chorus of *Ooohhh* bubbled like swamp water. With a grin that was pure bravado, Jay stood and saluted Mrs. Weismuller before ambling out the door.

Dean had no head for math in the best of circumstances. The only reason he'd taken calculus at all was because he thought it would look good on his transcripts. And with Jay promising to give everyone As, he hadn't tried very hard to grasp the concepts in the class.

These were not the best of circumstances. He could not focus on the equations and formulas projected on the screen, the numbers, letters, and brackets merging into a nonsensical mishmash of text. At some point, he just gave up trying to understand and stared down at his blank notebook as though something intensely interesting had appeared there.

With ten minutes to go before the end of class, Jay returned, his eyes hard, his jaw set. He stared in Dean's direction even as he handed a slip of paper to Mrs. Weismuller.

Mrs. Weismuller moistened her lips and shook her head as she read the paper. With an apologetic tone to her voice, she said, "Dean, they'd like you to report to Admin."

A fork of lightning speared Dean's heart, and his gasp for breath drowned in the gurgle of *Oooohhh* that erupted again. Mrs. Weismuller shushed them as Dean managed to stand and headed to the door.

Jay grabbed his arm on his way and leaned in.

"Don't speak to each other!" Mrs. Weismuller snapped in sudden alarm.

"Screw the prisoner's dilemma," Jay whispered, and then dutifully returned to his seat.

Dean staggered down the corridor to Admin, moving by muscle memory alone. His loafers slapped the linoleum, echoing in the empty hall.

At Admin, Mrs. Wistern gazed at him balefully before telling him to go into the principal's office.

The door was open. Dean stepped inside. He'd been in here before—at night, with Jay. They'd gone through Mr. Taylor's desk just for the hell of it, absconding with a pad of hall passes and a roll of breath mints for their troubles.

Mr. Taylor sat behind his desk in a charcoal-gray suit, the jacket slung over the back of his chair. His tie was a nubby magenta, squared-off. He had a full head of shaggy brown hair and a nose that could have stood in for an Olympic ski ramp. His eyes were frighteningly, piercingly blue.

"Close the door," he said evenly. "Have a seat."

Dean did as he was bade. As he sat down, he thought, *Screw the prisoner's dilemma.*

"We need to talk about what happened this weekend, during homecoming." Mr. Taylor did not seem upset or angry. He clasped his hands over his belly and leaned back in his chair. "You were at homecoming, correct?"

"Yes, sir," Dean said. "I heard the police come, but I didn't see anything, if that's what you're wondering."

Wow. The lie came out so smooth that it would have surprised Dean...

if he'd been in his body. Instead, he was floating just outside it, above and slightly to the left, looking down on himself as he spoke.

Mr. Taylor nodded as though he believed this. "The police did come. And they arrested Patrick Dearborn. He's your best friend."

It was passing strange that the principal knew who was whose best friend.

"He is," Dean said. "Look, I don't know if you know this or not, but his mom just died. So he's—"

"I'm aware." Mr. Taylor cut him off, his tone not unkind. And Dean realized: Mr. Taylor's boss, technically, was Jay's dad. Jay's dad was on the board of education.

"But what I'm interested in," Mr. Taylor went on, "is who else was involved. And I know you were."

Had Dean's focus been on Mr. Taylor, he most likely would have reacted to that comment with a weak grin and a stuttered, unconvincing laugh of denial. But most of his brain was busy churning through the epiphany that Mr. Taylor was Jay's dad's subordinate. How hard could they or would they actually come down on Jay? Especially given that his mother had just died?

They were prowling around for a scapegoat, he realized. Someone else they could dump this on.

"I don't know what you're talking about," Dean said with bewildered confidence.

His denial seemed to shake Mr. Taylor. "You expect me to believe that your best friend copied keys to this building and you didn't know about it? You're the SGA vice president."

Dean shrugged. "I don't know what Jay does when I'm not around, sir. I was having a good time at the dance, and I heard the sirens like everyone else. And I was really surprised later to learn that it was Jay."

Mr. Taylor pursed his lips. To Dean's astonishment, he realized that even *he* believed himself. That was *exactly* what had happened. A giddy, feathery feeling eddied within him; he was going to get away with this.

"We're not going to let this go," Mr. Taylor went on, a note of impatience ringing. "Do you think we can just let students roam a multimillion-dollar physical plant with impunity?"

"I would imagine not," Dean said. "Is Jay going to be in trouble?"

"Him and anyone else who was with him." Mr. Taylor glowered significantly.

"Look, if I knew anything, I would tell you," Dean said. *Screw the prisoner's dilemma.* Jay had told them nothing. He knew he could bear the weight of whatever happened because of who his father was. And because he was Jay, he was indestructible, and he would always win. "If I hear anything, I'll come to you. Honest."

Mr. Taylor said nothing for a moment, shifting uncomfortably in his chair. This conversation clearly was not going the way he'd imagined.

"Can I go back to class now?" Dean asked earnestly. At that moment, the bell to change periods rang. Mr. Taylor said nothing and did not so much as budge as the tones rang out over the PA system.

As the last clanging echoes died away, he nodded to Dean and said, "Yes. Go back to class."

## 50

# THE PRESENT: ELAYAH

"Look," Liam said, "we gave it a good shot. More than one. But we don't have a victim." He ticked off the point on one finger. "We don't have a motive—"

"Didn't you hear her?" Jorja insisted. "She *cheated*. On your dad!"

"With *your* dad!" Marcie interjected.

"*My* dad wasn't dating anyone."

"Oh, so it's all my mom's fault, then?"

"Guys!" Elayah clapped her hands for attention, then held them up, palms out. After their talk with Kim, they had convened in her garage, settled into old lawn chairs, with Jorja slumped in a threadbare lounger. Dad was at work; Mom was at the store; the house felt vaguely safe.

"Guys! Come on. This is, like, ancient history. It doesn't really matter who cheated on whom. Because where's the victim, then? I mean, are we saying Liam's dad was so pissed about Kim and Peej hooking up that he went out and killed...someone else? Doesn't that seem weird?"

Marcie and Jorja each nodded, somewhat grudgingly.

"What's really weird," Liam said with an utterly, forcefully guileless expression, "is that your parents hooked up and now you guys are hooking up."

Jorja surged up from the lounger, rage etched on her face.

"Take that back," Jorja said.

"Take it back? It's a *fact*."

"It's true," Marcie said. "It *is* a little weird."

Jorja flexed her fingers. "Just don't be a dick about this, Liam. Not this. Come on."

Liam shrugged. "Sorry."

It was just enough of an apology that Jorja sat down.

"I think we need to take a big step here," Elayah said. "I think we need to go to the sheriff."

"Are you mental?" Liam asked. "*Now* you want to do that?"

"*Now* you *don't* want to do it?" He'd been the one suggesting going to the sheriff from the very beginning.

"That was before we did a bunch of stuff that's either illegal, immoral, or just plain dumb," he informed her.

"But he's the only one we haven't talked to yet. Other than Marcie's dad."

"Maybe *Brian* got pissed that Kim and my dad hooked up. . . ." Jorja said, sitting up straight.

"Again, and killed someone *else*?" Marcie asked in such a withering tone that Elayah questioned whether their relationship would last the night.

"Look, we know some things the sheriff doesn't know. We *know* the handwriting on the note matches the postcards. It's like . . . it's like we have ingredients, but no recipe."

"And we don't even have a picture to know what the meal is supposed to look like," Jorja offered.

"Thank you for helpfully extending the whatever-you-call-it," Liam snarked.

"Metaphor," the other three all said at the same time, then did simultaneous double takes.

"We can give your dad what we know," Elayah told him. "And he can put it together with what *he* knows. And maybe this all gets figured out."

"And maybe I end up in deep trouble because none of us are supposed to be doing *any* of this." Liam flexed his fingers as though seeking something to clutch as a distraction. "Technically this could all be called obstruction of justice. We could get in big trouble."

They sat in silence, staring around at each other as though one of them would suddenly snap and reveal the solutions to all the mysteries.

"Who the hell would steal an old mixtape?" Marcie said out of nowhere, her tone beyond annoyed, as though the missing cassette were the worst part of this whole ordeal.

"Well, either it was a mistake or it's not a mixtape."

They all turned to look at Liam, who seemed shocked to find himself the subject of their attention.

"What? It's pretty obvious—you don't steal a mixtape. You steal, like, an important recording."

Elayah fumbled for her phone and brought up the pictures she'd taken the first day, on the hill overlooking the school. In the Before Times. When the world still made sense.

"Here they are," she said, studying one particular photo for a moment. "The two tapes. Look."

Pinching the picture larger, she thanked the ghost of Steve Jobs for the excellent camera in her iPhone, then held it out for the others to see.

Jorja squinted. "So the one Liam's dad gave back to you has writing on it. Song titles. The one that's missing has nothing written on it."

"It's a confession," Marcie said with unearned yet captivating confidence.

Jorja's eyes lit up, and it killed Elayah to slay her mood. "Doesn't matter what's on it. We don't have it."

Just then Elayah's phone chirped. "Indira," she said, and swiped to accept the call. Elayah put her on speaker.

"Hey, Elayah." There was something different about Indira's voice. Even at its huskiest, it possessed a bounce and a verve that communicated almost as much information as the words conveyed. Now it was low, soft, funereal. "Am I on speaker?"

"Yeah."

Indira asked to be taken off speaker. Raising her eyebrows at Liam, shooting a quick look over to Marse and Jorja, Elayah shrugged and complied.

"What's up?"

"I have to tell you something. This will be hard to hear."

Elayah tried to imagine what could be so hard to hear. What could be worse than what she'd already been through?

"We pulled your dad's blood type from the DNA you gave us. It matches the blood type on the report Liam showed us. AB. He's the only one of your parents with AB. Which means...well, it means a few things are possible. It could mean your dad struggled for the knife with someone and was cut."

"Or it could mean my dad killed Antoine. Or my dad is Antoine and killed Marcus. Because they'd both have AB, right?" Misery and nausea cloaked her. Mist filled her brain.

"Yeah," Indira said after a moment's hesitation. "I mean...yeah. Look, I'm sorry. I'm really sorry. If we had the blood from the knife, we could maybe pin down if it's your dad's blood or his twin's. Maybe."

"But it's one of them." She looked around. Her three friends all had furrowed brows. She felt as though she'd just been given bad medical news.

"Or someone else with AB," Indira pointed out.

Elayah shrugged. They were almost 100 percent certain that no one but the parents had put things in the time capsule. So it had to be one of the twins.

"I'm really, really sorry, Elayah," said Indira. "We'll, uh, keep digging on our end."

The call ended.

Elayah twisted in her seat to take one of Liam's hands in both of hers. She kissed the top of his hand and tasted the salt of her own tears.


As was traditional when her dad was on night shifts, dinner became breakfast in Elayah's house: On this night, banana pancakes and bacon, with a side of hash browns. Elayah pushed the food around, trailing a slurry of powdered sugar, butter, and syrup along the edge of her plate. Her appetite was nonexistent, and she couldn't even look across the table at her father.

"Something wrong, baby?" he asked.

*Yeah, you killed my father.*

He hadn't, of course. But she was having trouble disassociating the name from the role, the relationship. Was this something children of twins went through, and she'd missed out solely because of Antoine's—Marcus's?—disappearance? Regardless of the names and the faces, the people behind them remained the same.

She literally did not know who her father was, even though he was sitting right across from her.

"Just not hungry," she mumbled, still not looking up.

"Not feeling well?" he asked, and the sincerity of his tone rankled, dug its claws under the flesh between her shoulder blades, raising the hair on the back of her neck.

"Why do we have Aunt Jemima?" she snapped, dropping her fork onto her plate. "Didn't they stop making this stuff? It's racist."

"I found it on sale," Mom said mildly.

"If something's going on," said her father, his voice verging into disciplinary territory, "tell us. Otherwise, watch your attitude."

She couldn't do it. She couldn't be in the house with him. Not now. Not knowing what she knew.

Rising from her seat, she said, "I'm going to spend the night at Marcie's," and bit off and swallowed *if that's okay.* Because she wasn't asking, damn it; she was telling.

When she rounded the corner, she pulled out her phone. She didn't text Marcie, though—she texted Liam.

# 1986: MARCUS

With Brian tagging along, Marcus sought out Dean at home. They found him in his basement bedroom, where he'd erected custom-built cases for his burgeoning comic book collection. Marcus glanced around. Dean had described the setup to them all as he'd built it, in a manner that Marcus had assumed to be overly self-impressed. But he had to admit that the space was cool. If you were going to read silly crap like comic books, you might as well have a very nice, handmade walnut-fronted cabinet to store them in and a couple of comfy beanbag chairs to read them in.

"What's up?" Dean asked, flopping onto a chair.

Marcus squatted into the other beanbag and faced his friend. Brian leaned against the doorjamb and crossed his arms over his chest. "It's about Jay, man."

"What about him?" Something clouded Dean's eyes. Marcus thought it might be knowledge, trying to get out. Trying to break through.

"We're not happy about this," Brian said. "But we have to talk."

"He's outta control," Marcus said. "Even before homecoming. That stuff with the pizza guy..."

"That was my idea," Dean said quickly.

"Right," said Brian. "At first. And then you tried to get him to back off, but he was—"

"You know Jay," Dean interrupted. "He gets something stuck in his teeth like that, and he just can't let it go."

Licking his lips, Marcus shook his head slowly. This was the problem with Dean: Dean saw everything from every angle. He understood everyone's perspective. Dean read comic books, so he thought the good guys always won. Which was just one step away from not acting because, well, the good guys are going to win anyway, right?

It reminded Marcus of Dr. King's admonition about the moral arc of the universe bending toward justice. People were fond of quoting that, but they always neglected to mention that the arc bends because *we* bend it.

"I get that he's your best friend," Marcus said, plucking words with care and precision, like pomegranate seeds. "He's my friend, too."

"*Our* friend," Brian said with some urgency.

"But we gotta rein him in, man."

Dean wasn't buying it. "No one can make Jay do anything he doesn't want to do. You both know that."

"He's gonna get himself in trouble," Brian said, "and we're always around him, so we're gonna get in trouble, too. That stuff at homecoming...he could narc on us at any time. *All* of us. I know he's being cool now, but if they pressure him..."

"I hear you," Dean said, his tone rising. "But don't you think you're blowing this out of proportion a little bit?"

Marcus found himself licking his lips again, stalling as he gathered his calm. He did not, in fact, think he was blowing this out of proportion. Not a little bit. Not a lot. Not at all. The ease with which Jay had produced and wielded that knife concerned him. A split-second decision and Dean's suggestion to hit the high beams had been the difference between a crazy night and a night in jail for Jay and probably the rest of them. Marcus and Antoine, certainly. Just being crime-adjacent would be enough for the cops in Canterstown to slap handcuffs on two Black teens. Never mind that those same cops had no doubt cheered on Black Lightning during the countywides in the spring; at the end of the day, if he wasn't entertaining, he was dangerous.

"What do you think is gonna happen, if they find out we've been breaking in with him? You think you're gonna get good recommendation letters for college?"

"Plus, we've all been slacking off because Jay was going to fix our grades,"

Brian added. "And now it's too late to catch up. You want to be applying to college with lousy grades *and* a B&E on your record?"

"We need to make sure he keeps his mouth shut," Marcus said.

Dean pursed his lips. "That sounds like a threat, man. Come on. It's *Jay*. What do you want to do, go after him with this and make him promise to behave?"

*This* was a hunting knife that Dean plucked from the gun rack mounted over his bed.

"No one's saying hold a knife to his throat," Marcus said, then startled at his own words because now he *had* uttered those words.

"Reason with him," Brian suggested. "And if that doesn't work, we find a way to intimidate him."

Dean clucked his tongue as he flipped the knife around and around in his hands. "Jay's never been intimidated in his life."

Brian finally came away from the door and stood next to Marcus, putting a hand on his shoulder in solidarity. "He's never had his best friends gang up on him before, man. Come on!"

"What does Antoine think?" Dean asked suddenly.

The question snuck up on Marcus like the hands coming out of the mirror at the end of *Phantasm*. Because the question's innocuousness tilted out of balance with its core truth: He had no idea what Antoine thought on this issue.

Once upon a time, there would have been no stumble, no hesitation. He and Antoine agreed on most things, on the things that mattered, at least. And more recently, had he not sensed Antoine's position, he would have sussed it out or just asked.

But he hadn't spoken to Antoine about Jay because he hadn't spoken to Antoine much at all. Other than *Pass the salt* at the dinner table or *Did you steal my practice shoes?*, they'd hardly exchanged words since the argument in the locker room.

And what really gnawed at Marcus's sense of self and balance right now wasn't that he didn't know Antoine's mind on the issue of Jay, nor even that he hadn't asked.

It was that it hadn't even occurred to him to consider what Antoine thought until Dean—*Dean!*—posed the question.

"Antoine's not sitting in front of you," Marcus snapped, more harshly than deserved.

"What do you want to do about it?" Dean asked. "You know Jay—if we tell him to take a chill pill, he'll do something crazier than usual, just to make a point."

The beanbag beneath him tilted and made a shushing sound as Marcus leaned back. "I don't know. I guess we just wanted to know what was in your head."

"And whose side you're on," Brian supplied. "Because right now, there aren't any sides, but who knows?"

Dean shrugged. "I don't know yet. But I'll think about it."

Marcus figured that was probably the best he could hope for.

# 52

# THE PRESENT: LIAM

He picked up El outside her house. Grimacing, her lips set in a firm line, she didn't so much as peck him on the cheek.

"Let's go," she said.

He didn't ask where; he could tell she had no idea. *Away* was the only answer.

So he drove in silence. What must it be like, he wondered, to think your father could be a murderer? The evidence was thin but incontrovertible. It had always been likely that Antoine was somehow involved—his running away to Mexico seemed too convenient to be mere coincidence. But it had been an accepted piece of town lore, of family history, for more than three decades. A strong wall, built over time, reinforced with grief and certainty. It would take a hell of a sledgehammer to knock it down.

A sledgehammer made of DNA and handwriting analysis.

"I'm really sorry," he said.

Speechless and staring out her window, she sought him over the center console, settling a hand on his thigh. Instant electricity, instant shame. He drove with his left hand, his right resting atop her hand. The sky clotted with clouds, blocking out the moon and the stars. Purple-and-gray shadows saturated the buildings.

With no conscious thought, he guided them to the Wantzler factory. A single smokestack coughed black smoke against the charcoal-scudded sky.

"He'll be working tonight," she mumbled.

"Oh. Sorry." He put the car in gear and started to back out.

"No, it's okay. Just go around to the other side."

He steered them to the west-facing side of the building, a smallish parking lot bordered by three dumpsters. Liam killed the engine, and they sat listening to the car's engine ticking down to cool.

After a while, she spoke. "Back when they were kids, the night shift was as busy as the day shift. So he says. This parking lot was full, twenty-four seven."

"Things change."

"What replaces it, though?" she asked. She turned partway in her seat, her back to the door now, so that she could face him. "They keep laying people off. Cutting hours. Things change, sure, but when do they change for the better?"

He didn't know. He told her so.

"Do you think Kim was right?" she asked. "All our dreams, up in smoke?"

He put a hand on her closer knee. "I don't know. I don't want to think about it. We're supposed to have everything in front of us, you know? And I thought we did. Do. Did. Whatever. I mean, Jorja's gonna write and Marse is gonna run for office and you're gonna...be brilliant." He smiled at her. "I hear that pays hella good."

She shook her head. "But what if we're just hoping and dreaming? We think we're special, but what if we're just big fish in a small pond, and the big pond doesn't care about us?"

With a sigh, he leaned back, his hand still warm on her knee. A lifetime, it seemed, of wanting to touch her, and here he was, doing it so casually already, as though their flesh naturally sought each other's out. Living one dream, contemplating the death of others.

"I can't speak for any of us," he said at last, "but you'll make it, El. You'll get out of this town and make something of yourself."

"How do you know that?" Her voice, smaller than he'd ever heard it before. Needy in a way he'd heretofore thought impossible.

"Because it's you," he told her.

Grunting, she adjusted her position, twisting and contorting until her knees tucked under and she could lean into him, kissing him softly and sweetly on the lips. He closed his eyes and did not move. Passive, he lost himself in her lips, his head awhirl.

She broke contact, rocking back on her heels. He gazed at her.

They said nothing. They watched each other, seeing each other as though for the first time, despite their lifelong friendship. She was so. Goddamn. Beautiful. So beautiful and so perfect that it hurt. If he'd seen her on the street, he would have noticed her, maybe indulged in a momentary fantasy, but he was lucky. He was the luckiest man alive because he'd known her before. Before the beauty. Before growing up. He'd known her with *Ben 10* Band-Aids on her knees from recess scrapes. He'd known her with rainbow bows in her hair, with glittery fairy T-shirts, with Smurfs pajamas on PJ Day in school. He'd known her as the first kid in class to raise a hand during lessons on multiplication, the girl who danced—*so badly!*—to Beyoncé for the second-grade talent show. Who had brought in a microscope for show-and-tell and had students line up to see what lived on the ends of your hair.

He knew her from parties and dances, lunchroom sandwich swaps, and the regrettable blackface Barbie incident in third grade. Movie nights with friends, joint stag appearances at middle school dances. Before she was a woman, she was a friend, and he'd loved her then, too.

"Do you think we should have sex?" she said abruptly.

Fortunately for Liam, clueless comedy stepped into the breach.

"I don't think the back seat is big enough, but I'm up for it if you are."

Finally, *finally*, she cracked a grin, nudging his thigh with her toe. "Dumbass. I mean, do you think we're ready? And don't say *I'm always ready*."

"It's like you can read my mind." Truthfully, in that instant he *was* ready. Physically, at least. His entire body ached with need, one part in particular.

"I want you pretty badly," she admitted. "That's no secret, right?"

Forcibly and forcefully, he rejected a smart-ass comment. "The feeling's mutual. But I don't think we're ready. Not yet." He paused. "Was this a test?"

She laughed. "Sure, let's call it that. I think..."

Her phone bleated. Not a text or a notification—this was her actual ringtone.

"Has to be my parents," she said, struggling to turn in the seat, reaching for her pocket. "They're the only ones who—"

"Or Jorja," he reminded her. Jorja had an annoying tendency to use the phone for its original purpose.

She wrestled her phone from her pocket. It was, in fact, Jorja.

"You're on speaker," she told her.

Jorja didn't even ask who else was listening, nose-diving straight into a monologue. "I've been thinking about alternate theories of the crime. That's what they're called—a different way events could have happened that still fits the same facts.

"Remember Rumson, the pizza guy?" she went on, not waiting for affirmation or denial. "What if *he's* the one? What if your dad is still Marcus and *Rumson* had a fight with Antoine? I know you're thinking *why*? Well, we know *someone* was following Rumson around in the weeks before the burial and the disappearance. We also know that we can't find Rumson. I think Rumson was actually the victim."

Even Liam could see the holes in this theory.

"Why?" El asked. "And how did the knife get into the time capsule, then? And what about the handwriting on the note? And what about the cassette?"

Jorja did not so much as clear her throat to stall for time; she'd thought it all through: "Antoine wrote the note to apologize. Someone was following the pizza guy—what if it was Antoine? They met in secret. A fight broke out. Rumson was killed. Maybe with the knife, maybe not. Either way, Antoine is cut, too. Bleeds on the knife. Antoine, fearing reprisals, flees to Mexico. A Black man killing a white man in this town, especially back then? He knew he'd never get a fair hearing. No one would listen to him. So he ran."

Silence welled up and filled the car. Jorja stopped, as Jorja always did, without pronouncement or summary.

Liam had much to say, but this was El's family and her burden. He waited, watching her as she mulled it over.

"I don't know," she said after a few moments of cogitation. "How did they even know each other? Why would they fight?"

"Maybe Rumson was a dealer. Possibly steroids for track. Maybe Antoine was using." Jorja sounded both injured and exasperated. "Who knows? We don't *need* to know. All that matters is: Does this theory fit the facts as we know them? Yes."

"We're not in court." Liam couldn't stop himself from jumping in. "Beyond a reasonable doubt is nice, but it doesn't prove anything."

"I'm trying to give El a different perspective, okay?" Jorja snapped, and Liam immediately felt like an asshat. El was crushed at the idea that her father had killed her uncle and taken his place—Jorja was laying down a nice, fresh path for her to walk, one that avoided the bear trap of twin fratricide. And Liam was kicking dirt all over it.

"I appreciate it, Jorja," El said. Her voice was cheerier than her expression. "Thanks. That's a lot to think about."

After she'd signed off, though, she crossed her arms over her chest and scrunched up into the corner made by her seat and the door, staring out at the factory.

"What are you thinking?" he asked after he figured she'd had enough time to come up with an answer.

"I don't know if Jorja's right or not," she said slowly. "Probably not. But she's right about one thing: There's more than one possibility here. If we could just get Antoine's DNA. Something we *know* is his, that couldn't possibly be my dad's. We could compare it to the sample from Dad Indira has already, and we'd know once and for all if my dad is Marcus or Antoine."

"He's been gone for thirty-something years," Liam said as gently as he knew how. "Anything he touched or left DNA on would be hopelessly contaminated. So what else can we do? Is there another way to—"

"The stamps," Elayah said, sitting upright. "The stamps."

"What?"

She waved Liam quiet. "Uncle Antoine sent postcards from Mexico. He had to put a stamp on them."

"So?"

"So...back in the eighties, you couldn't just stick a stamp on something. You had to lick it."

"Can they even get DNA from that?" Liam asked.

He meant it as a rhetorical question, no doubt certain that there was no answer, but El charged on, already excitedly typing on her phone: "I don't see why not. The stamp has been stuck to the postcard all this time. So the DNA couldn't get out and no contaminants could get in. I'm asking Indira."

They waited as a gray bubble popped up on El's screen, throbbing with an ellipsis.

"Come on...." El muttered.

Then she held out the phone to him.

Indira: **Lab says they can try. Get me a postcard.**

Sucking in a breath, she nodded with more confidence and élan than she truly felt. They held each other's gaze.

"What are you gonna do?" he asked.

She said nothing, but her fingers flew over the glass.

**I'll get it to you.**


Liam had never seen one of the fabled Antoine postcards before. El sat on her bed, shuffling them. Mexican vistas flipped into sight and out of sight. "Which one should I give them?" she asked without looking up.

"Does it matter?" he asked.

"Probably not."

"Then just pick one."

"I can't." She kept shuffling through them, a blackjack dealer with ADHD. "You choose."

"Me?" She offered the stack of cards to him, and he recoiled, yanking his hands back toward his body as though a copperhead had hissed its warning.

"Yeah, you. Like you said: Just pick one." Her hand did not waver as she held out the postcards. "Please? For me?"

Well, hell. That wasn't fair.

Reluctantly, he accepted the cards. "I want it on the record that I'm only doing this because my love for you makes me incredibly weak-willed and you unfairly used your feminine wiles to manipulate me into doing your bidding, which is super unfeminist of you."

El grinned broadly. "So noted."

He spent a moment riffling through the postcards before settling on one that was blank white on the side that should have been a picture. It seemed to him that it made sense to keep the ones with pictures. At least they gave a sense of place, a way to situate Antoine in the imagination, even as it was impossible to locate him in the real world.

Turning it over, he read the handwritten note:

Mom, Pops, Marcus—

I'm sorry, but I can't explain this right now. Maybe later. I'll try. I've gone away. I

*have to do this. Please don't try to find me.*
*I love you all, but I can't be home right now.*

*Love, Antoine*

"I think this one," he told El.

She nodded. Together, they laid it out on the desk with good lighting and took pictures, just in case something happened to it. And then El tilted her face toward him and brushed her lips against his in the sweetest, truest kiss he ever had or ever would taste.

# ELAYAH

Days passed. She heard nothing from Indira. She was still avoiding her father, a chore made somewhat easier by his night-shift duties. He usually woke up around the time she got home from school, so she'd taken to arranging a series of study dates right after school ended. Anything not to go home until he'd left for work.

Today, she was at Liam's and neither of his dads were home. The house echoed with possibility and the soft murmurs in Elayah's throat as she and Liam kissed on the living room sofa. He traced a hot, wet line from her lips to her ear along her jawline, then dipped lower. She flinched as he tickled the line of her stitches—now dissolved, but still tender.

"Sorry," he mumbled.

"'S'okay," she told him with what little breath still lived in her. He'd sucked all the oxygen from her lungs, from the room, the house, the world. She lived anaerobically now, sustained by his propinquity, his heat, his touch.

"So, uh, how do your dads feel about…" She pointed from him to her and back again.

Liam's eyes widened in something like panic. "I haven't actually said any-thing yet. Is that okay?"

She laughed. "Are you asking me for permission to *not* do something?"

"I don't know."

"I haven't told my parents, either. It just..."

"Doesn't seem like the time," he finished for her.

"Yeah."

A silent wave rolled between them, and then Liam said, "Told them about Jorja and Marse, though. Holy crap, you'd think I told them someone cured cancer! They were *super* psyched!"

She leaned in to kiss him again. She meant it to be a quick peck, but apparently her mouth had other ideas, and soon they were glued to each other, eventually breaking apart for the cruel necessity of air.

"Should we..."

And she stopped. She'd been about to say, *Should we go into your room?* She ached for him, a very real pulse and throb at her core. The conversation in the car at the factory parking lot seemed like a million years ago. She was ready. She was ready right now. Mind, body, and soul.

As if he could read her mind, Liam's eyes flicked to the darkened hall that led from the living room to the bedrooms. "Oh," he said, and ran a hand through his hair. "It's just... I didn't make my bed this morning," he stam-mered. "And, uh, there's stuff all over the floor. Damn."

He exhaled a short, rueful chuckle. "All those times Pop told me to clean up because you never know when someone will come over. He was right all along, huh?"

And her phone chirped for her attention.

Because of *course* it did.

*Don't answer it don't answer it don't answer it*, she told herself. But she'd put on Do Not Disturb when coming over to Liam's, so only people on her VIP list could break through. That meant Liam, her parents, Marcie, Jorja...

And Indira.

"Who is it?" Liam asked, craning his neck to peer over her shoulder.

Elayah skimmed Indira's text, then stared at her phone until the screen locked and went black.

"Let me see," Liam complained.

It didn't make any sense.

She thumbed open the phone again and twisted away from Liam so that she could do more than simply skim this time. With her tongue jutting out between her teeth, she bore down on each word, accepting and assimilating them, not merely reading them. Surely she'd read too fast before. Surely a deeper meaning had eluded her.

But her initial, superficial perception had been accurate.

"It just..." She groped blindly for his hand, found it, clenched it hard enough that he drew in a sharp breath. "It doesn't make any sense. Indira says the DNA on the stamp doesn't match my dad's DNA."

Liam's eyes lost focus for a moment as he deliberated. "Isn't... isn't that a good thing?" He nodded, realizing. "Or, wait. Does that mean your dad is still Marcus, but Antoine cut him? Or—"

"No, no. That's not it. The DNA analysis shows that..." She consulted the phone so that she could read the exact quotation Indira had included from the report. " 'Subject's geographic origin fifty-six percent eastern European, forty percent western European. Detailed analysis to come.' Don't you get it?" she demanded when he only stared at her blankly. For the first time since knowing him, she was suddenly enormously frustrated that Liam was not as smart as she was. "No African ancestry. Or a really small percentage. The stamp wasn't licked by my dad *or* Antoine."

Liam's lips worked, but his throat produced only a dull, wordless groan, comprehension leavened with confusion.

"Who the hell licked that stamp and sent the postcard that my uncle was supposed to have sent, Liam?" A hot flash of anger scorched her insides, from where and directed at whom she could not say. As suddenly as it ignited, the rage burned itself out, abandoning her as an empty husk. Tears streamed down her face.

"Why, Liam? Why is it every time we learn something new, things make *less* sense, not more?"

# THE PRESENT: LIAM

The four of them agreed: It was time to go to the police. They'd gone as far as they could on their own.

El, being El, sat up late one night, compiling everything they knew into a dossier. She wanted to leave nothing to chance. There was no way she would let Liam's dad use some accidental omission to dismiss everything they'd learned.

So her dossier included their individual perceptions, notes of the discussions they'd had both in person and online with their parents and Kathleen Rourke. As well, she enclosed copies of her text conversations with Indira and the PDFs of the reports Indira had procured for them. She confined the scope to the knife, conveniently leaving out Lisa De Nardo and Peter McKenzie and the kidnapping. So far nothing but radio silence from the De Nardo/McKenzie end of things. No point rattling that particular cage.

When she showed the final product to Liam—printed and compiled in a dark green binder, one copy for each of them and one for Dad—he struggled to find something funny to say, then something sincere, then something deep. Ultimately, he settled for the only words that his brain formed in that moment.

"Damn, girl," he told her. "You're amazing."

Jorja paged through her copy, grunting in agreement. Marcie threw her arms around her best friend. "Nancy Drew's got nothing on you."

"Nancy Drew *solves* mysteries," El said dourly.

Liam drove them to the sheriff's office, where Dad was working his second shift in a row. The sun was going down over the Wantzler factory, salmon-pink clouds speckled with smoke on the horizon.

Dad sat behind his desk and listened very quietly, hands steepled before him, as El walked him through what they'd done, what they'd learned, what they still did not understand. The only time he moved or shifted his eyes from El was when she directed him to a specific page in the dossier. Then, dutifully, silently, almost respectfully, he would turn to the requisite page and stare at it as she spoke.

When she was finished, he said nothing, his face blank and inscrutable. Liam took El's hand, squeezed, braced for impact.

"Elayah." The word tumbled out of his father's mouth like tears. Dad knuckled his eyes and sighed like a man who has just given up the love of his life.

"Elayah," he said again, "I am *so sorry* you've been living with this. I wish you'd come to me sooner. I could have…" He groaned, softly, as though alone in a room with only his regrets for company. "I could have explained some of this, I'm sure. I could have at least helped you understand it."

"You haven't said *anything*." Liam was surprised at the intensity and the venom in his own voice. But this was about El, so maybe it shouldn't have come as a surprise at all. "You just keep your head down and work and don't tell anyone what's going on."

Whether it was the presence of his friends or the fact that his accusation rang true, Liam couldn't say, but the expected sharp rebuke never came. Instead, Dad said—with only the merest hint of pique—"Look, we haven't announced anything because there's nothing to announce. There's an ongoing investigation. And it will conclude when it concludes based on the evidence. Not based on Twitter or a podcast."

He tapped his copy of the dossier. "Or this."

"We deserve to know what's going on, sir," Jorja said. "Respectfully."

"This is about our parents," Marcie added. "So it's about us, too."

El ran a finger along the purple, bruised incision that had almost ended her life. And said nothing.

Dad buried his face in his hands. "You kids are gonna kill me. We got the guy who cut you, El."

"But he's not the guy who broke into my garage," El responded. "And he couldn't have anything to do with the knife, because it wasn't in the picture in the *Loco*. Which means there's someone else out there, someone connected to the knife. And as best we can tell, it has to do with my uncle."

"And a white person," Jorja said significantly. "Which means one of our parents."

Dad offered an indulgent smile. "I don't know much about…" He quickly consulted El's paperwork. " 'GenomiX Corp.' But I can't imagine their DNA workup is up to the same standards as a forensic-crime lab. These places take cheek swabs and blood samples in a medical environment and use them to analyze for congenital conditions and the like. It's a far cry from collecting DNA off a thirty-five-year-old *stamp*, for God's sake, in such a way that it's usable or reliable. And even *if* the analysis is correct and Antoine didn't lick this stamp, there are any number of explanations for it. He could have handed the postcard to someone else and asked them to mail it for him, for example."

"The handwriting analysis—" Liam started.

"Is amateur hour at best," Dad said, willing to be curt with Liam if not with the others. "I don't trust the results. Handwriting analysis is an inexact science under optimal circumstances, and all you kids had was a photo of a few words as one of your samples." He shook his head as though in regret, as though he'd held out hope that they would crack it, that this quartet would come to him with the case solved.

Liam's eyes burned. He was furious at his dad for shooting down everything they'd gathered, for pissing on all their achievements. But most of all, he was angry at himself because his dad was right. They had nothing. They'd worked themselves into a frenzy, and they had nothing to show for it.

Beside him, El touched his hand. He couldn't read her, not her face, not her body language.

"I'm sorry it's happened like this," Dad went on, speaking slowly and calmly, the way he had when Liam was young and not able to understand why he couldn't play in the fireplace or sleep on the kitchen floor or wear two different-colored shoes. "I've been trying to juggle my responsibilities as sheriff with my parenthood. And I've failed miserably."

It was the first time Liam had heard his dad admit to such a human failing. The words themselves were almost meaningless; the very real pain in his father's eyes spoke louder and more clearly than any words possibly could.

"Dad…"

He held up a hand. "Let me finish, Liam. There has to be a way to thread this needle. El, you need some closure. And all of you have questions that you should get answers to. So here's what I'm going to do: I can't tell you anything about the ongoing investigation, but I'll get the old gang together and we'll answer any questions you have. About what happened back then. About what we did. Prove to you that the knife thing is nothing and that in the end you'll see: It *will* turn out to be nothing. Is that okay?"

The four of them passed a look back and forth. "I feel like it's El's call," said Liam.

"Yeah," said El. "That's fine. Let's do it."

**54**

# THE PRESENT: ELAYAH

They met at Liam's house. The sheriff wore jeans and a polo shirt; folding chairs made a semicircle around the coffee table, where Wally had laid out crudités, homemade hummus with fresh-baked pita chips, and an impressive cheese board. When Elayah and her father arrived, Marcie was already there with both of her parents. Elayah couldn't remember the last time she'd seen them in a room together.

Jorja and her dad arrived last, even though they were just ambling over from next door. A slightly frosty air hung between them, still.

Elayah kissed Liam lightly on the lips when he approached her, much to the surprise of the sheriff and the obvious delight of Wally.

"Uh, when did this start?" the sheriff asked.

Elayah's dad shrugged out of his jacket. "You think she tells me things? C'mon, Dean. You know better."

The sheriff cracked a grin at that and took Dad's jacket, hanging it on a peg by the door. "Let's get comfortable and get started," he said.

Elayah sat on the sofa with Dad on one side of her, Liam on the other. The sheriff sat directly across from her. Wally lounged in the doorway to the kitchen, an observer to a past he'd never shared.

She took note of them all. The sheriff, who back then would have been just plain old Dean. Marcus, her dad, one half of Black Lightning. Marcie's parents: K. T. and Brian. And Jorja's dad, Peej, Patrick Jason Dearborn, who'd been called Jay back then. All of them in a room together.

Except for Antoine. The missing piece of the puzzle.

She suddenly realized that she couldn't remember the last time she'd seen them all together in a room like this. It had been years since the backyard barbecues, the joint birthday parties. The kids had stayed close, but the parents had drifted apart. She'd always thought of them as friends, but the truth was, they were more like acquaintances.

The sheriff opened his mouth to speak, but Marcie's mom uttered a stalling syllable and bent to retrieve something from the mammoth purse she'd tucked under her chair. "Before we start..."

She brandished her 1987 Canterstown High yearbook.

"What's that for?" her ex-husband asked, overtones of weary exasperation ill-concealed.

Kim blushed ever so slightly as she scanned the gathering. "Oh. I thought we were all bringing them."

"Mom!" Marcie groaned.

"Why would we need them?" Peej asked in a surprising tone of hauteur. Beyond his tone of voice, his posture and entire bearing were different around adults. He'd always seemed harmless and friendly to Elayah, but in this group, he clearly wanted to dominate.

"At least the rest of us have them," Elayah's dad said archly. Peej shut up.

"Why *don't* you have a yearbook?" Jorja asked her father. "Shouldn't you at least have one from 1988, when you went back to school after..."

She drifted off, clearly not wanting to say anything about the mental hospital, even though everyone knew.

With a dirty look sent toward Dad, Peej grumbled, but answered. "Because I never graduated. I dropped out when I got out of the hospital and got my GED, then went straight to college."

"That's why you're *Gone, But Not Forgotten*," El breathed.

"You didn't drop out," Kim snapped. "You were expelled. You had no choice."

"I was *going* to drop out anyway," Peej said hotly. "Look, it was a tough time, okay? My mom died, and then the school and police came down on me.... My dad was in a bind. He... he put me in that place. It was only supposed to be for a little while." Peej stared down at his hands, clenched together in his lap.

"You don't have to say any more," Dad said, a note of apology in his voice.

"That's how he got the charges dropped," Peej went on. "And then they... I ended up staying longer than it was supposed to be. I..."

He couldn't finish. He just shook his head and brought his forehead down to his joined hands. No one spoke for a while.

"Anyway..." Kim shrugged and handed the yearbook to Marcie, who flipped through it desultorily before handing it over to her dad. Brian didn't even open it; he just passed it along to Elayah's dad, who took a moment to page through.

"Check out your old man's hair back then," Mr. Laird said, leaning over to show Liam.

"Jesus, Marcus..." The sheriff groaned, running a hand through his thinning hair.

Elayah cracked a grin along with Liam as they looked at the book open across their laps. The sheriff gazed eagerly out of the photo, his hair shellacked into place with what had to have been a metric ton of hair product.

"You're an insult to gay people everywhere, Dad," Liam quipped. "I'm surprised they let you in the club."

"Me too." Kim said it. Quietly. Under her breath. Elayah wondered if anyone else heard it, if anyone else picked up on the injury and the insult in the tone. Thirty-five years later, Kim T. was still hurt.

It was so odd, looking in Kim's yearbook. It was the exact same book as her mom's—same pictures, same text—but altogether different at the same time. Different scrawls, different signatures, different in-jokes...

She went to pass it along to Jorja's dad, but Liam held it close, staring down at the picture of his young father. She relented and folded her hands in her lap. "Should we start?" she asked.

The sheriff shrugged as he bit into a carrot stick. "Sure."

Previously, the four of them had agreed to let Jorja start off. "First question: Who put the knife in the time capsule?"

Jorja's dad barked laughter. Liam's dad shrugged.

"It wasn't me," said Kim.

"Or me," said her ex-husband. They flanked Marcie, who seemed ill at ease between them.

"Right to the point, eh?" Liam's dad said. "Okay, let's settle this: Does anyone remember doing it?" He peered around the group. "Maybe right at the end, when we were throwing stuff in there? Brian, it was in your garage—was it maybe lying around and it got scooped up—"

"Not mine," Brian said immediately. "Hell, I know that for a fact. I had a knife like that, sure, but I lost it a year later on a camping trip. My dad was pissed."

"And that wouldn't explain the note with it anyway," Elayah piped up.

Jorja couldn't hide her exasperation. "So no one will cop to putting the knife in—"

"*None* of us did it!" her father exploded. "No one's hiding anything. The lock on Brian's garage door was busted for *years*. People knew."

Brian shrugged. "Yeah, it's true. My parents just never worried about it. Not back then. So anyone could have—"

"Okay, okay." The sheriff held up his hands, admitting defeat. "We'll move on. What about the envelope, the love letter from Lisa McKenzie?"

No one spoke. The sheriff cleared his throat and gazed significantly at Peej. "If you don't tell them, I will."

Peej grunted, shaking off his melancholy. "Oh, fine. That was me. I stole it from Chisholm's desk one night when Dean and I went into the school."

"Why'd you put it in the time capsule?" Kim asked.

"I don't know." Peej's expression and tone both exuded disgust, but it seemed self-directed. "I was stupid and angry at the world, and I really hated that guy." Here he paused. "I'm sort of the hero of this whole thing, really. He'd probably be on his way to the state senate if not for me."

A series of groans echoed around the gathering as Peej squeaked, "What? What?"

Elayah spoke up. "I want to be clear. None of you will admit to putting the knife in the time capsule. Or the note that was with it."

"We can't admit to what we haven't done," Liam's dad said gently.

She couldn't be sure he was telling the truth…but she also couldn't be sure he was lying. It was—frustratingly—possible that none of them had done it. That the blood on the knife matched her father's blood type...and a billion other people's.

"What about the cassette?" she asked. "There were two in there. One was a mixtape for sure, but the second went missing after someone broke into my garage."

Except for the sheriff—who'd read the dossier—the other parents reacted with shock. None of them had known about the theft of the tape.

"This is about a *mixtape?*" Brian asked. "Have you all gone crazy?"

Elayah clenched her jaw. Marcie's dad wasn't around much and didn't really stay in touch, so he'd missed out on most of the drama. "We think the missing tape had something else on it. Maybe something incriminating."

"Like New Kids on the Block?" Brian joked.

"They weren't a thing until eighty-seven, eighty-eight," Kim pointed out.

Brian rolled his eyes theatrically. "Oh, sure, right, of course."

"The tape is a strange one," Liam's dad admitted. "But I'm still not certain that it wasn't just misinventoried. I've already got someone looking through the evidence room at the station. What else have you got for us?"

The other parents were already checked out. Kim had withdrawn, gnawing at the cuticle on her left thumb. Marcie's dad had folded his arms over his chest early on—his posture since had become even more defensive, which Elayah would have thought to be impossible. Her own father slumped next to her, occasionally sighing. Jorja's dad kept yawning.

None of them acted like criminals. They seemed more like offended and irritated parents.

"Well..." Jorja held her phone up to Elayah and raised an eyebrow. *You think we should?*

"What about Douglas Rumson?" Elayah said, picking up on the item Jorja had flashed to her. Next to her, Liam still stared down at the yearbook; she was a tiny bit miffed that he, too, was checked out, and it came across in her tone.

"Who the hell is Douglas Rumson?" Her dad's voice rang out as though insulted by the mere name.

The sheriff sighed. This had been in the dossier. "The pizza guy."

"What pizza guy—oh." Dad's face contorted into mingled remembrance and shame. "What does he have to do with it?"

Elayah took a deep breath and explained the theory that possibly one of them—or all of them—had killed Rumson. Jorja chimed in with the drug angle.

Dad's jaw dropped. "You thought we killed the pizza guy?"

And then he started to laugh.

The laughter prompted something in the other parents. After a moment or two, they each began to chuckle, some of them shaking their heads at the sheer idiocy of it. Brian snorted and wiped a tear from his eyes.

"Stop it!" Elayah yelled, standing. "Stop it right now!"

To her surprise and savage delight, they did.

"You think this is *funny*? You all did lousy stuff when you were kids and never told us any of it, and now we're here trying to figure out why and what's going on and I had my throat cut because of it!" She jabbed a finger at her father. "I don't even know if you're my dad or my uncle!"

Tears streamed down her cheeks. Snot clogged her voice, but she kept going, shouting into her father's astounded expression.

"Did you kill your own brother and take his place?" The words wrenched from her with the force and pain of glass shards ripped from flesh. Her body and her mind went light as they punished the air between her and her father. After so many days of wondering, of fearing, of nausea and confusion, it was out.

Dad's eyes jittered and his lips twitched. "What?" he whispered.

No one spoke. Elayah's body vibrated, and Liam—damn it!—was still looking at the *stupid goddamn yearbook*!

"El, maybe—"

"No." Her dad rose, interrupting the sheriff. "Let me. Baby, let's step outside."

They pulled on their jackets and stepped out onto the front stoop. She wrapped her arms around herself, tucking in, like a hermit crab.

Her dad jammed his hands into his pockets and stared up at the night sky. Elayah seethed next to him. She barely needed the jacket—her anger kept her warmer than she'd anticipated.

"Is that what you think?" he asked quietly. "Is that what you've *been* thinking?"

In a rush, her life flashed at her. Like the moment of death. And there was her dad, running to her on the soccer field. Bellowing in the night as her throat bled. Charging into the garage the night of the second break-in. These and more, battering her, buffeting her like wind-driven waves against the hull of a ship.

"I don't know what I think," she said just as quietly. "Nothing makes sense anymore. Nothing."

Her tears began afresh. "I'm sorry" spilled out of her before she knew she would say it. "I guess I know...I guess I know you're exactly who...It's all been so...I'm sorry."

"Oh, honey," Dad said, his face fallen and gray. "Oh, baby. No, no, no. I'm so sorry." He clutched her to him, and for the first time in forever, she let him. "No. No. I swear to you: I have no idea whose blood that is. And I swear I never held that knife. And I'm sorry I never told you anything, but I promise you, I don't know. I just don't know."

He sniffled against her, loud and somehow comforting in her ear. She'd never seen her father cry.

"This is all my fault," he said. "Your whole life, I've always made so much of Antoine. Built him up to you. Made him a legend, when he was just a person. And that made it so that...so that you had to dramatize his disappearance. Make it something bigger than life. But, baby, it wasn't bigger than life. There's nothing dramatic about it. I loved him, but he was selfish. Selfish and wrong."

He disengaged and pushed her away. Gently. Dug into his coat pocket. Withdrew the frame she'd recovered from the time capsule.

"Been carrying this around since you dug it up. Same way I've been carrying around the past my whole life." He opened it and gazed down sadly. "But that's not right. You shouldn't be carrying my burden, Elayah."

She took his hand in her own, turned the frame so that she could see it, too. Mom and Dad on one side. Dad and Antoine on the other.

"Why did you put this in there?" she asked. "None of the others put anything really personal in there."

He sighed deeply, from the marrow of his bones. "Because every damn thing going in there was about white people. I wanted something to show we were here. We were real." He clacked the frame closed. "I didn't know it would be Antoine's last picture. I didn't know I would never see him again."

This time, she held him.

Back inside, the others were midconversation. Elayah peered around.

"Where's Liam?" she asked.

"Bathroom," Wally answered from his post by the kitchen, where he'd been keeping silent watch.

She and Dad sat down on the couch again.

"Have we solved the past yet?" Dad cracked hollowly.

Muted chuckles all around. The mood of the room was melancholy, rusted over.

"The past? Hell, the past was nothing. It was all about the future, remember?" Jorja's dad said somberly. "We all thought the future was open to us. We thought it would be easy."

"You *convinced* us it would be easy." Marcie's dad spoke for the first time in a long time, his voice smoldering. "We slacked off. We knew the grades would be changed at the last minute. And then..." He gestured with three fingers like an exploding chef's kiss. A magician's *poof.* "It all went away. Too late for our grades to recover."

"Colleges didn't look too kindly on seniors who slack off like that," Liam's dad said.

"It wouldn't have mattered," Kim said. "You're just all looking for a convenient excuse for what your lives have become."

"Speak for yourself," Peej said.

"You wanted to be a cop, Jay," she said, coming down hard on the old nickname. "How'd that work out?"

Peej moved as though to rise from his seat, but Liam's dad gestured him into calm.

"You know, sometimes," Elayah's dad said slowly, "sometimes I think the hardest thing... one of the hardest things about living in this world is understanding that it's not personal. Or directed. Good things happen. Bad things happen. And sometimes they're for a reason, but sometimes they just *are.*"

"And some mysteries never get solved," Liam's dad said soberly. "I have a slew of cold cases to prove it. This may end up being one of them."

Elayah glanced over to the hallway. Liam stood there, wan and troubled. He gazed right through her.

"Kids, no one died," said Liam's dad. "Am I one hundred percent sure of that? I'm never one hundred percent sure of anything, really. But I feel pretty confident about this one."

Marcie and Elayah locked eyes. Then Jorja. Lastly, Liam, who didn't flinch or change his expression in the least.

The room fell silent for a protracted moment that expanded to the border of discomfort.

And then Marcie's dad groaned out a breath, slapped his knees with his palms, and said, "Right, okay, so are we done here?"


# LIAM


Liam's spit dried up entirely as the parents all stood up and began doing that shoulder-slapping, guy-hug stuff that grown-ups did with people they pretend to be close to. His mouth clicked when he moved his jaw.

El caught his eye and tilted her head in a *What is with you?* direction.

Oh, God. She didn't know.

But she would.

He checked his phone again. To make sure.

Was he really going to do this?

El's dad shrugged into his jacket. Jorja stood off to one side, murmuring with Marcie.

"Could..." He heard the syllable escape from the dry captivity of his mouth. He cleared his throat. Tried to work up some spit so that he could speak. "Could everyone sit down again, please?"

Dad looked over. "Oh, good, just in time. Help Pop and me clean up when everyone's gone."

Liam shook his head. He had to do it. Everyone was here. He had to.

"Dad, remember you said everyone in town had a knife like that?"

Dad cocked his head, peering quizzically at Liam. Everyone else seemed to realize that there was something going on; a half dozen separate *so long* conversations fell silent.

"Are you all right, Liam?" Pop asked. "You look pale."

He didn't so much as flick an eyeball in Pop's direction. "Dad, you said everyone in—"

"Yeah, I remember."

"You said yours is probably up in the attic."

"Yeah."

"Show it to me."

Dad blinked rapidly, his expression that of a man who is only barely able to control his disbelief. "What did you just say?"

Liam choked a bit on the next words but managed to get them out. "I wasn't in the bathroom before. I went up in the attic. Looked all over, opened every box, but I couldn't find it. Just a bunch of your old comic books and some of Pop's stuff. So show me what I missed. Show me the knife."

A short blurt of an aggravated laugh escaped Dad's lips. "I said it was *probably* up in the attic."

"It's been more than thirty years," El's dad said. "I don't expect you kids to understand, but things go missing."

"What's going on, Liam?" El asked. She came to his side, reached for his hand, but he pulled away.

"You wrote..." Words became jumbled in Liam's head and on his tongue. But he had to get them out. "In Marcie's mom's—in Kim's yearbook. You wrote *I'm sorry about the prom, but I know you understand!*"

Dad threw his hands up in the air helplessly. He exchanged a half-wounded look with Kim. "She thought we were going to go....That was when I was figuring things out. I don't...Liam..."

"You always told me you didn't realize you were gay until college." Liam realized he was trembling, his teeth threatening to clack together with each word. "What were you *figuring out?*"

Pop approached him, put a hand to his forehead. "You don't feel warm. But you're shivering. I'm getting the thermometer."

"Don't," Liam told him, his tone commanding, his gaze unwavering.

"I matched it up," he went on. "Just like we did to compare the note with the postcard from Antoine." He held out his phone. "Three samples of the exact same words. Written around the same time. *I'm sorry.* And they all three match."

Pop jerked his hand away from Liam's forehead as though it had caught fire.

"Wait, *what*?" El's dad.

"Dean!" Peej yelled suddenly, startling everyone. "Dean, don't say a word! Not a word, you hear me?"

"What the hell?" said El's dad, peering around as though fog-swaddled. "What the hell is going on?"

But Liam ignored him, staring straight ahead at Dad, whose lips pressed together into a flat line, his expression unreadable.

"You wrote the note. And the postcards that were supposed to be from Antoine. And I bet it's your saliva on the stamp. So, Dad, seriously: Where is your knife?"

"I'm not your lawyer," Peej said, coming around the coffee table to stand between Liam and Dad, "but seriously, don't say a word."

In a severe, implacable silence, Liam and his father glared at each other over Peej's shoulder.

Pop said, "Sweetheart...?" in a too-high voice.

"And while you're thinking about where the knife is," Liam said, "maybe you can explain why I found this in your gun safe."

Digging into his pocket, he produced a pristine Wantzler cassette tape.

The room went utterly and deathly silent, so it was easy for everyone to hear El whisper, "Oh, hell."

And Dad sank into a chair and said, "Damn it."

# 1986: DEAN

**D**ean got to the hideout early and took measurements of the drafty window. By the time Antoine arrived, he was down on all fours, cutting lengths of weather stripping with his hunting knife. He'd laid out a cloth and a roll of masking tape, but it turned out he didn't need them.

"What are you doing?" Antoine had come in behind him, silent.

"Fixing the drafty window. Like I promised." He was in the middle of holding the stripping in place, so he didn't turn around, but he did excitedly wave a ribbon of the gray padded weather stripping over his head.

He slid the window open, bracing himself against the cold. With the knife in his teeth, he began stuffing the weather stripping into place, occasionally pausing to retrieve the knife and nick away a too-long piece.

When he finished, he turned around with a flourish and a *ta-da!* gesture at the window. Antoine was pacing the room.

"It'll be a lot warmer now," Dean said.

Antoine kept pacing. Dean knew what this meant—Antoine was excited about something.

"What is it?" he asked. "What's up?"

# 56

# THE PRESENT: LIAM

Liam, that's stolen evidence," Peej said. "As an attorney, I'm going to advise you to—"

"To hand it over to the cops?" Liam asked snarkily, indicating Dad, who sat staring at the floor.

"Just... just don't *do* anything with it. Or to it. I don't want you to get in trouble."

"Isn't it a conflict of interest for you advise father and son?" Kim said.

"Not now!" Peej barked.

"How did you—"

Liam interrupted his dad with a mirthless chuckle. "Like I said: I was looking for the knife. I've been able to get into your gun safe since I was eleven, Dad."

Pop groaned.

Liam shrugged. "Let's hear what's on it."

The family stereo was Dad's old receiver and speakers from college, along with a combo cassette/CD player that had last been used when George W. Bush was president. Liam snapped open the tape case, slid the cassette into the player, and hit Play before anyone could say anything.

"Liam," Dad whispered.

A voice boomed from the speakers. El's father gasped.

"My name is Antoine Louis Laird," said the voice. "This is my confession."

# 1986: DEAN

Antoine said nothing for a moment, his expression one of mingled delight and fear, trapped in that liminal uncertainty between the two. Dean gritted his teeth together. He wasn't up for a big, intense talk. Not tonight. All he'd wanted, after the chaos of homecoming, was a night with his...

His...

He still didn't have a word.

"Talk to me," he said. He tucked the knife into his belt and approached Antoine, holding out both hands. "Tell me what you're thinking."

"I...I'm just trying to think of how to..." Antoine's eyes flashed with excitement. His words tumbled over themselves and then finally he just said it:

"I'm leaving."

Dean blinked a few times. "But...but you just got here."

Antoine shook his head. "No, not here. *Here.*" His gesture encompassed the whole of Canterstown. "I can't take it anymore. I can't stay here. I can't do it, Dean. I have to go."

Dean stepped back as though someone had punched him in the chest. His heart thudded like elephant feet. "What?"

This couldn't be happening. This wasn't happening. He would not *let* this happen.

"You can't go," he said. "You...your family...Marcus..."

"They'll be fine. They'll get along without me. But I can't stay around here. My bag is packed. There's a bus leaving at six in the morning." He took Dean's hands in his own and stared into his eyes. "Be on it with me. Please."

Dean pulled his hands away. They were shaking. A bus. On a bus. With Antoine. Off into the unknown. Together.

He wanted it. He wanted it more than anything. It hovered before him, almost like a mirage.

No. No. *Exactly* like a mirage.

"You're just springing this on me. Come on."

"It's time. It's way past time, actually."

"Why now?"

Antoine sighed. The dancing light left his eyes, and he took a few paces away from Dean. His expression said that all this was going exactly as he'd predicted, not as he'd hoped.

"At school. In the storage closet." Antoine finally spoke.

"Yeah. I know. That was rough. But it worked out. We didn't get caught. Jay didn't tell the police or the school about the rest of us."

Antoine shook his head. "That's not it."

"Look, his dad is on the school board. He'll be okay."

"And *that's* not it."

"Then what *is* it?"

Antoine clenched his fists, his lips puffed out in frustration as he struggled for words.

"I was scared, too!" he exclaimed. "Cooped up in that little space, waiting for the cops to do who knows what."

"Me too, and—"

"And you held *her* hand. You comforted her."

Dean sighed. Fidgeted. He'd never even thought of holding Antoine's hand, and now the guilt hit. "I couldn't. Come on. You know that."

"You *wouldn't*." Antoine stalked toward him, suddenly seething. "I'm the guy you say you love—you should have been thinking of me. I was thinking of you."

Yes. He remembered Antoine's hand in the dark. Shame washed over him. He pinched the bridge of his nose.

"I'm sorry. I don't...I'm not doing this well." He knew he wasn't.

Daylight Dean and Nighttime Dean. He'd thought they could coexist, like alternate-universe versions of each other. But they were in conflict. Each dangerous to the other, like matter and antimatter.

"I'm still figuring it all out," Dean told him. "I promise you, I'm getting better. I love you."

"You can hide," Antoine told him. "You have that luxury. I can't. I haven't been able to hide since the day I was born. I have to walk in this world the way I am. How long am I supposed to wait for you to figure that out? Because I don't get to be real unless you decide to be real, and that's not fair to me."

This was it: the kernel of their dilemma. Even though Antoine thought he didn't, Dean *did* understand. Antoine lived in a world that had expectations and prejudices simply by virtue of his skin color. And Dean *knew* that. Dean *got* that. Just existing in his skin made the world dangerous. Antoine had lived with that danger, that constant threat, his whole life, so even though he knew opening up about his love was fraught, well, in the end it was just one more reason for the world to hate him.

For Dean, though, it meant sacrificing…everything. Why couldn't Antoine understand *that?*

"I'm so tired of hiding the half that I can," Antoine told him, tears glimmering in his eyes. "It's exhausting, man. It takes so much out of me. It feels like lying and cheating and…skulking around in the middle of the night. Pretending we're nothing to each other during the day. If I have to live like that, I might as well just leave."

"Don't do that," Dean whispered. His heart thrummed in double time at the idea of losing him. "Please."

"We have to be open," Antoine said, his voice gone so soft so fast. "We have to be out and real. Or we can't *be* at all. It's the only way to live. I know it'll be tough. I get that. But I can help you. I swear, Dean, I swear on my mother's life, I will always, always be there for you."

"I can't." Dean's own tears glistened now, blurring the edges of his vision, smearing wet rainbows on the periphery. "I'm not there."

"You have to make a choice. You're either with me in the open or you're with her."

"I'm not giving you up," Dean insisted. "You're the only thing in my life that's real."

"Then tell everyone. Or say nothing and come with me. But we can't keep living these half lives."

Dean shook his head back and forth and had trouble making it stop. No. No. That wasn't just impossible—it was insane. He couldn't do that. No no no no no no.

Antoine's expression softened at Dean's distress. "Look...look, at the very least...this isn't fair to her, either. You're cheating on her every minute of every day. You gotta let her go."

"I can't."

He knew he couldn't. Kim was his shield and his shelter. She staved off the arrows and spears.

"Please." His voice was less than a whisper. He wiped at the tears. "Please. I need more time."

Unbidden, his legs carried him forward, stumbling into Antoine's arms. "I'm trying. Please. Please don't leave."

Antoine held him. Strong arms around him. Dean wept.

Outside, the sound of a car's tires broke into the weeping.

**58**

# THE PRESENT: ELAYAH

"...knew that I had to make a decision," Antoine's voice went on from the stereo. "And that meant Dean had to make a decision, too."

They all sat in silence as the voice purled forth from the speakers. No one spoke as Antoine described his love for Dean, their relationship, their impasse.

And then suddenly Dad leapt up from the sofa and lunged over the coffee table, reaching out for Liam's father.

"What did you do to my brother?" he howled. "Tell me what you did!"

The sheriff leapt back. Brian was up from his chair faster than she would have thought possible, given his size.

For the first time, Elayah realized how huge Brian was. Her father still had the coiled, muscular build of a runner, but Brian was built like an alp. He interposed himself between the two men and held them apart.

"Everyone just calm down," he said. "Just calm down."

From the stereo, Antoine kept speaking. "...didn't even realize a car had pulled up until we heard the door close outside..."

59

# 1986: DEAN

What was that?" Antoine's head snapped up. He'd been nestled against Dean's shoulder, but now he peered around.

They still held each other. Looking around. Another sound.

The front door. Steps on the floor above.

They exchanged a look of fear. They were back in the storage closet again, terrified.

Unless Antoine had closed the basement door—and why would he have?—the light from their lantern would lead whoever it was right to them.

The steps creaked. As though through some silent, telepathic agreement, Antoine and Dean separated, but still held hands. They would face this together.

And then there was Brad Gimble on the final step, staring at them.

He gazed around the basement, taking in the sleeping bag on the floor, the duffel, the beer bottles, and the lantern. After an interminable wait, Gimble laughed a low, cruel, nasty laugh. "Holy crap. You two are *queer* for each other?"

They were still holding hands. Dean jerked his out of Antoine's grasp.

"What the hell are you doing here?" Dean demanded, as though he himself had any right to be in the same place.

"Marcus and Dean, two fairies in a fairy nest!" Gimble chortled. Antoine didn't even bother to correct him. "I wasn't expecting *that*! Man, Kim T.'s gonna be *soooooo* disappointed when she finds out those big ol' titties of hers are wasted on her boyfriend!"

Dean's fists clenched of their own accord. "Shut up, Brad. Why are you even here?"

Brad seemed to mull this question over for a bit.

"Let's just go, Dean," Antoine said quietly.

"What?"

"Yeah, what?" Brad said in a high falsetto.

"Seriously, shut up, Gimble!" Dean turned to Antoine. "What do you mean, *let's go?*"

"There's no point talking to this jackass," he said, gesturing to Brad. "Let's just get out of here."

Gimble crossed his arms over his chest. "No one's going anywhere until you tell me who pissed in my locker. Was it one of you two?"

Dean snorted. "Is *that* what this is about?"

Gimble grunted and set his jaw. "I've been looking to get one of you alone. Saw Marcus over there running through town on my way home from the movies and figured I'd follow him. After homecoming, everyone knows you guys broke into the school. So which one of you pissed in my locker?"

"It wasn't us," Antoine said wearily. "Now get out of my way."

Gimble actually stepped aside and let Antoine pass. Halfway up, he turned, expecting Dean behind him. When he realized Dean wasn't coming, he shook his head and disappeared up the stairs.

Dean couldn't move. His fists were so tight they hurt.

"Kim doesn't know, right?" Gimble said. "There's no way she knows. Oh man, when she finds out, she's gonna lose it. How does a *homo* end up with one of the hottest girls in school?"

"Just shut up."

Gimble laughed. "You know what? This is even better than finding out who pissed on my stuff." Then, turning to go up the stairs, he said with a pronounced lisp, "Thee you at thchool, thweetie!"

Dean growled deep in his chest and charged at Gimble. Brad was a football player and a wrestler, but those were games with rules. Dean just flat-out launched himself at Gimble, throwing all his weight into it. He caught

Gimble from behind, on the stairs. Together, they slid down and crashed to the basement floor.

"Shut up!" Dean howled. "Shut up!"

Gimble struggled against him. The element of surprise had given Dean the upper hand. "You...you getting all excited, Dean?" he managed. "Getting a boner?"

Dean reared back with his right hand and drove it into Gimble's stomach. Gimble *woof*ed out a breath and made a choking sound.

Dean saw it all flash before him: The look of disappointment in Kim's eyes. His mother's tears. His father's anger. His grandparents. All his friends. Everything he would lose.

Dean's vision went red. He raised a fist again, but Gimble was too busy catching his breath to notice or flinch.

Dean managed to shift his knees so that he was pinning Gimble's arms down. But Gimble was strong. Too strong. The shift and surge of his body under Dean's meant that it was only a matter of time before he threw Dean off.

He raised his fist again. The face this time. If he was about to get his ass kicked by Brad Gimble, at least he'd leave him with a black eye. But just then, Gimble jerked his lower body, trying to heave Dean off him. Dean lurched forward, tried to catch himself. His forearm lodged itself under Gimble's chin, across his throat.

This worked pretty well, actually. Gimble's chest hitched and he stopped laughing. Dean leaned into it, putting more weight on his arm.

*Shut you up. Shut you up. Shut. You. UP!*

Gimble started thrashing, but Dean knew he couldn't let up. He couldn't.

He pressed down harder. He had to scare Gimble enough that he would never ever threaten Dean again. Never ever say anything about—

Dean's arm slid suddenly. Something gave out beneath. There was a crunching sensation, the feeling of walking on layers of autumn leaves. Without realizing it was happening, Dean stumbled off Gimble and rolled to the floor.

Every nerve in his body hummed and sang danger. *Get up. Get up before he does!*

He rolled to his side, then heaved himself into a crouch. Gimble still lay there. Completely still.


Dean stared at the body for how long he could not say.

He'd killed Brad Gimble.

He'd *killed*—

He swallowed, hard, willing himself not to vomit. Bile burned in his throat.

What would he say? What would he do? When people asked why, what would he tell them?

*He was angry about piss in his locker. He threatened me. I fought for my life....*

No. No one would believe it. No one would believe that an angry Brad Gimble had attacked Dean and Dean had won.

*I jumped him. I started it. Oh, God.*

The bile rose again. He spat it out, his mouth gone sour.

Gimble stared up at the ceiling, unblinking.

*I killed him!*

What could he do? What could he do now?

He ran his hands through his hair. His palms sweated.

Nothing. Nothing to do. No apology to make. No way to take it back. No do-over.

There was no way forward from this. None.

It was over.

He was a killer.

There was nothing for him now.

Nothing but prison. A lifetime of horror.

He saw it before him. He experienced it in a rush.

No.

There was another way.

One way.

One way out.

He found a piece of paper in his duffel bag, along with a pen. He began to write.

It was the only way. He drew the knife from his belt.

Steps. Creaks.

"Are you two still—oh."

Kneeling on the floor by Brad Gimble's body, Dean looked up at Antoine, who stood, shocked and paralyzed on the stairs.

"What...what did you do?" Antoine asked, but Dean could tell he already knew.

"It was an accident."

"What did you do?" Screaming it this time.

"It was an accident!"

"You *killed* him?"

Dean struggled for words. "He was—he was saying—"

"So you *killed* him?"

"It was...I didn't..." Nothing made sense. Dean's thoughts whirled. He went dizzy and the taste of bile returned.

The only thing to do...

It was so obvious.

He looked at what he'd written so far: *I'm sorry. I didn't mean to kill anyone.*

He had more to say. How it had happened. How foolish he'd been. But none of it mattered. Not any longer.

Dean raised the knife to his throat. "I love you," he told Antoine.

Antoine startled. "Hey!" He held out a cautioning hand. "Hey."

"Say it back. Please say it back."

Instead, Antoine dashed toward him, channeling every bit of Black Lightning. His hand clenched Dean's wrist and the knife jittered.

"Don't do this!" he yelled at Dean.

Dean tried to draw the knife across his throat, but Antoine was too strong. They struggled, tugging back and forth. Dean's arm lost all its strength and it snapped back toward Antoine. He felt something give.

Antoine jumped back. His shirt was torn across the chest and blood seeped into the fabric there. "You cut me! You actually cut me!"

Oh, Jesus. Dean's eyes juked from Brad's body to Antoine's gash and back again. The knife clattered to the floor from his nerveless hand.

"Are you okay?"

"You *cut* me!" Antoine pressed a hand against his chest to stanch the bleeding. "Oh man, it burns."

"I'm sorry, I..." Dean sniffled. "There's no other way. There's nothing else to do. I can't...I killed him. I can't just...can't go *back*. Can't pretend—"

The room spun. It felt too hot all of a sudden. The air itself seemed speckled before his eyes.

Antoine hissed in a pained breath and stooped to gather up the note, the knife. He wrapped them in a bit of cloth from Dean's duffel bag.

"Listen to me," Antoine said. His voice came from very, very far away. "There's still a way."

**60**

# THE PRESENT: LIAM

They listened, his dad and El's dad staring at each other past the immovable block of Brian, as Antoine described the two of them dragging Brad Gimble's body from the house. Driving him to the rocky overlook out on Route 9. Antoine positioned the body with the chin hooked over the steering wheel.

They poured beer on him. They left bottles in the car.

They pushed it over the precipice.

"I knew that night that Dean would never come with me. That we would never be together. He was still tethered to his old life. I should have realized. I shouldn't have pushed him.

"I told him I was leaving on the bus in the morning, but the truth is this: I hadn't decided yet. I was ready to go, but I wanted him with me. I would have stayed, for him, no matter how desperately I needed to leave.

"And then he killed someone. He was so afraid of being found out that he actually killed someone. And that made my decision for me.

"I put it all in the time capsule. All the evidence. It was all I could think of to do. I had to protect Dean, but I also couldn't let these things go unsaid. So that's why you're hearing this tape, whoever you are. I had to unburden myself. But I also had to protect Dean, so I spoke the truth and then I made sure it would be buried.

"And in fifteen years, someone will dig it up. Or they won't. I can't control that. I can only control what I do now. Which is..."

"Which is try to start over."

The tape clicked into silence.

No one spoke. Pop sat on the floor, his expression dazed and broken.

Liam sought out El with his eyes, but she was staring at her dad. After a moment, Mr. Laird felt around behind himself and sat back down on the sofa.

"Oh, dear God," he whispered.

"He called me." Dad twisted his hands together, staring down at them. "From the bus depot. He told me he'd done this. I...I barely even remembered the night. I was in shock. The knife...all of it. He told me it was in the time capsule, but there was no way....It was too late by the time he called me. We were burying it in a couple of hours....I just had to...leave it there. And hope."

Liam nearly gagged. If he hadn't insisted on digging it up to spite his father...

Dad did not move for a long time, his hands dangling at his sides as though nerveless and useless. Finally, he reached for his phone. His hand trembling noticeably, he held it out to Pop, who stared at it as though it were an alien life-form before accepting it.

"Honey," Dad said, his voice sounding astoundingly like Liam's grandfather's in that moment, "could you please call the station for me and tell them to send a deputy over to make an arrest? I'd prefer Riley or Gonzalez, but whoever's available."

Pop took the phone.

"Where?"

It was Mr. Laird.

"Where is my brother, Dean? You wrote the postcards, right? So where did he really go?"

Dad finally looked up, gazing at Elayah's father with helplessness radiating from his eyes. "I swear to God, Marcus, I don't know."

**61**

# 1986: KIM

Bearing shovels and a pickax, they made their way up the hill that morning. Jay had the gait of a condemned prisoner who knows he's guilty but believes he should have gotten away with it anyway. He'd been suspended, and the rumor was that his father, in a political move to preserve his board role, was pushing for an expulsion in exchange for the county agreeing not to press charges against his son. But the singularly dour expression on Jay's face curbed her desire to ask him about it.

Marcus carried the pickax as well as, in a moment of chivalry, Kim's shovel. Jay hadn't even offered.

Dean and Brian waited for them at the top of hill, the time capsule standing on one end between them. Dean leaned against it precariously.

"Was it heavy?" Kim asked.

Dean and Brian shrugged. "Nothing we couldn't handle."

Brian flexed a little. Whatever.

"This tree?" Brian pointed.

Dean yawned as he consulted a sheet of paper. "Yep."

Brian unsheathed his deer knife and carved a capital *B* in the bark of the tree as high up as he could reach.

While Brian carved, Marcus punched Jay in the shoulder and asked the question Kim had been avoiding: "Hey, man. How's it going? What's new with the police and the school and all that?"

"I don't know. My dad's working something out." Jay's expression was vacant and distant. A stare into an abyss that seemed more welcome than threat.

"Hey," Dean said to Marcus, scouting around them. "Where's Antoine?"

Marcus flashed a grim, angry mask. "Who the hell knows? I don't think he came home last night. He's been sneaking out lately. He's…" Marcus licked his lips. "Can I tell you guys something? He's been acting real weird lately. Not just the not-talking thing, either."

"Should we wait for him?" Brian asked, and Dean nodded.

"Look, he's been checked out for a while," said Marcus. "If he's not here, it's because he doesn't want to be here. Let's just bury the damn thing. I think he might've hopped a bus to New York. To see our cousin again. Mom is sitting around at home, waiting for a call from my aunt." He shook his head. "He's an idiot."

Jay grunted something like agreement. "Is it all sealed up?" He jerked his head at the time capsule.

Dean thumped its top. "Yep."

Kim frowned. "I thought we were going to finish the inventory first," she said.

"Oh, come on," Dean said. "We have enough." He brandished the piece of paper they'd used to list the things they added to the time capsule, then folded it and tucked it into his pocket. "I'll stash it in the yearbook room so we can get to it when the time comes."

Brian rubbed his chin. "I don't know, man. Twitchy said—"

"Who cares what Twitchy said?" Jay growled. His eyes had sunken into black-and-purple hollows and his hair was limp. "Let's just bury this thing."

No one spoke, the five of them gazing around at one another, the woods behind them, the sun, the sky. And then, with a shrug, Dean took up the pickax and swung the first blow at the earth.

---

TRANSCRIPT BEGINS

INDIRA BHATTI-WATSON, HOST:

This is *No Time Like the Present*, an NPR podcast. I am Indira Bhatti-Watson, reporting from Finn's Landing, Maryland.

(SOUND BITE OF MUSIC)

BHATTI-WATSON:

Today we're coming to you from the steps of the courthouse in Finn's Landing, the county seat of Lowe County, Maryland, where the state's attorney has just announced charges being filed against Dean Malcolm Fitzroy, the sheriff of Canterstown and the man who had been conducting the investigation into the attack on Elayah Laird.

Late last night, word came that the sheriff had confessed to—among other things—being the individual who broke into the Lairds' garage, allegedly to steal evidence from the time capsule. This, because Fitzroy *also* confessed to having killed Bradley Simon Gimble in 1986, then faking Gimble's death as a drunk driving accident. The crime scene was bulldozed in early 1987, so no evidence has been recovered, but the sheriff is cooperating with authorities.

Details are still sketchy, but we have learned from sources that the evidence in this case comprises items from the time capsule, ironically unearthed by a group including Fitzroy's own teenaged son. The letter that drove Martin Chisholm to attack Elayah Laird was placed by someone else, entirely coincidentally.

Keep listening after this word from our sponsor for much, much more.

**62**

# THE PRESENT: DEAN

He was given the third holding cell from the door to the detention area. With typical cop irony, they all called it "The Suite." Someone had measured it once—it was six inches larger in one direction, and the single barred window somehow let in more light than the other cells'.

It was a kindness and a consideration Dean knew he did not merit.

The cot was as uncomfortable as detainees had always complained. Dean sat on the edge of it and watched the shadows of the window bars as they ticked the minutes away, leaning farther and farther east as the sun traveled west.

And so it ended, as it had to end. His entire life had been one big cover-up, even becoming sheriff in order to keep a lid on his crime. He never thought anyone would actually dig up the damn thing.

He never imagined his own child would be the one to unravel it.

It had all gone wrong. Not that last night with Antoine—long before that. It had gone wrong when he was born, when Antoine was born moments after Marcus. When Jay was born, and Kim, and Brian. It had gone wrong when the world threw them together as they were, then told them not to be who they were, to suffer in silence, and to never ever show weakness.

And someone died. And families fell apart. And Black Lightning... forked.

"Uh, Sheriff?" It was Riley, one of the deputies, standing just on the other side of the bars.

"I don't think that's my name anymore," Dean told him.

Riley's mouth gaped and shut, gaped and shut, like an astonished goldfish. "Right, sir. Right. Uh, there's someone to see you."

"No visitors," Dean told him sternly. "You know the rules."

"Yeah, well..." Riley shrugged and went to the door that opened out into the rest of the building. He walked out and ushered Wally in.

Dean clenched his jaw, holding back tears. Wally was not so successful; tears streamed unfettered down his face.

"Goddamn it, Dean," he said as he stood before the cell. "Goddamn it."

Everything Dean could think of to say danced unused on the tip of his tongue. Could he say he was sorry? Sure. He *had* already. It was useless. Could he say, "You were never supposed to know"? Yes. And what of it? Nothing he could say meant anything now. No words could mend the damage.

"I can't believe you...." Wally sniffled and pulled at his hair. "How could you do this? How could you?"

*It was an accident.* More words he could say. More words that wouldn't matter.

Dean stood and walked to the front of the cell. He wrapped a hand around one of the bars.

*I love you.* The biggest words to say. And still meaningless.

"Do you remember when we met?" Wally asked.

Of course he did. One of the first commercial flights after 9/11. They'd ended up seatmates on a flight out of BWI, bound for Cleveland. The flight hummed with nervous energy and black humor. For once, no one wanted to ignore the person next to them. Dean was a deputy sheriff, heading to a symposium on community relations. Wally was interviewing for a chef's position at a seafood restaurant.

"Who goes to Cleveland for seafood?" he'd asked somewhat rhetorically as they chatted, staving off the fear with comity.

By the time the short flight landed, they'd exchanged names and numbers. They met up in Cleveland that night for a drink, then Dean puckishly suggested seafood for dinner.

Wally tanked the interview. Maybe on purpose. Dean never asked.

"I knew from the moment I saw you," Wally told him, fighting for breath and composure. "I knew you were the one. The love of my life. I knew we would be together. That we would marry. Even though it wasn't legal yet. I thought to myself, *I'm gonna make it legal if I have to go to law school and get a degree and get on the Supreme Court myself. I will marry this man.* I knew all of that. The first time we met."

He said this all looking over Dean's shoulder, staring into the shadows of the cell. Now he finally fixed his gaze on Dean.

"I didn't know you would break my heart," Wally said, choking on his own words. "I didn't know you'd already broken my heart before I even met you. How could you do it? How could you promise me a life? How could you bring us a child?"

How?

They'd been kids, and they'd thought nothing they did mattered. They'd been *told* it didn't matter. But thirty-five years go by and suddenly it all *does* matter, just as you were starting to forget it, just as you were thinking maybe it was a dream you'd had once, long ago, in another place, when you were another person.

But you were the same person after all. All along.

You have this notion that your life doesn't start until *you* say it does. That nothing counts until you look in the mirror and decide you've grown up. But everything you did, you did. Everything you said, you said. It's all real and it all matters, to someone, if not to you.

If, Dean wondered, he'd been able to see the future, to see the parades and the court decision and the *pride*...would it have mattered? Nothing had really changed. Except everything had changed.

He didn't know.

All of that, true.

None of it answered Wally. Not in the way that mattered.

Wally put his hand over the end of Dean's fingers, the parts that wrapped around the bars. He didn't squeeze Dean's hand, just laid his hand there.

"I'll always love you. And for what you've done, I will hate you until the day I die."

*    *    *

Later, despite the regulations, Riley returned. This time with Liam.

Dean began to tremble at the sight of his son. Liam's eyes were sunken, bloodshot. It had been only sixteen hours since his arrest, but Liam looked as though he hadn't slept for weeks.

It was one thing to see Wally. Wally was an adult. Wally had lived a life of joys and disappointments, cares and troubles.

Not Liam. Liam was…

"Did you think you'd get away with it?" Liam asked abruptly, his jaw set.

Dean fought against the reflex borne of years of struggle with Liam. "Did I think…? Liam, I *did* get away with it. For thirty-five years."

"Because you're always the smartest one in the room, right, Dad?"

Dean took a deep breath. Counted to ten. He knew he needed to do this when he spoke to Liam, but in the moment—in the fire of the present—he often forgot.

"It didn't start out like that. Trying to get away with it. I…I really…I panicked. And Antoine had this great idea. I thought it would work. But as soon as you kids said you were going to find the damn thing and dig it up… I knew. Deep down, I knew I couldn't stop it all from coming out, no matter how hard I tried."

They glared at each other in silence. Dean remembered to count to ten this time. And then he did it again. Because this next part was risky.

"The tape, Liam."

Liam startled as though wakened from a deep sleep. "What? What about the tape?"

"You have to destroy it."

The command and the implication hung between them like gun smoke. "Dad…"

"Listen to me." Dean pressed against the bars with urgency. "That tape is the only evidence connecting Antoine to Brad's death. No one who heard it last night is going to talk. They just won't. Peej can fall back on attorney-client if he has to. Sure as hell none of the rest of them will say anything to hurt Antoine."

"It's been thirty—"

"There's no statute of limitations for what we did!" Dean couldn't hold back the explosion of anger. Why couldn't Liam just *understand*? "Second-degree or negligent homicide, it doesn't matter. He's still on the hook as long as that tape exists."

"He didn't kill anyone, Dad. You did." Liam seemed to take a savage satisfaction in saying it.

"Doesn't matter. He covered it up. He's an accessory after the fact, and he's in just as much jeopardy as I am. He's just as culpable...unless you destroy that tape."

Liam said nothing. He pondered, his expression unreadable.

Tears, then. Dean didn't expect them, but there they were, gathering at the corners of his eyes. "Liam, listen to me. Antoine is still out there some-where. And wherever he is, I don't want him to wake up to US Marshals kicking down his door one morning. I did this. He tried to save me. I deserve punishment. He doesn't. If you destroy the tape, he's free. Like he always wanted. Give that to him."

"Where did he go?" Liam asked. "You have to tell the Lairds. They deserve the truth."

"I don't know where he is, son. I hope wherever it is, he's happy."

Liam snorted at the sentiment. "Then why the postcards, Dad? Why even bother?"

Dean sighed. "You don't...He was just *gone*, Liam. He left nothing behind. He vanished. And his family was so distraught. A week went by. Then two. And they thought he was dead, and they were so...I thought that I could at least...I could at least let them know he was alive. And maybe if they thought he was really far away, they'd stop looking.

"But even there, I screwed up. That first one. I bought a blank and sent it to my pen pal in Mexico. Then I thought about it and instead I started send-ing him money and had him buy the postcards and stamps. He'd send me the postcards, I'd write them, send them back for him to mail. I told him it was a school project. It's not like I was a master criminal, Liam. I was a scared kid doing my best to pretend everything was fine. Just a kid who kicked off something he couldn't control."

And it was true, but it also didn't matter. None of it mattered. The truth was out and even *that* didn't matter, because it didn't fix things. It didn't heal things. He'd thought he could spare the Lairds a specific pain, and instead all he'd done was inflict another kind for thirty-five years. And then came the original hurt, like a boomerang returning through time. To say nothing of the Gimbles, who had left town shortly after Brad's "accident," but who now were lining up their lawyers.

It was a chilling sort of funny that in the years since, he'd thought less and less of Brad Gimble, and more and more of Antoine. Brad's death meant damn little to him compared with Antoine's disappearance. The law had a different view.

"All this because you had a boyfriend." Liam shook his head. "You had a *boyfriend*, and some jackass was going to maybe, possibly, out you to your girlfriend. Jesus, Dad! So what?"

"It was—"

"Don't tell me it was different back then!"

"It was!" Dean roared, lunging at the bars. Despite the steel between them, Liam took a step back. "It was different! You got to grow up in a world where people argued over whether it should be called *gay marriage* or *marriage equality*. I grew up in a world where gay kids got beaten to death!"

"That's *bull*, Dad!" Liam shouted, now leaning in close enough that Dean felt his breath. "They're still beating up gay kids. It's not something that only used to happen back then."

"The difference is that back then, no one gave a damn. You don't understand. In 1986, the only thing in this town worse than a Black faggot was the white faggot who was in love with him."

Liam staggered backward as though struck. He'd never heard his father speak that word, other than the time—as a very young boy—when Dean had lectured him on certain words and why not to use them. *And this is one of the worst*, Dean had said, and told him the word and its history and why it was so very, very bad, and why it should never be used. Especially not in *this* house.

To his shame, Dean took an almost barbarous pleasure in shocking his son this way. He'd tried for so long to have the final word with Liam, to have his son finally capitulate and admit, *Yes, Dad, you know some things I don't know. You know some important things. I'm listening, Dad. The world is serious, Dad. I get it. I understand.*

The wounded, dumbstruck look on Liam's face was, Dean figured, the closest he would ever get.

He'd never understood why he and Liam had such contention between them. Shouldn't a blissful and respectful relationship with his child have been the natural reward for the long, hard-fought slog to have a child with Wally? The adoption paperwork and legal negotiations. The surrogate interviews. The endless rounds of artificial insemination. The string of checks and credit card charges that depleted his life savings. And then one day, he'd gotten the call and rushed to the hospital. Wally had arrived an hour later, still in his chef's whites, spattered with bone broth and tomato seeds. Liam was born after six hours of labor at 3:22 in the morning, a squalling, howling ball of outrage and pitiableness, shivering, blue hands and feet, wrinkled. Scraggly black locks of hair that would eventually fall out, to be replaced by blond. His eyebrows were invisible, his lips folded in except when he screamed his disapproval at being expelled from the comfort and safety of the surrogate.

And Dean had—much to his shock and pleasure—fallen in love instantly. And hard. They had agreed that since Dean was the donor, Wally would get to hold the child first. But in that moment, Wally had put a hand on Dean's shoulder and said, "Take him, Dad."

A nurse placed the wailing newborn in his arms, and in an instant, Dean saw Antoine standing before him, for the first time in years. Just for an instant. Tears gathered and spilled, and he knew that he would do anything for this boy, that he would suffer anything to protect this child. He knew in that instant why he'd become a cop—to protect the helpless and the vulnerable. The people like himself as a kid, a kid too scared to come out of the closet, and who could blame him? He'd lived a life of fear for too long; he wanted the world to be a safe space for everyone, but now especially for his son.

And yet from the first day, Liam had protested Dean's love. Hurled it back in his face. His boy had always clung to Wally, and Dean admitted that he came to resent it. Liam was *of* Dean. Dean made him. Why did he not cleave to his biological father?

For the longest time, Dean blamed the boy, but as the years wore on, he came to see that the problem was in him. It was in his talk, his walk, his mere existence. He'd committed the ancient sin. And all the good in his life could not make up for that. No one else could see it, but Liam could. Liam, who was his blood. Liam knew. Liam knew all along that there was a rotten, corrupt mass at the core of the sheriff of Canterstown. That the safe space had been purchased at the cost of a human life and a lifetime of lies.

And with that realization came a relief. If someday Dean had to go away, he knew that Liam would still have Wally. His loving Pop, who could not have cared for him more had Liam been of his own flesh.

"You're going to be okay, son," Dean said quietly. "Probably better than if this had never happened at all."

And that truth, Dean realized, hurt more than all the others.

**63**

# THE PRESENT: LIAM

Monday morning came. Liam could not be certain if he awoke from a fitful sleep in which he dreamed he was awake or if he'd never slept at all. One seemed as likely as the other, and his exhaustion offered no answers. He stared up at the ceiling, his phone's alarm music running over and over.

His father was in jail. Nothing else seemed to matter.

The song played and played and played. Then it looped and played some more. Eventually, he shut it off and rolled out of bed. When he sat up, his head swam with exhaustion and grief and a dull fury, his emotional gyroscope broken to bits.

School would start soon. He wouldn't be there. How could he?

He composed a text to El, deleted it, started over, deleted it, again and again and again, and then sent nothing.

His grumbling stomach prodded him out of his room in a pair of boxers and an old T-shirt. The door to his fathers' room was ajar; Pop lay on his stomach on the bed, above the covers, which seemed undisturbed. Liam couldn't tell if Pop was asleep or just lying there and decided, in a moment of emotional barbarism, that he really didn't care.

In the kitchen, he poured cereal into a bowl. It was some kind of wheat crap for old people and had no taste until he doused it with sugar. After three spoonfuls, he lost his appetite and resisted the urge to hurl it against the wall.

Pop padded silently into the kitchen and regarded the bowl with resigned dismay. "Do you want to talk?" he asked.

Liam pushed the bowl to the center of the table, as far as he could. "Why?"

"I don't know. But they always tell parents to talk to your kids and get them to talk during times of trauma."

"Who's *they*?" As if it mattered.

Pop gestured theatrically to the air, the ceiling, the sky beyond, the universe. "Them. Mommy bloggers and all that."

"Well, that's your first mistake, because there are no mommies around here."

Pop started crying, and Liam felt about two inches tall. But he couldn't convince himself to stand and put his arms around his father. He couldn't even make himself stop staring at the stupid bowl of cereal, just beyond his reach.


By the time night fell, Liam was unable to think through the welter of memories and emotions colliding within him. He was a tornado inside, a monsoon. Nothing connected to anything else, and nothing stuck long enough for him to cling to it. It was like watching a movie sped up at 10x, dropping context, eliding the unfamiliar and the unknown.

One thing penetrated like a laser: El.

A text wouldn't do it. Couldn't do it. He had to see her.

He drove to her house. Sat in the car at the end of the block, with a clear line of sight to her front door. It occurred to him that his father had probably done something similar the night he'd broken into the Lairds' garage.

**can i see u? im down the block**

No response. Not even a gray bubble with a throbbing ellipsis.

But after a couple of moments, the front door opened and El stepped out. She looked up and down the street, spied his car, and walked without hurry toward him. He got out before she gained him and leaned against the driver's side door.

"Hey," he said to her. And wanted to hold her and kiss her and hold her some more, but did not.

"Hey." She stuffed her hands into her pockets. "How, uh..."

"I'm okay," he lied. "How about you?"

She shook her head and pressed her lips into a fierce line. "Don't ask me that," she told him.

He held up his hands in surrender. "Okay. Okay. Sorry."

"Do you have any idea...," she began, then shook her head again.

"I have to..." He wasn't sure how she would deal with this next part, but he had no choice. "The tape."

"What about it?"

"I know it's your uncle's voice, but..." He rubbed the end of his nose in distraction. No one knew what he'd done. How he'd popped the tape out of the stereo that night while no one was paying attention.

And given it to El.

He figured it belonged with her family.

And now...

He told her what Dad had said. About destroying it. And why. And he knew that the last thing she wanted was to be given marching orders by the guy who made all this happen in the first place, but the hell of it was, Dad was right. It was the only thing to do.

She glared at him.

"Look, I can't fix any of this. I can't change any of it. But none of it..." He paused, knowing that if he continued he would start to cry. Then decided the hell with it and plowed through, letting the tears come. "But none of this is about us. You and me. And right now that's what I care about."

The urge to take her in his arms was too powerful. He could no longer resist. He needed her against him. But she stepped out of his arms as soon as he opened them to her.

"It's not...I can't just..." She was crying, too, now. "Your dad knew. He *knew* and he said nothing. He just fed us lies. Do you know what he did to my family? To me?"

Liam groaned. He didn't need a recitation of his father's sins. He knew too well. "He didn't do anything to *you*. You weren't even born yet. You didn't even know your uncle."

Her fuming, fearsome glare told him everything he needed to know. She wanted to slap him so badly that he could feel the strike already. He decided he would let her. He wouldn't budge.

"It's probably best…" She hugged herself and looked off into the distance. "It's probably best if—"

"Don't say it. Please." He wiped his eyes.

"Just for a little while. Until things are better. Or calmer. Or whatever."

"I don't like that."

She nodded in agreement. "I get it. But you don't have a choice."


Liam's backyard was small and weedy, but it had one thing in its favor—a tall, very effective privacy fence. He found an old basketball in the garage and headed outside. The house was both too empty and too full at the same time, Pop's grief and memories of Dad cluttering the air and choking each breath like smog.

He wondered what El had decided about the tape. He wondered if he would ever know.

He thumped the ball a few times and took a lazy shot at the hoop mounted on the side of the garage. Pop had once entertained dreams of Liam playing ball, but that had always felt like too much work. Liam's jump shots were so-so, his dribbling passable. If he'd *applied himself*, maybe he'd've gotten better.

As things stood, the best he could do with a basketball was dribble it fiercely and hurl it at the hoop in an attempt to fling his anger out of him.

Didn't work.

The back door to the house squeaked open; Marcie squeezed through, followed by Jorja, who gestured for the ball. Liam decided hell no and instead tucked it under his arm.

"What's up?" he asked, his voice toneless. It wasn't a put-on. He couldn't figure out how to give a damn. Or why.

"We wanted to see you," Jorja said.

He believed *she* wanted to see him. Not Marcie, though. Not El's bestie.

"We know things are bleak right now," Jorja said. "We're here for you, Liam."

He didn't even want to look at them. Their happiness corroded the air. No one should be happy right now, he decided. No one in the whole world.

Turning away from them, he dribbled and drove the ball toward the net.

Jorja moved like lightning, smacking the ball out of his control as though taking a pacifier from a sleeping baby. She ducked under his flailing arm, oriented herself without even looking up, and shot the ball up high. Nothing but net.

"Screw you," he muttered.

"I can dance with you all day on the court," she said calmly. "If that's what you need. But I think you need something else."

"El needs time," Marcie said. "But it's going to be okay. Give her some space."

"We know you've been calling and texting," Jorja added. "You have to knock it off. It's only been a couple of days. Don't go all stalker-y."

"What the hell? You hook up and suddenly you're relationship experts?" Liam recovered the ball from behind the air conditioner, where it had ended up after Jorja's basket. He passed it to her and watched her effortlessly shoot another two-pointer. "Not like I have a choice anyway."

Marcie shrugged. "It'll work out. Trust me."

Liam watched the ball roll to Jorja's feet. "Yeah, well, I'm having trust issues these days."

"Trust *us*," Jorja said. She snatched up the ball and fired it back to him. "And I've been telling you for years—try not to lead with your left leg when you go for the layup."

# 64

# THE PRESENT: ELAYAH

Cross-legged on the living room sofa, she stared ahead at precisely nothing. She'd done the right thing.

She was crazy.

It was the right thing because how the hell could she be with him right now?

It was crazy because Liam had nothing to do with it, it was ancient history, shouldn't they heal and move on?

She'd wanted him for so long. Had him. Her fingers in his hair. His hands on her hips. Lips pressed to lips. What else was there? What else mattered?

It had been four days without him, and it felt like centuries.

She went into the kitchen. Dad sat at the table with a beer open before him, its level undiminished.

"I heard…" She stopped. Started again. "Marse said that Liam got in to see him." Avoiding the name. "Maybe you could go, too."

Dad shrugged.

"You know."

"I don't want to talk to him. I have nothing to say to him."

He hadn't moved since she'd come into the room.

"Well, I mean, closure…"

"Closure? No such thing. No such thing."

She didn't know what to say to that.

"I know you want to be with him...," Dad began, still not looking up. "I get it. I need you to know that I don't know if I'll ever be able to look at that boy again."

"You can't blame Liam. It's not his fault."

Dad tilted the bottle this way and that, watching the beer within slosh from side to side. "We're always supposed to just take it," he said with acrimony. "We're always the ones to forgive and forget. Give up today and hope that since we did, tomorrow will be better. Not this time. Not. This. Time."

He snatched the bottle from the table and abruptly stood, then took two steps to the sink and dumped the beer down the drain.

"You heard the tape. You heard it. He drove Antoine away. I never got to know my brother. He stole that from me. I never knew the most important part of him, who he really was. I never got to be angry at him and then ask for his forgiveness, and he never got to give it."

Elayah absorbed this. Felt the truth of it. Let the *real* filter through her, as though via osmosis.

Thought of the tape, in her desk drawer right down the hall. Her father could hear his brother's voice again. All she had to do...

"It's not like...I'm not asking you to forgive his dad. Just Liam. It happened a long time ago, before he was even born."

Her father regarded her with sad, envious eyes. "Oh, baby. It *all* happened a long time ago. Before any of us were born."

He came over to her, and for a moment, she expected a hug, a kiss. Instead, he simply put a hand on her shoulder, squeezed once, and then left her alone there as he wandered out into the dark hallway.


The next day, Jorja and Marcie came to visit. They sat on Elayah's bed, holding hands. She faced them in her desk chair.

They'd known each other for pretty much all their seventeen years, and Elayah had never seen Marcie look so relaxed, so at peace, so...happy.

She recognized the look. It was like gazing into a mirror that reflected emotions from the past. She'd experienced that bliss for a finger snap of time, and now feared she'd never reclaim it.

"He misses you," Marcie said. Needlessly.

"You should call him," said Jorja, who had suddenly become the lesbian Dr. Drew. "Not a text or an email or a DM. Call him. Let him hear your voice."

"It's not that simple." She swiveled the desk chair in a truncated arc. Back and forth. Back and forth.

It was the emotions, yes. And the history, yes. And now, also, the tape. And the choice of destroying evidence—breaking the law—or putting a target on her uncle for the rest of his days.

"He feels alone," Marcie was saying. "His dad's in jail; his other dad's a wreck. He needs us. All of us. But especially you, El."

She thought of her father's hand on her shoulder. Of the sadness in his eyes that drove out the anger and was somehow worse.

"I don't know what to do," she admitted. A tear came out of nowhere and traced a too-warm runnel down her cheek. About Liam. About the tape.

"What do you *want* to do?" Jorja asked.

She didn't know that, either.

**65**

# THE PRESENT: LIAM

Liam gave a lot of statements to the police. It seemed as though every couple of days, they called to see him or ask him to come to the sheriff's office or the county courthouse to answer questions. The questions were always the same, and he knew what they were doing—making sure his story didn't change.

It didn't. It couldn't. It was the truth.

More than a week after Dad's confession, he was alone in the house when the doorbell rang. Thinking it *had* to be El, he dashed to the door.

It wasn't El.

"Aunt Jen?"

His father's sister gazed at him from the other side of the doorway, her graying hair done up in a bun. She refused to color her hair, no matter how often Dad had badgered her about it. His aunt had been the most significant female relationship in his life—he adored her, and right now he couldn't bear the sight of her.

"I talked to Wally," Aunt Jen said. "Took some time off work. I thought maybe I'd stay for a few days...?"

It was strange, having her ask permission. Of him. He noticed now a roller bag just behind her. She gazed into the house with something like wistfulness.

"You can come in," he told her. "But I'm not good company these days. Not even for you."

"I get it."

She rolled her bag in and stood there in the living room, clearly wanting to hug him. Resisting. Good. He knew he would fall apart, and he didn't want to fall apart.

"I'll only stay as long as you're okay with it. But no matter what, I have to tell you something, and you have to hear it, Liam."

Liam shook his head. "Unless you can prove my dad was brainwashed by the CIA into confessing to a crime he didn't commit, there's nothing I really want to hear right now." It was hollow and brainless and stupid, and he was ashamed of himself for even saying it.

Aunt Jen put a hand on his arm. He flinched.

"I just wanted to tell you something that I bet no one is thinking to tell you in all this: You're a good guy, Liam. People are going say a lot of things about your dad. You're gonna hear a lot. And people will want to take care of you. People like Wally and me and others. And you should let us. But sometimes we'll forget to say it, so it's important you know: *You're* a good guy."

Liam watched his toes as she spoke. He couldn't let her see his eyes. Swollen permanently from crying. Tearing up even now.

He should have said something. Should have thanked her. But instead he just shrugged, turned, and went down the hall to his bedroom.

**66**

# THE PRESENT: ELAYAH

She met him on the hill overlooking the school twelve days after the arrest. It had been a long twelve days. Her throat was almost entirely healed, and the air had gone from almost-fall to almost-winter. She wore a purple knitted scarf with a matching hat and her middle-weight jacket.

She remembered him climbing the hill with her, both of them bearing shovels. His spitting into the grass. Then, later, her hands on his dirt-caked, sweaty back. Their first kiss still a dream.

Everything still a dream.

Dressed in jeans and a plain blue hoodie, he sat near where they'd unearthed the time capsule, knees to his chest, elbows on knees. Staring off into the distance. The Wantzler factory had gone to a four-day week, and the smokestacks were idle. There were no more reporters in town; even Indira had left. They would return for the trial, she knew. If there even was one. Rumor had it that Liam's dad planned to plead guilty to manslaughter and something to do with mishandling human remains.

She didn't ask Liam about that. She didn't say anything at all at first. She didn't tell him how she'd gotten a butter knife and broken open the plastic shell of the old Wantzler cassette, about the fire she'd lit one cold morning by the trash cans on the concrete pad in the backyard, the way the ribbon of tape had curled in and in and in on itself as it burned into a black smudge that could hurt no one.

Would she ever tell him?

Purple shadows bulged under his eyes. He was thinner, noticeably so even when hunched and folded in on himself. His hair was longer, unkempt. Couldn't be bothered. His beard stubble was uneven and too heavy to be stylish.

"Aren't you cold?" she asked.

He shrugged.

She sat next to him. Close enough to touch. And—oh!—how she wanted to touch.

Still wanted.

This boy.

This *almost-a-man*.

His flesh called to hers. They were two halves of a perfect whole.

Not touching.

The intolerable, infinite silence stretched on. She broke it.

"I've been having weird dreams," she told him. "Since it happened. Every night. Not the same dream, but all my dreams are about fire. Sometimes just, like, a match is lit. Sometimes it's all around me. Always fire. Do you think that means something?"

He regarded her with nearly empty eyes and shrugged helplessly. Then returned to staring off to the horizon.

"I can understand," he said after a while, "if you can't be around me. I get that. But, man . . . I can't handle you hating me."

"I don't hate you." The thought was impossible. The words didn't belong in the same language, much less the same sentence. "I just haven't figured out how to be around you. How to reconcile everything."

"I guess I don't see what there is to reconcile. Yeah, my dad, he, you know. And your uncle, too. And I've been in love with you forever. Why can't that be what matters to us instead of the stuff that happened before we came along?"

"I don't know. Not entirely. But I know that we have to learn to live with the past. We can't avoid it and we can't change it.

"We carry it with us. Into the future."

A slow nod from him. "I don't know how to make it right."

"Maybe you can't. But maybe understanding is just as important."

He shifted his position, leaning back on one elbow so that he turned to her, his hand now resting on the dying grass between them, only a finger's width from her own. She thought she could feel the sensation of him through the air, the ground, the ether, the spirit plane, whatever medium there could be.

"What happens next?" he asked. "For us, I mean. Is there even a chance?"

His hand, next to hers. The shivering touch.

She did not take his hand.

Neither did she move hers away.

"I don't know," she told him. "Time will tell."

# EPILOGUE

It happened more than a week after she saw Liam on the hill.

Ten more days as the story spread.

She was home with her parents. Missing Liam. Wishing to live in a different world. Knowing she was stuck in this one.

Dad actually cracked a grin at something on TV. That was something. Progress. She and Mom exchanged a brief, knowing, relieved glance, then pretended they hadn't noticed.

Dad's phone rang during a commercial. He stared at the screen. "I don't recognize this number."

Elayah sighed heavily. "It's spam, Dad."

But he answered anyway. Because there was some Gen X reflex to answer a ringing phone that he was powerless to conquer.

"Hello?" he said.

And then: "What did you say?"

And then: "Yes, this…"

And then his breath hitched in his chest. He trembled. Elayah noticed it first, choked out a warning to Mom, who spun around from her place on the sofa. Dad was shaking now, completely out of control. Tears began to stream down his face.

"Dad!" Elayah shouted. He was having some sort of fit. A seizure. Oh, God, a stroke?

Mom was up from the sofa and at his side. "Marcus? Marcus, honey, are you okay?"

Elayah's heart slammed at her ribs and then—in an instant—she saw it.

The tears.

Were tears of joy.

Her dad, weeping, said one word.

"Antoine?"

## Acknowledgments

There are so many to thank with this book in particular. I want to begin with the four sensitivity readers of ethnicities and orientations that are not my own, some of whom read a rather ramshackle version of this story and provided their thoughts. They are anonymous to you because they are anonymous to me, as it should be.

I'd also like to thank my early readers, Rana Emerson, Eric Lyga, and Morgan Baden, who helped me—among other things—keep the timelines straight and the mystery consistent.

My agent, Kathleen Anderson, once again led the charge in getting this book into the right hands. Those hands belong to Alvina Ling, my editor now on eight books, who did her level best to wrangle my intentions for your reading pleasure. I hope you find our compromise enjoyable.

The team at Little, Brown has been in my corner for ten years now, and I am indebted to them for their faith in me. My thanks to Megan Tingley, Ruqayyah Daud, Marisa Finkelstein, Victoria Stapleton, everyone in Production, Marketing, and Sales. And a special shout-out to Chris Koehler and Jenny Kimura, who put together a really striking cover that I loved the moment I saw it. (Those of you who know me know how rare that is.)

Many thanks to the experts who guided me but who could not prevent what I am sure are many liberties I've taken with reality: Dr. Deborah Mogelof, who answered my questions about our frail human bodies, and

Cara Lewis of the Carroll County state's attorney's office, who guided me through Maryland law in 1986 and now.

A big Jersey shout-out to Bruce Springsteen, for allowing me to realize the dream of using his lyrics in a novel, as well as to those who secured those permissions for me, Alison Oscar of Jon Landau Management and Mona Okada of Grubman Shire Meiselas & Sacks, P.C. I raise my kid's toy guitar to you in salute.

Last but not least, my thanks to Supreme Court Justice Brett Kavanaugh, whose obscene blend of sniveling cowardice, convenient tears, abject dishonesty, and blustering toxic masculinity turned this project from a simple thriller into what it is today.